WHEN TRUTH COWERS

G. M. BA

Library of Congress Control Number: 2025905921

Hardback ISBN 979-8-9915412-0-6

Paperback ISBN 979-8-9915412-1-3

eBook ISBN 979-8-9915412-2-0

Edited by Vallie O'hara

Cover design by G. M. BA

✾ Created with Vellum

For the people with PTSD who read thrillers as
therapy.
I see you. I'm one of you.

Before You Read

CONTENT WARNINGS

This book contains on-page instances of murder, bodily harm and blood, injuries, ableism, family discord, discussion about sex (but no sex), and a few swear words. There are also references off page to self-harm, bullying, child abuse, and police brutality.

AUDIENCE

This book was written for a young adult audience —particularly around the ages of 16-20.

With all of this information in mind, feel free to decide if you'd like to proceed with this story.

Character Guide and Map
For Your Convenience

Truth or Dare Contestants:

Caitlee "Cai" Ito
[kayt-lee "k-eye" ee-toe]
(she/her)
Truth or Dare Signature Colors: bright yellow and black

Analisa Patel
[ah-nuh-lee-suh puh-tail]
(she/her)
Truth or Dare Signature Colors: light pink and black

Lian Patel
[lee-in puh-tail]
(he/him)

Truth or Dare Signature Colors: green and black

Sevyn Evans
[seh-vin eh-vehn-z]
(they/them)
Truth or Dare Signature Colors: neon blue and black

Brandon Jiu
[b-ran-duhn j-yoh]
(he/him)
Truth or Dare Signature Colors: red and beige

Solana Díaz
[so-lah-nuh dee-ah-s]
(she/her)
Truth or Dare Signature Colors: bright purple and black

Ever Wright
[eh-ver right]
(xe/xem)
Truth or Dare Signature Colors: brown and white

Jared Farley
[j-air-ed far-lee]
(he/him)
Truth or Dare Signature Colors: plum and black

Joane Lu
[j-own loo]

(she/her)
Truth or Dare Signature Colors: lilac and white

Eric Foucault
[eh-rick foo-cull]
(he/him)
Truth or Dare Signature Colors: navy and brown

Daraja Jones
[duh-rah-zh-uh joh-nz]
(they/she – they most of the time)
{Clementine – [kleh-men-tie-n] – he/him – protector and introject alter
Didi – [dee-dee] – she/her – child alter
Bridget – [br-ih-jet] – they/them – gatekeeper and ex-persecutor alter}
Truth or Dare Signature Colors: neon green and white

Flutura Leka
[flew-too-rah lay-kah]
(she/her)
Truth or Dare Signature Colors: orange and white

Truth or Dare Referees:

Comedy
[kah-meh-dee]
(she/her)

Truth or Dare Signature Colors: bright yellow, pink, and white

Tragedy
[tr-aa-jeh-dee]
(he/him)
Truth or Dare Signature Colors: faded purple, black, and silver

Cai's Family:

(Auntie) Tera Ito
[teh-ruh ee-toe]
(she/her)
Cai's human great-aunt

(Gram) Aru Ito
[ah-roo ee-toe]
(they/them)
Cai's human grandparent

(Grampa) Dix Ito
[dih-x ee-toe]
(he/him)
Cai's human grandfather

Alexis Ito
[uh-lehk-sis ee-toe]
(she/her)

Cai's human mother

Kiran
[key-rehn]
(they/them)
Cai's alien parent

TRUTH OR DARE CABIN LAYOUT

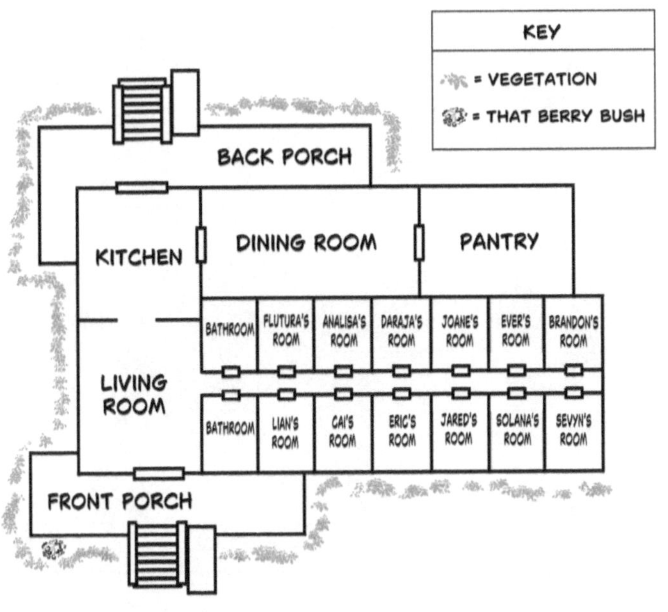

Truth or Dare Rules
Also For Your Convenience

Dear Player,

Here are the rules of Truth or Dare for your reference. Don't worry, you can look these up at any time in the game without penalty.

- (12) Twelve people spend (6) six days in the simulated forest cabin. Each player who remains in the game until the end is allotted $500,000 to their winnings.
- On the first day, each player gains (1) one accusation for every other player, totaling (11) eleven accusations. The accusations are cumulative, so if a player chooses to save all (11) eleven of their accusations from the first day, they may have (22) twenty-two accusations on the second day. Note that these accusations can only be applied to the

respective players—in this case, (2) two per player.

- The accusation process starts with the question: "Truth or Dare?" The accused player must respond with either "truth" or "dare" within the minute, otherwise the accuser chooses for them. After the accuser states the truth question or dare, the accused player is given a time limit to complete the accusation by the referees.

- If the accused player doesn't complete the accusation within the time limit, the player is issued a warning. For every warning a player is issued, $100,000 is removed from their potential winnings.

- If a player completes the accusation within the time limit, a prize amount determined by the referees will be added to their winnings. The prize amount awarded per accusation will be somewhere between $0 to $100,000.

- If the referees question an accusation's entertainment or extreme level, it will be put to an audience vote. If the accusation is denied due to audience vote, the accused player does not need to complete the accusation and the accusing player isn't reimbursed an accusation. If the accusation is approved, the player must complete the accusation as usual, with additional prize money as compensation.

- Besides an audience vote, the only way an accusation can be negated without penalty to the accused player is by the accusing player retracting the accusation. If an accusing player retracts an accusation, they are not reimbursed an accusation.
- A player may start a vote for the audience to remove another player from the game. If the latter player is removed due to audience vote, their winnings are given to the former player. If the latter player is spared due to audience vote, the former player is removed, and their winnings will be given to the latter.
- For a player removed from the game for any reason, besides an audience vote, the prize amount accumulated by that player is divided evenly among the remaining players. This is added to the prize money gained from completing accusations and receiving winnings from player removals.
- The referees reserve the right to adjust the rules and hold audience votes at any time.
- The No-Liability rule applies. As a summary, anything you admit or do in the game cannot legally be held against you, or anyone involved in the production of Truth or Dare. Please see the attached Terms and Conditions and Privacy Policy for details.
- Everything is televised. Every conversation. Every truth. Every dare. What is seen will

remain online even after the game's
completion.

We hope you have the time of your life in this round
of Truth or Dare. If you have any questions, feel free
to contact us.

Your Referees,
  Comedy and Tragedy

Chapter 1

I kicked the avocado plushie off the bed again while I slept. It looks up with that smiling face, judging me silently.

My contact lenses notice that I'm awake. Logos and notifications cross through my sharpening vision. It makes it difficult to gauge the distance from the floor as I swipe at the plushie. I scoop it up as unread text messages overtake my eyes. The text swarm after waking up isn't unusual, but seeing multiple missed messages from Analisa worries me. Did I forget a date?

An impulsive smile forms as I read her inquisitive texts: "Good morning, beautiful. Awake yet?" "Cai, do you remember what today is?" A GIF of an animated clam with googly eyes follows the texts. Clams are one of Analisa's favorite creatures. As she puts it, they've got even fewer limbs than she does, but they get through life just fine.

Knowing that she's likely saying these messages out loud makes it feel more personal. She won't trust the generative writing in her contact lenses for much of anything. She even wrote her most recent physics paper by dictating it in the middle of the mall.

I say, "Yes, I'm awake. Why?'" The text ripples across my eyes as it sends.

Analisa responds with: "Yay! Updates in thirty minutes!"

The tree bark on my back warbles in nervousness. Ugh—my alien parent likely thought it was a gift for some of my skin to be like theirs. Sure, the way the bark rubs together to make noise is cool. And when my parents taught me that it's called warbling, it stuck with me as something that could've been neat. But if my skin were to make that singing kind of noise in public, someone might question whether I'm fully human.

The whole reason I'm nervous enough to warble is because I forgot that Analisa wanted to go to Updates today. It's where everyone goes to get checkups on their contact lenses. At certain ages, people can upgrade the information, places, and privileges accessible with their contacts. Since Analisa and I are both eighteen, we can update our contacts to Version 20.

I set the avocado plushie on a pillow and leap out of the bed. I fling on my yellow robe and step over my comfy corner of plant plushies covering the beanbag. My desk chair almost trips me again since I attempted to hop around the folded, clean clothes I left in a pile by the foot of the bed.

I snap my fingers for more light. The bulbs strung across the ceiling flash on. My little plant-shaped lamps also illuminate the furniture. The electronic wall wakes from its night mode, igniting with digital photos and posters. I can't help but smile at the several photos of Analisa and me. For years, we've commonly taken selfies to show off our outfits, commemorate when we find posters for game shows, and capture silly moments.

When I enter my personal bathroom, I snap again to turn on the bright lights. My elbows press against the marble counter as Analisa sends, "Remember we're just visiting. We don't have to do it today. If at all." An uneasy shiver runs across my skin, but fortunately, the bark doesn't warble this time.

I suck in a breath of lavender-scented air, trying to calm my mind as I arm my toothbrush with toothpaste. Despite her claims that this is only a visit, I know Analisa's ready to update her contacts. Usually, I tried new things when she did, like when we got our matching carnation tattoos. But the idea of actually going through with Version 20 is a whole new kind of commitment.

Another text: "Hey, Cai? We can go another day. I don't want you to feel pressured into this."

I give an exhausted glare at myself in the mirror as I finish the onerous task of brushing my teeth. I don't feel pressured; I feel stupid for agreeing to this visit and suddenly getting cold feet.

Oh great, my green skin is starting to show. I have to apply skin gradient every day, since it wears off after enough time—or after using enough cleaning supplies. The bark texture on my chest is easy enough to hide with a shirt, but I need the skin modification to make myself look fully human. Why is it so easy for me to change my skin, but it feels difficult to change my contact lenses?

My fingers trail over the glass door entrance to the skin modifier pod. As the pod is just big enough for me to comfortably stand inside, it doesn't crowd the bathroom. Fortunately, I was able to purchase it after winning a local kids Trivia game. I have my history fixation to thank for helping me win that a few years ago.

I step into the pod and close my eyes when the chiming countdown starts. Music plays as steam ripples over my body. As the music diminishes, the soft drying jets blow warm air. My eyes blink, wary of the vapor drying on my lashes. Relief settles into my tense muscles when I see the light tone on my arms. I step outside the pod and admire the change in the mirror.

My fingers work to put in the gold leaf promise earring that matches the one I gave Analisa. My anxiety grows as it takes me a few extra seconds than usual to pinch it into place. I push open my closet doors and slide the hangers around, considering my black outfits. The scarf with neon yellow highlights was a gift from Analisa, so I choose that as part of the look. I pick through my clean clothes pile for the blouse that matches the scarf best. A black jacket would be good. Damn it—my usual pants for this outfit are in the hamper.

My mind lingers on the Updates visit as I pull on ripped leggings. Getting Version 20 might not be so bad. The main advertised appeal is that it gives a person access to applying to serious game shows. All the local, barely-televised kiddy games are left behind—no more Hide and Seek, Hot Potato, or Trivia. Version 20 allows people to apply for broad-casted game shows like Mother May I, Never Have I Ever, and Truth or Dare. The last one has been my favorite for years, since it was the first show I watched with Analisa.

Playing well-funded games like those means more money to win and more notoriety to gain. If I want to keep my alien parentage a secret, staying away from attention-grabbing things like those shows would be best.

Aside from the game show aspect, Version 20 is appealing for different reasons. With Version 20, I'd be treated more like an adult. I could drink alcohol and take pills. If I had the money for it, I could apply for off-government housing. I've even heard that there's better service at restaurants as a teenager with Version 20. That's probably why Analisa's excited about it.

But she's been awestruck by the serious games since she was little. She's joked that we could win something big together on one of them. Am I so nervous about this Updates visit because I'm scared of her applying to one of the shows?

I'm wasting time thinking. I snatch buckled, black boots out of my closet and pull them on.

Another text from Analisa: "How about I try it today, and if you feel more comfortable with it, you can try it later? Who knows, I might play something and win enough to get you to DU." She adds a cartoon clam GIF with a heart.

She would be willing to play a serious game to get me into Darilek University? I've had my eye on the place because it has one of the best history departments in Tribu Amalricus; it's arguably one of the best schools in the entire North American Region. And it's right here in the city. If I won a major Version 20 game, or even a few small Version 20 games, I could pay for tuition.

But the cost of winning depends on the game. To start, you have to sell yourself on how interesting you are to become a contestant. Then, whatever happens in the game is on your online record. If I do something embarrassing or say something horrible, my reputation could be ruined. The games guarantee that players can sue if someone discriminates against them based on what's revealed. Still, I don't feel secure enough about that being enforced.

Regardless, Analisa wants to upgrade to Version 20 today. I should be there to support her.

Analisa's supported me countless times throughout my years in New York. Her encouragement has been even more resolute since she learned that I'm a lab-created being. My alien parent, human mom, human grandparents, and Auntie Tera are the only other ones who know. Gram and Grampa made sure to delete any online evidence of me as a kid with green, barky skin. They're cool like that. My parents—who used an incubator with a random-generated characteristics blend—are not.

I let a bot apply my makeup and a metallic gold sheen to my dark brown hair. After I have my contact lenses add yellow flecks to my brown irises, I say, "Command, text Analisa."

I do a final mirror check. The reflection now shows an East Asian Amalrican teenager dressed up in typical New York fashion. Without the green skin and bark on my torso showing, I look like my human mom. No one would question my humanity.

I send a message to Analisa: "You should get your update today. I'll be there in ten to support you."

Chapter 2

My flat shoes slap against the sunny sidewalk. Updates isn't a far walk from my apartment; soon, I'm standing outside the store. I appreciate the warmth of the sunlight on my face—it'll give me some extra energy. The wind licks at my scarf, encouraging me toward the sidewalk edge.

I lean against the railing as I look down at the water-filled streets carrying jet skis, SUBs, and boats of all kinds. The whooshing of the water and engines beneath my feet is calming. As interesting as a pure, sea-street city like Houston was, I prefer having more space to walk above it all.

"Cai!" Analisa squeals.

My chest lightens as she strides over to me with her walking stick. I squish her until she pokes my stomach, laughing at me to let her go. As energizing as the sunlight is, nothing beats the wholesome feeling I get from Analisa's touch.

Her glittery, metallic eye shadow is so on point—she always applies it herself. She went with gold in her contacts today, complementing her brown skin. I'm tempted to touch her hair, which has flower braces wrapped around the pink streaks. Interesting, she's even wearing her favorite dress and fishnet tights, showing off her curvy figure. I knew she'd be excited to go out today, but I didn't anticipate this much.

"Someone's looking especially beautiful today." I give her an obvious glance-over.

"I know! My girlfriend has such good style." Analisa shoots that look back at me. It shifts into an adorable smile that tries to mask her sheepishness.

"Me?" I wrap my arm around her shoulder and point at a nearby shop. "You see those mannequins? They try to sell people the idea of beauty. But you? You're the perfect twenty-third-century princess. Wonderful in every way."

She rubs her head against my shoulder. "Wow. Seven months in and you're still a sweet talker. What did I do to deserve you?"

Giddy that my arm-around-the-shoulder tactic worked to get her closer, I suddenly lose my ability to speak. "I..." Is there a cute pun I can make here? Or something cool to continue the banter? "Uh." I know I don't need to impress her, but I would prefer some ideas over none.

"Looks like I spoke too soon." She laughs and takes my hand. "It's okay. You don't need to be nervous. Is the upgrade idea still bothering you? If so, let's go to the mall instead. We could look at jewelry to celebrate the new semester. Lian told me to get him some more fabric anyway."

I shake my head as I stare at the Updates sign. "You wanted an upgrade, so you should get one. I don't want to miss out on your special day."

Her eyebrows slant with concern. "Are you sure?"

I step toward Updates, lifting our held hands. "Of course. Ready?"

As soon as I walk into the sleek salon with all its black marble and pristine mirrors, my discomfort fades. Now all I want to do is sit in a cushioned chair. I don't even know what I was so worried about.

When the stylist plucks our contacts out, the dry chill around me makes my eyelids squeeze shut. I coerce my eyes open while our stylist works on our contacts. As my gaze wanders, there's no time blinking in the top right, no text notifications, no desktop, no Internet access, no email, no dictionary, no calculator, no books or movies... nothing.

Analisa giggles. She's futilely outstretching her arm like she's trying to manipulate a part of her vision. "So weird! What do you think, Cai?"

I nod. "Definitely weird. It's like my eyes are naked."

"Oh, how scandalous!" She covers a hand over her temporarily brown eyes, peeking through her fingers a bit. "Don't look, Cai! I'm indecent!"

I roll my eyes, trying to hide my smile. "Like you care when I see you indecent."

"Wow, you make it sound like we're indecent around each other a lot." She wiggles her eyebrows.

Warmth flushes to my cheeks. We're far too asexual for that kind of thing. Kissing, holding hands, and cuddling are normal for us. After enough times of Analisa complaining about sex scenes in movies, we figured out that we were both disinterested in sex. Apparently, that doesn't stop Analisa from teasing me. "I just meant we change clothes around each other a lot."

Before Analisa can think of something else embarrassing to say, our stylist approaches. I cool my face with the back of my hands. I try not to look at Analisa, but I know she's watching me because of her little giggle.

The stylist opens a couple of shiny cases, containing the upgraded contacts. After the stylist gently sets lenses in Analisa's eyes, their gloved hands insert my contacts as well. My vision sharpens. All the icons load onto the desktop bar at the side of my vision, the time blinks in the top right corner, and everything else boots up... including the new app that connects to Version 20 games.

We test out the contacts, confirming that everything works the same. After we send our payments, we leave the salon. Now, when I look at Analisa, her public profile lists "Version 20" beneath her name and pronouns.

"You want to get some food? I swear, I got dehydrated just from having the contacts out for five minutes." Analisa laughs lightly.

"Yeah, that sounds good," I agree.

She's got an extra spring in her step now. "We did it! Now we can apply for Version 20 jobs. We could even play the major games if we wanted to."

We did it. A breathy grin forms on my face. "Yeah. I guess we could."

No way I'm playing any of those games though.

Chapter 3

Analisa gapes at my plate. "They gave you fries!"

A bit of bile circulates at the back of my throat. "Yep."

She whirls toward the automated food desk. "Hey, she didn't ask for fries! We need a new steak here, and maybe a mechanic. Gotta fix up this doofus of a machine!"

The automated desk robot tilts its serving tray arm, as if questioning her.

I tap her arm. "It's fine. I can just eat the steak."

"Okay, but if I were a mechanic, I'd piece you apart right here and now!" Analisa points at the machine. "You know those Gen-Ren people? I'd fix you up quicker than them, you piece of work!"

As I guide her away, the serving tray arm gives her a middle finger. It's for the best that Analisa doesn't notice.

Analisa leads the way through the crowded tables

in the food court. The buzz of overlapping conversation blankets the environment, encouraging me into a trance-like state as I focus only on avoiding people. Analisa has always been better at pushing through crowds; I still haven't figured out how to mimic her bold presence.

We reach a small table that a couple of people just left. The hovering cleaner robot finishes sweeping the trash and drying the sanitized table before we sit. I quickly thank the robot as it chirps and flies away.

Analisa gives an exasperated sigh as she sits. "You know, your Gram and Grampa could probably fix that food server bot. By Gret, if only I were an engineer."

"Maybe Grampa could," I note as I sit across from her. "Gram is more like you. They prefer physics."

"Ah, so it runs in your family to be attracted to physicists." Analisa lilts her voice jokingly. "That explains a lot."

I roll my eyes. "Sure. My family explains a lot about me—that much is true."

She places her hand on mine. "It only explains as much as you want it to." After the pause that comes from thinking about my parents, Analisa continues, "Speaking of, what are you going to do about those fries?"

"You can have them," I suggest. "It'd be a waste to throw them away."

Her mouth twists in the way it does when she wants something but wants to deny it. I've seen that expression when we order food at a place with decent vegetarian options.

"Have them. You really don't have to only eat meat around me," I insist.

Her unsure eyes flicker between me and the fries. "Well, it's our first day with Version 20. I'll make an exception today, because wasting food is bad for the environment. And because that idiotic machine gave it to you."

The machine stops what it's doing to give Analisa another middle finger. While I glance over Analisa's shoulder, she scrapes the fries onto her plate.

"Do you want ketchup?" I ask. The packets are nearby; I might as well offer so she feels better about eating a vegetable in front of me.

Her eyebrows pinch incredulously. "Of course not! Ketchup is made from tomato."

"Mustard?"

"That's also a plant."

"Mayo?"

"Who puts mayo on steak?"

She's so stubborn. It's ridiculously cute. "Relish?"

"Made from pickles."

"Tartar sauce?"

"Also has pickles."

I grin. "You're an omnivore, Analisa. You can get away with cutting out animals from your diet, but you can't cut out plants, even if it's only when I'm around. You've gotta pickle your battles."

Her face becomes deadpanned. "You did not do that whole spiel just to set up a pun."

"I may-o may not have done that."

She shakes her head. "No."

"You have to ketchup to my level, Analisa."

"No."

"I'm relishing your reaction right now."

"Ugh. I'm dying right now. You are literally killing me." Her forehead rests on the table.

"You can't even mustard the energy to look at me?"

She slides down into her chair, so much so that her head goes beneath the table level. She dramatically reaches her prosthetic right arm toward the ceiling. "Still dying!"

A crackle of static tickles my ear, followed by a wrinkly voice. "Oh, dear. It seems Cai is killing her girlfriend. Cai, why would you do that?"

Grampa hacked into my headphones again. My grandparents could call people instead, but since they're technologically confident enough to link their headphones to other ones—and they enjoy surprising me out of nowhere—their voices often jump into my life.

Now I'm the one to set my forehead on the table. "Grampa, what are you doing?"

Analisa's excited voice rises as she sits up. "Grampa! She's killing me with puns again. Please tell her to stop."

"Cai, why would you do such a thing? We didn't teach you to be like this." Gram Aru jumps on the line too.

"Excuse you, sweetie, but puns are the ultimate

charming method," Grampa Dix argues. "After all, you're with me."

"Wrong. I am with you *despite* your unfortunate infliction of puns."

Analisa whispers, "What are they saying?"

"They're bickering," I relay as I sit up. "And yes, Gram Aru's on your side again."

"Yes!" She balls up her fists victoriously.

"This wasn't what we called for," Gram Aru redirects the conversation.

"Yes, but your comment about puns was uncalled for," Grampa Dix undirects.

"Sweetie, I'm going to block your voice unless you settle down." After allowing Grampa Dix to grumble for a moment, Gram Aru asks, "Cai, my dear, how are you?"

"I'm doing alright," I say. "I'm getting food with Analisa."

"Ah yes. A few stores away from Updates."

I rub my forehead. They know.

"What are they saying now? Anything about..." Analisa points at her eyes. I shake my hand in front of my neck, which makes it clear to her that she's right.

"Well, did you do anything fun today other than dining out?" Gram Aru asks.

I rub my forehead. I haven't mentioned the idea of upgrading to Version 20 yet to my family. Upgrading is something that normal families can talk about without it being a big deal. It's just a common aspect of growing up as a human, like being excited to drive even the short trip to the grocery store after getting a boating license, talking an in awkward cluster of friends at a school dance, or having a first sip of alcohol only to hate the taste but appreciate the independence. I've only experienced those instances vicariously via television shows, but my argument still stands.

With my family, anything that associates me with change is often followed by an argument with my parents. "Alright, I know you know, Gram. I'm sorry I didn't bring it up. I just thought that it was time." I sigh. "Do Alexis and Kiran know?"

"It's about time you upgraded. I thought you didn't like new technology for a couple years. It scared the heck out of me," Grampa Dix exclaims with a relieved laugh.

"What your Grampa is trying to say... is that it's alright; you didn't have to discuss it with us. And no, we haven't told your parents. We thought you should tell them yourself. Perhaps tomorrow when they're in town?"

"Tomorrow?" I planned on trying to hide the upgrade for at least a week.

"Your Grampa Dix and I can create software to change your Version number to 10 in front of your parents. Still, you should tell them soon. Hiding things from those you care about never turns out well."

They're such cool grandparents. Especially when I've learned about what they've been through. I grew up listening to how they became engineers, broke down the Houston government, and handled their friend who once took over the world. Hearing their stories about the past is what encourages me to read about history. And Version 20 might help me pay for the tuition to study history in college.

"Okay," I respond. "I'll try to tell them next week, at the latest."

"Good," Gram Aru says. "Now put me on speaker. I want to say hi to Analisa."

I blink the controls to change one of my headphones to speaker mode and set it on the table. I rub my ear, appreciating how it feels to remove the headphones every so often. Usually, I keep them in so I can put on music whenever there's annoying or overwhelming noise in public. That also means more opportunity for my grandparents to talk to me on a whim.

Gram Aru's voice emerges. "Hi, Analisa!"

"Hi, Gram!" Analisa leans over the table to respond.

"Has Cai been treating you well?"

"Cai's been wonderful. She came with me so I wasn't alone when I got my update. I'm afraid I might've coerced her into getting one too. I'm sorry."

"No need to apologize, dear. We saw the footage; it appears that it was Cai's own decision. I'm glad to hear that you're both treating each other well."

Of course they watched the footage. I wouldn't be surprised if they're watching us now through the mall's food court cameras. I say, "I mean no offense,

Gram, but most people of your generation don't hack into security cameras anymore."

"How else are we supposed to make sure our only granddaughter and her girlfriend are doing okay? What if you were kidnapped? You know, back in our time, we were kidnapped by a terrorist group. They hijacked the security cameras, so no one knew."

"Didn't we willingly go with them? They hijacked the security cameras so no one knew we were traitors," Grampa Dix corrects.

"Oh, right. Well, what choice did we have? We had to get away from that dangerous so-called politician my birth father worked with."

"Dude, you're getting off-topic again."

Analisa giggles. "Cai, your grandparents lived such interesting lives! I can't believe they're so cool."

"Look at that, we're still cool," Grampa Dix says, a bit of pride in his old voice. "It's not like people still have me tattooed on their arms, but whatever."

Analisa gasps. "Did someone really do that?"

"It was one person you met in an airport. Get over it, dear." I can hear Gram Aru roll their eyes. "Did we have anything else to tell them?"

"There was something else. Your Aruzheimer's is kicking in."

"I don't have Aruz—Alzheimer's! I thought there was something else."

"A thing about a game, maybe? Oh, a birthday gift?"

"Cai's birthday is months away."

"A game?" I ask, the word getting my attention.

"Oh! Yes." The uncertainty fades from Gram Aru's voice. "Be very careful about the Version 20 games. Although your Grampa and I did some dangerous things at your age, these games are unnecessarily cruel. I warn you: don't take part in too many, or any at a high scale of risk. A person almost died playing Truth or Dare last week, and I don't want you or Analisa to get seriously injured. Do you two understand me?"

I haven't seen last week's highlight video yet, so I don't know whether Gram is being overly concerned. The dares on Truth or Dare can get semi-dangerous— it's part of the entertainment value. Although the show occasionally produces severe injuries, no one ever dies on the show. Still, trying to explain that to Gram isn't worth the worry it might cause them.

Analisa nods toward the earpiece, indicating she'll side with what I say. I nod back, saying, "Yeah, we understand, Gram. Thanks for telling us. We'll keep that in mind."

Chapter 4

Our two-week break from school just ended. The history classes concluded before the break, so today, I start my next chosen history class: Fashion History. I even get to take it with Analisa.

Students meander around the school's reception area. Their voices overlap as they dictate and type assignments at the last minute. I squeeze into one of the large elevators along with several students. My class is on the fourth floor above the main city walkway, so I press against the wall until the students from the other floors leave.

I step out of the elevator on the fourth floor when someone waves at me out of the corner of my eye. Ah, it's Lian—his hair is shorter since I last saw him. His profile divulges that his name is Lian Patel, he uses he/him pronouns, and he has Version 10. I know him as Analisa's twin brother.

"Hey." Thin, neon green lines cover his jacket

today. He set his iris color to green, accenting his relaxed eyes. Even though the contact lenses correct his vision, he wears oval glasses for style. His Indian accent is stronger than Analisa's. "I'm glad to see someone I know. Do you know where room 450 is?"

"Yeah. That's my next class." I raise my eyebrows. "Did Analisa not tell you where it is?"

"Ah, no. Did she know this whole time?" His voice sounds irritated and amused like there's a joke I'm missing.

I gesture for Lian to follow me as I walk down the hall. "She's in this class too."

Lian gapes. "She did not tell me!"

I shrug. "She's probably just messing around. Or she's trying to surprise you. I didn't realize you'd be interested in this class."

"Are you kidding?" He gestures down at his outfit. "I dress up for school! Sewing this was not inexpensive. It took me two years of tutoring to finally make a week's worth of clothing I truly like."

His dramatic voice gets me to smile. He's always able to carry on a conversation, even with someone as generally reserved as me. "I just mean... I thought you already knew a lot about all this."

"Ah, yes, I do. But it's a class credit with a topic that I am interested in, and knowing more can't hurt." He squints at me. "Say, what is your favorite color, Cai? Mine is green, in case you can't tell." He gestures to his outfit.

I tug on my yellow scarf. "Yellow. It's bright and positive."

"Hm!" His eyes widen. "Interesting choice. You don't hear too many people say yellow, but it is a good color, isn't it? It makes quite the statement." He leans closer, as if sharing a secret. "Needless to say, I like your scarf."

My smile grows wider. "Thanks. Although, I'll have to credit Analisa for giving this to me for our six-month friendiversary a few years ago."

"I see!" Lian nods emphatically. "Don't tell her I said so, but her fashion sense isn't terrible. I still cannot believe that she did not tell me about this class."

I pause at the open doorway, gesturing. "Here it is."

"You first. I insist." Lian holds out his hand.

I nod in thanks and step inside the classroom.

Students talk with each other in clumps around the room. I recognize a few acquaintances among many strangers. There's no one here that I'm all that comfortable with. Keeping to myself is what I'm used to anyhow.

I slink into a seat in the back row. Desks and fashion event posters pack the sunlit room. The large windows reveal the metallic urban environment around us. It's reminiscent of the bright view I saw when I went to school in Houston—at least, on the days when it wasn't pouring rain.

Lian's face lights up as he approaches some of our classmates. They quickly welcome him into their conversation. It's impressive how he can talk with anyone.

I blink my visual desktop into view and click on a song by Heka. Grampa Dix introduced me to her music a few months ago, and now I'm immersed in her albums from the 2200s. The orchestra seeps me into a calm atmosphere, making this classroom feel like a setting in a musical. The day would be more entertaining if my classmates started dancing and singing like in the movies Analisa adores.

My face lights up when Analisa walks into the room. She waves at a few of our classmates and asks how their break was. I blink the volume down on my headphones so I can hear her peppy voice.

When she walks over and slings her backpack onto the floor, I eye her pink platform boots with amazement. "You never cease to amaze with what you can walk in."

"What can I say?" She takes my hand as she sits down, swinging it between our desks. "My balance is better than ever. You've seen my medals."

"How could I miss them?" I ask, thinking about the recent line of gymnastics medals in her bedroom.

"Well, it's one of my many talents. Speaking of talents..." She holds up my hand, examining the gold nail polish I applied last night. "I love this. Your hand's gotten much steadier."

"Thanks." I squeeze her hand, lifting her red nails. "The red goes well with your outfit."

"I know! I still enjoy dressing a little extra for the first day back from breaks." She laughs.

Lian slips into the seat next to Analisa, clearing his throat with his chin high in the air. Dressing up special for the first day of school seems to run in their family.

Analisa rolls her eyes as she turns to face Lian. "What is it, Lili?"

"You did not tell me where this room was. I told you I was in this class." Lian tips his head up higher. "You ignored me."

"Not ignored. I jested." Analisa reaches her non-prosthetic leg over to kick his calf.

Lian gapes before dusting off his pants. "Rude."

Analisa and I part hands as an older person steps into the classroom. I read our Fashion History teacher's profile while she introduces the class material. I double-blink to screenshot some of the slideshow images.

About midway through the class, the teacher pauses, listening to something in her earpiece. She blinks a few times before continuing with her presentation.

Analisa picks up her backpack. Lian too. As they walk to the door, Analisa looks back at me with her eyebrows raised.

After the two of them leave the classroom, a message pops into my vision from Analisa. "Called to the office. We're being picked up early for some reason. I'll keep you updated."

I blink to give the message a thumbs-up. An unexpected early pickup on the first day after a break is odd given how school-emphatic their parents are, but it's probably fine.

When the bell rings, I lift my bag and turn up the

music in my headphones. I have twenty minutes until my next class. I've got time to journey to the moderate-volume library. There, I sit on the balcony overlooking the book-filled environment. I mutter, "Command, text Analisa: 'Everything okay, question mark.'" The text appears in the middle of my vision as it sends.

I close my eyes and pluck a random book from the history shelf. My fingers trace a title about the Acceleration in the late 2040s. I know the general gist of the events when the effects of climate change skyrocketed, but I don't know them well.

I spend my remaining break time reading. My contact lenses send the words into my earpiece, allowing me to listen while my eyes parse the book. Sometimes, my eyes skip lines and flip some of the letters around, so I appreciate the extra help.

By the time my timer goes off, Analisa still hasn't replied. I tab the page in my contacts and check out the book. Then I head to Mathematical Archaeology. Then lunch. Then Journalism in New York City. Then another twenty-minute break. And finally, Chemistry in Art and Artifacts.

When school finishes, I turn up the music and leave the building. Auntie Tera doesn't get off work for another few hours, so she can't pick me up from school. Usually, I walk with Analisa and Lian, since their apartment is on the way to Tera's. I'll be at the building in about three songs.

The corner of my eye catches the jetskis and SUBs surging on the streets beneath my feet. I peer over one of the bridges, watching the traffic in the water flowing beneath the sidewalk. I catch an involuntary smile, realizing that the sight doesn't ever stop being neat.

I pass under a canopy with public water fountains lining the edges. A ruggedly-dressed nomad sits on a bench, strumming a guitar and singing to a small group of children. I lower the volume in my headphones to catch some of the familiar folk tune. After I meet eyes with the nomad and offer a smile, they grin and change the next lyric from "kindness of a stranger" to "kind smile of a stranger." The acknowledgment sets off a delighted warmth in my chest as I continue walking. Brief, uplifting interactions with strangers are part of why I like this city so much; it feels so human.

The apartment building is in sight. Auntie Tera is well off enough to stay on a floor to herself since she works in the Tribu Amalricus government. She was even able to take me in after the break with my parents a few years ago without it straining her finances. Even though she can't tell me what exactly she does, I imagine that she's important.

I should get some groceries to make her something. She liked the dumplings I prepared a few weeks ago. We've got to make something anyway since my parents are visiting today. I veer in the direction of the grocery store before I forget.

I journey through the aisles, blinking ingredients off the list as I place them in a cart. I need enough to feed all four of us, but the amount is getting too big to fit into my bag. I also get a six-pack of flavored water, ensuring my alien parent has enough to drink.

I glare at the half-full shopping cart. Although the shipping fee is only fifty dollars, it still seems silly to have the store fly this stuff a few blocks away. Regardless, it's too much for me to carry alone. I sigh as I select the drone delivery option and charge it to the bank account Tera opened for me.

Before I arrive at the apartment, I receive a notification saying my bags have been delivered. Once I'm inside, I put the ingredients away. Since Tera hasn't come out, she's either busy or not home. Or maybe she's got on the noise-cancelling headphones that Grampa Dix made her.

In my bedroom, I boot up my electronic desk and work through assignments for my classes. Midway through filling out an introductory questionnaire for the fashion class, Analisa texts, "Sorry for responding so late. Can you talk?"

"Sure," I respond.

Analisa starts a voice call. She's sniffling. "Hey, Cai."

"Hey." Concern tugs at my chest. "Are you okay? What happened?"

"I—uh, well... no." Her voice drops, although it tries to stay near its usual pitch. "Is Tera nearby?"

Tera can hear everything within a few miles of her because of some technological experiment she went through as a kid. If Analisa's asking about that, she probably has something serious to say. "I don't think she's in the apartment, so she probably wouldn't pay too much attention to my voice right now if she's in the city. Why?"

"I don't... I want you to know. But I also don't want to tell a lot of people." She sniffles again. "I don't know."

"I'm here. I'm listening," I assure. My eyes stare into the wall as if my focus could traverse the streets to comfort her.

"My father has cancer. I'm in the hospital right now. They say it's bad. And rare. He collapsed earlier, and now he's—" Her voice cracks. "I don't know what to do. Apparently, it's been around for a while, but maybe he's been hiding it or not dealing with it. They say the treatment is so expensive, and insurance won't cover most of it. He might... they're saying he might not make it, Cai."

My heart jerks at her voice. Although I'm not close with her father, he's always kind whenever I go to their apartment. From how Analisa talks about him, he's been a positive influence in her life. "That's horrible. I'm sorry, Ana. If there's anything you need right now—food or delivering something, whatever you need—I'm here."

She sniffles. "Thanks, Cai. I seriously think... I'm thinking I need to apply for Version 20 games. If I win enough prize money, it might pay for the treatment."

My throat tightens.

"I know it sounds insane," she adds quickly. "I mean, my mom might hate me for doing something so public, but I've been watching the shows for years.

I know all the ins and outs of them. I might be good at it. It couldn't hurt to apply, right?"

I cover my open mouth, stopping myself from saying something too soon. If I were to do something so impulsive as joining a Version 20 game, doing it for her feels like a worthy reason.

"Aren't you going to tell me it's not worth it?" She gives a sad laugh. "I know it sounds insane, but I don't know..."

"Wait until tomorrow to apply." My dry throat has a difficult time swallowing between my words. "They're more likely to pick people who know each other for games like Never Have I Ever and Truth or Dare. Take the night to think."

"Yeah. I don't think Lian would do it though. I'll ask him, but still. He doesn't really watch the shows."

"What I mean is..." My mouth stutters as I admit something I might regret. "I don't want to jump into anything, but I might apply with you."

"You would do that?" Her hiccupped tears are clear enough from her despondent voice. "I can't ask you to take that risk for me."

"If we both apply, you're more likely to be chosen. And if we're both chosen, then that's twice the possibility of winning enough for your father to get treatment. If we apply tomorrow, they still might put us in a game next week." The more I talk, the more resolved I become. "Is there anything else you need? Otherwise, I'm going to start preparing for my parents."

"No, I'm—thank you for even considering it. You're

too sweet, Cai." She sniffles. "Good luck with your parents. Talk tomorrow morning?"

"Yeah, thanks. I'm sorry this is happening, Ana. I'll see you tomorrow." My hands rub together to knead out their unease. "I'll have an answer for you by then."

Chapter 5

As I cut the dough, I hear the locks on the front door disengage. Even though no one can enter this floor of the building without authorization, Auntie Tera is extra careful with the living space portion—where we relax and sleep.

I continue shaping the dough pieces into circles as Tera walks in. "Hey, Auntie."

Her eyes are always distant like she's not quite able to pay attention to the people around her. She always tries though, even if she's distracted by the sounds in the city. Since she's able to hear everything within a few miles of her, I'm surprised she hasn't gone insane.

She smiles. "Cai." She pats my shoulder. "It looks like I arrived for my favorite part. Do you need help pleating?"

Non-verbal cues reach her faster, so I nod, gesturing to the dough. She helps me pat little clumps of meat, vegetables, and noodle filling into the dough. When we let them sit in the steamer baskets, Tera collapses onto one of the clean couches in the living room. She adjusts her hearing aids—probably to make them block out more noise.

I heat some meat without any plants in it for myself. Using metal chopsticks, I push the ground beef around the sizzling pan, letting myself get lost in the mesmerizing act while the meat changes color.

My thoughts return to the Version 20 games. Analisa and I are lucky to be in New York, which is the biggest hub for the broadcast games. But playing any of them might expose some things to the world. I focus on my beige hands, still pushing the meat in the skillet.

I can apply multiple layers to my skin tone. Hopefully the gradient would last at least a week before starting to fade. I don't want to think about the possibility of it running out before we finish a game. The games themselves tend to last less than a week. They can be longer when combined with introductory interviews, closing ceremonies, and other events.

"Cai," Tera's voice calls from the couch. I turn to look at her. "Thank you for cleaning."

So she did notice my efforts from this morning. Since she's letting me stay here for free, I try to keep the space clean for her. I smile. "You're welcome."

She stares at me, squinting. "Ah. Version 20."

My skin shivers. Grampa Dix's software should

prevent my family from seeing that I have Version 20. "Yeah."

She leans back with a sly smile. "Interesting. It still says Version 10 on your profile."

I tip my head up, slightly irritated that I let that slip so easily. She must've heard Analisa and I at Updates. "Yep. I wanted to tell you and my parents before you saw it."

She stares into space, shrugging. "It's become the norm to have Version 20 for many reasons. I don't think you need to ask us for permission. Especially if you're using your own allowance from cleaning the apartment."

I squint, wondering if I've forgotten that I have an allowance. My face slackens when I realize what she means. It's a defense against my parents, saying that I worked hard for what they might call an unnecessary expense. "Thanks, Auntie."

As I package the cooked meat, Tera asks if I want to play one of her old combat video games. Since we've got several minutes until I need to reduce the heat on the dumplings, I change into a tank top and shorts.

By the time I'm ready, Tera's stretching with the remote system strapped on and the television set up. She might be in her late fifties, but she still clings onto an intense exercise regimen.

I strap on the remote system. When I click on my saved character, the resistance bands tighten.

The video game screen returns us to our next quest. We jog our characters into a dungeon and punch, kick, and jump through fantasy monsters. I find myself smiling as Tera and I work together, moving through it all.

She's still quick. Gram Aru has shown me videos of Tera from her younger years—she learned to fight well, and I bet it's still in her muscle memory. Glancing at her, I know it's embedded in her form. Although I'm not certain if I want to learn martial arts, I imagine she'd teach me if I asked.

After a few minutes, the steamed dumplings are done. While I pack the food, Tera passes me a wet towel. I wipe it over my shoulders and neck as I go change into clothes that cover my barky chest.

By the time I leave my room, Tera's in a more casual outfit. I pick up the heavier bag of food and Tera lifts the other one before we leave the apartment. She adjusts her hearing aids while we walk to the park.

Tera confirms in her earpiece that the part of the park we usually go to is "closed for eco-friendly renovation." Because of Tera's connections, there's even an invisible cloak over the hill where we'll meet my parents so no one can see us from afar.

It's all out of precaution. Hardly anything surprises anyone living in New York City. Plus, most people know by now that there are aliens living on Earth. The concealing effort is probably for the best though. People still tend to get scared of a walking tree.

Tera's handprint allows us through the park barrier. My parents already sit on the hill we usually picnic on. They've got a checkered blanket laid out, and they wave as we approach.

My mom, Alexis, is human. She cut her hair short again, but she's still wearing that long, green coat she found a few months ago at a thrift store. As I hug her, she beams. Her voice does the gravelly thing it does when she squeezes me. "It's so good to see you, my little sapling!"

I admit a slim smile. She's gotten nicer over time. Maybe this picnic won't feel too awkward.

Kiran, my alien parent, warbles as I hug them. My arms reach about halfway around their trunk. Their branches brush against my back. Although my parents tried teaching me both English and warbles, my understanding of the warbles isn't as certain as it used to be.

As they hug Tera, I unpack the dumplings and flavored water onto the blanket. There's already some flavored water, potato salad, a pack of grilled shrimp, and an unseasoned omelet in containers on the blanket. I smile at the last two odd things—probably trying to cover their bases for whatever I might feel like eating.

We pass around the food. Tera points out that I did most of the effort on the steamed buns, and my mom compliments my cooking. Before touching the ground beef, I eat the omelet to be polite. Kiran opens some of the flavored water I brought and pours it on their trunk. They warble something about how good my choice of water is.

Tiptoeing through lighthearted conversation feels

odd. Still, the more time I spend apart from them, the more hopeful I feel about mending our relationship. After all, they're not talking negatively about my choice to appear as a human. Maybe it's a sign that they're trying to accept how I want to present myself.

I slide off my shoes and socks to match my mom. I grew up walking barefoot on the dirt floor of our house in the Houston outskirts, following my mom's footsteps. She'd praise the callouses I developed, telling me all about how my tough feet would carry me wherever I wanted to go.

The game show possibility lingers in my mind. Is that where I want to go now?

If I'm considering whether to enter a televised game, I shouldn't leave it as a surprise to my parents or Tera. I should bring it up. But I prefer the light-hearted conversation about harmless things—how their plane trip was, how Tera's been feeling about work, how my first day back at school was.

At least, that last part seems harmless. But when I tell them that Analisa's dad is in the hospital, I realize how close I am to talking about the games. If I'm going to tell them, now is the time.

Kiran warbles in concern. They say something about how they hope the parent improves—Analisa's father, I realize.

"It's really bad from what it sounds like." My fingers rub each other anxiously. "Analisa's even thinking about entering a Version 20 game to raise the money for his treatment."

Tera's eyebrows rise. I'm not sure how present she is right now, but with the context that I have Version 20, I wouldn't be surprised if she knows where this is going.

I glance at my parents, trying to gauge how they feel about what I said.

"That poor girl." My mom lowers her food. "Going to such lengths for her parents. It's admirable, although I hope she's careful."

Hope rises in my chest. "Agreed. Which is why I'm considering applying to the games with her."

Kiran's branches shiver. My mom's face freezes, a careful concern in her eyes. My heart yanks forward, knowing that face—this won't end well.

Tera stares into the distance, perhaps hearing something that distracts her. Her blank expression could be in reaction to my words. Either way, I have to sit in the uncomfortable silence.

"Caitlee, your contacts are still on Version 10," my mom says. She's deflecting to avoid confronting my words.

"I got Version 20 yesterday. It's just hidden," I say.

The implication makes my mom's eyes widen as she looks at Tera.

"She's eighteen. I learned to grow up when I was younger than that," Tera says.

"Not everyone is you." My mom tries to smile, doing her best to avoid her darker voice. "I merely mean that she shouldn't have to grow up so quickly." She faces me again with a softer tone. "The Version

20 games come with a lot of publicity. I thought you didn't want that."

My skin stings, feeling like my preference is being twisted. Does she think I don't know the risks? Trying to keep my voice level, I say, "I generally don't. But Analisa is more likely to be chosen if I join. They like choosing people who know each other—especially family and romantic interests. I want to help her."

Kiran warbles unsurely. I can't quite tell what they're saying—the words aren't familiar enough.

My mother says, "Exactly. I don't think it's a good idea to do this just for her. Analisa's a nice girl, but you've only been dating for six months. Your whole future might change if you enter one of those games."

I hold back from correcting the months to seven. "I've been best friends with her for years. She's supported me the entire time I've been in New York, and now I want to support her."

My mother's eyebrows shoot up. "We would've supported you too if you hadn't moved so far away."

I tip my head, heat flushing into my face. "This isn't about—You pushed me away. I told you that I wanted to look human for years, and you wouldn't listen to why. I had to win a Version 10 game to buy the machine that would do it for me."

She scoffs with a gaping frown. "What is so wrong about wanting your child to be near you? What is so wrong about wanting to raise your child like any other parent?"

"Because you won't accept that you aren't

normal!" Pain bleeds into my voice. "And I'm fine with that part. But I'm not fine with being bullied and having my parents tell me to just get over it."

"We didn't tell you to just get over it," she hisses.

"Repeatedly," I emphasize. "You said that I shouldn't listen to what they say. Meanwhile, Kiran's telling me to not fight back and keep my head high. That sounded a lot like, 'Let them bully you.' So I did, until Gram and Grampa heard what I was going through."

"Caitlee!" Her fingers curl into the picnic blanket. "Do not bring your grandparents into this."

I shrug, my arms outstretched. "Why? Because they're the only ones who cared when I was bullied? Even Tera—"

She's right here; I shouldn't bring her into this unless she wants to get involved. She leans back on her arms, looking at me with concerned eyes.

"Even Tera what?" Alexis' voice rises. "Tera—as wonderful as she has been for taking you in—is not your mother."

"So why is she more supportive of me than you are?" I ask.

Finally, Alexis pauses with a hurt expression rather than an angry one. Why does that feel satisfying?

This wasn't how I wanted this to go. I wanted to be honest—to communicate my intentions and feelings. How did it deviate so quickly to this?

I grab my shoes and socks before standing. "I'll see you later."

While I walk away, Alexis starts to shout something, but stops mid-sentence for whatever reason. I need some space. I'll come back in a few minutes, or maybe I'll go to my room.

The dusk sky carries a chilly breeze across the city. The lights shining from the sidewalk edges and square windows keep everything well lit. Even the dark clouds above glow. My bare feet don't mind the cold ground.

The water rushing below the sidewalk keeps me moving in the direction of the apartment. Worry crawls up my throat. My family isn't healing. If encounters like these are all we have, then will we ever change? For a few strange moments, I'm disconnected from the world. Aimless.

Chapter 6

I don't want to return to the park yet; my disapproving parents and Tera are there. Analisa's at the hospital. It's not like I can fly to Houston to see my grandparents. I'm not close with anyone else.

I enter the apartment and approach the cushioned beanbag corner of my room. The plant plushies compress as I sit. The succulent-shaped pillows provide my back with support while my shoulders slouch. Although my limp body doesn't want to move, I manage to lift my hands to scroll through the call contacts list in my vision. I'm an hour ahead of T-Territory, so it shouldn't be too late to call my grandparents.

I hesitate before texting to check if they're available. My heart yearns for support. I thought my parents could help me with that at some point, but we're just not there yet.

My lip trembles at the thought. "Yet" might be optimistic.

I pull my knees to my chest, allowing my feet to knead the blanket by the beanbag until my legs are comfortable. My arms wrap around the big, squishy avocado plushie—it's the perfect size to rest my chin against while I curl up here in my comfort corner.

My mind swims through the possibility of Analisa and me entering a Version 20 game. We can participate in any of the games without a guardian's consent. Even if my parents don't want me to do it, it's ultimately my decision. They won't even have to spend a dollar on us; the games will take care of housing and food for the duration of our time on the show. If we play along, we can only win money from there.

Of course, the cost would be handing over our secrets and clean records. That gets the Version 20 games so many views. When people confess or do things in the games, they can't be legally held accountable for anything they admitted or did. Players can even press charges if someone discriminates against them because of what they said or did in the games.

Will it be worth it?

Will. I take a deep breath at the word. My mind is solidifying its opinion.

There's a knock on the door. Tera calls out, "It's me."

My back warbles. This might be difficult. "Come in."

Tera crosses the room at a steady pace. Her hands grip the bed frame as she lowers herself to the ground beside me. She sighs as she rests her back against my mattress. "Can I hold the clover plushie?"

As I pass her the four-leaf clover, my eyes find it easier to look past her knees—not anywhere near her face. "I'm sorry I dragged you into it. I shouldn't have done that."

Her fingers gently pet the clover plushie as she passes it between her hands. "Did I ever tell you that I can hear heartbeats?"

I give a slim smile. That's kind of cool. "It wouldn't surprise me."

"It makes me helpful for lie detecting. And generally interacting with people—telling when they're genuine." She blinks for a moment. "Oh, and no worries. I would've spoken up more if I registered the rest of the park conversation quickly enough." She pokes my hand, getting me to meet her eyes. "I was prepared to take you in for a year because my sibling and brother-in-law advocated for you. During that time, I found that your heartbeat was always genuine. It's why I've supported you beyond what I initially anticipated."

"Is it still genuine?" I ask.

Tera nods. "Ultimately, I have no place in telling you how to live your life. And your mother's right— I'm your great-aunt, not your mother. But I hope that you take it seriously when I say that I trust you to make your own major decisions about your life." Her eyes close. "I give you more free rein than maybe I should. But as a kid, I was sold as a slave. Then I was rescued and reunited with Aru right before I developed my enhanced hearing. I never want you to have to face a difficult life like mine, so deprived of decision."

My heart dampens when I hear about her past. Guilt crawls up my throat when I acknowledge how fortunate my life is in comparison.

Before I can think of what to say, she continues, "So, if you want to support Analisa, then I'll support your decision. Let me know how I can help."

And she does help. The next day, Tera sets up a makeshift recording studio in one of the school's break rooms. Analisa, Lian, and I film our application videos for Truth or Dare, Mother May I, and Never Have I Ever. We consider other shows, but Mafia is too physical, and shows like Two Truths and a Lie don't pay enough. If we can get one of the big shows to accept us, we might be able to raise the $1,900,000 Analisa's father needs.

While Analisa and I take Lian to Updates, one of Tera's friends edits the application videos. Before the end of the day, Lian has Version 20 and we submit our polished applications.

The next morning, we already get rejection emails from Mother May I. After school, we walk to my apartment with snacks. Our plan is to watch reruns of Never Have I Ever and Truth or Dare. But then we receive rejections from Never Have I Ever.

Analisa stops in the middle of the sidewalk to read

the email. She growls as she continues walking toward my apartment. "These people don't know entertainment!"

"At this rate," Lian says as he glances at the cloudy sky, "should we even review the footage?"

"There's still Truth or Dare!" Analisa shouts as if Lian's question is wildly out of line.

I unlock the door to the apartment building. Analisa gives a quick "thank you" before stomping inside to the elevators. Her trembling arms and pinched eyebrows retain most of her irritation. Even so, I can sense the expletives in her mind.

Lian doesn't seem too concerned, but his expression doesn't look hopeful either.

I seriously thought for a while that one of the shows would accept us. And yeah, Truth or Dare is still an option. But given that we received two rejections so far, an acceptance feels less and less likely.

The three of us carry the groceries inside my apartment. While I put away Tera's groceries, Lian helps Analisa bring snacks to the living room.

Analisa swipes through the controls on the coffee table. The television screen brightens as it wakes up. "Truth or Dare is the most interesting one anyway."

"What do they even do for seven days?" Lian sits on the couch facing the television.

"It's six days in the arena," Analisa corrects as she sits beside him. "But there will be an opening ceremony before and a closing one after, so the whole ordeal is eight days."

"But how does it work?" Lian lifts his arms in a wide shrug. "I have not seen any of this before."

Now done with the groceries, I squish into the corner of an adjacent couch. "You know the elementary version of Truth or Dare?"

"You ask someone 'truth or dare,' they pick one, and you tell them to answer or do something, yes?" Lian asks.

"Exactly." Analisa clicks on a small hologram, navigating the television to the Truth or Dare channel. "It's that, but more. Truth or Dare thrives off of revealing deep secrets and getting people to do ridiculous dares. It picks up as the competitors learn more about each other—then they can dare each other to do things tailored to each person. You want to keep the audience entertained enough to want you in the game."

I settle into the couch. "You're guaranteed $500,000 if you make it through the six days. You can get more from completing accusations—which are the truths and dares. But if you don't complete the accusations, you lose money. And if another player gets the audience to vote for your removal, you don't receive any money."

"Why would anyone try to remove someone else?" Lian asks.

"Oh, you innocent child." Analisa pats his shoulder. "Where do you think a person's accumulated winnings go if they're forced to leave the game?"

Lian stares at the wall, not following.

"To the player who called for the other one's removal," Analisa answers.

"But," I add, "it's important to be careful when you do that. Because if the audience votes to keep the competitor in the game, the one who called for the vote gets kicked out instead."

"So it's a gamble. And the odds are determined based on how the audience feels about the two players." Lian's eyes widen.

"Exactly," Analisa says. "Which is why it's important to watch for the player's motivations. Players tend to be in it for the money rather than the fame—they could get fame from less socially risky games. How much money they want—that determines how far they might go in the game. For Truth or Dare, the referees are called Comedy and Tragedy. Those two decide when the audience gets to vote to steer the game, like if a specific truth or dare might be too extreme."

"Comedy and Tragedy? That's a little dramatic, isn't it?" Lian asks.

Analisa grins as she clicks up a search. "Wait until you see their outfits."

She finds a few pictures of Comedy and Tragedy. Together, they've got an interesting clash of colors that they love to show off.

Comedy, a tall, white woman in her early thirties, embraces yellow and white dresses while styling her pink hair in gold bands. Gold chains line her knee-high boots.

Tragedy is a Black man about the same age as

Comedy. The soles of his boots are thick to make his height match Comedy's. He often wears gothic-inspired black outfits with silver and purple accents. He's even got silver cuffs in his locs, which he styles differently in almost every photo.

"They're beautiful." Lian gapes.

Analisa nods. "They're quite the hosts. Truth or Dare has held the title for highest live viewership for years. My guess is that it's due to their commentary. And their choices for players. Their arena is also top-notch. It might look like the cabin is in the middle of nature, but everything in the arena is composed of shapeshifting technology. It's how they change the cabin surroundings each game." At that, Analisa sinks into the couch. She blinks at the ceiling—I recognize it as one of her expressions for holding back tears. "I've always wanted to see it in person."

I rub her arm, encouraging her to lean forward as I wrap an arm around her shoulder. "We'll figure something out."

An email notification appears in my vision. Analisa jolts forward at the same time. The email sender is labeled as "Comedy & Tragedy."

I blink it open.

"No way."

Chapter 7

Wild electronic music pulses through the hall, echoing from the stadium.

"Is this really happening?" Analisa waves her hands in front of her face, careful to not damage the professional makeup.

Her rose petal perfume is especially noticeable with her pink outfit. Her stylist team went for a fancy, flowery dress and mismatched boots based on her usual look. They even decorated her prosthetics and walking stick with gemstones. She's been staring at the gems like they're going to fall off in a few minutes.

I brush my fingertips against my yellow nail polish. I'm glad my stylists took my input on using the bright color and giving me pants instead of a skirt. They made me nervous when they considered how much cleavage to show. Fortunately, I convinced them to go with something that would cover the bark on my chest.

They might've got the idea that I'm conservative with my clothing though, hence the sleeved jumpsuit look. It's loose enough to be comfortable, even if the embroidered layers make it bolder than what I'd normally wear. They styled my hair in a high ponytail; it amuses me that I can feel every bit of movement as I tip my head.

We stand in line with the other competitors for next week's Truth or Dare. All twelve of us wear upscale outfits that utilize our assigned color schemes. We each look different enough to be memorable—just as Comedy and Tragedy promised when they emailed us details of our acceptance a few days ago.

Lian's eyes travel around everyone as if analyzing their outfits. He did a little spin earlier when he walked out of his changing room in a classy suit with deep green piping. He stopped at a mirror to admire the shiny eyeshadow his makeup stylists applied. Analisa and I had to drag him away from the mirror on our way to the line.

Now, we stand by the wall, listening to the excited murmur of the audience beyond the yellow and plum curtain. Even with the darkness surrounding us, the shine beneath the curtain provides enough light to see with. The metal and sequins in our outfits create dancing bits of reflected light on the wall. It's like everyone here glows.

Analisa clasps my hand. Although her arm trembles a little, her smile is more energetic than I've ever seen. Not one of her barely-passing physics exam experiences compare to her current vigor. "I'm so glad you're here, Cai. I love you—you know that?"

Even with my stomach jittering from the thought of being on stage, knowing that Analisa's here makes it worth it. "I'd kiss you if it weren't for the makeup."

"How are you two so calm?" Lian grits his teeth through a smile. His arms shake at his sides.

I raise my eyebrows. I thought Lian would be the least nervous of us.

Analisa rubs his shoulder. At my expression, she mutters, "It's the crowd. He doesn't like performing or public speaking if he can't see the people clearly."

I nod in acknowledgment. I'd try to reassure him, but I don't know how to calm my own stress about the crowd.

Analisa clears her throat. "Lili, look at me." When he turns his head, she says, "You look fabulous. And you're about to talk face to face with *the* Comedy and Tragedy. They're gonna think you're fabulous too. They wouldn't have chosen you otherwise. Just have fun, okay?"

"It's true, they've got style." His head sways unsurely before landing in a resolute nod. "Okay, yeah. I'm just talking with them. Not in front of a giant audience. And cameras. Which will be recording."

Even at a distance, Comedy's laugh is unmistakable. It's the sound of someone who values showmanship.

The crowd laughs with her, enticing Analisa into

trotting toward the curtains. Caught between returning to the wall and beckoning me over, she does a wide, conflicted stance until I tiptoe beside her.

I peek through the thick folds of curtains with Analisa. Even though it's Comedy on stage, she wears a faded purple and black outfit, like something Tragedy would wear. Even her hair and makeup are dark.

"Ahem." From across the stage, Tragedy clears his throat. His arms cross as he looks Comedy over. "I believe someone has stolen my look."

"Oh, have I?" Comedy looks down at her frayed dress, lifting some of it as if to inspect it. "Well, I wonder what the audience thinks. Should we ask them who wears it better?"

While the audience laughs, Tragedy raises his eyebrows. "Unfortunately, we'll never know the answer." As he crosses the stage, his platform boots resound through the ground. He shoves Comedy.

As she flails, her hands find the ground and push herself into a flip. The torn pieces of the dress mend with a shimmer as the color transforms into a bright, sparkling yellow. She lands on her feet with a bright grin, showcasing even her makeup and hair that change to a bright pink.

My eyes widen, unsure how the transformation happened so quickly. When the audience cheers, I find myself clapping with Analisa.

"Hey, we have to stay by the wall." Lian pulls our

shoulders, gesturing toward the approaching security guards.

I scoot away from the curtain and find my spot in line again. Fortunately, the security guards don't chastise us as they walk past the line of players. Some of the other players are close enough to the stage that they can peer around the curtain from there. Our spot isn't quite so close. I count that I'm ninth in line, with Analisa and Lian following me.

As I rest against the wall, the person next to me leans forward, getting my attention. Their profile jumps into my vision. Daraja Jones. They/she. Twenty-one years old.

That's all my contact lenses can see for now. The player profiles have been limited for the sake of not revealing too much. For the game's duration, our contact lenses can only sharpen our vision and show the limited player profiles. We have to learn about each other by interacting.

Daraja's pretty; I wouldn't admit that in front of Analisa, of course. Their stylists dived into a bright green and white theme for their sporty outfit. The glittery, green makeup complements their dark brown skin. The silver cuffs in their long box braids are engraved with music notes.

If only I could tell something about another player from their clothing. Looking at mine, I'm not sure what I would deduce about me if I were another person. I can't deduce much about Analisa or Lian either. Lavish first impressions done up by fancy stylists aren't helpful for speculating.

Daraja's dark brown eyes catch my attention as they whisper, "What did you see?"

Oh, they mean behind the curtain. "Comedy came out in Tragedy's colors. She did a flip and the colors changed back to yellow and pink."

"Ooh." Daraja covers their mouth. "That would've been nice to see. It is a shame that the players don't get to see the theatrics." They hold out their hand. "You may call me Daraja. May I call you Cai?"

"Of course." I shake their hand. They've got manners too. People are supposed to ask first before using information from a profile, but not everyone checks like they're supposed to. "How do you want your pronouns used?"

They twirl their hand nonchalantly. "Most of the time I prefer 'they.' I won't complain if you use 'she' though—it's easier for some people."

I nod. "I'll go with 'they' then."

Daraja smiles softly. "Thanks. I'll be honest—I'm glad I'm not the only young person here. I was worried I'd be surrounded by a bunch of older people. And you seem nice, so I'm not as worried anymore."

Being on good terms with the other players would be best. The more we view each other as human beings, the less potentially harmful accusations we might give each other in the game. "Well, if you want to know more young people..."

I turn toward Analisa, who's rubbing Lian's shoulder as he stares at the curtain in a daze. Without needing an additional cue, Analisa steps forward, holding out her hand. She whispers, "Hi! I'm Analisa. May I call you Daraja?"

"Of course." Daraja beams. "I'm glad to meet such nice players. Do you two know each other?"

I nod. "Analisa is my girlfriend."

"Oh, lucky!" Daraja looks at the ceiling, a flopped smile on their face. "Having a person here you trust is bound to make it more fun. I wanted my brother to apply too, but he's got work. And that's understand-able. We need to pay rent, so."

I try to log that information in my memory. Remembering as much as I can about the other players would be for the best.

"Well, if you want to know another player, I have my brother here too." Analisa jabs a thumb over her shoulder.

Daraja's eyebrows rise. "That's even better than I thought. Three people make quite a team."

Analisa steps aside so Lian can do his meeting-people thing. At least... I *thought* he'd do his meet-ing-people thing. He keeps staring at the curtain with a dumbfounded look on his face.

"His name is Lian," Analisa introduces. "He gets nervous around crowds. He's a lot better with one-on-one conversation." She pushes his shoulder, trying to induce a reaction from him. "Usually, at least."

"In that case, kid, try something out for me." The last person in line snaps her fingers to get Lian's attention. "Imagine your deepest, darkest secret that brings you shame. Now, imagine that everyone in the audience has a secret like that, and you know all of them. They're vulnerable, but there's no danger to you. Imagine that those are the people you're talking in front of."

The last person in line is a white woman with orange hair and an outfit to match. Her height is flattered by the placement of her buttoned blouse, white pants, and tall, bright orange boots. Her profile reveals that her name is Flutura Leka; she's thirty-nine years old. And apparently, she gives odd pieces of advice.

"Like..." Lian rubs the back of his neck. "Talk as if I know their secrets?"

"Avoid doing so in a creepy way, but yes." Flutura's gaze travels slowly across the curtain. "I've attended my fair share of crowded events. That vulnerability technique usually helps me talk openly during interviews."

Interviews and crowded events. Is she a publicized figure? I'm not sure I recognize her as someone widely famous, but I could be wrong. I tend to listen to things about famous people more than watch them.

"Thank you," Lian says. "You may call me Lian."

"Call me Flutura." She sighs as she leans against the wall. "And don't worry—audiences tend to sympathize with nervous people if you acknowledge how you feel. Just stay on the stage until the hosts tell you to leave."

Comedy's voice lightens. "And now, without

further delay, allow me to introduce our first player! Meet Sevyn Evans!"

The first person in line steps onto the stage. From here, I glimpse a tall, Black person in a black suit with bright blue pinstripes. The suit has shiny gear that looks like protective armor for their shoulders. Their profile says Sevyn Evans, they/them, sixty years old. They don't look more than forty years old. The profile disappears as they walk away.

I go back to the curtain, hoping to see more from there. Every glimpse helps my hammering heart prepare for walking onto the stage.

Comedy gives a wild, gaping grin as she encourages Sevyn to their seat. Her voice reverberates through the speakers as she says, "Your name sounds like an alter ego, you know. You're not a superhero in disguise, are you?"

Sevyn gives a soft smile. "Well, I do certainly have the armor for it."

"Yes, I appreciate seeing some of your own creation on your shoulders tonight," Tragedy says. "It lightened some of the load for your stylist team."

"While placing more of the load on my shoulders, yes." Sevyn shrugs.

Comedy grins. "Ha! I love it when players are comfortable enough to make jokes! Do you mind talking about your profession?"

Sevyn runs a hand over their trimmed beard. "Not at all. I've been working as a metalsmith for twenty-four years. I started out as an apprentice for someone in west NE-Territory and later moved to a workplace here in the city. Our specialty is in wearable metal, including armor, jewelry, and chainmail."

Comedy and Tragedy continue talking with Sevyn as if it's an informal chat. It's relieving to witness.

"And on that note," Tragedy says, "thank you for coming out here, Sevyn. We look forward to seeing what shenanigans you bring to the table."

As Comedy and Tragedy stand, Sevyn waves to the cheering audience. They look predominantly stoic, only with the slightest hint of a smile.

Tragedy waves on the next player, an East Asian Amalrican man whose short hair flutters as he hops onto the stage. Besides the bold, gleaming pattern on his red shirt, he looks like he's on his way to an office job.

As his interview starts, the things the previous player said begin to fade. I try to seize every piece of new information, but the conversation moves so quickly that I'm not sure what aspects are most useful to remember. Something about how he works for Kola-Cola. He can chug a soda can to amuse his five-year-old daughter. I can't even remember the name of Office Job Guy at this point, but his excited grin lingers.

The interview moves on to an overweight, white woman with vibrant pink and purple hair. As sharp as her black dress is, her heels are even more impressive. She's prickly in response to the questions, but she hopes to win money to pay for medical treatment for her brother.

Even without knowing much about this player, my chest lightens in sympathy. She's also hoping to help someone she's close to.

At this point, my head can't retain most of what's being said. Nerves jolt through my arms as if cold hands press on my shoulders. I resolve myself to not paying attention unless I feel like it. I can always find out more about the players later. There's no need to keep track of everything now.

The fourth person is called on. An old, Black person in an electronic wheelchair crosses the stage. Xir brown jacket, button up shirt, graying hair, and round glasses remind me of how I'd picture a grandparent. From xir answers, I glean that xe loves xir family.

The next player is a thin, Brown man with a plum shirt, a sports jacket, and pants with purple stripes. As passionate as he is about botany, he talks even more about his partner. He met her over a year ago at the upscale restaurant she works at. When Comedy mentions how the winning money could pay for a wedding, the botanist guy shushes her, saying that he hasn't saved up for the rings yet.

The next player twirls onto the stage—a short, East Asian Amalrican woman with her long hair pinned with flowers that match her lilac dress. She kicks up one of her sandaled legs as she kisses the botanist guy on the cheek. Blushing, he waves to the cheering crowd as he exits the stage.

To my left, Analisa giggles. "That's pretty cute."

So Analisa and I are not the only players in a

romantic relationship. I take her hand, gently rubbing her fingers. As dazzling as this all might be, I need to keep in mind who I'm doing this for.

The seventh player strides onto the stage. He's a tall, white boy with wavy, brown hair and a saturated blue suit. He seems to be proud of his smile since it doesn't waver for a second. He's a sophomore at Darilek University, pursuing a dual degree in business and political science.

So this is someone who made it into that school. I know it's a popular school, but it's also gotten competitive to get into over the past few years. Asking him about the school could be helpful for writing my college admission essays.

Daraja is next called to the stage. I return to my spot in line, now near the edge of the curtain. I can't see as well from this direction, which makes my heartbeat pound louder in my head.

My chest feels whoozy from seeing the shaded audience and the bright stage and dazzling Comedy and curious Tragedy and the chair Daraja's sitting in. This is more terrifying than I thought it would be.

Daraja's words barely make it into my mind. Something about how they've worked a ton of jobs in customer service. They want to win the money to achieve an easier life for themself and their brother. They enjoy singing. At that, Comedy asks for a tune. Daraja belts the Truth or Dare theme, adding in several vocal runs. The audience jumps to their feet, clapping and cheering and whistling with approval.

Please don't make me follow that. My skin wants to crawl out the door.

"And with that beautiful tune, I have to thank you for coming out here, Daraja. We look forward to seeing what shenanigans you'll show us." Comedy laughs with a wide grin as Daraja walks off the other side of the stage. A pit forms in my stomach as Comedy throws an arm out in my direction. "Now, introducing our ninth player, Cai Ito!"

I'm here for Analisa. My frozen feet remember that as they stutter forward. My gaze drills into the chair as I home in on it. After a deep breath, my focus drifts.

Comedy grins with an exaggerated excitement. Tragedy smiles, tipping his chin up in approval. As I approach them, the reality of this moment becomes more surreal.

I'm about to sit with Comedy and Tragedy, the hosts of New York City's Truth or Dare. I'm being interviewed in front of a dimly lit audience that stretches so far back and up that I can't count the rows. It's a stadium full of people clapping so much that their hands sound like a wave of water crashing into my head.

"I love your outfit." Comedy wraps an arm around my shoulder. Her firm hand sends nervous shivers down my skin. "We match pretty well, actually. Perhaps the stylists knew I should pay attention to you. Now, this is important..." Comedy stares at me intently. "Have you considered dying your hair pink?"

Numbness covers my whole body. I never thought

I'd be talking with these two. I watched them on television for years; now I'm with them on the television. I wonder if there are preteens out there watching me, dreaming of being in my position—like how Analisa and I grew up.

I'm here for Analisa. I can't freeze. I've got to press my limits. I need to be more outgoing, like Analisa and Lian.

I manage a suspecting expression. I state my words slightly slower than usual to avoid tripping over my tongue. "Comedy, you know I can't possibly try to take your look. I couldn't pull off something so spectacular."

A warm feeling emerges in my chest when the audience laughs. Even Comedy laughs. Maybe I can do this.

"Well." Comedy tips her head. "It *is* spectacular, but you wear yellow so well, I couldn't help but ask!" She gestures her hand in invitation as she sits down.

As I sink into the chair, my tense muscles ease slightly. My fingertips glide across the velvet chair arms until they find a comfortable spot. I should keep my posture open.

"So, what do you think of yellow? Not many ask to wear it as their main color." Comedy leans back in her chair. Her fingers maintain an elegant pose as she talks, like she holds an invisible drink. "But I hope to see more of it. It always brightens my day to see a nice yellow, you know?"

I nod. "I agree. It's my favorite color, actually."

"Oh, is it?" Comedy's eyes widen with her grin. "Why is that?"

"It's bright and positive." I take a breath, considering how to elaborate. I don't want my answers to be too short, otherwise, it'll sound curt. "Like sunlight. I know sunlight isn't technically yellow, but its representation in media almost always is. And I like plants, so the connection to sunlight is another reason for me to like it."

Tragedy nods as he leans forward. "Plants make for good companions, I've found. Do you have any plants where you live?"

I nod. "Yes, I take care of quite a few in my apartment. Well, it's not exactly my apartment. It's my auntie's. I try to do as much cooking and cleaning as I can to help her out."

"That's good. Do you two live in an apartment here in the city?" Comedy asks.

I sense the possibility of a family question. Comedy and Tragedy try avoiding questions that could be uncomfortable for the player during the interview. So, if I act comfortable with talking about my family, they'll ask. That wouldn't be ideal.

But if I indicate that I don't want to talk about my family, then that's also not ideal. Other players could use that as a question in the game. I'd rather they not get the impression that asking about my parents could lead to an intriguing answer.

"Yes," I respond. "It's just my auntie and I here in New York. I've got a couple of grandparents in Houston, T-Territory who I talk with regularly. Although, I feel like they like calling particularly when my girl-friend's around." I give a playful smile. "We've been a package deal for the past few years."

"Your girlfriend—that's right. The lovely Analisa," Comedy says, raising an eyebrow as she turns to the audience. "It would be nice to meet her, wouldn't it?"

The audience lights up with delighted whistles. They know it must mean that Analisa's a player.

"Now, speaking of Analisa." Tragedy's voice quiets down the audience. His soft voice continues, "When we saw your application video, we were inspired by your motivation. Could you let the audience know what you plan to do with your winnings?"

I swallow, knowing that Analisa said it was fine to talk about this. Still, it feels vulnerable.

But vulnerability means the audience might provide extra donations during the closing ceremony. I won't pass up that opportunity. "I've been in a romantic relationship with Analisa for seven months, but we've been close for years. She's the only one outside of my family who I've trusted to know all about me. I'd do anything to make her happy."

I turn, hoping I can see Analisa in my periphery. Although it's difficult to see her past the curtain, I smile in her direction.

Turning back to Comedy and Tragedy, I continue. "This week, her father was diagnosed with a rare cancer. The treatment itself is expensive, and then to send her parents to stay at the facility across the country is a lot. Analisa thought her best hope for curing her father would be to raise the money from a show like Truth or Dare. I'm here to support her, and to contribute my winnings to her father's treatment."

Tragedy's clapping leads the way, encouraging the audience to applaud in support. He nods, an acknowledging weight in his sharp eyes. "Thank you for sharing that, Cai. What a noble cause. I'm sure Analisa is pleased to be with such a loyal partner."

A warmth spreads through my chest. "I'm certainly pleased to be with her."

As an "aw" sweeps through the audience, Comedy clasps her hands in front of her chest. "Isn't that sweet?" Her teeth gleam as she smiles. "Now, is there anything else you'd like the audience to know? Perhaps an extracurricular, a favorite song, or something mysterious to leave us with?"

Thoughts swirl in my head. Alien parent. Famous grandparents. Hoping to be a history major. I adore plant plushies. I like Heka's music.

Ultimately, my decisiveness wins. "You should know that this is the most talkative I've been with someone outside of my family and Analisa's."

"Oh." Comedy leans back, her eyebrows lifted with an impressive tilt. "I wouldn't have guessed. You've got good improvisation skills, Cai."

"Agreed. I'm curious to see how that will change the game," Tragedy says. "Thank you for coming out here, Cai. We look forward to seeing how you'll contribute to this show's shenanigans."

"Before you leave." Comedy stands. "Perhaps we could witness a moment between you and our tenth player. Now introducing Analisa Patel!"

As Analisa strides onto the stage in her boots, the spotlights cause her outfit to shimmer. The gemstones on her walking stick sparkle with her flowing dress. Her pink smile captivates my attention. Her glittery eyelashes blink as she adjusts to the light.

Pride emboldens my chest as I stand. We've made it here.

Analisa sets her arms on my shoulders before kissing me. Her rose petal perfume immerses me in her embrace under the warm spotlight. Audience cheers blur into the background. My hands pull her back closer, tempted to prolong what should be a quick kiss.

When our lips part, her glittery eyes bat at me, holding back tears as she gives an excited smile. She tips her head toward the crowd, reminding me that I need to go offstage.

I squeeze her hand as I wave to the audience. Then I walk across the wooden stage, leaving behind the wave of cheers.

Huh. The interview is over, and I'm still alive. It actually went kind of well.

Once I'm offstage, escorts direct me to an empty elevator. Once I pass through the whizzing doorway, Analisa's chipper voice continues from the elevator speakers. The wall displays the live video of her radiant smile and bubbly laugh. As the elevator surges me upward, reassurance blooms in my tense chest. Analisa will do well in her interview, and so will Lian.

Now we need as much support from the audience as we can get to stay in the game. As long as none of us get kicked off the show, and we keep completing truths and dares, we'll accumulate plenty of money for Analisa's father.

Relief settles in my stomach as the elevator stops.

Chapter 8

"I can't believe I said that," Lian grumbles. As he walks, his mortified fingers wrestle with his hair.

"They were flattered. Besides, Comedy and Tragedy have heard much weirder things." Analisa pats Lian's shoulder abruptly, startling him into lowering his hands. "Now, back to what I was saying. From what I saw earlier, there's a pool, a ping pong table, a bar, a kitchen, arcade games, a spa, a mini-theater, and some lounge areas. It's all in the same open space, trying to entice players into interacting with each other."

"A bar?" Lian's eyebrows rise.

"Yeah. Version 20 means we can drink, remember?" Analisa says. "But if we do, only one drink. We don't want to be hungover for the first game day. Those players don't get a lot of audience sympathy unless they're *really* funny." She sighs, trying to slow down her quick-paced breaths. "Now, we've got the advantage, since the three of us know and trust each other. We can defend each other's secrets. Certain ones that we don't want revealed."

From what I know, I'm the one of us three with the biggest secret. Sure, human astronauts are interacting with aliens, and there are some aliens on Earth. However, most aliens don't interact with people on Earth without a disguise. Kiran only does because they live with my mom on the outskirts of Houston. Everyone knows each other there. Because Kiran only interacts with a few people, they don't care how they're perceived. But as a human/alien hybrid, I grew up being treated more alien than an alien.

Lian only found out yesterday. I doubt he believed Analisa and me about the green skin, but the bark warbling on my stomach shocked him. His reaction wasn't as bad as it could've been. I'm sure that it's not as bad as the world finding out and having it be on a permanent online record. This could all easily go wrong.

Analisa waves her hands, recapturing my attention. "That's why we need to befriend other players. That way, we can be kind to them, and they can be kind to us. If we put on a good show, no one will care if we don't reveal everything super deep about ourselves. Daraja feels like a good start. Maybe Flutura too, since she helped Lian out. And she's a famous dancer —she's bound to know how to hide secrets."

"Eric seems like he could be nice to talk to," Lian

considers. "And Solana's cause is like ours. Although, she is a bit intimidating."

I don't remember which one Eric was. I think Solana was the one with the sharp heels though—the aloof one who wanted to raise money for her brother's treatment.

"Lian." Analisa stops in the middle of the hall. I stop with her as she puts her hands on his shoulders. "You're our greatest asset when it comes to talking with people. We need your A-game. You can't let anyone intimidate you."

Lian nods, taking a breath and closing his eyes. He hops in place, readying a smile. Even his voice solidifies. "I know. I've got this. We've got this."

Analisa nods. "Good." Then she turns to me. "I know it might be hard, but we need you to be as outgoing as you can. Whenever you need some time alone, tell me you're tired, and I'll go with you for a while, okay?"

I pull her shoulder close and kiss her cheek. "Don't worry. I'll do my best."

Even if I've conditioned myself into not standing out, I'm now a player in a major Version 20 game. I need to let go of trying to blend in.

The floral carpet ends at two ornate doors. Brass swirls around the doorknobs, illuminating while the doors swing away from us.

As we step inside, my attention sweeps through the luxurious expanse of a room. Everything Analisa described earlier is here. The pool is in the middle of the floor, surrounded by couches. Since I don't know what alcohol can do to my body, I intend to stay away from the bar.

The arcade games capture my focus. They're archaic, with only visors linking some of them to recent decades. I'm fairly certain that arcade games with styles like these emerged in the late 1900s. With a few modifications, they've maintained their resurgence since the 2210s. Despite competition in recent technological entertainment, these games still attract attention. I even see Kid Isaac: Genesis Uprising—is it free to play it here?

Analisa rubs my hand, capturing my wandering attention. It looks like the other romantic pair are here. The two purple-dressed partners talk excitedly as they sit at the pool edge. Like us, they've changed into their prepared pajamas. It won't be the last time I see them in plum and lilac. We're all going to wear our opening ceremony colors for the whole week, making it easier for the audience to remember each player.

Analisa tips her head toward the two of them and parts from me. Dividing and conquering, as planned.

As Lian stares at the Truth or Dare memorabilia on the walls, the arcade games reclaim my attention. I recognize most of them. Considering Comedy and Tragedy's collection of amenities, I was half expecting to see a Galaxa game here. They might not be able to include the game currently used to recruit for the Galaxa space program. That's the most popular space program out there—Gram and Grampa are friends with one of the founders. As far as I know, the Galaxa astronauts haven't visited Kiran's planet yet, but they've been to a ton of places in the Milky Way and the Andromeda Galaxy.

"Fascinating, isn't it?" A deep voice appears behind me.

I turn, facing the player with the proud smile. He's the one who goes to Darilek University. He's got bluer eyes than I expected. His profile says his name is Eric Foucault. Ah, so that's who Lian mentioned getting to know. Convenient.

He pats one of the arcade games called Sharp-shooter Straights. "We've got one of these on campus. The CS majors keep stealing it, so we keep stealing it back. We being the poli-sci majors, I mean. Do you have a favorite game?"

Time to be outgoing. I try matching Eric's energy as I look around. "Wow, how direct. Isn't there supposed to be a lead-in question before you ask a truth like that?"

Eric laughs. From the way he's squinting, it seems like he's receptive to lighthearted conversation. "My bad. I haven't even introduced myself before asking something so personal." He bows, looking comically formal while in his dark blue pajamas. "You may call me Eric. May I call you Cai?"

"Of course." I look at the games again. "Since we now know each other, I might as well say that I'm partial to Kid Isaac: Genesis Uprising. It isn't the most accurate to the mythology, but it's still fun to see how far I can play."

"Ah, yes." Eric walks over to the arcade game,

watching the graphics bounce across the screen. "That's the one where you have to defeat Jesus, right?"

From the way he's talking, he doesn't seem to know much about the Christian mythology. I suppose not everyone looks up weirdly specific historical details. "Jesus isn't in the game; that's just a rumor someone spread on the Mainframe. God is the final boss."

Eric's face scrunches in confusion. "Which god?"

"Just God." I shrug. "Whoever came up with it wasn't the most creative."

Eric laughs again. "Well, as tempted as I am to know how much you know about other mythologies, I'll settle for a possibly less controversial question. If I teach you how to best play Sharpshooter Straights, will you teach me how to play Kid Isaac?"

I raise an eyebrow. "You seem confident. How can I be sure you know how to best play it?"

Eric gives an understanding shrug. He grabs one of the fake guns attached to Sharpshooter Straights, straps on a visor, and clicks the start button.

His avatar jogs through a ruined city on the screen, firing at barely distinguishable creatures. My eyebrows raise as he hits his targets without fail. His focus and stance are more serious than a minute ago when he would hardly let go of that grin. I wonder which expression feels more comfortable for him.

Since I can examine him without his attention on me, I look for anything I didn't notice before.

Now that he's right beside me, I can confirm that

he's tall. If I'm five-nine, he's got to be at least six feet. He's muscular, indicating that he works to keep it that way. I don't see any scars, tattoos, or other unique aspects to his skin except some acne on his forehead. The makeup must've covered it well for me to not notice earlier.

Eric lifts the gun as the game's music twinkles and an announcer calls out the next level. "You have to anticipate the lag at the beginning of each level. If you don't, it'll swarm you in fifteen seconds. Want a try?"

It's not like embarrassing myself on this game would have any detriment. If I'm bad, the vulnerability might make him feel like I've let my guard down around him. I nod as I accept the fake gun.

As he guides me through the buttons, his proximity is somewhat unnerving. When his fingers nearly touch mine on the trigger button, I take a step back, raising a shocked eyebrow.

"Sorry." Eric shakes his head with an embarrassed laugh. "I'm not trying to flirt with you. I just get a little excited about this game. And if it makes you feel better to know—I like guys. I'll be more careful with my distance."

As he shuffles back, he does seem genuine. "Okay, good," I say. "Analisa likely wouldn't appreciate it."

"No, I know. You should've seen her face a second ago. She looked like she considered vaulting across the room." Eric stares past me.

I look over my shoulder, seeing Analisa chatting with the two purple partners. She waves coyly, making me smile. I turn back to Eric. "You were saying something about watching for the red light on the characters?"

"Yeah." Eric gives a relieved smile. He explains a bit more before handing me the visor.

The game graphics fill my vision. I lift the fake gun, ready as the countdown begins. Analisa's a lot better at the shooting range, but I can at least hold a toy gun. I suck in a focused breath.

It's as overwhelming as it looked from the outside. I swing the aim as my finger rapidly clicks the trigger. My heart jerks when a few monsters approach too close for comfort, but I keep my character alive until the end of the level.

I pull the helmet off with a short breath. Eric smiles, holding up a hand. "Not bad!"

I high-five him as Daraja runs up to us, holding a tray of brown cubes with oven mitts. The smell of warm chocolate wafts from the dessert. "Hey! Oh, I'm glad there are other people I've already met out here. It makes this a little less awkward. When I saw there was a kitchen, I had to make brownies. I haven't had sweets in ages." They give a bubbly laugh. "Do either of you want some?"

"You seem nice, but I do have to wonder if you're trying to drug us." Eric scoops up a brownie piece.

Daraja's eyes widen. "Oh! No, not at all." They pick up a piece and bite into it. After they swallow, they say, "In case that helps. They do it in the movies."

Eric shrugs as he bites into his brownie. Covering

his mouth, he says, "Well, I'm not going to refuse free food. Also, this is really good."

"Thanks!" Daraja grins. "Cai, do you want any?"

Brownies have a lot of plant matter in them. Although I could physically eat them, the thought feels questionable. "I'm actually allergic to wheat."

"Oh!" Daraja yanks the brownies away from me.

"Not *that* allergic," I correct. "I just can't eat it."

"Ah." They relax their arms. "Well, sorry about that. Is that your only allergy? I can try making another dessert you can eat."

The discussion is going to come up anyhow. "That's okay. I'm actually allergic to a lot. I have to take supplements to get most of my nutrients." That's what Analisa and I came up with for the game, at least. I've got a ton of "supplement" packages in my room, ready to be brought to the cabin tomorrow. They're packets of flavored water, but Lian printed labels to make them look medically assigned.

"Oh wow." Daraja's eyes widen. "I haven't met someone who primarily takes supplements before. I won't ask about your business, but that's really something. I didn't know people could live like that."

Eric tips his head, giving a knowing look to the ceiling. "Well, that's science for you."

"You seem confident about that for someone studying *political* science." Daraja's stance shifts, their eyelids drooping with faux suspicion.

"Just because I'm more interested in those subjects doesn't mean I haven't taken my fair share of science courses. I'm not surprised that Cai can live off supplements. People can be lab-grown with specific requested characteristics now. And people can even have clones of themselves created with their memories implanted. If things like that exist, the human body can do anything with the help of technology."

Their ability to form thoughts quickly is a lot better than mine. If I want to keep up with Eric and Daraja's conversation, I need to give in to instinct. It's hard not to doubt my ideas for words when they're close to thoughts I'd rather leave undisclosed.

Daraja shakes their head. "I'm just trying to pay rent. Stuff like that isn't even in my life, you know? I'll bet you'd have to be richer than rich to get someone to grow a whole human for you."

Like my grandparents. Given their political status and engineering days, they don't worry about money anymore. They could even pay a lab to grow their granddaughter based on my parents' wishes.

Eric raises an eyebrow as he finishes off his brownie. "I don't know. I think it'll be more accessible over time. All technology follows that trend. There are people our age in space who go out and meet aliens on other planets. We've got technology in our eyes, which is partially paid for by the Northeast Territory government." He looks at me with a smirk. "You look like you have thoughts on this, Cai. Don't worry, we won't think it's controversial."

I smile, going for an embarrassed innocence. "No, I'm just quiet because I don't know much about all this. I tend to be more focused on history than the future."

Eric asks, "You're interested in history, huh? I guess that makes sense with the mythology knowledge."

"I've always thought of mythology as more of a culture thing," Daraja says. "But yeah, I guess culture goes hand-in-hand with history."

"A lot of war was actually because of mythology," I say, my passion starting to bleed into my voice. "People held to their beliefs so much that they thought they needed to subjugate anyone who believed in anything else. People were willing to kill and die for it."

Daraja's eyes widen. "That sounds..."

"Brutal." Eric's forehead scrunches. "At least nowadays war between humans is primarily because of resources. And we don't even kill each other. It's just robots fighting until one side decides the war is too expensive."

Sure, most wars aren't fought with human life. But there's still a horrible, hidden realm of violent crime that hasn't faded into history; Tera knows that well, having been sold into slavery as a child. But I shouldn't bring my family into this discussion.

Daraja shakes their head in disbelief. "I guess humans do progress eventually. People could do better with spreading wealth though."

"Agreed. We could use some legislation to help with that." Eric shrugs with a forced grin. "It shouldn't take too long to get that to happen, right?"

I laugh lightly at his dramatic expression. My body starts to feel fatigued from talking with strangers for a while, but I want to stay in this conversation. Talking with these two doesn't feel difficult anymore.

Analisa taps my shoulder, signaling before she wraps her arm around mine. Warmth fills my chest, re-energizing me. She smiles softly. "Sorry, I hope I'm not interrupting at a bad time. I smelled those brownies though, and I thought I should ask if stealing one is allowed."

Daraja beams, holding out the tray. "Steal as many as you want!"

Analisa grabs a brownie and delicately bites into it. I'm glad she decided to eat plant matter in front of me during the game. It would be a lot harder on her body otherwise. "This is good, thanks. I also might have eavesdropped a bit. I agree with Daraja—I'm all for spreading wealth."

"Right, your father needs the expensive medical treatment." Daraja nods, recalling. "I'm glad you got in. Hopefully the winnings the three of you get will be enough for it."

"It should be, yeah." Analisa lowers her gaze. "Assuming we don't get voted off the show."

Eric makes an incredulous expression. "Who would want to kick you three off? You and Solana have the most noble causes out of all of us."

His reaction is reassuring. Still, Analisa plays up her concern with a sad smile. "Yeah, I hope it stays that way. I've got to be entertaining enough."

"Girl, I've got your back," Daraja assures. "If you

need to strike up a dramatic conversation with me or something, go for it. I'll help you out."

"Same here." Eric crosses his arms, considering the ceiling. "The whole thing is meant to be entertaining, so we're not held liable for anything we do in there. Just go all out, and the audience will want you to stay in the game."

"Are those brownies?" Lian's head peeks over Analisa's shoulder.

Analisa bites into her brownie. She covers her mouth while saying, "Ask Daraja if you want one."

Daraja holds out the tray before Lian says anything. Delighted, takes a bite of a brownie and hums with satisfaction. "These are great, Daraja! Thank you very much. Also, do any of you want to watch a movie?"

"Sure." Eric starts walking toward the movie screen.

"Oh good, I can set the tray down. I'll get more snacks." Daraja bounds off to set the brownies among the theater seats.

Analisa looks up at me, her shiny eyes encouraging. "How are you feeling?"

Resting in my assigned bedroom would be the most comfortable for me right now. But getting to know the others would be in our best interests. A movie means a bonding experience.

I take a deep breath, gauging my body. It's not too exhausted yet. I can always hole up in my cabin bedroom tomorrow. "I'm up for it."

Chapter 9

The arena looks like someone dropped us into the middle of the woods. Inside the dome, the panels of simulated sky display clouds in the place of skyscrapers. Instead of water or concrete beneath our feet, there's dirt. The simulated sun hovering in the east guides us toward the cabin.

The twelve of us group together, traveling in casual outfits that match our assigned colors. My lightweight, yellow fabric feels weather-appropriate given the humid air. My skin rejoices from the extra water vapor. Even the simulated sun is accurate enough to replenish my energy.

The surrounding forest is impressive. Technology is weaved into every fiber of what I'm seeing. It enables Comedy and Tragedy to redesign the forest layout every game, so I'm not sure what they've got in store for us. Usually, there's some kind of water, like a pond, a waterfall, or a river. The plant life changes each time to accommodate different people. The arena from two weeks ago had sequoia trees with massive trunks. These trees are slim by comparison, but there are a lot more bushes.

Lian trips over a root on the edge of the path. He stumbles into Analisa, making her pat his shoulder with an overdramatic smile. "Come on, Lian, we're not even to the hard part yet."

"Define 'the hard part.'" Eric looks back with a grin as he walks. Everyone has a heightened energy, ready to jump into conversation at any opportunity.

"Oh, it won't be so bad," the grandparent person says with a gentle laugh. Xir profile lists xir name as Ever Wright. Xir wheelchair whirs as it wheels across the path. "We're just getting to know each other."

"I'll be honest—I'm worried that you will all find me weird." Botanist guy wearing a plum button-up shakes his head. Jared, his profile says. I seriously can't keep up with remembering all of their names unless I look at them. He's the one in a relationship with—

Joane takes his hand with a playful smile. Her fleecy, lilac sleeves catch up with her swaying arms. "Don't worry. I know you're weird, but I still like you anyway."

"Only *like*?" Jared asks, rubbing the back of his neck with a bashful smile.

"There's more behind the word than you'd think," Analisa assures.

"I think she's right." Office Job Guy points at Analisa,

his mouth gaping in amazement. Brandon Jiu, the guy in the red polo. So many names to remember. I'm barely able to keep up with the conversation as I try remembering everything that everyone says. There's no way I'll be able to remember enough to use later for accusation questions and dares. "My wife would likely agree."

"Likely indeed." Joane smiles mischievously as her fingers pinch her purple skirt.

The group lights up with incongruent responses of appreciation. Not exactly a standing ovation in response to the joke but attempts at being friendly.

"Oh no." Analisa groans. "We've got another pun-maker."

"Oh?" Joane looks between Lian and me. "Is there someone else with the gift?"

I lift my hand. "Present."

Eric snorts at my quick thinking, even rushing a hand to cover his mouth. It's the best reaction out of the acknowledgments of my humor—his response was too immediate to be fabricated.

Joane pauses walking to hold out her hand. I accept her firm handshake and reciprocate her amused smile. When she lets go, her eyes widen at the path ahead. "I think I see it!"

Sevyn—metalsmith person, wears bright blue and black—nods from the front of the line. "Yep. The cabin is up ahead."

"Oh, good." Solana—sharp heels, raising money for her brother's treatment—huffs out a sigh. "These shoes are killing me. I tried convincing my stylist team to give me arch support, but no—looking good is more important to them."

Her prickly nature was clear enough in the opening ceremony interview yesterday. I'm not sure how to respond to it. For someone with such a caring cause, she seems less kind than I would expect.

Ever looks up from xir wheelchair with a sympathetic smile. "We're almost there, child. I'm sorry that I cannot offer you shoes or a ride. My wife would beat me to the cursed lands if I did."

Solana's expression softens, although her voice still has a sharpness to it. "Yeah, well, thanks. I'd rather you not tick off your wife. I've accidentally been a homewrecker to one marriage before—I'd like to keep it to one."

I try taking mental notes on everyone, but it's hard to keep track of all the details they've shared so far. I hardly remember their names until I look at them and see their profiles. Maybe I need to be less tense. I don't need to keep track of everything. Analisa and Lian can help me remember what I miss about the other players.

We emerge in a dirt clearing around the place we're going to inhabit for the next several days. Some bushes and sparse trees create an atmospheric canopy around the log-style cabin. Hopefully the logs are fake wood. Even if Earth trees aren't directly related to my alien parent, the thought of living within husks of trees for six days is unsettling.

Regardless, the cabin is pretty, and there are lots of windows. It stretches a long distance since it has bedrooms for all of us on one floor. There are stairs and a ramp leading to the porch. The porch has rocking chairs and a television next to potted pink and purple flowers. The tall bushes nearby the porch are full of dark berries.

"Oh cool!" Brandon—the office job guy in the red polo—picks off some of the berries. "Free blue-berries."

The botanist's eyes widen. "Don't eat those!"

Brandon's eyebrows scrunch in confusion. "Huh? Why?"

The purple-dressed botanist—Jared—steps closer to the bush, delicately pinching the leaves. "I haven't seen these in the North American Region before. The berries contain toxins. Eating them in moderation is fine, but enough of those in your system might cause your heart to stop. You see the spear-shaped leaves? If you see this leaf with these berries clustered near the bottom of the bush, it's likely one of the wartime-engineered plants from the Highlands. It was made to be toxic to humans. A historical find, really."

My eyes widen. I don't know about these particular bushes, but plants were indeed experimented on in recent centuries. They were used as defense against potential enemies, surrounding places like the High-land Castle in the 2100s.

Comedy and Tragedy tailor the arena environ-ment to reference different players. The potted flowers on the porch, for example. The purple flowers could reference the flowers in Joane's hair. Likewise, the pink flowers for Analisa. Solana's hair is dyed bright pink and purple, so the referees likely had her in mind too. These berry bushes combine the interests of botany and history, appealing to Jared and me.

"Woah, you really know about this stuff?" Brandon backs away from the bush.

"He's a botanist, remember?" Sevyn—the metal-smith—says. "I'd take his word for it."

Brandon drops the berries. He smears his hands on his khaki shorts.

"That's way neg. What if one of us dares someone to eat those?" Solana asks, her jaw dropped with distaste.

Concern shifts in my stomach. Although we can dare each other to do risky things, the point is seeing if we can get away with the dare without putting ourselves in definite danger. Daring someone to eat poisonous berries would be blatantly dangerous without any entertaining risk. Still, there's no rule against it.

"Why would anyone do that?" Lian asks with a legitimately dumbstruck expression.

"Look, I don't trust any of you." Solana narrows her eyes at Lian. "I'm on my own here, unlike some of you. So yeah, I'm going to be concerned about a dangerous plant parked outside our living space."

"Again, it's only dangerous in large quantities," Jared clarifies. "It would take maybe thirty berries—"

"I don't care." Solana brushes past him, stepping up the ramp to the porch. "I'm tired, hungry, and really don't need to argue about this right now. Do they even have enough food for all of us to last six days? I would hate to ration."

I don't feel comfortable around her flippant attitude, but I do want to explore the inside of the cabin. I join the stream of players going up the ramp to the porch. Solana walks through the automatic doors before everyone else. The rest of us follow through the gaping doorway.

The dim atrium opens to a spacious living room with enough couches and chairs for the twelve of us. The technology is limited to an electronic fireplace, a television that fills half a wall, and a game table with a holographic projector screen. There are also clear tubes coming out of the ground beneath the coffee tables to deliver drinks. The earthy tones in the couches and rug make the room feel cozy. The thick logs composing the walls emphasize the vintage aesthetic, reminding me of history book pictures depicting homes post-WWIII. My fingers brush against the soft couch fabric, satisfied by the feeling.

"Velvet. The good stuff. Not cheap." Lian raises his eyebrows as his fingers graze across the couch.

Flutura is the first to collapse onto one of the couch chairs. Her wispy, orange hair flattens as her head leans into the couch pillow. She's a famous dancer, according to Analisa. All I know of that first-hand is that she's acclimated to interviews. Her thin legs cross while her tired eyes stare at the ceiling. "This is New York's Truth or Dare."

"And yet, I was expecting something more upscale." Solana purses her lips as she looks around.

Her pointy, purple fingernails poke at an embroidered lantern shade on the wall—it changes color with each tap.

Daraja gawks. "But this place is huge! And it's in the middle of a forest."

While looking around the room, my eyes catch the places where the cameras should be. I generally remember the spots in the cabin, but my memory is hazy on where they are outside. I need to remember that I'm always being watched. Every moment, every word, every action.

"Exactly!" Brandon rubs his palms on the couch. His hands look like they've got old scratches on them, particularly on his left hand—scars from field work? Maybe he wasn't always in an office job. He gapes at Lian. "You said this was the good stuff?"

"Yeah. Even the way it was sewn—it's made to be durable." Lian smiles at Brandon's eager expression.

"Well, that's great!" Brandon ducks into the kitchen. "Then I've got to see the food!"

"Food is important." Ever nods, xir wheelchair peeking out from the hallway that I know leads to the bedrooms.

"We should take stock of it. That way we know how much the twelve of us can consume per day." Sevyn flexes and unflexes their fingers. Have they always had a metal pinky? I must've been too far away to notice it during the opening ceremony. That's one way to advertise their wearable metal.

"Shouldn't there be plenty of food? They've done this show several times." Botanist guy—Jared—says.

"There also have been plenty of food-related dares on this show. If enough people overuse the food, we might find ourselves low on it. Taking stock might help prevent that from happening."

Sevyn makes a good point. There was a Truth or Dare round when food ran out in the cabin. Fortunately, Comedy and Tragedy always create edible plants out in the forest for dares. As a result, the players were able to keep themselves alive until the end of the game. They lost weight, but they recovered. We should be able to avoid running out of the cabin food if we keep track of it.

"This might be a silly question." The woman in lilac—Joane—looks around blankly. "But wouldn't they send us more food if we ran out?"

"The no-intervention rule is strict." Flutura blows a wisp of orange hair out of her face as she stares at the ceiling. She doesn't seem to speak much, but she chose to give Lian advice to calm his nerves yesterday, so that's a positive in my mind. And based on her confidence about the no-intervention rule, she's familiar with Truth or Dare's rules.

"She's right." Eric combs a hand through his brown hair. His smile is less showy now. "Truth or Dare operates as its own government that way. Anything goes here since you can't be held accountable for it after the games are over. Part of that means that only the players can enter the arena until the six days are up. We can't leave until then either."

"Look at you, poli-sci. You're actually helping out."

Daraja elbows Eric's arm, inducing a light laugh from him.

"It would help more if people joined me in taking stock." Sevyn's gaze moves around the room, seeking volunteers. "I don't want to be blamed if something were to happen to the food."

"How about we all go then?" Solana pushes past people to reach the door. I catch Analisa's arm as Solana bumps into her.

My eyebrows scrunch, even as I try to calm my voice. Analisa's frown propels me to say, "Next time could you maybe... ask us to move?"

Solana looks over her shoulder, her pink and purple hair sweeping past her unimpressed gaze. "She can walk, can't she?"

Analisa mimics Solana's drooping eyelids. "Sure, but not everyone walks the same." She's trying so hard to not jump to irritation on the first day.

Players often enter Truth or Dare with a strategy about how they want to be perceived. I don't know whether it's a conscious decision, but Solana's strategy appears to be to stand out in a rude way. Pushing around the other players can intimidate them into not giving harsh accusations. Another benefit is that the audience often views the rude players as the most honest, so that can increase their popularity.

But the rude player strategy can lead to other players escalating the accusations. It can also make the player too unapproachable for the audience. I've never understood why someone take the risk on using that strategy. Players who are kinder and the most humiliated on the show tend to collect more winnings anyway.

What's even stranger in this case is that Solana is raising money for her brother. Could that have been a lie to gain sympathy? Or perhaps the use of the rude player strategy with her goal is to make her more relatable. Either way, it's difficult to react to.

"Then you could've moved when you saw that I was clearly walking across the room." Solana turns, dismissing the conversation. Her heels clack against the wooden floor, changing pitch as they hit the kitchen tile.

Analisa's eyes widen at the wall. She swallows back the inclination to say something else. I'm tempted to encourage Analisa to use her walking stick to trip Solana the next time she walks by. But there's no benefit to escalating the situation. It's only the first day.

I wrap my arm around Analisa's shoulder, trying to remind her that I side with her. Lian has his fists balled up on the couch. The rest of the room contains a silent tension.

Ever sighs as xe slowly crosses through the living room. Xir wheelchair bumps over the small threshold at the kitchen entrance. "Well, I think we should follow Sevyn's reasoning and go see that food. I, for one, look forward to breakfast."

"Hey, perhaps we should we all eat together? That could be fun," Botanist guy—Jared—suggests.

The mood lightens as we walk into the pantry

room. Several shelves are stocked with cubbies of food—from starches to snacks. The walk-in fridge is full of fresh produce, meat, dairy, drinks, condiments, and frozen food.

We estimate that we have around a week and a half of food for each of us—more than enough for three meals a day per person. If we don't use up too many ingredients for dares, we should be fine.

We start grabbing items that we want to incorporate into our first meal. Analisa and Lian team up to make rava dosa, one of Lian's comfort foods. Daraja asks if they can have some in exchange for some of the fruit they were slicing. The kitchen has enough counter space to where most of us can work without bumping into each other too much. Some talk in the long dining room that the kitchen joins with the living room.

After a half hour, we're all gathered at the long dining table. Sunlight passes through the swaying curtains. The buttons on the windowsill indicate that we could change the outside view. I'm glad no one brings it up; I like the forest environment.

Although the ceiling is much lower than my old house, it reminds me of the conditions I grew up in. We wouldn't use electricity in the day if we could help it. The breeze was always dense from being near the coast. Unlike most roofs around our area, we went with the hurricane-prepped glass that urban Houston has on all their skyscrapers. I could see the stars through the ceiling. When my grandparents visited, they'd point out where their friends have traveled in the sky. My alien parent would sometimes point to where they were from—a planet abundant with mobile and immobile plant life, somewhere in Aquarius.

Analisa rubs my shoulder, recapturing my dazed attention as she hands me a "supplement" pack. I thank her and unscrew the top of the pouch. I drink some of the flavored water inside, staring at the table to avoid eye contact with the others. The ridges in the wood start to interest me. My eyes try to convince my mind that it's fake wood. It would be creepy to eat off a corpse.

"Are you not hungry, Cai?" Joane asks, her thin eyebrows pinched in concern. Her light purple sleeves bounce as she picks up a bowl of scrambled eggs and holds it toward me. "There's plenty of food."

Despite knowing my prepared answer, a shiver of worry runs over my shoulders. It's like my body thinks they'll somehow know that I've got alien traits. I shrug in hopes of appearing like I've answered this a million times before. "I'm allergic to most types of food, so I primarily consume supplements for my nutrition. But I'm okay to be around food—I just can't eat it."

The people I haven't told before react with various levels of muted or engaged surprise. I internally reprimand my arms when I notice how tense they are in my lap. It causes a ricochet of noticing other tensed-up portions of my body.

"Oh, no wonder you're so thin." Joane's eyes look

genuinely concerned, but I don't know why—she's thinner than I am. "Well, is there anything I can get you? Some water?"

"You're not allergic to water, are you?" Brandon asks, leaning forward with wide, curious eyes.

"Hey. Maybe dial down the personal questions," Eric says.

Analisa and Lian are the only ones here I trust. Yet I'm surprised at how easily that previous statement made me feel appreciative. It's especially weird given how silly that statement should be in this game.

"No worries, that's what this is all about, right?" I smile. The more open I seem about this, the less likely anyone will use it for a truth question. "Thanks, but I'm alright for now. I make sure to stay hydrated. So, yeah, I'm not allergic to water."

"How can a person be allergic to water anyway?" Daraja asks, possibly to direct the conversation away from me.

Daraja and Eric are following through with trying to be good allies. That's especially helpful since Analisa and Lian are letting me handle most of this for the least suspicion.

Ever chuckles lightly, shaking xir head. Xe has an old age kind of laugh, reminiscent of Grampa Dix's— like xe's seen some dark things. "If you meet enough people, you'll find that there are plenty of dangers in the world. Including water."

"Yes, there are people allergic to water, believe it or not." Solana lowers her eyes at the table, pursing her lips as her fork stabs at her omelet.

I raise my eyebrows, not knowing that. I'm also surprised that Solana has said something indicating that she's aware of other people.

The conversation subsides as everyone focuses on their food. Small conversations pop up about the food, our professions, stuff like that. It continues for a few minutes. It's a pleasant tone, but still with an underbelly of awkwardness. What a familiar feeling. I sip more water, trying to avoid dwelling on the last conversation I had with my family.

Lian clears his throat, putting on a slight smile. He's going for an awkward angle, from what I can tell. "So, I'm new to all this. How, or when, do we start the whole accusation thing?"

The conversations pause as eyes focus on him, the wall, the table.

"I imagine it can start at any time, on anything. Given that we hardly know anything about each other, it might be difficult to personalize the accusations." Sevyn folds their hands beneath their chin, done with their food. "But as we ease into the game, I imagine we'll become more entertaining."

"But why be unentertaining until we know each other better?" Solana asks, leaning back in her chair with raised eyebrows. "I say we up the stakes now."

Sensing an accusation coming, I look past Solana's shoulder. I don't want to make eye contact or look like I'm actively avoiding it. If Solana wants to up the stakes, attracting attention to myself now isn't the way to go.

"Okay. I'll bite." Eric leans over the table, his large

arms crossing. "What level of stakes are you aiming for?"

The corners of Solana's pink lips lift as her narrowed gaze homes in on Eric's unflinching eyes. She asks, "Eric, truth or dare?"

I swallow, feeling a sense of awe at the first accusation being held... at least, as far as I know. It's possible that an accusation might have happened already that I didn't hear. If only Auntie Tera could be here to listen.

Eric hums, tilting his gaze toward the ceiling. "Let's go truth."

"If you were guaranteed to get away with it, out of any person in the world, who would you kill?"

Chapter 10

Eric sucks air between his teeth. He doesn't answer right away. As he considers, it sinks in how troubling the question is. For a question like this, a person might not know their honest answer. Even so, the dome technology translates our brainwaves and catches even the slightest doubt. The timer won't disappear until we answer with what the technology detects as the full truth.

A hologram pops up above the table. It's a countdown from two minutes.

Eric smirks at the ticking time. "Well, ladies, lads, and gentlepeople, it seems we've officially started."

We really have. A question like this is strong for starting out. I don't know what I'd answer. There isn't anyone I hate enough to want to kill them. But if someone asked me and I doubted my answer, the timer would continue going until I figured out my feelings.

Eric gives a light sigh through the fingers laced in front of his mouth. "There's a certain group of COfficials and judges who abused the law because their drunk friend caused a car accident. They tried to blame it on the victim, whose car got T-boned. The victim... her car hit a pole and flipped. She was plugged into tubes and unconscious for weeks. The cops tried to claim that she consented to a DUI test and had alcohol detected in her. When she finally woke up, she couldn't stand. She bit part of her tongue off because she couldn't control her muscles anymore. It's been three years, and she—my cousin—can't move most of her body anymore." His jaw sets, lost in his thoughts.

The timer continues. He hasn't stated an answer yet. I don't blame him for taking his time on this one. It doesn't sound like a pleasant memory to parse through.

Eric sighs, looking at the ceiling. "My aunt and my father have been dealing with so much paperwork. And so many calls to so many incompetent people who keep denying my cousin treatment and disability compensation because they're abusing the patient privacy rule. My aunt is having to take care of my cousin's baby. All three are dirt poor and out of state, and their government won't do shit to help them." A slight smile of disbelief flashes on Eric's face. "And all because the cops didn't want to admit their rich friend hit someone when she was drunk and speeding. She's dead now; apparently died of a heart attack a year ago, and never tried to advocate for my cousin. If I had to pick anyone, I'd bring her back to life to kill her."

My eyebrows lift. It's quite the story.

Eric's going to school for business and political science, learning the tools to understand economic and political power. I think I have more context behind that choice now. Although... I wonder if understanding would be enough to prevent something like his story from happening again.

"Now there's a good answer." Solana flings out her hand with a bright grin. "Hateful government bullshit. I can certainly relate to the paperwork and phone calls. The cops don't know what to do with my schizophrenic brother either. They'll taze him and throw him in jail when he's having an episode, instead of putting him in psychiatric care like his lawyer keeps advocating for. But anyway." Her eyes lull to the side. "Fun questions, fun answers. Fun dares, fun accomplishments. That's how I think this should go."

"Asking someone who they want to kill counts as a fun question to you?" Lian asks somewhat incredulously. He seriously needs to learn to keep his mouth shut.

"Do you want something livelier?" Solana homes in on Lian with a smirk. "Lian, truth or dare?"

Lian freezes up. He holds Solana's gaze. Typically, dares can result in embarrassing actions, but truths can result in division among players. I don't know which would be worse for Solana to exploit.

"Dare," Lian says.

Solana hums with satisfaction as if that's what she was hoping for. "Let's play matchmaker. I dare you to make out with someone for ten seconds."

Lian looks like he's about to be hit in the face with a frying pan. At least he's single. But I also don't know if he's ever kissed anyone before—has he been in a relationship or hooked up with anyone?

He rubs the back of his neck, sheepishly looking at the table. He attempts an easy smile, but it falters quickly. "Uh, yeah, so most of you are... older. So that might be weird. Analisa's my sister. Cai's with her. So, uh..."

Leaving Daraja and Eric. They both seem to notice. Daraja's eyes widen. Before they say anything, Eric grins, raising his eyebrows. "It's okay. You can admit if you want to kiss me. I think I have that effect on people."

His arrogance gives me a twinge of surprise. Lian might be into it. At least, I haven't seen Lian make such a tightly embarrassed expression before. Maybe Eric was trying to make it easier for him to decide.

A holographic timer pops up for two minutes. Lian narrows his eyes at it, taking a moment to prolong his consideration. "You all don't have to see the dare while I'm completing it, right?"

"Right," Analisa says, her voice light. She's probably trying to gauge how comfortable Lian is with this.

Lian nods and takes a breath, his eyes boring into the table. Then he stands up and walks toward the nearest hall, the holographic timer following him. Barely turning back, he points at Eric. "You. Follow me."

As Lian continues down the hall, Eric's eyebrows raise with his delighted smile. "Yes, sir."

I engage in a quick eye-movement conversation with Analisa. Then I follow her grinning lead as she perches beside the hall entrance. I crouch on the floor beside her, grasping her hand so I know if she intends to walk somewhere. We're careful not to peer too far around the wall's edge.

Solana leans her hip against the other side of the hall entryway. While looking at Analisa, her index finger deftly points down the hall and to her pink lips. Ah. She's asking if it's Lian's first kiss. Analisa shrugs with a nod—she thinks so.

Daraja, who was sitting with their leg partially leaving the chair, kneels on the ground by Solana.

"Ah, what a nice precedent to set," Flutura says sarcastically as her eyes flit between the four of us.

I'm too curious to not hear how this goes. And if I'm too curious, Analisa's definitely not leaving her post.

"Perhaps..." Jared's hands gesture like he juggles an invisible object until he finds the rest of his sentence. "Perhaps we could talk about some of the amenities here? I'm sure we could do some fun things while we're here, besides the accusations."

"Ooh, I overheard a dinner with one of the arena's engineers. They said that there's always a water source in the game. I've always wanted to swim in a pond, or even a river," Joane jumps in, supporting Jared's attempt at introducing a new conversation. "I've been too scared to go in the water though—so many creatures. My sister was stung by a jellyfish once, you know."

As they speak, I press a hand over my right ear. They're conversing to cover up our spying, but it makes it harder to hear Lian and Eric.

Then I catch Eric's voice. "We can go to my room if you want to be sure—"

"No! I mean, nope. Here is fine," Lian's tight voice responds.

From Daraja's widened eyes and Solana's curved smile, I think I'm hearing correctly.

"The timer is right here, so we can easily keep track. We don't have to do this any longer than ten seconds," Eric says.

Lian releases a light, almost scoff-laugh. "So, have you done this a lot?"

"What? No. Timed kisses don't tend to come up a lot."

"No, I mean..." he sputters.

The passing of time itches. It makes me question whether I'm hearing everything. Fighting the urge to peer forward more is painful.

"I haven't kissed a guy before, if that's what you mean," Eric admits, his voice less enthusiastic than his usual stage-presence pronunciation. "It's not that I never wanted to. I just don't have a lot of time for dating."

Lian clears his throat. "So you're not dating anyone?"

Eric hums knowingly. "You seem a little too delighted by that."

"You're the one who encouraged me to kiss you."

"Yeah, well, would you rather kiss your sister?"

A noise of disgust from Lian. Looking up at Analisa, I see the tongue-out, silent expression of that disgust. Lian continues through a laugh, "Ack, you're gross."

"I'm just trying to build rapport. I figure I should do that before kissing someone I barely know, although a minute isn't a lot of time for that."

"We have a *minute*? Shoot, shoot, shoot."

"I'm not going to judge you, okay? I don't really know how to do this either. And it's only ten seconds." Eric sighs. "Can I kiss you?"

I raise my eyebrows, unsure whether they're kissing or if Lian is standing there with a tight, embarrassed expression.

"It's not you. You're not the issue. You're great. I mean, you're alright. Not—" Lian groans. "That's not what I meant."

"Hey, this is your dare, not mine. I won't lose anything by not kissing you. Well, other than missing out on kissing a handsome guy. But more importantly, you want the money for your father, right? This dare is a step closer to that."

"I guess that's true. How serious were you about calling me handsome?"

"Lian, we have twenty seconds. Can I kiss you?"

"Oh. Um, yes."

At the silence, Analisa's face creeps forward above me. I grip her hand tighter, making sure she's balanced as I lean forward.

First off, the height difference is adorable. Eric is nearly as tall as the bedroom doors surrounding them in the narrow hall. As he leans forward, his wavy hair rests over his closed eyes. One hand is cupped around Lian's jaw as they kiss. His other hand rests at his side, holding Lian's glinting glasses. The yellowed hall light catches the red on Eric's ears.

A wave of second-hand embarrassment shudders through me at seeing Lian's hands. They're trembling and raised as if he wants to hold Eric but isn't sure what to do.

"Put your hands somewhere, you idiot," Analisa mutters.

Lian seizes Eric's resting hand, making Eric laugh airily during his next breath. He gently encourages Lian's back against the wall. Lian's face flushes even more when his spare hand rubs the back of Eric's neck.

Just as they start to look more comfortable, Eric leans back. The corners of his mouth rise as he mutters, "Ten seconds. The timer's gone."

"Oh." Lian's residual smile fades as Eric hands back his glasses. "Right, yeah. Thanks."

Analisa's hand pulls on mine, yanking me out of the hallway frame of sight.

"If you need help with an accusation in the future, let me know," Eric says.

"Thanks. I'll keep that in mind." Lian sighs. "I'm gonna find my room. I don't need them staring at me, knowing that... that is now online forever."

"That's understandable. I'll go back to the group. Hopefully it'll help get the attention off you."

"Thanks. Hey, uh," Lian starts. "If there were someone who wouldn't mind minimal dating, what would their chances be? With you."

I look up at Analisa, her mouth an o-shape like mine.

"With me?" Eric hums in consideration. "Well, he'd have to be handsome. It helps if he's a little awkward. And if he asks me for a kiss without a dare associated with it next time, I'd like his chances."

At the sound of steps, I lurch to my feet, helping pull Analisa back to her seat. Daraja and Solana speed to the table as well. By the time Eric steps into the dining room, we're acting engaged in discussion.

Of course, the conversations audibly dip when Eric stands in the hall doorway. His arms cross with a smug frown directed at Analisa. His eyes glance at me as well. Then he swivels to Daraja and blinks at Solana.

Daraja catches a laugh in their throat, blocked only by a wavering smile. They become the primary target of Eric's silent stare.

"See?" Solana dares to speak with such a grin. "Fun truths and dares aren't so bad."

Eric nods, his eyebrows rising to add to his

relenting agreement. "Sure. Spying isn't very sports-manlike though."

Analisa takes a deep breath. "If you're serious about considering my brother as a potential dating mate, you'll need to know that he's really weird." Staring right at Eric's unmoving face, she goes on and on. "He likes fashion. Don't worry, he won't make you do coordinated outfits, but he does like little matchy things like the promise earrings Cai and I wear. Despite how awkward he was just now, he's popular at school because of how sociable he is. He makes fun of grand romantic gestures on television, but I think it's because he's jealous of the characters. He's good at chemistry and math too, so feel free to use him as a reference. He sometimes works as an encyclopedia too, but don't push it too much on physics, since he's got a sore spot there. And if you really want—"

"I'm going to stop you there." Eric holds up his hands. "Thank you for the support, but we just kissed. On a dare. I'm not expecting anything more from—"

"He asked you out!" Analisa flings her arm toward the hall. "Sure, it was in his dorky way where you could misinterpret it as mere semi-interest, but I'm pretty sure it was more than that." She clicks her tongue. "You're as thick as he is. Now I have to support this."

I jump in with, "If it helps, we won't spy on you next time."

"Really?" Eric narrows his eyes at Analisa.

"Don't be gross." Analisa shakes her head. "It was his first kiss. I don't need to spy on him more than that."

Eric leans against his chair. "Ah. I see."

"Alright. Credit where due." Analisa swivels in her chair, facing Solana. "I admit it, since Lian seemed okay with it, that was fun. I give you points for that."

Solana's chin tips up. "Thank you. And I wouldn't have spied if you hadn't gotten up first."

A new bond seems to solidify from across the room. Even I can admit feeling a little better about Solana now. Sure, she's brash, but maybe she's not bad.

"Hey, Solana," Eric says. "Truth or dare?"

Solana's amused smile grows. "Dare."

"Jog a couple laps around the cabin. You could use some payback for forcing Lian to kiss me."

A timer pops up beside Solana. I suck air through my teeth at the twelve minutes allotted.

"Joke's on you. I jog in my free time." Solana's hand nudges Eric's head as she passes him. As she flings off her heels, her finger scans over the group. "If any of you were fit, you'd join me without needing a dare."

"There are motor carts outside," Sevyn remarks, their chin placed on their folded hands.

Eric points at them. "I like the way you think. You all hop in the motor carts, cheer her on. I'll go tell Lian in case he wants to join."

"Evil. You're all evil." Solana cackles as she jogs out of the room.

My chest lightens as Analisa pulls me up with an excited grin. Her brown eyes gleam, reminding me to relax. It's like we're on a paid vacation with a bunch of people we're getting to know.

I join the others on motor carts to cheer and shout about how relaxing it is to ride carts around the building. Meanwhile, Solana jogs and cusses us out with a breathy smile.

Chapter 11

"This time, we're not giving you food unless you let us in. Don't make me dare you to leave the room." Analisa taps the door with her walking stick. The wall helps support my back as I balance a few empty bowls on my forearm. My fingertips press against the rim of the steaming bowl of vegetables and rice.

"Then I'll choose truth," Lian calls out indignantly through the door.

"I don't think you'll like my truth questions either." Analisa taps the door again. "Come on, let us in."

"Who's us?" Lian asks.

"Just me and Analisa," I respond.

"Yeah, we're not mean enough to bring your future boyfriend by," Analisa says. Her voice sounds less like she intends to mess with Lian, and more that she thinks it a matter of fact. With the way her bored eyes stare at the door, she seems used to Lian holing himself up in a room.

The door swings open. Lian glares at Analisa and gives us space to enter the room.

Analisa steps inside with an eye roll. I follow, feeling her dramatic wake rub off on me. She settles onto the bed and grabs a pillow to wrap her arms around. It reminds me of the way I hold my avocado plushie during a vulnerable conversation. I sit beside her, carefully setting the bowls on the bed as Lian shifts his position. The blanket crumples around him while he rests his head in his folded arms.

I pull out one of my "supplements" and sip on the flavored water.

Analisa snuggles beside me, linking her arm through mine until her fingers find my hand. She stares at Lian. "Look, I don't get it, so explain it to me. What's going on with you, Lili?"

Lian looks up, his eyelids drooping. He sets his head against his arms again. "It's stupid."

"What is?" Analisa scoops some veggies and rice into a bowl. She pokes Lian's head with the spoon handle until his head snaps up.

"I'm not the kind of person to jump into things. What was I thinking—kissing him like that?" Lian's palms rub his eyes.

"You had to kiss someone," I say. "What else could you have done—give up on $100,000?"

"Yeah, but I didn't expect to like it that much. And I don't even think I did it right." He buries his head into a pillow.

"So, wait." Analisa holds up her spoon. "Is it that you want to kiss more, or is it that you want to kiss *Eric* more?" Lian mumbles something. "Head out of the pillow, Lili."

Lian's head pops back up. "The second one." He groans. "Which makes it worse. Like, if I wasn't attracted to him, we could just move on. I actually dread the thought of seeing him again. I'm so embarrassed."

"Sure, you're awkward. And yeah, I get to make fun of you for that." Analisa shrugs. "But you aren't embarrassing. You're outgoing, everyone likes you, and you're cute in a kind of nerdy way. Right, Cai?"

"Right. And Eric seems like he's at least attracted to you too," I note. "And I don't think you should worry about what he thinks of you anyway."

"But I've got to be around him for five more days." Lian slumps over again. "And then what, anyway? What am I expecting?"

"Lili, look at me." Analisa pokes his head with the spoon handle again. He bats it away but does look up. "Just have fun, okay? We aren't obligated to do *anything* over the next few days. Accusations pass the time, sure, but think of this as a vacation. Once we get back, we'll have enough money for Baba to get treatment. So don't get trapped in the insecurities inside your head."

"You can start by going to the group event," I suggest. At Lian's curious eyes, I explain, "Ever suggested we all make s'mores at the firepit. It's a big group, so you could sit next to Eric." At the increasing panic in his expression, I correct, "Or not. But I don't want to have to dare you to show up."

"I'm staying away from dares forever," Lian mutters.

"And food too, apparently. What would Amma say?" Analisa waves the bowl of food in front of Lian. "She could be watching you reject your food right now."

Lian's face flushes. He groans into the blanket.

"You just reminded him that his mom might've seen his first kiss," I say.

Analisa covers her mouth, having a difficult time not laughing. "Yeah, I didn't think."

"Now I'm going to be thinking about that all week! Thanks, you stupid clam." Lian snatches the food bowl and spoon, burying his attention into his food. At least he's eating, even if it's angrily.

"So..." Analisa pokes his arm. "You going to the s'mores thing?"

Glaring at the blanket, he mumbles something through his food. Analisa seems pleased by it, so I think it's a confirmation. We sit in silence while Lian finishes his bowl.

"You done?" Analisa asks, staring at Lian's cleaned-out bowl. She tugs on his arm. "Come on— the campfire awaits! And Eric. But I'm sure you know that."

Lian whacks her with a pillow, his grumbling not nearly as loud as Analisa's persistence.

"Don't worry, I already told him about you. He

seemed kind of interested, even!" Analisa insists. "Come on, Lili, it'll be fun."

I sweep up the bowls before they become casualties in the tug-of-war and pillow fight hybrid of a squabble.

We freeze at a knock on the door.

"Hey, Lian, are you alright?" Eric asks through the door.

Lian buries himself under the pillows. Analisa whisper-hisses, "Get up or I'll tell him you like him."

His head pops out of a pillow, whisper-hissing back, "You wouldn't dare."

"Oh yeah? Truth or dare, Lili?"

Lian's jaw clenches, unsure. "You're not going to make me tell him, are you?"

"Of course not. I'm not that mean."

I drift toward the door, preparing to possibly answer it.

"Hey, Lian, are you in there?" Eric calls out.

Lian whines. "Dare."

"I dare you to go talk with Eric at the s'mores campfire thing. Talk about whatever. Just don't run away from it, alright?" Analisa nudges his shoulder. "I swear, things will be less awkward if you don't treat it as awkward."

A thirty-minute timer materializes beside Lian. It follows him as he slides out of the bed. His hand hesitates by the doorknob. After a deep breath, he opens the door and dashes down the hall. "Eric, wait!"

Analisa giggles. "About time."

I sit next to her and offer her a hand. I'm not sure if it's because of something in my expression or her own inclination, but she sighs. "Yeah, I know, I'm a little harsh on him. He just holds back so much, you know? He doubts himself."

"That sounds familiar," I admit. "Based on how he acted, I think he appreciates it."

She kicks up her legs playfully. Her smile seems self-conscious. "I'm kind of pushy to you too."

"Maybe. But I wouldn't have gotten the courage to apply to all this if it weren't for you."

The unease melts from her as she presses on her walking stick, getting to her feet. She tugs on my hand. "Come on. Don't you want to see if Lian crashes and burns?"

I shrug, walking with her to the door. "If someone as awkward as me can manage to convince someone as hot as you to love me, I think Lian has a shot with an Eric."

"So you think Eric is hot, huh?" Analisa's teasing voice returns as she swings my hand down the hall. I wait for her to turn around to see my glare. She doesn't indulge me. "What a silence. Do I have some competition here?"

"Never. I was playfully glaring. It's your fault for not looking back." I lightly nudge her shoulder.

"Hey, you know that Norse myth? The Orpheus and Eury..."

"If you mean Eurydice, that's a Greek myth," I correct.

"Right, yeah. All Orpheus had to do to get both of

them out okay was to not look back." She slows down, matching my pace. "So I plan to keep looking forward."

After we turn the corner into the living room, a shrill shout sends a shiver down my tensing arms. I peer through the kitchen entrance, focusing on the glass doors to the patio. Near the campfire outside, Solana screams at a frowning Flutura.

"Ugh." Analisa shakes her head. "I thought we finished with the Solana drama."

Flutura appears more reasonable for being composed. Then again, it's possible Solana has a good reason for being dramatic. Heck, she could be acting over-the-top to retain the audience's attention. Regardless, I'm curious to know what the timer and the other number next to her entail. The number is four, and she's got about a minute and a half left on her timer.

Chapter 12

"My ears!" Office Job Guy—Brandon, I mean—scurries up to Flutura. I really should remember his name without having to peek at his profile by now. "What did you ask her to do?"

"How dare you question what I'm doing here?" Solana's hands flail toward Flutura. "Should I ask why a famous dancer like you is on this show? Not everyone has the world handed to them—"

"Solana. Solana! Calm down." Eric's voice is suppressed by Solana's volume. "You don't have long to answer whatever it is."

"Why don't we all sit down? The s'mores are ready! Solana, you can have this one." Joane desperately holds out a s'more toward Solana. It's a futile attempt since Joane frequently flinches away from Solana's waving arms. Jared shimmies himself between the two, encouraging Joane to a safer distance.

Lian drifts toward Analisa and me on the porch. Analisa tugs on his sleeve, whispering, "What's going on?"

"I'm not sure. I wasn't here for the accusation," Lian mutters.

Ever approaches Solana, xir hand rising as if trying to tame a wild horse. "Child, what did she ask?"

Solana glares at the ground, her face red. Only now do her tightly-pursed lips obstruct her words. She only has forty seconds left.

"I asked her if she's really here to raise money for her brother's treatment," Flutura says.

Silence envelops the group. It's clear what the issue is. Solana would've easily answered yes if it were true.

My respect for her diminishes. How could she lie about something like that?

"Are you serious?" Analisa asks. "Answer the question, Solana."

Solana scoffs. "You can't imagine what I'm going through—"

"I can't?" Analisa's voice raises, matching Solana's. "I'm actually here for my family. My father needs the money from this show. What can you possibly say for yourself? Did you want pity points from the audience for something that's not even real?"

Solana smacks Analisa across the face. I snatch Analisa's arm as she stumbles into me.

Concern stabs through my body at how much the force made her stagger. As she catches herself against me, my fear for her is replaced by a searing resentment.

"What is wrong with you? You can't hit my sister." Lian pushes Solana's shoulders. She pushes him back.

Sevyn tangles Solana's arms behind her back faster than I can detect. "Stop it. We're all going to get along here. If you can't answer a simple question, then that's your problem. Don't take it out on everyone else."

The timer reaches zero seconds. It turns red before disintegrating silently. Solana's arms slump as she stares blankly at where the timer was. She just lost $100,000 from her potential winnings.

Flutura has a seat on a log positioned by the growing campfire. How did she know to ask about Solana's motivation?

More importantly, what incentive could be so bad that Solana doesn't want to reveal it? Most people don't care if players join for money or attention. But it could be so self-serving that Solana thought she'd lose favor with the audience.

Fire builds in my chest while I hold Analisa. She hasn't moved, staring at the porch with wide eyes. I mutter, "Solana, truth or dare?"

Solana's head lifts. "What?"

I raise my voice. "Solana, truth or dare?"

Her eyes narrow. She tips her chin at the number four floating next to her. "Well, I was dared to only accept truth for the next four accusations. So, truth."

"Are you really here to raise money for your brother's treatment?"

I know I'm creating needless risk. The animosity in me thrives on it. Despite Solana's piercing eyes, I don't retract the accusation. If she breaks out of Sevyn's grasp, I need to be ready to fight back.

Analisa's grip strengthens on my arm; she's bracing to move as well. Lian looks like he's ready to jump in. And... we're not alone. Other than Flutura sitting down, everyone surrounds Solana. Against her, with us. When did this happen?

As the timer counts down from two minutes, Solana says, "Retract it."

I shake my head.

"Answer the question," Daraja adds.

Solana's gaze flits around the group; her eyebrows change positions as quickly. "You all don't get it." She laughs nervously. "I'm not a bad person!"

"Then it should be easy for you to answer the question," Sevyn states.

"Without smacking or shoving anyone," Eric emphasizes.

"What's the point?" Solana glares at me. "What do you get out of this?"

I'm not sure if she's directing her words toward me or the group. To label the bundle of emotions in me as irritation would be limiting. "You're running out of time."

Solana stares at the minute remaining on the timer. Her head droops with her next exhale. "Finnigan's dead." The hostility in her voice has faded.

Confusion destabilizes my anger. "Who's Finnigan?"

"My brother. The police manhandled him during

one of his episodes last week. I came on this show to get money for an assassin to kill the officer who choked him to death." Solana directs her voice to the side. "You can let go of me now, sweetheart. There's no point in me playing this anymore. Thank you all for alerting my brother's murderer about my plan. You can sleep well knowing that cop will still be out there."

Solana slips out of Sevyn's arms. As she walks by, my skin itches to back away from her. Since Lian and Analisa don't move, I don't either.

The automatic patio doors slide open for Solana. As soon as she steps inside the kitchen, she grabs a ceramic bowl and hurtles it into the wall. My shoulders flinch at the shattering dish. She walks into the living room with an eerie steadiness.

The tension in my chest reduces now that I can't see her. My anger wants to feel justified, but baffled remorse sneaks into my mind, inciting a headache. Was provoking Solana worth it?

The guilt vanishes when I notice Analisa's cheek. Beads of blood indicate a thin scratch below her eye.

"As uncomfortable as that all was, perhaps we can return to our dessert," Ever suggests.

Flutura slides a burnt marshmallow off a stake with graham crackers. She bites into it, content to focus on her snack. Her indifference feels oddly stabilizing. Light conversation returns among the people passing out the s'more materials.

"Ana, your face." Lian gapes.

Analisa's fingers hover over the light purple mark forming. "It can't look that bad, can it?"

"Hang on, I'll get some ice." Lian steps up to the glass doors.

I encourage Analisa to a patio chair by the fire. Before I can sit beside her, the patio doors slide open again, killing the gentle conversation. Solana stands in the doorway, blocking Lian. His fists tremble, but he doesn't step aside.

"Cai," Solana calls out.

The rustling of the forest leaves at the edge of the cabin's clearing overwhelms my ears. Solana may captivate my gaze, but the wind bellows a more threatening omen. Any moment now, I feel like I could be swept away like a discarded leaf.

"Truth or dare," Solana finishes.

This is the consequence of my actions.

She probably wants to ask me something revealing—something that could hurt me as much as I hurt her. I can't imagine how she could get close to the truth about my alien parentage, but it's possible. I can't take that risk. "Dare."

"Cai, I dare you to have sex with Lian. I recommend about an hour to get that done." She walks back inside. The screen doors shut behind her.

Chapter 13

An hour-long timer appears beside me. Shock roots me into place. My thoughts vanish, replaced by a muted panic.

"You can't do that!" Analisa yells.

The screen doors slide open again. Solana crosses her arms. "Really? There aren't any rules against it. Just because you're in a relationship with Cai doesn't mean she can't have sex with someone else."

"How can you make us do something that—like that?" Lian stutters. "It's—it wouldn't be consensual."

"It's as consensual as the kiss with Eric, isn't it?" Solana leans against the doorway, her glower unchanged.

"No, actually. We did consent to that," Eric's firm voice objects. "But if they're resisting this, it means they're not consenting."

"You're taking this too far, Solana," Joane's voice quivers, horrified. "They're brother and sister."

Solana rolls her eyes. "Cai and Lian aren't siblings."

"No, but you're telling Cai, who's dating Analisa, to sleep with Analisa's brother." Daraja rounds on her. "It's gross and just plain weird! Aren't you thirty? How sick are you to ask eighteen-year-olds to have sex?"

"They're right. Retract the dare, Solana," Jared agrees.

"Did Cai retract her dare?" Solana throws her arm toward me. "No, she didn't, even after I begged her to. Why are you giving special treatment to this team of teenagers?"

"You were acting suspicious, and they were mad because you lied using the reason that they're actually here for," Office Job Guy—Brandon—argues. "I'm with the teenagers."

"You don't know if that's actually what they're here for."

Analisa throws out her arms. "Ask me. I dare you."

"Ahem." Sevyn taps Analisa's chair. "Analisa, truth or dare?"

"Truth."

"What do you plan to use the funds for Truth or Dare for?"

"First and foremost, it's for my father's treatment. If we've got extra funds, then Lian and I can travel to the hospital across the country with our parents. And if I'm lucky enough to have any personal winnings left, I plan to give them to Cai so she can pay for tuition to Darilek University." Analisa takes my shivering hand. "She's helped me so selflessly throughout all this—I'm hoping I can give her something back for it."

Her words are warm. If only I could feel them past this chill. The timer beside me continues ticking.

Sevyn nods, satisfied. "There's your answer, Solana. You're picking on a selfless person. If you truly want justice in the world, you're not off to a good start."

"You took away my justice. I really don't care about yours." Solana flicks her hand toward Lian. "I'd get to it."

My fuming emotions don't melt my frozen exterior. I don't know what to do.

"If you won't retract the dare, then we'll put it up for an audience vote." Analisa throws up her arms. She shouts to the sky, "Comedy, Tragedy, you know this is messed up. We may be legally able to play Version 20 games, but we're not nineteen yet. This is child pornography—the dare deserves a vote!"

Unfortunately, laws from the outside don't apply to what we do inside Truth or Dare. Legally, they don't have to initiate an audience vote. Even if they do, the audience could vote for us to enact the dare, and the game wouldn't be held liable for it.

Disturbing thoughts begin to surface. If I were to have sex with someone, my skin might be revealed. My bark would be noticeable if I were naked. I could wear a top...

But I also don't have a vagina or an anus. Sure, I could participate in sexual activities without those and without sexual urges, but if the other players somehow find out that I don't have those, that's one step closer to finding out about my parentage. Would revealing that stop the dare from happening, or would it not make a difference?

The timer beside me stops. A few seconds pass without it continuing.

Notifications pop up next to us: "An audience vote is being held for Solana's dare to Cai. Allow five minutes for the votes to be cast."

A five-minute timer starts.

Hope worms its way into my fear. Would the audience be sympathetic toward us, or would they desire more drama?

Analisa's fingers grip mine. Her jaw clenches—she's also feeling the pressure of the conflicting possibilities. If the audience votes to cancel the dare, we don't have to do anything more.

"You're all making this a bigger deal than it needs to be," Solana says.

"No. You're being petty," Eric accuses.

"Oh yeah, sweetie? Truth or dare."

"You already used your accusation on me today, remember?"

"Shame. I was going to dare you to ram your head into a wall."

Daraja stands up. "You really are a sick person, you know that?"

"Yeah? Truth or dare, Daraja?"

"Stop it!" Joane shouts. Her hands clamp over her ears, her fingers running through her stringy hair.

Daraja's eyes widen at the ground. Their mouth stutters, not quite deciding between dare and truth. They manage, "Truth."

"What's the deepest, darkest secret you have that you were going to take to the grave?" Solana offers a sly smile.

A five-minute timer appears beside Daraja. It begins counting.

Daraja slumps into a patio chair, their braids swaying across their rocking back. Their fingers lace over their mouth.

Everyone else is too scared to speak. Anyone could be Solana's target now.

"Retract it, Solana. This isn't fun anymore," Eric insists.

"It's fun for me." Solana flicks her fingers at him. "As soon as the misery is turned on you all, you start to care. So why couldn't you care to not prod into my business?"

"It was a simple question that, if you didn't initially lie about it, should've had a simple answer," Eric says.

"What else was I supposed to do? The refs asked me what my motivation was for being here, so I told them a lighter version of it. It's not my fault that you're all so self-absorbed to not leave well enough alone!"

"Um. I think I'm ready to answer." Daraja's soft voice cuts through everyone. Even Solana waits for them to speak. "Or, as ready as I'll be."

It's not fair for Daraja to have to answer this. I

was the one who pressed Solana. Even if I hate what she's doing, I could've avoided this.

Daraja continues, "I have a condition. It's called Dissociative Identity Disorder or DID for short. I haven't told anyone about it because of all the depictions of it in movies and stuff. People are more interested in making it look bad than accurate. And there's just not enough of us with influence to change that narrative, even after at least a century of trying." They press their hands against their forehead as they stare at the ground.

"Um..." Joane's voice sounds delicate, reluctant. "Sorry, but what is DID?"

"Oh. Right." Daraja gives a quick chuckle. "So, I have a single body, right? But I have more than one personality inside my head. We each take control of the body at different times. Daraja is awake the most. We've also got a child alter—personality, I mean. Her name is Didi. Bridget helps guide the switching between who is in control of the body. And uh, I'm Clementine. I'm a protector alter who's based on our older brother."

Their mouth stutters again before closing. They rub their eyes while my chest tightens. The timer doesn't stop.

They clear their throat before continuing. "We each have our own preferences, behavior, internal appearances, and stuff. We also have different memories. Like, when I'm awake, I remember what happens when I'm awake. When Daraja's awake, she's able to remember what she experiences. But it's harder for us to recall each other's memories. Since we've started communicating with each other in a healthy system, it's gotten easier to access different memories. But I swear, we're not dangerous. We're just... us."

Although the words are a lot—really, too much for me to completely absorb—they feel genuine. Even though they seem worried that we'll be afraid of them, I don't fear them. I just feel bad for them for having to unload that in this messy situation.

"So, Clementine?" Eric kneels beside them. "Is that how you'd prefer to be called?"

Their shuddering subsides. They give a light laugh. "Wow. I've never been called that by anyone else. Huh. For now, 'Daraja' works for all of us. But thank you."

"Okay, no problem. Let me know if that changes," Eric says.

Words compose themselves before I can even think. "I believe you, Daraja. That you're not dangerous. You're our friend."

"Yeah," Analisa joins in. "It's like we get four new friends in one."

Daraja sniffles. Their tears roll down their face, dripping over their breathy, uncertain smile.

"I hate to bring this up, but if you don't want your truth to go to waste... there might be something else you need to admit." Sevyn gestures to the ongoing timer beside Daraja.

"What? How can that not be it? We've never admitted—" Daraja's eyes gloss over in realization.

"Oh. Well. It could be…" Their hands clasp over their mouth. Their silver eyebrow piercing catches the fire's light as their pinched eyebrows quiver.

"Hey, it's okay," Eric assures. He kneels on the ground, his bare knees digging into the dirt. "We've all got things we don't want to admit. Whatever it is, we're here with you."

Daraja's hands hover inches from their mouth like they want to catch their words before we can hear them. "I'm not sure exactly what it is. But something tells me I might be on the right track."

"Then guide me through it." Eric's voice remains even.

"Well, we used to cut our thighs with a razor. Specifically, Bridget thought we deserved it. Back when we were all so depressed that we didn't know what it was to deserve." They stare at the timer.

My breaths are short. I've watched players parse through their emotions before, digging for the truth. But this is the first time I'm witnessing it in person. And this is with someone I've started to get to know. It hurts my chest.

"Our father died when we were young," Daraja relents. "And our mom just… wouldn't take care of us. I remember one time she locked us in a closet—it's a feint snapshot of a memory. But I think we started talking to ourselves around then. Maybe when we were seven? I don't know. It's so hazy. But we never told anyone, even though we knew it was weird. It was only when I saw one of the movies that had someone with DID… when I resonated with the killer, because they were the first person I'd seen who was like me. And I was so scared of that. So scared that it was what I was destined to be. But part of me thought it was good, because maybe then we'd not be so afraid of everything anymore. It felt good—thinking people might fear us instead."

The timer beside Daraja disappears.

I thought Solana and Eric's truths were dark, but Daraja's immerses me in this game. This isn't supposed to be a fun experience for the players. It's supposed to be dramatic, enticing, and entertaining for those watching. How did I not realize that from outside the game?

Even before the audience vote timer disappears, a cynical sentiment submerges my heart. The result is in.

The audience permits Solana's dare. I have to have sex with Lian.

The hour-long timer restarts.

Chapter 14

Analisa shuts the door behind us, her chest wheezing. Noticing that Lian and I are the only other two in the bedroom, she taps Lian's shoulder. "Move just like... three steps back from Cai, please."

Lian jumps across the room at the prompt.

My jittery limbs lock in place. My heart rattles in my ears—or maybe that's my shivering making that noise.

"Okay, you two spend the next fifty minutes figuring out a loophole. Sex means a lot of things, so figure out a way that is as least... bad... as you can." Even through her purple bruise, sickly green taints her cheeks. "Yeah. Don't do anything until the timer runs down to about fifty minutes. I'll try to convince Solana to retract the dare before then. I'll let you know as soon as I do that." Her resolve barely keeps her shaking knees standing. "I'll be back soon."

I want to tell her to stay. I really *really* want her

to stay. My mind is so obstructed with general panic and hate for Solana and love for Analisa and disgust at the thought of all this and—

Analisa shuts the door as she leaves. My trembling muscles respond to the startling noise by scurrying to the nearest wall. Lian and I scrunch into opposite corners of the bedroom.

Fear sinks into my terrified skin. What if he starts to want to complete the dare? Could his human desire overrule his better judgment?

"Please stop looking at me like that." Lian's voice wavers. "I don't want to do it either."

"You promise you won't try..." I can't finish that thought coherently.

"I promise. It's consensual or nothing. And I don't consent," he insists.

Some ease returns to my tense shoulders. Still, I don't leave my corner. If only it were my comfort corner, with all my cozy plant plushies. I already miss my familiar room so much.

"So, any ideas?" Lian asks.

"I'm asexual. So... no," I respond.

"But... you do know how all that works, right?"

"I don't—" How much can I admit here? Lian knows that I'm partially an alien. If I say I don't have a vagina or an anus, it's not like he's going to give me a truth about why. Admitting it on television is uncomfortable, but if we're looking for loopholes, it might be important to admit. "I mean, I don't really have experience. I also don't have a vagina, or... uh..." Discomfort strangles the end of my sentence.

Sure, it's possible to be a human born without an anus. But the more I admit, the more of an anomaly I might seem to the audience. Will they pester my public profile with questions about my anatomy for the rest of my life?

"I mean, I don't have a vagina or experience either. But I get how it works."

I scrunch my eyebrows. "Are you trying to be funny right now?"

He recoils in his corner. "I'm sorry. Humor is my coping mechanism for uncomfortable situations."

Embarrassment seeps into my words. I manage to push through it. "I mean, yeah. I get how it works to a certain extent. I haven't really researched nuanced ways of doing it. Have you?"

He glares at the wall.

"Have you?"

"You can't just ask someone that on live television, Cai."

"Look, this is awkward for both of us. But if we want to come up with a loophole, we need to consider what qualifies as sex. Solana didn't specify that we needed to do a certain thing, so if we were to do... *something*... it would count. But since I don't have a vagina, I think... we might need you to... well... use your, uh... yeah."

He grips his jacket hood and yanks it over his head.

"You have an idea?" I venture.

"Not any good ones, no," his muffled voice says.

Even though we're dragging ourselves into being

productive, the situation feels hopeless. An icky feeling chews at my insides.

Someone knocks on the door. The hope that it's Analisa drives me out of my corner. Lian and I bolt for the door, then do this awkward dance of bumping into each other and making grossed-out faces while we dash back to our corners.

"Sorry. You answer it," I say.

"No, you can. I insist," Lian says.

"Hey, Lian? Cai? Are you two... Can I come in?" Eric's voice says.

Lian's hood is over his head again, so I venture, "Yeah."

Eric pokes his head through the doorway. Seeing us in the corners, he sputters a laugh.

Lian groans. "This isn't funny!"

Eric shuts the door and crosses his arms. "I agree. But I heard that you're trying to think of loopholes, so I'm here to help."

"You know a loophole?" Lian asks.

"Not off the top of my head, no. But if we talk about it enough, I might be able to think of something."

Fear stirs up suspicion in me. "Wait, why... Eric, truth or dare? Say truth."

Eric raises an eyebrow. "Okay, truth."

"What do you get out of helping us?"

His mouth flops into a frown. He tips up his head as a timer appears beside him.

"Come on. What is it?" I prompt, my suspicion growing.

"No, it's not weird. I just..." He covers his face, rubbing his forehead.

"Okay, leave." I point at the door. "If you're not going to help us for good reasons—"

"No, it's embarrassing, that's all." Eric sighs through his hand. "If helping you means you two don't have sex, then that's good for me."

"Why?" I ask.

"Because I'd be jealous if you did."

I raise my eyebrows. "Oh."

"Wait, what does that mean?" Lian asks.

Eric stares at the floor as his ears redden. "It means I don't want you to have sex with Cai. I would be jealous."

"But... why?" Lian asks.

A twinge of amusement lights within me. Now I see the appeal in humor during uncomfortable situations.

Eric sits down in front of Lian, waiting. Lian still has his hood on.

"Take the hood off, please?" Eric requests.

Lian hums uncertainly. "I like it on."

"Then can I use it instead? I'm mortified."

"At my hood?"

Eric buries his face in his hands.

Do I have to translate? After a few seconds of silence, I muster, "Lian. Eric doesn't want you to have sex with me. If he doesn't want that... what do you think that means?"

Lian guesses, "He thinks it's gross to make us do that too?"

"Sure, and?"

Lian goes quiet.

I don't know exactly what words to use here. I don't know if Eric likes Lian, wants to hook up with him, thinks he's attractive, or what. This is where Eric should say something, but he's sitting there as stubbornly as Lian.

Lian pokes up his hood, watching as Eric sinks further into his hands. "Um, Eric. Are you attracted to me?"

"Yes," Eric says through his hands. "I mean, the feelings are new, but I think so."

"Feelings. So... do you like me?"

"Again, *new* feelings. Very new. But maybe," Eric grumbles. "All I know is that I'll feel horrible if I don't convince you away from doing this."

The timer disappears, but the secondhand embarrassment doesn't. Sitting in a corner watching all this is painful.

Lian shuffles off his jacket and drapes it over Eric's back. "You can use my hood now."

Eric gingerly tries to put it on without looking up. His arms are too big for it, so he resigns himself to keeping the jacket draped over his back. "It's a nice hood."

"It doesn't really fit you, does it?" Lian asks.

"It does."

"No, it doesn't."

"I still want it."

Lian smiles tightly. "Do you want me?"

Huh. There's some of his confidence returning.

"Yes," Eric admits.

Lian's eyebrows raise as his smile grows. "The timer's gone, by the way."

Eric's head snaps up to confirm that. "You let me go on..." He trails off when their eyes meet. "Ugh. You get a pass for that. Only because you're in a difficult situation."

I glance at the forty minutes left on my timer. "Speaking of... can we figure a way out of the difficult situation?"

"Right—we need to decide on a backup plan in case Analisa doesn't convince Solana to retract the dare." Eric messes with the zipper on Lian's jacket.

"Great. Do you have ideas?" I spur.

"Well." Eric rubs the back of his neck. "Sex is a broad word. What does it mean to you?"

"Something I don't do."

Eric gives me a flat expression. "Come on. You can come up with a more precise definition than that."

It takes a moment of making a disgusted expression before coming up with, "Sexual beings stimulating each other in a way that might result in reproduction?"

"Okay, that's a start. But oral sex doesn't result in reproduction. Same with anal," Eric says.

"You're not suggesting..." The icky feeling bubbles back up in my throat.

"No. I'm not pitching ideas yet. Just focus on creating a definition. That's how we might find a loophole."

I adjust the definition. "Sexual beings stimulating each other's reproductive parts?"

"Again, oral and anal."

"What?"

"Try, sexual beings stimulating reproductive parts. Sure, it's broad. But it means that sex doesn't require both beings to be stimulated at the same time. And in that sense, you might not have to touch each other much at all for it to qualify."

"I'd rather not touch her at all," Lian contributes.

"Likewise," I add.

"Okay, then do you think masturbation counts as sex?" Eric asks.

"I don't have..." While I trust Lian to not ask questions about why I don't have any reproductive or excretory parts, I'm not sure about Eric. "I don't like this. Can we stop talking for a minute?"

While I press my forehead onto my knees, bundled up in my corner, I don't hear anything from Lian or Eric. It feels like there's fire beneath my skin, burning with irritation and mortification that I can't handle. I want to dig a hole in this floor and bury myself in it.

"It can't be worth it," Lian mutters. "I know it's your money, Cai. But I don't even think 100,000 is worth it. You'll still get 500,000 from completing the game, right?"

But it's not just 100,000. Solana lost that much initially, and I pressed her with the same truth because she didn't complete it. My body shudders— my muscles tighten, prevent my chest bark from warbling. "What's to stop Solana from daring us to do this over and over for the rest of the week? We could be in debt by the end of this game if we don't placate her."

At their silence, I look up. Lian's wide eyes stare at the ground, considering the possibility. We went into this game to win money for his father. We could instead leave with debt we could never have a way of repaying. And that's if we refuse to do the accusations. We could do Solana's accusation, and whatever else she has planned. The thought of doing accusations like this feels worse than the thought of debt.

Eric shakes his head, his jaw set. "You could answer only truth after this. Or you can avoid Solana. She can't give you an accusation without you being within her distance of understanding, right?"

"What? What's that rule?" Lian asks numbly, hardly moving his mouth.

"It's in the Terms and Conditions. It's got a more detailed list of how the accusations can happen than the general rules. For example, because of the possibility of deaf and blind people on the show, the way the accusations can be given is vague. But essentially, the technology in the show can determine whether someone fully understands that an accusation is being given to them. So, if Cai is far enough to not hear herself being accused by Solana, she doesn't have to complete the accusation. If we get you to avoid her for the rest of the week—"

"How are we all going to avoid her?" I ask. "The cabin's only got the porches, living room, kitchen, pantry, dining room, bedrooms, and bathrooms. It's hard for just one person to avoid another in that condensed space. But I'm not the only one she has on her radar. She did this to hurt Lian and Analisa too. Then she gave Daraja a messed-up question." I fling my arm at Eric. "And she literally said she was going to dare you to run into a wall."

"Run my *head* into a wall," he corrects.

"Doesn't matter. Yeah, I'd rather throw away this dare. But unless we get everyone earmuffs, I'm not sure how we can all manage to avoid someone..." My voice trails out as my head starts to hurt. It's like a finger jabs into the side of my skull.

I want to let the timer run out and avoid Solana. I don't want to think this hard. But it's going to come back to bite me if I don't think all this through, isn't it?

There's a frantic knocking on the door. Analisa shouts, "The dare is retracted!"

I whip my head toward the timer. Wait, when did it disappear?

Relief swells through me. I nearly tackle Eric and Lian in a hug. We're all laughing on the ground when Analisa cracks open the door. My body feels like it's floating.

"Hey, you didn't do anything, did you?" Analisa asks, her voice nervous.

I lurch to my feet and hug her. "Nope! Well, I mean, those two flirted while I sat in a corner. But no sex."

"Oh! Good." Analisa is swept into our collective breathy laughter. Deliriousness leaves me clinging onto her. I'm so glad to feel her ruffled blouse beneath my fingers, her pink hair running over my hand, her relieved figure pressed against mine. I don't want to be near anyone else but her.

"How did you do it?" Eric asks.

"Oh." Analisa's gaze flickers between the ground and me. "I'm sorry, Cai. I told her about your procedure. The genital removing one."

I already implied that out loud, so that's not the worst. Solana knowing about it isn't great, but it's still not anything directly about my parents. I'm just glad it's over for now. "It's okay. I'm surprised that convinced her."

"Yeah, she was doubtful. But then she just claimed it wouldn't be fun for you and retracted the dare." Her unsure eyes flit to the wall. "I can't imagine that's why she gave up though. Maybe she calmed down and wanted a reason to change her mind, or she's planning something worse."

Huh. I don't understand Solana, and part of me doesn't want to. Now I know that we need to watch out for her. "Sounds like this might be a long week."

Analisa nods. "The others are picking up the s'mores, and they said we should head to our rooms so Solana doesn't try anything else."

Now that the dare has been retracted, the full feelings of the last hour return like cold waves. The first wave is the residual relief from the dare being retracted. Then the recent memory of how panicked that dare made me washes over my skin. A kinder, warmer current runs through me, flushing the panic away with encouragement. The past few minutes haven't been all bad. Lian and Eric sort of communicated their feelings. We proved that we could make it through a bad dare situation. But there's still the matter of Solana. We need to be wary of her. "Daraja. Is someone with them?"

"Sevyn said that they'd stay with them when I came here to help out," Eric says.

"You... help out." Analisa gasps, her eyes wide with glee. "Aw, you have Lili's little jacket! I told you —I told both of you! I approve of this pairing. Cai, aren't they adorable?"

Lian tugs on Eric's arm. "I feel like we should go somewhere else now."

Eric raises an eyebrow. "I don't know. I kind of like seeing you flustered."

"I'm gonna bolt regardless of whether you're with me."

"Okay, okay. Take me with you."

I wrap my arms around Analisa, inhibiting her swinging limbs from following Lian and Eric as they dash down the hall. After she stops trying to chase them, I rest my head on her shoulder.

"That was scary, huh?" Analisa mutters in my left ear—the ear with my promise earring, matching hers.

"Yeah." My feelings start pouring out of my mouth. "You know, as gross as the thought felt in of itself, I hated how it would've made you feel more."

She hugs me tighter. "I love you, Cai."

"I love you too, Analisa."

Chapter 15

"Oh, something I forgot to mention." Analisa sighs as we walk down the bedroom hall, on our way to check on Daraja. "Well, Solana was arguing on the basis of how nothing is illegal in the game, right? So, I kind of... started beating her with my walking stick. Maybe I should've stopped sooner than I did, but I guess it's payback for my face."

A bit of pride stirs in my chest. Maybe it shouldn't feel good to hear this, but I don't hesitate to squeeze Analisa's shoulder with a slim smile. "Thanks for telling me. I'm more worried about you right now. Did you ice your face?"

"Yeah. It got too cold, so I'm giving it a break. I'll get the bag from the freezer."

Flutura and Sevyn sit on the couches in the living room. Sevyn gives us a light wave with their partially metal hand. Flutura's eyes are closed as she lies with her head tipped back. While Analisa retrieves an ice bag from the pantry, I'm tempted to ask Flutura what prompted her to ask about Solana's motivation.

I glance down the bedroom hall. It doesn't look like Solana is nearby, but I don't want to risk irritating her again. Instead, I look at Sevyn. "Hey, do you know where Daraja is?"

"They're by the fire pit. They wanted some space, so I'm keeping an eye on them from here." Sevyn gestures to the patio doors. Simulated dusk paints darkness over the world. Illuminated by the bright patio lights and the hovering lanterns, Daraja sits by the smoking hunks of wood.

Guilt compels me to approach the patio doors. Daraja doesn't look up as I step down the creaky patio. I clear my throat, trying to let them know that I'm approaching. They still don't move.

What if they're angry with me for all this? Maybe I deserve it. Regardless, Daraja deserves an apology.

I carry a patio chair over to the fire, sitting at an angle across Daraja. My voice begins softly, "Hey, Daraja?"

Their head jerks up. They laugh, embarrassed. "Sorry, I got lost in my thoughts."

Their relaxed demeanor toward me is comforting. My fingers knead the loose, yellow fabric of my pants. It's easier to focus on that than to dredge up something that might change Daraja's expression. "No worries. I wanted to apologize to you. For earlier."

Their eyebrows rise. Why do they look surprised?

Oh, the memory thing. "Sorry, do you remember what happened with Solana today?"

Daraja nods at the ground. "Yeah. I wasn't fronting—in control of the body, I mean. I was co-conscious though, so I saw it happen. We really admitted something we weren't going to tell anyone." They chuckle. "It feels better than I thought it would. To let that secret be free, you know?"

Astonishment leeches onto my skin. It drains my guilt, leaving me with numb confusion.

Daraja meets my eyes with a calm smile. "Don't worry about apologizing. The accusation wasn't your fault. And now, I'm a little grateful that I was forced to reveal that. No one's treated me all that differently yet. Eric, Sevyn, and Joane were really nice about it. And you too. Analisa and Lian as well. I know you had to deal with the dare Solana gave you, but even during all that, you still insisted that I'm your friend."

"I mean, yeah," I admit. "We haven't known each other all that long, but I want to be friends with you. Eric too. I haven't made much connection with the others, but this all could be fun if we didn't fight so much."

"You mean if we don't provoke Solana."

I grimace, trying to resist the urge to look around.

"Right. Maybe don't mention her." Daraja leans back in their chair. "I don't want to walk around on eggshells anymore. I feel so free right now. I'm not sure there's anything Solana could really do to hurt me."

I glance at my fingers rubbing the yellow fabric. My skin isn't green right now. It's been coated a few times to hopefully last for the week. With how rapidly things have escalated on the first day, I'm worried that I'll have to reveal my alien parentage.

But with how Daraja looks at the sky with such relief... would it be all that bad to admit that here?

I clench my jaw, trying to dispel the thought. If I want to walk around in human society as a human, then revealing my physiology on this show would ruin that. Most Truth or Dare contestants are forgotten by the general public, only occasionally becoming celebrities or people with a decent social media following. But I don't think an alien hybrid would get away with going unrecognized. Walking the streets of New York wouldn't be the same with strangers staring.

"You ever think about outer space, Cai?" Daraja asks.

I tip my chin up, staring at the darkening blue sky. The dim stars become more apparent the longer I observe them. "Not much, no. There's enough going on down here for me to be concerned with."

"Yeah, that's true." Daraja laughs. "Sometimes I dream that I'll be an astronaut though. I want to float."

"Have you tried swimming?" I ask.

They laugh harder. "Not like that! I want to be in a tiny little satellite where I can breathe and float without a suit on. Just to be. Untethered. You think people would ever trust someone like me to go up in space?"

"I don't see why not. You could apply to one of the space industries. If they don't hire you because of your condition, you can sue based on the rules of this show. That's one good thing we get out of all this."

"Man, Cai, you're funny. You think I have the money to go to court?"

"You might by the end of this," I suggest.

"Oh yeah. But then I'll feel bad for you, Analisa, and Lian for spending all your winnings on medical bills. I might have to donate my winnings to charity or something."

"Don't be silly."

"No really. I might chip into the medical bill treatment. That way you three don't have to use so much of your winnings on it. I bet some of the others might help."

I shake my head, finding myself smiling at the stars now too. "You know these stars are fake, right?"

Daraja tosses a ball of unused newspaper kindling at me. "Don't ruin it for me, Cai."

I toss the kindling back at them. Past their shoulder, I spot Analisa sitting inside the cabin. Through the glass doors, she gives a thumbs up while lifting the ice bag on her cheek.

A shriek snatches my attention. It came from the opposite side of the cabin. Outside.

I glance at Daraja, trying to gauge what they think

of it. They look as concerned as I feel. That shriek could've been a benign one, reacting to a dare of some sort. Even so, it sounded unsettling.

Analisa hurries through the sliding screen doors, her footsteps shuffling onto the porch. Her wide eyes lock on mine. "Did you hear?"

"Yeah, someone screamed," Daraja confirms. "It sounded like it was from the side of the cabin."

"It was definitely outside," I add.

Another shriek—shriller this time. I think it was from someone else.

The three of us rush inside the cabin. Sevyn and Flutura aren't on the living room couches anymore—I find them standing past the front porch.

"What's going on?" Lian asks from behind me. Eric is at his side.

"I don't know," I say. "We just heard a scream."

Most of the players are already here, circling around one of the tall, poisonous berry bushes. The porch lights illuminate the grassy area.

I step around the people present, trying to get a better view of whatever we're looking at. Past everyone's legs, there's a pair of shoes casting a stark shadow over the grass. Then the slacks of the legs. A red shirt.

When I'm in a clearer spot, my joints lock. It's Brandon lying on the ground. His wide, waxy eyes stare up at the bush he lies beneath. He's motionless.

Sevyn pulls a pair of thick, brown gloves out of their jacket as they kneel beside Brandon. They gently tip Brandon's head and hands. "It appears that he went into cardiac arrest. He's passed away."

"He's holding..." Joane covers her mouth.

A few dark berries rest in Brandon's purple-stained right hand.

Chapter 16

"Jared, what kind of symptoms do these berries cause?" Sevyn's authoritative voice cuts through our shock.

"It stops a person's heart, sure. But from what I've heard, it would take maybe twenty to thirty berries before something like that could happen." Jared stares at Brandon, his mouth slightly agape.

Sevyn steps away from the berry bush. They stand at a distance from the group as their gaze examines the cabin.

I glance at Brandon's unmoving body. I'm hardly able to keep looking, yet unable to completely avert my eyes. Grampa Dix and Gram Aru's warning returns to my memory—someone nearly died in Truth or Dare recently. But an actual death in the game is unheard of.

"Did he... do that himself?" Daraja's shaking fingers linger near their mouth. Their knees almost buckle under the scrutiny of the group. "Look, I don't know!"

A shiver goes down my back from considering their words. Would Brandon have committed suicide on live television?

"Why would he?" Flutura's mouth twists into a bitter scowl. "He has a wife and a kid he adores. Plus, parents he sends money to. It sounded like he was doing well in life."

"We all have our secrets," Ever mutters. Xe lifts a berry from the shadowy dirt, examining it with a somber frown.

"I don't think he committed suicide," Sevyn says. They cross their arms as they stare directly at Brandon.

I raise my eyebrows. Sevyn sounds certain.

"Then... what happened?" Lian mutters. His eyelids flutter, his gaze unfocused.

"All I know is that the berries and juice stain are in Brandon's right hand. Given that he was left-handed, why would his left hand be clean?" Sevyn asks.

My eyes check for confirmation. Brandon's right hand is indeed the one that has the berries and the berry stain. His left hand is clean.

"You're right. He'd open bottles with his left hand," Eric adds, his eyebrows pinching.

Unspoken questions linger in the air, circling the idea of what happened to Brandon. The most disturbing question surfaces in me—did someone kill him?

"It's certainly possible that he died from an accident. But I doubt it's from consuming the berries on purpose. And if that's the case, that means someone staged him here." Sevyn crouches by Brandon, their unwavering expression focused on his hands. "It doesn't necessarily mean he was killed by someone else. Perhaps he died from a dare, and the accuser thinks we'll blame and torment them for the rest of the week. But still, I want to make everyone aware of the possibility that someone did this on purpose."

Unease squeezes my chest, tightening my breaths. Analisa's hand grips mine, worry getting to her too. My gaze sweeps over the group, attempting to glean clues from them. Including Brandon, there are eleven of us present.

"Guys, Solana isn't here," Lian notes.

Ever emits a surprised grumble. "I don't think the child would do such a thing."

"Yeah, but it's looking like someone did. We need everyone here to figure this out," Eric says, his shoulders turning. "I'll—"

"No. Stay here." Sevyn stands, their stern expression stopping Eric. "I don't want any of you disappearing. We'll question Solana later. For right now, who was the first to find Brandon?"

There's silence while everyone either stares at the ground or others in the group. I catch Joane looking up at Jared, who looks uncomfortably conflicted. He manages to voice, "Um. I just—" He jolts as everyone stares at him. "I don't want to be a suspect. But I did find him here. You probably heard me."

"Then answer a truth for me, Jared," Sevyn suggests. Their analytical gaze flickers over Jared. "Truth or dare?"

Jared nods nervously. "Truth."

"Did you kill Brandon?"

"No. Definitely not." A timer counts down from sixty seconds as Jared explains. "I was wandering the forest. It seemed like a good time to explore since everyone was quieting down for the night. I like to examine flora alone, see, without anyone interrupting my thoughts. No offense—I'm an introvert." His hands circle each other as if trying to refocus. "Anyway, I came back to the cabin. Then I saw Brandon lying on the ground, right where he is now. I thought he was resting, but when he didn't respond—I had called out to him, but he didn't move. Seeing him like that—it startled me so much that I... well, made that noise. Joane came outside when she heard me yell, and then the rest of you came."

The timer beside him disappears. He told the truth. If he had tried to omit anything, the arena would've sensed it and kept the timer running.

As bleak as Daraja's truth experience was earlier, utilizing the accusations for this situation twists the game into something more disturbing.

"Excellent. Thank you." Sevyn clasps their still hands behind their back. "I'd like to go around the circle to ask everyone about this. Please respond truth when I ask you to. That way we can put everyone's minds at rest. Joane, truth or dare?"

Joane rubs her reddened eyes. "Of course. Truth."

"Did you kill Brandon?"

"No. I was in my room. I'd brought in one of the potted plants—one of the purple ones, since it reminded me of the ones in our apartment. I know it sounds stupid, but I get homesick. So, I—" When she glances at Brandon's body, she grips her shirt collar. Her cheeks twinge with a sickly color. "I was cleaning the dirt off my hands in the bathroom when I heard Jared scream. I came running to make sure he was okay. You saw that—and I'm sorry for running through you," she says to Sevyn. "That's when I saw Brandon... like that. Then, well, you probably heard my reaction."

Joane shudders and slams her hands over her eyes as her timer disappears. Jared wraps his arms around her shoulders, embracing Joane without letting her see the quiver in his terrified eyelids.

"Thank you," Sevyn continues, their voice level. "Ever, truth or dare?"

Ever swallows with a solemn nod. "Truth."

"Did you kill Brandon?"

"No. I was inside my room, taking my eight o'clock medicine for the evening. The—"

Notifications appear beside each of us. The text reads, "New rule: no player can use an accusation to determine the cause of Brandon's death."

Speaker feedback squeals through the arena. A

large, glowing, holographic version of Comedy materializes above the cabin. She waves down at us. "Sorry! But you can't ask truths like that. Nothing about who killed Brandon, or if anyone knows anything about his death. You can't use any dares to ask someone to draw, indicate, or otherwise express it either." She offers a nervous laugh and a limp shrug. "I suppose it does make things more interesting. Good luck."

Chilled irritation seeps into my blood. I shouldn't be surprised. Earlier, the audience determined that they weren't looking out for my well-being, or Lian's, or Analisa's. The show staff want to make money and retain views. This new rule adds drama by keeping us scared and, potentially, in danger. It's clear now—the show staff and audience aren't looking out for any of us. We're on our own in here.

Whatever, or whoever, killed Brandon could kill another one of us. Comedy and Tragedy are letting it happen. The audience must be curious to see what happens if we can't figure it out from the accusations.

I glance around at the group. Based on the timing of the new rule, at least one of us would have answered the question with useful information.

"What are we supposed to do now?" Daraja's voice wavers as they fling up their hands. "Now any of us can lie about this."

If only Auntie Tera were here. She could hear the heartbeats to tell who was genuine. But I'm trapped in a game for another five days with a possible murderer, and I don't have a way of knowing who it could be, if anyone.

"We should at least move him." Flutura's eyelids lower as she rolls up her white shirt sleeves. "If they're serious about keeping us here for the remaining days, then they likely won't take him until then either. I, personally, would prefer to not pass him by the front of the cabin every day. Especially as time draws on, his body will become more noticeable."

"While I don't like the thought of moving him from the scene, you're probably right about them not taking him." Eric sighs, his gaze downcast. "As his body breaks down, we'll start to smell it."

Joane shakes her head fervently as she backs away from the group. "I can't. I don't think I can touch him."

"I don't think you'll need to. Eric, Flutura, Jared, would you be willing to accompany me in carrying him into the forest? If we place him by the river, the smell might drift downstream," Sevyn suggests. "Anyone else is welcome to join us. I want enough people around each other to maintain alibis and protect each other, in case anything new develops."

"I'll go with," Lian says. Eric gives him a slim smile.

Analisa's not the best at walking on uneven ground. I tip my head toward the cabin, trying to gauge her response. At her slight nod, I say, "Analisa and I will stay at the cabin."

Daraja nods. "I'll stay with you."

"Same," Joane says.

"I'll stay too." Ever wheels up the ramp to the porch. "We should try to find Solana while we're here. She should know what's happened."

Chapter 17

Those of us at the cabin prepare a light supper for ourselves. There isn't as much sharing as there was earlier. The thought of berries being involved with Brandon's death has me on edge. I haven't been consuming anything here except the flavored water. As long as no one manages to sneak berries into that, I should be safe. But Analisa and Lian are at risk.

After eating, Ever and Joane go to the bedroom hall to find Solana. Daraja wants to witness whatever conversation they have. Analisa and I sit in the dining room, keeping our distance from Solana. The back of my neck prickles at the empty room. It feels like we're too exposed here.

Brandon's body lying limp doesn't go away. My mind flashes the memory behind my eyelids every time I blink.

My tense fingers rub my arms. My knees implore

me to stand. Nerves swarm beneath my skin like flies, asserting that the killer could attack us at any moment.

Only, is there really a killer? It's possible someone didn't kill Brandon. There could be some other reason why he was positioned to look like he committed suicide. That's assuming he was positioned. It's possible he used his non-dominant hand. The show staff could have added the new rule purely to scare us, knowing that we weren't in danger.

There's too much unknown in this situation for my comfort.

"Do you think there's a killer?" Analisa asks, her voice low.

We were thinking on the same wavelength. Between sips of water, I mutter, "I don't know. I don't like this."

"Me neither. There could be more than one, too."

The thought alarms me. "What makes you say that?"

"Comedy and Tragedy like teams. Lian, you, and I were one from the start. We might have Daraja and Eric with us too now. Jared and Joane are clearly together. There might be more teams than we know. Some of them might've formed after the game started but were bound to happen." Analisa squints at the ceiling. "I know Ever is sympathetic toward Solana, and she's a little less rude to xem. I wouldn't gauge Sevyn and Flutura as a team, but they were asking each other truth questions when you and Daraja were outside. They seemed to share some kind of mutual respect. But I don't have any idea who Brandon was connected to, if anyone."

"So, are you suggesting that he's an easier target than the rest of us?" I ask, trying to decipher Analisa's thoughts.

"Maybe. He also could've had a connection with someone that we don't know about—a connection that could've been exploited. If he was fed twenty to thirty berries, then he could've been given a drink of them blended, or some kind of food with the berries cooked in. He might not have suspected anything of it, especially if he trusted the other person. It would hardly leave a trace."

We're in the dining room, right next to the kitchen.

Analisa bolts to her feet before I do. We dash through the doorway, only to hesitate once we're inside. I'm not even sure what exactly we're looking for. Something with berry residue? Something that indicates recent cooking?

"Brandon was at the s'mores event." Analisa pinches her forehead. "He was there when I tried convincing Solana to take back the dare. I don't think anyone was cooking around then, but I might not have heard them."

"Who else was there when you were with Solana?" I ask.

Analisa shakes her head. "I barely remember. I was in the living room, but I wasn't facing the kitchen most of the time. I remember seeing Brandon's red shirt outside, at least around the start of when I confronted Solana."

"The colors." I look down at my yellow pants. We're all in our assigned colors. "Do you remember which ones weren't there?"

She shakes her head again. "No. The red was noticeable enough for me to be certain that Brandon was there. But I'm not sure who wasn't." Her frantic fingers stop the running dishwasher. "At least half of us were outside still. Some went back to their rooms, I think. Or at least, I thought. It would've been around when I went to tell you that Solana retracted the dare—that's the window when Brandon had to have..." She pulls out the steaming dishwasher rack. "Damn. The dishes are already too clean to tell what was in them."

"What would you make out of berries to disguise a death?" I ask.

Analisa throws up her arm. Her grin leans toward being more incredulous and panicked than amused. "I don't know—a pie?"

"Too big. Defensive plants were usually bred to enact poison quickly, if I'm remembering my history correctly. That means Brandon wouldn't have likely gotten through a pie—even a small one—without leaving the rest of it. If someone poisoned him, what would they have done with the remains? Throwing it away would be too easy to find." I check the trash anyway. No pie or pie container in there.

"So it would most likely be something kind of small and possibly disguised. Since Brandon knows those berries are poisonous, he might've been at least a little suspicious if he knew berries were involved." Analisa catches onto my brainstorming wave.

"So maybe a sauce? Or a drink?"

"Those are looking more likely. They're easy to dispose too." She peers into the sink. "It looks clean. No dishes in it either."

There's pieces of a blender in the drying rack. I snatch the clear cartridge. It doesn't look dirty.

"The blades are harder to clean." Analisa seizes the bottom portion of the blender and squints at it. "I can't see any residue though."

I marvel at the blender cartridge in my hands. Could this really have been an instrument to kill someone with?

I face my prickling back to the kitchen corner while my eyes dart to the window and doors. Someone could discover us poking around right now. If we were right about someone using this kitchen to poison someone, what would they do if they found us here?

"There are too many options that they could've gone with," I say. "Even if they prepared something for Brandon to eat, I don't think we can figure it out from how the kitchen is now."

Analisa inspects the countertops. "Maybe. But I have to look. I can't just... not."

After a few more minutes of investigating without finding discernable clues, we give up.

As spacious as each bedroom is, Analisa and I decide to sleep in one together. The single bed is large enough for both of us to lie comfortably.

It's not long before Lian knocks on the door. He and Eric bring in sheets and pillows and lie on the floor. Same with Daraja. It's a twisted form of comfort—a sleepover created from fear. None of us want to sleep alone.

Chapter 18

The blinds divide the sunlight, casting streaks across Analisa's shoulder. Her hair presses against the pillow with a couple of the flowery metal braces still secured. Sunshine highlights the shiny, pink sleeves on her flopped arms. Her eyes are closed. Although it might be unlikely, I hope she's sleeping well.

Slowly, I sit up and peer over the edge of the bed. Lian's limbs stretch across the floor, taking up so much space that Eric leans against the wall. Daraja is curled up like a cat on the other side of the room. I'm glad they trust me—and each other—enough to feel safer together.

Brandon's dead body flashes behind my eyelids again. I flinch from the reminder. Something like that should've been a nightmare, not part of yesterday.

I blink open the rules of Truth or Dare in my contact lenses. Besides the censored player profiles, the rules list is the only thing I have access to. The rules are rather simple. I even dig through the Terms and Conditions. What's unnerving is there doesn't seem to be a rule against killing someone else. And a player can't be legally held accountable for breaking any laws that apply outside the games. So... the only thing that might discourage a player from killing me is my physical capability to evade them.

I consider Analisa again. She's taken gymnastics to be able to walk and maintain her balance better than the doctors told her she could, but I don't know if she can run.

I've been decent at running in school sport's days, but I'm not that strong. I'm not sure how long I could carry Analisa, or how fast I could be with her. Lian isn't that strong either. I don't know about Daraja. Eric looks like he could carry any of us.

I want to trust my new allies, but I need to consider the possibility of them deceiving us. Could those two be dangerous?

Then there's everyone else. Under the truth accusations, Jared, Joane, and Ever said they didn't kill Brandon. Well, Ever's answer might not have counted. Is it possible that they were involved in his death without directly killing him? Analisa did bring up the possibility that there's more than one person involved. That then could leave Solana, Sevyn, and Flutura as options for who did the killing.

Or Daraja or Eric. I shouldn't let my thoughts eliminate them, even if I don't want them to be the killers. Or even...

I watch Lian. Beyond what Analisa's told me about

him, I know he's popular in school and awkward when it comes to his romantic feelings. He doesn't know much about the broadcast games. He couldn't be involved in this, right?

Then there's Analisa. I've known her for several years. I can't imagine her killing someone unless it were in self-defense, and if she did, she'd tell me. If she knew something about Brandon and was dared to stay silent about it, she'd have a timer around her.

I don't like this. Why am I questioning the people I care about?

Analisa shifts her position. My shoulders tense up, nervous that I'll wake her. Fortunately, she turns onto her back and relaxes again.

My chin tips toward the ceiling. Although my vision wanders in a slow daze, my muscles itch to move. I don't want to wake the others, but I also don't want to leave the room alone.

"Psst." Eric waves.

I wave back. It must feel as silly to him as it does to me because we both grin stupidly from our odd exchange. He mouths something. I shake my head, my eyebrows pinching in hopes that he'll repeat himself.

He points between the two of us and whispers, "Make breakfast for them?" He points at the other three. Ah.

I type a note on the bedside notepad, letting them know where Eric and I are going. The two of us tiptoe out of the room.

The hall full of bedroom doors is empty. Even with

the light coming through the sunroofs, I glance over my shoulder as we walk.

"Feeling uneasy too?" Eric notes.

I nod as we turn into the living room. "We've got to be here for five more days. I hope that whatever happened yesterday doesn't happen again."

Eric freezes at the kitchen entrance. I didn't mean to spook him.

"Sorry, yeah, we should focus on making food for them. I think I remember how to make Lian's comfort food if you want to score points with him."

Eric tugs on my arm, pulling me into the kitchen entrance.

Dark red splatters litter the white tile floor. The crisp, metallic smell stings my nose. It's smeared across the glass patio door. A thick amount of dried blood is on the porch too.

We were just with them. Still, I scramble to the bedroom with Analisa, Lian, and Daraja inside. Eric matches my pace. I wrench the door open.

They're all fine. No red covers this room. The door startles Daraja wide awake. Analisa throws off the blanket with a jolt. Lian's groggy face tips toward the doorway with a questioning mumble.

So, someone else is hurt. My breaths are shallow, making it difficult to speak. "There's blood in the kitchen. A lot."

Analisa hobbles to her feet, snatching her walking stick in time to stabilize herself. "Whose?"

"I don't know."

The five of us return to the kitchen. Analisa

covers her mouth, her cheeks green from the substantial amount of blood. I haven't seen this much at once before—maybe it's fake. Before Daraja can step toward the porch door, Eric shouts for them to stop.

"We don't want to be caught near whatever happened without more people around," Eric says. "And use napkins to touch things, if you can. Anything but your bare hands."

We grab fistfuls of napkins while Eric shouts down the bedroom hall, getting everyone to come to the kitchen. Soon, we're joined by Sevyn, Flutura, Joane, Jared, and Ever.

That's everyone except one.

We open the patio doors and follow the trail of blood. It looks like someone was dragged around the cabin. Off the porch, around the side...

Solana's purple and black pajamas are ripped through the middle, displaying her shredded stomach. Her bruised, sawed-open neck looks stretched away from her torso. Her wide eyes and gaping mouth face the lowest branches of the berry bush. She holds a few berries in her bloody hands.

A soft warble trembles out of my back. My eyes dart toward Analisa, hoping for confirmation that no one associated the sound with me. Her eyes are wide, focused on Solana. Her hand holding the walking stick shakes.

No one would blame Analisa for this, would they? Solana was targeting Analisa, Lian, Daraja, Eric, and me the most. The other players must notice that her removal from the game would be to our benefit. But blaming us for it would be a stretch. No way we'd be so obvious as to kill her so soon.

I reprimand myself internally for thinking like that. This isn't some game of Mafia, where the goal is to enact or solve a mock murder mystery. This isn't even Truth or Dare anymore.

Sevyn kneels beside her. Their gloved hands pinch the fabric to examine Solana's stomach.

"Several puncture wounds from something thin and relatively short—like a knife. Choking bruises. I can't tell if the bruises around her side were from the attack or from when she was struck yesterday. Regardless, we're too late to help her," Sevyn confirms. "Solana must've struggled. There's blood beneath her fingernails. It could be someone else's. I want everyone to change into a tank top and shorts. She might've left a mark on someone."

A tank top won't cover the bark on my upper chest and back. I did say in my submission that I have skin scarring; I can continue that lie. The alarm from that feels numb. The situation I'm in now is so much bigger than keeping my alien parentage a secret.

"You're going to be changing too, right?" Daraja asks, their skeptical voice deeper than usual.

"Of course," Sevyn responds.

"Okay good." Their thick eyebrows scrunch. "Because you seem to be taking control of all this a little too comfortably for me."

Sevyn indeed seems to be taking command. They did yesterday too. Although it isn't suspicious in itself, the killer would be in a good position if they were to call the shots in how we investigate the deaths.

"I have experience in taking control of dangerous situations," Sevyn assures.

"Yeah?" Daraja crosses their arms. "Truth or dare, Sevyn?"

"Truth."

"What do you mean you have experience in taking control of dangerous situations?"

"It means I had a classified job that required keeping a cool head when things got dangerous. I won't be explaining more than that, even if it means losing money for it," Sevyn clarifies, shooing away the timer counting down three minutes. "Now seriously. Meet in the living room in ten minutes in your tank tops and shorts. If you don't, I'll personally drag you there."

I step back onto the patio deck, encouraging Analisa to follow. I don't want to see Solana in this state. She was irritating, but she didn't deserve this.

As we walk down the hall, Daraja mutters between Lian and me, "Doesn't less fabric make it easier for someone to stab us? And it's less to use to clot blood. I don't like this."

"Yeah, but they're right that the killer could be hiding a wound with their clothes," Eric says. "The less clothes, the less we can lie. And it's harder to hide a weapon."

"Tank tops don't sit well with me," Lian says.

"Oh yeah, they show off your puny arms." Analisa tries to muster a joking smile.

"I, for one, would enjoy seeing your arms," Eric adds to the lighthearted conversation. Lian stares at Eric's muscular arms. "You can touch them." Lian doesn't decline the invitation; he mutters something in Hindi.

"He thinks your arms are sexy, Eric," Analisa translates.

Lian gapes. "That's not what I said!"

"That's *so* what you meant." Analisa goes into her room. "Cai, could you wait for me while I change?"

"Sure." I lean against the wall by her door. I've helped her change quickly for gym before, but most of the time she prefers changing alone. Even if I'm nervous about leaving her side, I'm content to guard the room for her.

"Lian, you want to help me pick out a tank top?" Eric asks, even after Lian practically follows him into his room. The door shuts. They act like the silliest newlyweds.

"How am I the only single person among you singlets?" Daraja crosses their arms. "Sorry, but could you watch my room too? I just want to change in peace."

"Yeah, of course," I say.

Then I'm alone in the hall.

The long, wooden walls begin to disorient me. Without the clock in my vision, I can't tell how long I've been waiting. The environment feels extra old-fashioned with our contacts only seeing the Truth or

Dare rules and our limited profiles. It can't have been long since the four of them went into the bedrooms.

Sevyn exits one of the rooms at the end of the hall. They're dressed in a tight, black tank top and bright blue shorts. I press my back against the wall, giving them more space to pass. They nod at me as they walk by. There's an unnerving silence in my head while I wonder if I should say something.

They pause a few feet away and turn around. My heart rate accelerates as I wonder what they're doing.

They clear their throat. "Cai. You said you like plants, correct?"

They don't think I'm the killer, do they? Or do they suspect that I'm hiding something related to my alien parent? I keep my voice level. "Yeah. How'd you know?"

"Your interview with Comedy and Tragedy. I was wondering if you'd know why someone would repeat the same staging with this plant. Is there some clue you can glean from it?"

I can't tell if they distrust me. My thoughts go darker than I'd prefer. "Honestly, the first thing I think of when I see it is a calling card for serial killers. As a way of claiming their... what they did without giving away their identity. They'll keep some element of the method the same. The berry bush might be that." At their unchanged expression, I add, "I'm interested in various parts of history. I don't know a lot of serial killer facts, but I see random stuff like that in my online feed."

"I don't suspect you, Cai," Sevyn clarifies. "Thank you for your help."

Stress swirls in my stomach as Sevyn walks away. Do they really not suspect me? If so, I guess that's good.

Daraja exits their room, wearing a sporty neon green and white outfit. They fling out their arms. "I was the last to go. How long does it take to change for you people?"

"Analisa's got a prosthetic arm and leg, and she generally has a difficult time changing quickly," I remind.

"Well, okay, she's exempt." Daraja knocks on Eric's door. "Come on! I want to get this inspection out of the way."

If we do get an idea of who the killer could be from this, what do we do with them? Does this game turn into Mafia, where we have to use our brute strength to corral them and tie them up? What if we blame the wrong person? Then we'd be giving them to the actual killer.

Analisa cracks the door open. She leans out of the doorway in a pink tank top with flowers on it. The cuffs of her shorts stop higher than where her prosthetic leg connects to her skin. The tank top shows both the end of her prosthetic right arm and the red carnation tattoo on her left shoulder. I find it hard not to stare at the intricate joints on her prosthetics. She looks beautiful wearing anything. "Yeah, I forgot that I haven't worn something this short in a while. Do I look okay?"

"You look beautiful," I assure.

Her wary smile grows into her usual grin for a second. Then she seems to remember the situation surrounding us. "Right. I'll watch your room while you change. Are you okay with wearing a tank top?"

Over the past day, I've already admitted so much about myself. It's the nature of the game, accelerated by our need to figure out what happened to Brandon and Solana. Nervousness flutters in my stomach, but my feelings don't matter now. "I'll be fine."

"Ah, are you not comfortable in a tank top?" Daraja asks. "You can bring a cover to wear after we check for injuries."

"It's just that I have this scarring on my back and chest. I don't like answering questions about it. I'd rather not dredge up my feelings on it, if I can help it." I walk into my room. "Make sure Eric and Lian are all right. They might just be making out, but still."

Analisa takes the cue to slam her palm on Eric's door, shouting questions about if they're being safe in there. She hollers about how she doesn't have any condoms on her, so they better have them if they need them. Eric laughs as I shut my door. Even with the door closed, I hear a mortified Lian yelling at Analisa, asking if she's going to be like this all week.

My closet is full of bright yellow, black, and white —the signature color palette my stylists gave me. As I slide off my shirt, the fabric snags on some of my barky skin. I suck air between my teeth, hoping I didn't damage this free clothing. After enough careful shimmying, I get a tank top and shorts on.

WHEN TRUTH COWERS

Wearing less clothing makes my whole body feel lighter. It's like my skin can breathe better. Seeing the carnation tattoo on my right shoulder makes me smile. Then I consider my chest in the mirror, wondering if there's an inconspicuous way to cover the bark. If I walked in wearing a cover, that might draw more attention than the bark alone.

My hand rests on the doorknob. The voices of my friends outside entice me. Whatever is coming is going to be difficult. At least I'm not alone in all this.

I turn the knob and meet them outside.

Chapter 19

Everyone wears tank tops and shorts. It's awkward with the older people. Jared fidgets with his shorts, trying to stretch them into being longer. Joane keeps her legs crossed tightly, her arms locked across her chest. Ever taps xir wheelchair armrests, xir expression a blend of discomfort and mild amusement. Flutura lounges with her arms stretched on top of the couch. Sevyn leans against the wall by the fireplace. Maybe older people generally get uncomfortable about wearing less clothing in public as they age?

Meanwhile, Daraja doesn't seem to mind their athletic wear. Eric is comfortable showing off his arms and legs—like damn, what's his workout regimen? Lian sits next to him, ears red while he glances between the ground and Eric's calves. Analisa and I sit beside each other, my legs pressing against her thick thighs. The warmth of her arm around my shoulder and being so close to her chest comforts me. If only we weren't in such a grim situation.

"I understand that this isn't the most comfortable. But I suggest that we each prove to the group that we're uninjured. And if we are injured, we can provide an explanation for it. I'll start." Sevyn stands and slowly turns, their arms raised. "I have scars from working with metal for several years, but as you can see, they're faded." They lift their shirt, showing their muscular abs with a scar slashed across their side. "Nothing new."

"Wait, do we have to show our stomach?" Joane's eyebrows pinch in concern.

"Does that bother you?"

"I don't even wear bikinis to the beach. Yes, it bothers me to show my stomach to a group of strangers." She covers her face with her hands.

Jared wraps an arm around her shuddering shoulder and cradles her head. She starts sobbing. Why is this such a big deal? I have to show the bark on my stomach—I doubt she has as worrisome of a thing to hide.

Now that I think about it, we saw two people die in the last twenty-four hours. How am I not crying out of nowhere right now too?

"Hey, we won't judge you. No worries there, I promise." Daraja stands and twirls around. They lift up their shirt. "See? I hate showing my belly, but it's just for a few seconds, yeah? Just to show I don't have any recent wounds."

Joane seems to be out of commission, so Eric

follows Daraja's lead. If the situation weren't so serious, I'd make fun of the way Lian stares at Eric's abs.

Solana's body flashes behind my eyelids. Again, why am I not taking this seriously? Is my mind really so distanced from what's happening?

After hesitating to stand, Lian goes next. Flutura doesn't have an issue standing, spinning around, then flopping back down on the couch. I need to go soon so I'm not last. Last means I'm more noticeable.

Analisa pushes herself to her feet and points out the light bruising on her face from when Solana slapped her. I stand to help her sit.

Now that I'm up, I step into the center of the couches and turn around like the others. I lift my shirt. "I was born with scarring on my back and chest, so that's why it looks weird."

Fortunately, no one asks questions about the bark. As I sit, Ever expresses that xe would like help standing. Eric and Sevyn rush to xir side to help xem. No injury on xem either.

Joane has stopped crying by now. She stands and, with her mouth trembling, lifts her shirt. She doesn't have any injuries. Jared hugs her, then does the same thing. No injury on him either.

No one has any injuries that aren't accounted for. We're not a step closer to determining who killed Brandon and Solana.

"Are we the only ones in the arena? Maybe they put in an extra player and didn't tell us," Lian suggests.

"It's possible, but I'm less inclined to think so from

the staff behavior so far. They've been sticking to their rules and telling us when the rules have changed," Sevyn says. "Flutura, may I test something on you?"

Flutura flicks her hand, indicating that she's ready.

"Say truth, please. Truth or dare?"

"Truth."

"Do you know anything about Solana's death?"

"Unfortunat—"

Comedy's hologram flashes into the room. Her nervous laugh spreads startled jolts through the group. "Anything we said yesterday that you couldn't do regarding accusations about Brandon's death—that applies to Solana's death too. And any... potential future deaths." She clasps her hands together and opens her mouth as if to say something else before disappearing.

Flutura glares at the space where Comedy was. "As I was saying... unfortunately, no. It seems that she was killed this morning, and I was sleeping in."

Sevyn rubs their creased forehead. "Okay. Comedy confirmed what I thought was the case. Thank you for your cooperation, Flutura."

Eric grunts as his fingers clench his hair. "Is this a prank? Are we actually in Mafia right now?"

Joane's trembling fingers clasp her thin arms. "They're not going to leave us in here with a killer, are they?"

"They have to let us out." Jared squeezes Joane's shoulder. His set jaw and frozen, wide-eyed gaze reveals his growing dread. "There must be a loophole in the rules."

"The only way to get a player out is to have the audience vote them out," Analisa mutters. She pulls her walking stick into her lap, her fingers nervously pinching the cylindrical metal.

Joane points at Analisa, gasping hopefully at her words. "Then we'll vote each other out!"

"But if we did that, eventually, the numbers would reduce until it's the killer and a handful of people. Maybe even the killer and one other person," Sevyn says. "We would be letting the audience choose who might die. And clearly, they find it entertaining for us to face that prospect. They wouldn't vote out the killer. I wouldn't be surprised if they decided to vote out the strongest of us until the killer has a group they can more easily kill."

"In addition—not that it's the most important priority—a player voted out will lose all their potential winnings," Ever reminds. Xir fingers tap a nervous, uneven rhythm on xir legs. "I, for one, don't want to give my winnings to a murderer."

If I could get Analisa out of here by staying, I would. But if I started an audience vote for one of us to leave, the audience could choose to keep Analisa in the game instead. I couldn't leave her here alone. I don't like the idea of doing that for Lian or Daraja either. If it were Eric or me, he might make it out, but then we'd lose the strongest of us five.

I scroll through the rules, hoping to find a hint for what to do. My eyes widen at one of the bottom points. "For a player that is removed from the game for any reason besides an audience vote, the prize amount accumulated by that player is divided evenly among the remaining players." I stare at the rug between the couches. "Is someone killing the other players to get more money?"

"That's sick." Lian scowls at the ground.

"Or smart." Flutura shrugs at our incredulous expressions. "If we want to find them, we'll have to start thinking like them."

"So, is it someone who desperately needs the money?" Jared poses.

I shake my head, knowing where this could easily go. "We can't assume that's their main motive. Something else we can take out of that point is that a player can be removed from the game without an audience vote. The rules don't specify how. If we could figure that out, we could get out."

Sevyn clears their throat. "It could refer solely to accidental deaths. But as it doesn't explicitly say death, you're right that we have a potential opportunity there."

"The referees can change the rules using an audience vote too, right?" Lian asks. "So, we could suggest an audience vote on whether we continue playing. Or if the killer should be taken out of the game."

"I like the second one better. It was almost fun before all this happened." Ever frowns.

Holographic notifications emerge in the room. Five-minute timers soon accompany the messages. An audience vote is being held—it's about whether the killer will be forced out of the game. So, as obtuse as it might sound to consider otherwise... does that mean for certain that there is a killer?

Solana's body should be proof enough. Even if I didn't see what happened, there's no way she got like that without being stabbed by someone else. It still feels like a distant concept—the idea that someone in this room killed someone else. No one here looks like a murderer, yet we're experiencing the proof that someone is.

Muscles tense up all over my body. Even if the killer is voted out of the game, would they really walk out of here without hurting anyone else?

And if they're put outside the game, would they get away with what they did? My teeth mess with my tongue, hoping to channel my anxiety into a small motion. I can't think about what happens to the killer after the game. Safety should be our priority for now.

As the seconds continue in silence, we stare at the ongoing timers. Would we be alerted about who the killer is, even if they're voted out? Should we prepare to run from them?

"Ugh, I'm bored," Flutura blurts out. "Sevyn, truth or dare?"

Sevyn blinks rapidly, perhaps confused and suspicious. "Truth."

"Oh, shame. I was hoping you'd say dare so you could make me a sandwich real quick. How about this then: what's your favorite food?"

What is this sudden outburst? Is she the killer, trying to divert attention from the timer?

She rolls her eyes at our silent stares. "No, I'm not the killer, but I'm nervous and I'd rather not pass this time silent. Also, I'd be eating right now if it weren't for all of this. My dietician doesn't recommend that I eat a lot, so I enjoy food when I can. Sevyn, you got an interesting dish you like?"

"Pelmeni. It's a Russian dumpling kind of dish. Add some dill and sour cream on top and it's the best." Sevyn considers the ongoing timer. "One of my close friends said she grew up with her grandmother making the best pelmeni. Whenever we'd travel to a restaurant that had it, she'd have it and it would remind her of home. She got our friend group to eat it at one of our reunions, so now, I eat it to think of them." Sevyn's timer disappears.

Flutura nods with a slim smile. "That's nice. I'd eat trileçe for every meal if I could. And a half a gallon of hot chocolate with it. Similar reasons as you. My mother had a restaurant back in Albania. She'd let me have the leftover trileçe at the end of the day, back before the move and my extensive diet." The corners of her mouth droop. "I hope we all get to eat our favorite foods one day, after all this."

The timer on the audience vote runs out.

The killer has been voted to stay in the game.

Chapter 20

"I suggest everyone do what they can to ensure their own personal safety," Sevyn recommends. "Don't act on hasty judgments but defend yourselves."

"You sound confident," Daraja says, their voice accusatory.

"I can generally take care of myself. I've faced worse things than you all," Sevyn assures. "I can carry Solana to the river. Anyone who would like to come with is welcome. I'll also work to clear the blood from the kitchen. I would appreciate the help, but it's not expected."

Sevyn leaving spurs the rest of us to our feet. I don't want to leave the cabin, as I don't want to be far from Analisa. I also don't like the idea of cleaning blood out of the kitchen, but I'd rather not leave Sevyn to do that on their own.

After a few seconds, the room is clear except for Analisa, Lian, Eric, Daraja, and me.

"Do you think they saw us?" Analisa asks. At my quizzical expression, she says, "The kitchen. Do you think they saw us poking around, and that's why they left so much blood covering everything? Maybe there was something we missed."

"The kitchen?" Daraja asks.

"Analisa and I think that Brandon was maybe poisoned by someone he trusted enough to accept food from," I explain. "Maybe a smoothie or sauce or something that included the berries in it. We couldn't find any definitive evidence for that though."

"Do you think someone tried the same thing on Solana?" Lian asks.

"I doubt she'd trust anyone that easily," Daraja says.

"Exactly." Eric's head lifts, his eyes wide with an idea. "The person could've offered something poisonous, and Solana could have declined. Killing someone by stabbing them makes it more likely for the killer to be caught. Poison would be more ideal to try first. Then in a kitchen full of knives—"

"The weapon." Lian's jaw drops, his mind prompting a new string of thoughts. "There wasn't a knife or anything on Solana."

"This is an enclosed dome. Nothing leaves from it until the end of the week. The weapon has to be here somewhere." Analisa clasps her fist. Her narrowed gaze sweeps across the floor. "Maybe someone has it. Or they left it somewhere they could find it. Keeping it somewhere like a bedroom could be too incriminating. Maybe someone else's bedroom—

but that risks someone else finding a weapon they can use."

"So even if we find it, we won't know who used it." Daraja shakes their head with a wide frown. "Do you think we could find fingerprints on the weapon and truth someone into revealing it's theirs?"

"I'm not sure the refs would think it's distanced enough to not be related to Solana's death. Even if we can bring up an accusation about it, I'm not sure anyone would recognize their fingerprint on sight," Eric says. "We can try based on the fingerprint shape though, assuming there's a print clear enough for cocoa powder and tape to show."

"I approve of doing it if we can find the weapon, but..." Analisa holds up her thumb next to Lian's. "I know we're the only twins here, but there are ten of us. There could be other people here with similar enough fingerprints that we could falsely accuse someone. We shouldn't get any assumptions in our head about particular people unless we get everyone gathered to look at each other's fingerprints. And given how everyone split off, I'm not sure we'll be able to get everyone together again."

"Besides Brandon, is anyone here left-handed?" I ask. "The grip would look different. It's a long shot, but we could possibly determine something that way."

"I haven't noticed anyone else using their left hand as their dominant one except Eric," Analisa says.

"Wait, you're left-handed?" Daraja asks. After

Eric's little wave of confirmation, they shake their head. "Huh. But if I were trying to kill someone and cover it up, I wouldn't even use my dominant hand."

"I wouldn't use my bare hands at all. I'd use gloves. If Sevyn's able to bring their own welding gloves, any of us could. Which probably makes the fingerprint method beyond the scope of what we can use anyway," Eric says. "And if you're trying to kill someone who's struggling for their life, you'll want every ounce of strength you've got. So using your non-dominant hand might not be an option."

"Oh." Daraja lowers their head with an embarrassed smile. "Yep. I'm stupid."

"No, you're not," Analisa says. "We're brainstorming possibilities anyway."

"Out in the open," I note. The other players seem to be a decent distance away. But it's possible that the killer knew about Analisa and me in the kitchen, and we didn't think anyone was watching then. They could know about our conversation here too.

"Good point." Eric gestures, encouraging us to walk down the bedroom hall. "I don't know how comfortable you all feel right now, but I like the idea of camping out in a bedroom. If we can block the door and the window, and maybe get some supplies and weapons in there, we could make a decent fortification."

A twinge of discomfort makes me cringe. Weapons stocked up in a small room. "Um, well... hang on, let's go to my room before we talk more."

We return to my room and close the door. We

settle on the pillows and sheets. Their attention is on me.

I shuffle my legs into a different position, granting myself a little more stalling time. I don't want to break the almost comfortable friendships we have. "I want to trust all of you. But for my peace of mind, could we dare each other to not physically hurt each other for the rest of the week?"

"I get where you're coming from." Daraja bites their lip. "I just met all of you a couple days ago. I really want to trust you too. So yeah, hit me with the dare, Cai."

"That sounds good to me," Lian says.

"I'll do it too," Analisa adds.

"Of course." Eric holds up his hands defensively. "And I don't want to ruin the trust, especially since I know none of you killed Solana. I couldn't sleep all night, so I know you didn't leave the room. But keep in mind that the killer isn't necessarily motivated by money. They seem to be playing the game now, but once their odds are better, I'm not sure they'll have any reason to complete accusations."

He's right. Completing truths and dares was supposed to be a given. Now, we're playing a completely different game.

"Okay. How about we stay up all night tonight?" Analisa asks. "Time your restroom use carefully because no one leaves without everyone else. Then if something happens, and we're all together, we can trust each other."

Eric makes an unsure face.

"What?"

"There could be more than one killer," he says.

"If you're so sure that we're not the killers, why are you even arguing with me?"

"Because I don't want to leave anything unconsidered. We need to be prepared for anything. I don't think one of you is a killer. But if I slip up and one of you is involved in all this, then I'm screwed if I don't at least think of the possibility."

"Same goes for all of us," Daraja says. "I want a surefire way to trust you all, but the truth accusation timer might be our only way. And I don't think we can determine that one of us isn't the killer without relating it to Solana and Brandon."

I blink, staring at the floor. Now I understand Sevyn's lack of expectation for considering something that Comedy might shut down in a second. Still, I want to try it. "Can I ask you a truth, Daraja?"

"Yeah, sure," they respond.

"Have you ever killed a person?"

A two-minute timer begins counting down beside Daraja. No way. Did that stupid question work?

"Wait, they're allowing *that*?" Eric stares at the timer incredulously.

"Maybe they're being nice for once." Analisa grimaces. She's dubious of this too.

Daraja shrugs with a hopeful laugh. "I don't know, but I'm taking it. No, I haven't killed a person before. I should clarify—I'm Daraja. Clementine, Didi, and Bridget haven't killed anyone either. Trust me, our communication is solid."

The timer disappears. A bit of optimism pauses the worry churning inside my chest.

"Quick, everyone, ask each other before the refs change their minds," Eric says. "Lian, truth or dare?"

I ask Analisa, she asks Eric, and Lian asks me. All our timers initially set for about two minutes.

"Okay, I'll be quick." Analisa's words hasten. "No, I've never killed a person before. Um, what else… I guess, I admit that I drove a SUB into a shark once. They darted toward my boat before I could swerve, and I might've killed them. I don't know for certain though, so I hope the shark is okay. I haven't driven since." Her timer disappears.

"I've never killed a person. I haven't even gotten into a fight before, but my mom made sure I'd be ready for one." Eric's voice trails off as his palms tip toward the ceiling. "I don't know what else to elaborate on for this." His timer disappears.

"I've also haven't killed a person before. I do kill bugs though." Lian rubs the back of his neck. "A bunch of moths ate the first thing I remember sewing when I was a kid, so I'm a little more malicious toward bugs than I maybe should be. Is that enough elaboration?" His timer disappears.

"I've never killed a person before either." I glance at the ongoing timer. My hesitation at my phrase feeling too short is prompting my anxiety, which is likely continuing the timer. I let my terrified thoughts tumble out. "I'm worried about what we might have to do in self-defense here. If we're trapped in this cabin with the killer, we might end up needing to kill them before they can kill us." My thoughts trail off. "But yeah, I've never killed anyone. I don't want to either." My timer disappears.

Analisa squeezes my hand, encouraging me to meet her soft expression. She always tells when I get overwhelmed; her touch soothes my troubled mind. "Now we know that none of us killed Brandon or Solana. Hopefully, we can sleep better tonight."

"Better, yeah," Eric says uncertainly.

Analisa purses her lips. "What now?"

Eric winces. "One of us could be an accomplice to the killer."

Lian whacks Eric with a pillow. It encourages the rest of us to throw our pillows at Eric, which lightens the mood. Eric even joins the laughter while lifting his arms in a minimal effort to deflect our comical blows.

Then we plan our assignments. Eric and I will help clean the kitchen, and we'll bring back whatever we can use as weapons. Analisa, Lian, and Daraja will stay in my bedroom, working to convert it into a space suitable for all of us. They'll gather our clothing and toiletries, scoot a second bed inside, and break down wood from our furniture to fortify the door and window.

When Eric and I enter the kitchen, Sevyn is kneeling on the floor in a different outfit than earlier. They scrub the tile with a large, reddened sponge. At our footsteps, their gaze snaps up. "Are you hoping to grab something from the kitchen or to help?"

"We're here to help," Eric confirms.

"Oh, good. I grabbed extra supplies in case. I wiped most of it up already, but there's plenty of residue left. Anywhere you see red, scrub at it with the stuff in the buckets. It won't completely come out, even after the stain remover. But if we can make the kitchen useable, that's ideal."

I grab a sponge and wipe the counters. The bubbly soap lightens the red.

"So, Sevyn." Eric helps scrub the floor. "Do you have much experience cleaning up blood?"

Sevyn chuckles. "I'm not the killer, Eric. But yes. My friends often injure themselves."

Their friends often injure themselves. They had a classified job. They have a metal pinky. Even if I won't get an actual answer, I'm tempted enough that I ask, "Do you work in the mafia?"

Sevyn bellows with laughter, making my arms jolt. They shake their head, wiping their eyes with the edge of their bright blue shirt. "Whoo—imagine your great-aunt in the mafia."

Shock prevents my hands from moving. "You know her?"

"She's one of my closest friends, Cai. We've known each other since we were teenagers. She's got quite the hearing."

Auntie Tera got her enhanced hearing during her teenage years. "Were you one of the people who experimented on her, resulting in the... hearing?"

"No, I was like her. Instead of good hearing though, I've got a good memory." Sevyn raises an eyebrow at me. "Did she say she got the hearing because she was experimented on?"

I blink, confused. They're reacting like they know more about this than I do. With their authoritative demeanor, I'm starting to believe it. "I guess I always assumed that's how it happened."

"Ah, not exactly. But that's another story." They continue scrubbing the floor.

It's too much of a coincidence for them to be here and to know Auntie Tera. "Could you answer a truth for me?"

"Depends on what it is, but I'll try."

"Truth or dare?"

"Truth."

"Why did you apply to Truth or Dare?"

Sevyn nods like they understand something I can't. "Your aunt was worried about you. She doesn't know much about these games but still wanted to support you a little extra. She asked her *special* friends if they could apply to the same games you did. I'm the only one Truth or Dare accepted, likely because I claimed that I have an excellent memory. I thought your aunt was being overly cautious, but here we are, stuck in a game with a murderer. So, I'm here to protect you, and by extension, your friends." Their timer disappears.

It sounds like such an Auntie Tera thing to do. I smile, feeling a sting behind my eyes. I rub my eyes with my wrist, keeping the soapy residue away from my face. "Why doesn't she talk about you?"

"Remember that classified job I mentioned? My

closest friends—including your aunt T—are all part of that. She's also getting older, and with so much to listen to, I can't imagine we're all that interesting to talk about without explaining all our history. Maybe she didn't want to pain you with the things we went through. You've got to get out of here to ask her about all of that—you understand?"

My eyes gloss over again. I rub my nose, trying to avoid sniffling. I miss her so much that my chest hurts. Instead of dealing with all of this, we should be talking in my comfort corner, or playing a combat video game, or preparing food. I'd do anything to be out of here right now, just with Auntie Tera, Analisa, and Lian—even Daraja and Eric. I want to go to the mall with them, play games with them... I miss experiences that haven't even happened. "I'll try."

"No, more than that. You *will* get out of this alive, Cai. I need you to understand that. You can't give up here."

Their insistence solidifies something in me, preventing me from crying. "I understand."

"Good. Now, I don't have a lot to work with, since most of the metal here is junk too thin to protect anyone. But I'm working on getting some plates together to make it a little harder for someone to stab your torso. I'll try to get those finished for you and your friends today."

"Thank you," I respond. Eric adds his thanks.

"You're welcome. I'm afraid that we're all in a tough-to-resolve situation." Sevyn sighs. "The kitchen is as good as it'll get. I'll apply the stain remover once this dries. You two can leave. Grab some knives and lighters before you go. The skewers we used for the marshmallows could come in handy as well. Don't forget blunt objects like the fire extinguisher."

"Yeah, we'll do that," Eric says. "Any ideas for objects that are less... short distance?"

"Unfortunately, I haven't found material suitable for bowstring, otherwise I would suggest utilizing all these trees to whittle arrows and bows out of the branches," Sevyn says. "I'll keep you posted on ideas. For now, I trust that you're gathering defense for your room."

Eric and I carry as much as we can from the kitchen. We explore the cabin, searching for various large and sharp objects to use. When we return to the bedroom, we find Analisa, Daraja, and Lian hammering wood blocks to the wall. Soon we'll be able to cover the door with removable planks.

Eric's eyebrows raise with a hopeful smile. "Oh, you found hammers."

"The toolkit objects are small, but they could be helpful." Analisa holds up a kit with collapsable shelves. "I'm more impressed that Daraja moved the bed in here by themself."

"Hey, I helped," Lian insists.

Analisa rolls her eyes. "You got stuck in the door."

The two of them bicker, making it clear that Lian wanted the stuck-in-the-door part hidden from Eric. Daraja rubs the back of their neck and asks, "Anyway, what'd you two find?"

We place the weapon-like objects along the walls of the room and on the bedside tables. The idea is to keep the items within reach wherever we are in the room.

After we successfully construct a wooden plank system to wedge the door and window shut, we acknowledge our hunger. We decide to stock up on food that requires little preparation. Eric and I lift one of the microwaves in the kitchen and shuffle it into the bedroom. Then we haul back several boxes of microwavable things and a cooler packed with water bottles. By the time we're eating macaroni and cheese, apples, and flavored water, we've got a decently constructed compound of a room. We shouldn't need to leave except for bathroom trips.

Beyond the window, the day darkens. Brandon was killed around dusk. Solana was likely killed before sunrise. I don't want to wonder who could be next.

My chest stings when I think about Sevyn. They're facing this alone. They sounded confident that they could take care of themself. Still, I wouldn't have thought Solana could've been killed in the kitchen without anyone hearing it. Whoever we're dealing with seems to know what they're doing.

If the killer is discreet enough to have killed Brandon—and to have killed Solana so violently—without anyone witnessing it, we're probably facing someone who's killed before. I hope Sevyn can survive someone like that.

I hope my friends and I can too.

Chapter 21

"Okay, let's do a final stock-up for the night," Eric says. "Usual teams?"

"Yep. We're good." Analisa stuffs a metal wrench into my jacket pocket. "Do you have everything?"

Due to Analisa's persistence, my jacket pockets are stuffed with tools. I've got the largest kitchen knife we could find strapped into a makeshift holster on my leg, an inch from my fingers. Eric is equipped with the same things, except he has a fire extinguisher instead of a knife. After a debate on wearing shoes for extra defense versus wearing socks for sneaking capability, we choose to wear shoes. Who knows what could happen here—I'd rather be heard than step on a nail without a shoe on.

Lian and Daraja lift the wood planks barring the door. Eric and I squeeze through the doorway, journeying outside with a couple of bags to retrieve more food and water.

The hall light is off. The sunroofs only offer dark-ness. Eric finds the switch on his flashlight, casting a bright beam onto the floor. He scans both ways down the hall, and even at the ceiling. There's light under a couple of the bedroom doors, but the hall is deserted. Some of the fear clamping around my lungs alleviates. My flashlight quickly joins his.

Our shoes creak no matter how gingerly my toes graze the floor. My head keeps turning. My breaths bounce between being successfully steady and then too quick.

Eric's nerves are visible too. His Adam's apple bobs while his eyes dart around quicker than mine.

As we step closer to the living room, the metallic smell of the blood from the kitchen seeps into my nose. I set my teeth together, trying not to react rashly. It's just the stuff from earlier. I can't believe the cleaning smell didn't overcome it.

Eric's hand grips my arm, jolting me to a stop. His wide eyes stare at the flashlight beam lingering by the living room entrance. The living room light is off. Is he scared of the dark? If so, my jittery skin understands.

But stopping now isn't going to get us food and water. Having more gathered for the next few days would be beneficial. We won't want to leave the room tomorrow if we can help it. I press my arm forward, trying to tug him along.

Eric's fingers tighten around my arm. Under his breath, he mutters, "It's fresh."

The intensity in his voice locks my knees. "What?"

"The smell."

It couldn't be. Not someone else, so soon. I can't even hear anything from that direction.

We might not have time to decide what to do before the universe shoves more variables at us. Faint snapshots of Brandon and Solana emerge in the darkness inhabiting the living room.

In a flash, my mind imagines visions of a possible future. If I'm not careful, Eric could be the next person I see beneath the berry bush. Daraja, Lian, or Analisa could be there instead. Or they might find me with my stomach shredded and eyes wide.

When Eric next tugs on my arm, I relent in following him back. I'm glad I'm not alone. Moving feels worse than freezing near the end of the hall. Every creak in my step sends tremors through my legs. We quietly give the secret knock we decided on this time, and Lian lets us back in.

"That was quick..." Analisa's voice trails off when she stares at the empty bags. "Did the others take all the water?"

Eric shakes his head emphatically, too spooked to speak.

"We didn't get to the living room." Fear clamps around my throat, preventing my words from rising in volume beyond a mutter. "There's fresh blood out there. Enough that we could smell it from the hall."

"Shit," Lian whispers.

Daraja huddles with their knees to their chest on the conjoined beds. "Did you see anything?"

I shake my head. "The living room light was off. It

was completely dark." Looking back on it, I was too scared to move. I couldn't even bring myself to lift the flashlight.

I don't know whose blood it was, or who caused it to happen. Either could've been Jared, Joane, Flutura, Ever, or Sevyn. I don't remember which rooms had light on under their doors. I should've pointed the flashlight to read the names on those doors. But even if I had, it wouldn't have told me much. What happened in the living room could've involved any of them.

A heavy fear sits on my shoulders, waiting to be acknowledged. The more I consider it, the harder it presses into my skin—the possibility that Eric and I could've helped. Whoever's blood that was... they might not have been dead yet. We might've been able to help them if we had gone into the living room. But I'm still trembling at the thought of being in the hall. That blood could've been ours.

I wonder if the victim is being dragged to the berry bush now. Are they being positioned under there, face up, with berries placed in their palm?

Jared creeps into my mind. He's a botanist. I know that shouldn't necessarily make me think he's the killer. But the bodies keep being placed under that berry bush—the one he identified as poisonous. If he's the killer, the bush and his botany connection seem too obvious; maybe he's counting on that.

Or perhaps the killer is Joane, his fiancé. They could be working together. Or she's hoping the others will assume it's Jared by putting the bodies next to the berry bush.

Wait, neither of them killed Brandon though. They still could have killed Solana.

The first killer could've been different than the second killer. If Brandon's death made someone else realize that they could get away with killing on this show too, then the deaths might not be connected. That could explain the difference in how Brandon and Solana were killed. And the second killer could've positioned Solana similarly to Brandon to make it seem like the same killer. But why?

I need my brain to slow down. What do I know?

I don't suspect Sevyn, even though maybe I should. It's possible they learned about Auntie Tera and are using that information to gain my trust. They said that they have a good memory. I believe it—they retained things that we said during the interview. They could store information that they find useful to befriend everyone.

Flutura is still a mystery. She's a dancer who speaks rather spontaneously. Everything she does seems bold—asking Solana about her intentions, asking Sevyn about food during the audience vote... She seems so aloof that its suspicious, but that also could be how she is.

Although I hardly know anything about Ever, I don't suspect xem as much due to xir need for a wheelchair. Not that it means xe can't kill people, but I don't find it as likely because of how violently

Solana was killed—she would've fought back. Unless xe doesn't need the wheelchair? I can't believe I'm in a situation where I'm questioning whether someone needs a mobility aid.

The five of us here said under the truth accusation that we haven't killed anyone, so none of us killed Brandon or Solana. We couldn't have killed whoever it was out there, with the fresh blood in the living room. Eric was with me the whole time. Lian, Analisa, and Daraja were in the bedroom. Even if one of them snuck out the window and ran to kill someone in the living room, the timing wouldn't work to where there would be that much blood when Eric and I arrived. And if someone from the bedroom left, the other two would've said something. I trust that the people around me haven't killed anyone.

"I wanna sleep for hours and hours." Daraja curls up on the bed, their voice soft. They pinch one of their braids, playing with the end absentmindedly. "I don't wanna leave this room. I wanna pretend it's a slumber party and there's no outside world right now."

Their words increase a longing in me that I wasn't aware of. I want to block out the world too. As I scoot onto the bed, I mutter, "Yeah, let's do that."

Analisa lies beside me. Eric practically falls asleep as soon as his head hits the pillow. Lian snuggles up beside him. Although the two-bed situation has us a little squished, it's nicer than sleeping on the floor.

While we're huddled together, my mind attempts to convince itself that we have a chance. If I could bargain with the universe, none of this would've happened. As a result, my logic tells me that my hopes change nothing. Yet, that doesn't stop me from internally pleading: let us all make it out of this alive.

Chapter 22

There's a willow dripping sap from its trunk, catching flies while singing lies. Somewhere in the forest beyond it, a banshee screams.

I wake as soon as I realize the sound isn't from my dream. The shrill wailing comes from outside.

Analisa sits up, her pink and brown hair flinging over her shoulder as she looks toward the window. I turn to face the other three. They're all here, wide-eyed and awake.

The cry from outside decreases in volume. The sound elicits sympathy more than fear in my tense fists. If I had to guess, it's someone grieving rather than being attacked. I can't see much through the wood blocking the window. Soft morning sunlight creates disjointed bars of gold across the floor. We made it through another night.

"I don't think we should leave the room yet." Eric grips the fire extinguisher by the foot of the bed.

Analisa nods, her eyelids drooping. "I agree. But I'm tempted to know what happened. It would keep us informed and narrow down the options of who the killer could be."

"If we stay in here for everything except food and bathroom runs, we'll be safest," Eric insists. "If we leave, we expose ourselves to a greater chance of being ambushed."

"I know. But say we're out on a bathroom run and we're the only ones left besides the killer. Say they walk up to us and pretend that the others are still around. I want to have all the information we can to catch them in a lie."

"Yeah, I agree." Lian clutches his shirt, his fingers kneading the fabric. "And when we go outside is important. The killer might've left the next person by the berry bush again. Whoever saw them just now might move the person. We won't know who it is if they get moved."

"Moved to the river," Daraja notes. "If the bodies keep being moved there, we can do a check each day, when there's enough light outside."

"I agree that daytime is the best time to leave the room if we have to," Eric says. "The killer hasn't attacked anyone in the day yet, and we have more visibility then. But the bodies might not all be brought to the river, so checking later might not keep us informed. At the same time, running into whoever is grieving right now might not be great, especially if..."

Voices approach from down the hall. Relief hits my

chest when I hear Sevyn. They say, "You shouldn't do anything rash."

"I was going to buy her a ring. I was going to propose after this week." The pitch in Jared's voice rises and falls. "I never should've encouraged her to apply to this."

Our door rumbles with knocking.

Eric swings off the bed with the fire extinguisher. We all follow his lead, grabbing whatever is nearest. I find myself unsheathing our best kitchen knife.

"Cai!" Jared yells, causing my skin to shiver. "I know you were outside earlier! What do you know? Did you do it—did you kill her?"

Based on how he's talking, Joane is dead. Images of how she might look swim through my mind, making me grimace. Why would he think I had something to do with it? The others look at me, a blend of fear and confusion in their expressions.

I shake my head, muttering, "I've been in here all night."

We stare at the door, teetering on the edge of decision. How do we respond?

This is my room. As far as Jared knows, it's only me in here. I put my finger over my mouth and meet eyes with the others to make sure they know to stay silent. I approach the door.

"Cai!" Jared repeats, jolting me a step back.

"I'm here, Jared." Prickles on my thigh announce the gruesome proximity of the knife in my grip. Jared's threateningly loud voice compels the blade to whisper a warning: be ready. My arms jitter in response, but I maintain my voice's composure. "I've been inside my room all night. What do you think I did?" My legs spasm at a slam on the door.

"Jared, this isn't helping," Sevyn admonishes.

"Sevyn?" I call out, hoping for an explanation.

"You had to have seen it!" Jared yells. "You had to have known. How could you just leave her?"

"Cai," Sevyn says. "Joane is dead. She was stabbed several times and decapitated. It appears that she was killed in the living room and dragged out to the berry bush."

A chill rolls over my skin. She was the victim from the living room? She was so worried about me when I didn't eat. My stomach twists, flipping over.

No, wait. I haven't seen it myself. Even though I want to trust Sevyn, I can't let myself completely believe it. Under this premise, Joane was killed in the living room yesterday.

"What makes you think it has to do with me?" I ask.

"Truth or dare, Cai?" Jared asks.

Dare could lead to me having to leave this room. As long as I answer truth, I don't have to leave. "Truth."

"What are your supplements for?"

A three-minute timer appears beside my shoulder. What does that have to do with Joane's death?

Saying I don't know would be a lie. The supplements are flavored water, brought in to deflect suspicion from me when I don't eat. Would it matter to say that I'm partially an alien at this point?

Could telling the truth incriminate me somehow? Not answering is an option. Analisa and Lian know why I'd lie about it. But Daraja and Eric don't know. I don't want this to ruin our trust.

I glance at Analisa, wondering if she's got an idea. Her expression is hard to read—alert, afraid, sympathetic? Lian offers a quick shrug, his frown unsure. They're leaving it up to me.

"Can I ask what this has to do with Joane?" I ask.

"We found one of your supplements in the living room, cut into. It was on top of a bloody table," Sevyn clarifies.

On top of the blood. Indicating that I had seen the blood and was there at least after Joane had been killed. "It sounds like someone planted that then."

It is weird that someone could've had access to my stash of 'supplements.' They're all in here. So, either one of the people in here put it out there, or someone took one from my bedroom before we fortified the room. I haven't noticed any of the batch missing, but I wasn't keeping count of how many I've used. If only one or two were stolen, I probably wouldn't notice.

"Answer the question, Cai," Jared insists.

I stare at the timer. Jared has no way of knowing whether I answer with the truth. The timer will go red and fizzle if it runs out before I answer fully. Because there's no noise with it, Jared won't know either way.

But Daraja and Eric will. I can explain to them later. I'd rather lose the potential money than do something that increases Jared's anger, getting him to do something rash.

"They're prescribed by my gastroenterologist, so I don't know what's in them. All I know is that they keep my strength up," I answer. The timer continues counting down. "Satisfied? I didn't put it out there, so it sounds like someone is trying to frame me."

"I think you're lying," Jared says. "If you can drink water as you claim, how could you not recognize flavored water?"

My grip on the knife strengthens. I don't want to use it. But if Jared acts impulsively, I don't know what I'll need to do. "I drink flavored water sometimes. What does that have to do with this?"

"That's all the supplements are! I tasted what was left in the packet. It's just water."

I bite my lip, unsure how to diffuse this situation. Maintaining the pretense is my first inclination. "It had to have been replaced then. The stuff I drink is thicker than water."

"Stop lying to me!" The locked door rattles, making all of us tense up.

"Jared—"

I'm interrupted by Jared's frustrated growl. "Stay away from me! All of you!" Footsteps clatter down the hallway.

The timer beside me turns red and fizzles away.

Sevyn clears their throat. "Stay safe in there, alright?"

"Yeah. You too." The resolve drains from my voice. Now that Jared is no longer there and Sevyn walks away, fear climbs my back. Did I do the right thing?

Slowly, I cross the room and place the knife on the nightstand. I glance at Daraja and Eric, anticipating their suspicion.

"So, can I truth you?" Daraja's eyebrows pinch as I meet their unwavering gaze. At my nod, they ask, "Truth or dare, Cai?"

"Truth."

"Did you leave the room last night?"

I shake my head. "The last time I left was when Eric and I went out for supplies. I didn't put the supplement out there." The timer disappears.

Daraja nods, their thankful eyes softening. "Good. Do we get to know why you lied?"

"You know that I couldn't have killed Joane. Based on the smell of the blood in the living room, I was here with you all during the time she had to have been killed. None of us could've taken part in it."

"Yeah, I got that." Daraja curls up on the bed. "I don't want any lies between us. It makes me feel more suspicious. And I don't want to be, I swear. You just weren't sure what Jared would do with the information, right? Please tell me there's not anything weird happening here."

Analisa sits on the bed by Daraja, rotating her walking stick between her fingers. Lian adjusts his shirt. They don't know what to do either.

"I don't want to keep secrets from you," I insist. "And I swear, if we weren't televised, I'd tell you both right now."

"Both." Eric looks at Lian. "So, I'm guessing Lian and Analisa know whatever's going on with the supplements."

Lian's jaw clenches. He's not going to reveal my secret, even though he'd rather put Eric at ease. It would be easiest if they knew.

"Look, it's not a comfortable thing for me. It's an identity thing. Kind of like Daraja's. That's why I'm not comfortable revealing it on television. It's..." I lose track of my words as my closed throat snatches them up. I'm not able to capture breaths as fully as I want. Air goes partially in, more in, and out, in again, out a little, never hitting the comfortable boundaries of fully in and fully out. I snatch a pillow and sit in a corner of the room. "Please, give me a minute."

I bury my head in the pillow. The silk case rubs against my cheeks, smothering my nose in a way that forces my warm breaths to slow. If only I could keep my face covered like this. It's been so much easier being unnoticed as a human.

Back when I was in elementary school, I didn't change my green skin. I practiced warbling my bark, compelling it to speak the way Kiran's bark can. I thought it was neat; my classmates did too.

But the older kids decided these features made me a target. On their milder days, they only pushed me into the wall. Some days, they dunked my head into a toilet and told me to drink the water from there. The worst days were when they force-fed me flowers and spinach and cacti, laughing when I spit or threw it all up after. I flinch at the memory of the school nurses removing cacti needles from my mouth. The anesthesia wouldn't work, so I jolted at every needle yanked out with tweezers.

Soon, the classmates who once liked my unique traits wouldn't talk to me. Even though I told the teachers what happened, they wouldn't chastise the older kids. It took me a few years to realize their lack of action vocalized their silent agreement that I was too different for them to protect. I wasn't a child to them—just an alien.

It was hard to tell Analisa about those experiences. But after she told me about how some kids picked on her once, I stuttered through what happened to me. I pointed out the bark on my chest and the faded skin on my palms, looking a little green by the end of that night. While I cried in my comfort corner, she cradled me, kissed my forehead, and thanked me for telling her. She told me she loved me—as more than friends. This was only seven months ago. Now, we're closer than ever before.

I don't know how the world would react now. Would admitting this part of myself make me a target again, or would people sympathize?

Fear flutters through my chest. My heartbeat, loud in my head, persists. The dream I had—of the five of us hanging out after all this—could be shattered with my words.

An arm gently wraps around me, pulling me from the wall far enough for the other arm to find its way around my back. Analisa whispers, "I love you, okay?

Nothing's ever going to change that. I'm here for you, whatever you say."

"Would it be easier on you if we guessed what it is?" Daraja asks, their voice closer than I expect.

I peek from behind my pillow, finding everyone sitting around me. They don't have weapons, suspicious expressions, or anything threatening. They're simply waiting.

"Trust me, you won't guess this one." Lian sends a knowing smile to the floor.

Eric scratches his head as his glance jumps between my eyes and the wall past my shoulder. "Is it an eating disorder?"

Their voices are light—not accusatory, but curious. Dread clamps around my heart at the thought of their voices changing. I don't want to hear what their anger sounds like when directed at me.

If we're going to get out of all this, we need to trust each other. I can only hope that Eric and Daraja will be accepting.

Chapter 23

"You know about the supplements being flavored water, but that I eat meat. The skin condition I was born with, too. And that I don't have a vagina. Those things are related," I start. My chest tightens as my body acknowledges what I'm about to do; I'm willingly about to admit something I never thought I'd bring up publicly again.

The four of them wait patiently with soft gazes. Eric and Daraja pay attention, but based on their behavior, I don't feel pressured to rush my words.

I continue through a stammer. "I know you two know about how people can be lab-grown. Well, I'm lab-grown to have a mix of traits from both of my parents. One of my parents is human. The other... isn't."

Analisa rubs my hand, encouraging me to lock my fingers with hers.

"So wha—who... is your other parent?" Daraja asks.

"They're an alien. As in, from another planet." My throat pinches around my voice. I clear my throat, forcing out my words. "If you saw them, they might seem kind of like a moving tree with a canopy covering their upper leaves."

I glance between Daraja, Eric, and the floor. My words don't hit them with as nearly as much shock as I expected.

"So you're partially human and partially... a moving tree?" Eric asks, his mouth twisting a little. He fights to keep a straight face.

His amusement destabilizes my fear. "Are you laughing at my parent being a mobile plant?"

"Cai, you just told me that one of your parents is essentially a tree." Eric covers his mouth as his gaze darts to the floor. "Sorry, it's just... of all the things. Is that really what you were hiding?"

Daraja's mouth is a thin line. They don't seem to believe it.

An incredulous spark urges me to lift my shirt, showing the barky skin on my stomach. I compel my skin to warble.

Daraja flings themself backward in shock. Their legs kick the air as their back hits the ground. My spasm of worry relaxes as they release a cackle-like laugh.

Eric gapes, the corners of his mouth upturned.

"That's how my alien parent talks. Their bark warbles." An odd mix of feelings resurfaces. Pride?

Defensiveness? It's familiar, like hearing a song I haven't thought about in years.

"See? That's a reasonable reaction." Lian points at Daraja—they're still laughing on the floor, holding their quivering stomach. Lian crosses his arms at Analisa. "And yet, you made fun of me for jumping when Cai first did that."

"That's actually really cool." Eric grins. "Why didn't you want us to know though?"

Part of me wants to say, *if you were an alien hybrid, would you go around telling people about it?* My mouth pinches closed. He's being nice; I shouldn't be mean back.

"She wasn't treated well as a kid because of it." Analisa frowns at the ground. Her fingers rub mine. "Bullies got under her skin."

"Shit." Eric's expression sours. "I'm sorry."

"Don't be." I shake my head, not wanting him to be sorry. Eric and Daraja aren't reacting harshly to my admission. "I should mention that my skin is naturally green since I have chlorophyllic blood. I use a machine to spray my skin with a more natural human color every day. I applied a few layers a few days ago, in hopes that it would last to the end of the game."

"Okay, so... recap." Daraja rolls onto their side so they can face me from the ground. "You eat meat and drink water. Your green skin talks. Your physiology is different. And it's because you were a lab-grown kid with traits from your human parent and alien parent. Anything else we should know about that?"

"The talking is specifically called warbling. And..." What else is different? "I get most of my energy from sunlight and water. But meat and sleep help. I guess that's it."

Eric rests his chin on his hand, staring at me with narrowed eyes. "Now I'm curious about how you'd look with green skin."

"I know!" Lian throws up his arm. "She'd look even better in yellow with green skin, don't you think?"

My chest lightens with giddiness. "That's your first thought about all this? You don't have questions about my parents?"

Eric shrugs. "I'm up for listening to more, but I'm satisfied with what you told us."

Daraja points at him in agreement. "I mean, I've always wanted to meet an alien. I thought they'd be more obvious, with how... non-human they look in interviews. I know Galaxa astronauts are talking with them on Mars and everything, but I didn't think I'd meet one on a game show." Their eyebrows shoot up. "Wait, do you have some special skill you could use against the killer? Can you warble them unconscious or something?"

I shrug. "I don't think so. I'm more human than alien, in that sense."

"Ah, okay. It's all good."

Analisa leans against my shoulder with a soft smile. "How do you feel?"

"Not bad," I admit. "I'm happy you aren't scared of it."

Daraja gapes. "Why would we be scared? I was scared you had some dark confession, but your body's just a little different."

Daraja and Eric aren't like the kids who bullied me. I grin, feeling a stinging behind my eyes again. I don't want to cry right now. I tip up my head, encouraging my tears to subside.

Analisa wraps her arms around me again. Daraja tackles us in a hug. Lian and Eric pile on top of us, forming a warm sprawl of a group hug. I laugh, feeling high on relief.

I wonder what Tera would think—would she be proud? I don't know how my parents would react. Would they be irritated that I took so long to admit my parentage, or pleased that I finally acknowledged the alien part of me? I'm not sure. All I know is that my four friends are here with me.

We heat some microwavable food for a brief breakfast. After our meal, we decide to investigate the living room. We divide into our usual teams, with Eric and I exploring outside the room. The idea of the teams is twofold: to protect the bedroom and to keep Analisa from having to run. If need be, Daraja or Lian can carry Analisa out of the room while the other defends. Eric is the strongest of us, so he's most likely to be able to defend himself outside the room. I'm an average mix. Since we determined via a lifting-Analisa contest that I'm not strong enough to carry Analisa for as long as the others, I'll go with Eric.

The two of us walk down the lit hall, armed with our usual defense objects of choice. It's difficult to keep my shoulders from tensing as we approach the living room. The smell of cleaning fluid ambushes my nose.

The violent splotches are obvious as we enter. Sevyn scrubs the hardwood floor, but one of the couches is still stained with a deep, brownish red. The table beside it has dried blood crusted across the glass.

"No." Sevyn points at us. "Stay in the room."

I shake my head. "We need to stay informed about who the killer could be."

"Well, it's certainly not Joane." Sevyn's frown deepens as they continue scrubbing the floor.

A dark thought scratches my mind. "Could it be Jared?"

Eric grimaces. "It would be quite the cover."

"If it is, it's dedicated. He said he was with her for a year and two months, and she didn't contest it," Sevyn says. "But we can't rule out the other two yet. I haven't seen Flutura or Ever this morning. They could be dead by the river now, for all I know."

"Is Joane's body still at the berry bush?" I ask.

"As far as I know. I was going to clear the blood in here before taking care of her body. Jared is holed up in his room. If he's innocent, I imagine he doesn't want to see her in that state. I'll take her to the river."

"Is there anything else you figured out from… this?" Eric gestures around the room.

"Her body was stabbed more than Solana's, and she was decapitated. Her body was positioned outside, berries in hand—same as the others. Only, her head was in the living room earlier, next to your supplement bag." Sevyn pauses their scrubbing. "It was difficult to tell from her state, but it appeared that there were bruises around her neck, similar to Solana's."

So, she was killed like Solana. But her head was in here with my supplement pack; both are gone now. If there are multiple killers, then it's likely that whoever killed Joane is the same as Solana's killer. Regardless of if it's a single killer or multiple, the deaths are becoming more violent.

"Okay, thanks." Eric gestures to the door. "I say we check it out. Then we can get some food and head back."

Sevyn stands, sighing. "If you're going outside, then I'm going with."

Eric raises an eyebrow. He must be keeping suspicion of everyone in mind as well.

Sevyn gives a slim smile and takes off their decorative shoulder plate. It lodges into the wall faster than I can see the throw. I jolt, realizing that it came from Sevyn's outstretched hand.

"Trust me, if I were the killer, I wouldn't take my time." Sevyn yanks the metal plate out of the wall. It leaves a dent in the wood. "I'm going with you to offer strength in numbers. I wouldn't have any more advantage over you two outside versus in here."

There's so much about the nature of the killing that I don't know. Sevyn's words should be reassuring, but I don't know what advantage there is to killing someone inside versus outside. There's less space to run inside, perhaps. Still, I gesture to the door. "Alright, let's go."

Inside versus outside. A thought nags at my mind... we still don't know where Brandon was killed. Solana and Joane were killed inside—in the kitchen and living room respectively. Would finding where Brandon was killed lead us to a clue?

We step onto the porch. I grimace at the lilac dress stained with red splotches. Eric covers his mouth, turning away when we're close enough to see her full body. She's holding berries. Her skin is slashed into shreds. Her neck is a bloody, sawed-off stump.

"Her head." Sevyn whips their gaze around, searching the ground. "I placed it with her body. It was here thirty minutes ago."

I glance between Joane's body and the porch. I'd help Sevyn look through the nearby bushes, but I might have a heart attack if I find Joane's head staring through the leaves. It feels surreal to look at her now. Seeing something like this should only be in horror movies. It's like she should be a prop.

Eric rubs his face, also finding it difficult to look at Joane's body. He manages, "Do you think the killer realized there was a clue on it?"

"Maybe." Sevyn squints toward the forest. "I should move the body now. That way I can check on the remaining ones."

I haven't seen where the other bodies are yet. "Eric, I say we go with."

"I say you don't," Sevyn says. "I'll escort you back to your room. I can take care of the body alone."

"Even if that didn't sound suspicious, Cai's right—we need to be as informed as we can about all this." Eric hesitates before shrugging, not quite selling an aloof confidence under Sevyn's stare. "And if you're coming with, we stand a better chance of defending ourselves."

"Say the killer jumps us in the middle of the woods, while we're carrying the body." Sevyn's chin tips down, but their wide-eyed gaze drills into Eric. "Are you confident that you can defend yourselves long enough to run the three minutes back to the cabin? Because I don't think that's a risk you should take."

"The killer has only killed inside the cabin so far," I note. "At least, Solana and Joane were killed there. It's almost like whoever's doing this is showing off how efficient and quiet they can be. There wouldn't be a point doing that in the woods." I don't know if that's true. But I do want to convince Sevyn that we should go.

They look past their shoulder. "I don't have shields for any of you. I tried to gather material, but someone cleaned out the cabin's common rooms. The useful metal is gone. Pots, baking sheets, furniture—

even the damn motor carts have disappeared. I get the feeling they aren't underestimating my specialty." A flicker of doubt crosses their expression before resolve takes over. "But if you're going to insist, then let's hurry."

Eric lifts Joane's feet while Sevyn lifts her by the shoulders. My head turns constantly as we trudge into the forest. My back tingles from the feeling that, at any moment, someone could appear where I'm not looking. My fingers brush against the sheathed kitchen knife on my thigh.

The daylight provides some reassurance. Past the still trunks, I can see across the flat forest. The leaves chatter as the branches shift. No people around, as far as I can tell.

The whooshing of the river catches my ears before I can discern it. It's not wider than maybe ten footsteps. It doesn't look deeper than my calves. On its rocky bank... there's Brandon and Solana. They look sickly and dry as they lie a few feet from the water. A strange, unpleasant stench makes my nose crinkle as we approach.

Sevyn and Eric lower Joane's body beside Solana's. Joane's head isn't here.

Sevyn examines the bodies with gloved hands. "I don't see any further manipulation of their bodies. If anyone's touched them since I helped move them here, they must have as powerful a memory as mine to put them back as they were."

"Oh." I make the connection to Sevyn's persistence. "That's why you've been bringing them here."

"Yes. I hope to utilize my memory where I can. I couldn't research anyone the night after the interviews, as our online access had been restricted. They wouldn't even let me call anyone. So I have to rely on gleaning everything directly from the players during the game." Sevyn begins to walk the path back to the cabin. We follow, not straying further than a few feet from them. "The person we're dealing with is experienced. This isn't the first time they've killed someone."

I'm curious for their reaction. "So, if we determined via truth accusation that Analisa, Lian, Daraja, Eric, and I haven't ever killed anyone, that would mean we're all in the clear, right?"

Sevyn raises an eyebrow. "I wouldn't clear out anyone, Cai. But I don't think any of you are actively involved. I suspect that there's more that we can't determine here on our imagination alone."

After we walk back, Eric and I help Sevyn clean the rest of the blood on the living room floor and the table. The couch is harder, but we try cleaning that too. There are still dark stains coating everything. Now the living room is like the kitchen—tainted by a physical reminder of the agony someone experienced.

As I pull supplies off the depleting pantry shelves, I freeze. My palms and fingers are much greener than they were. Two days of scrubbing with cleaning supplies has accelerated the fading process.

I shove the remaining food into a bag and clench the handle. "Okay, back to the room now?"

Chapter 24

It's the evening of the third day. We have to endure three more days.

The system that we have so far is working. Only us five have been in the bedroom. We take turns going to the bathroom in teams. We've explored outside the room for information during the daytime.

While dusk arrives, we're determined to stay inside. We'll keep the lights dim so we can sleep, but bright enough that we can see the whole room.

Even though I'm lying with my friends, my heart-beat thuds against my forehead. It's so quiet. I should be sleeping, but I jitter with every rustle in the sheets from one of my bedfellows shifting. I don't like my back being to the window, so I turn toward it. Facing my back to the door feels even worse, so I flip the other way.

Analisa wraps an arm around me, tracing her fingers over my tattoo. She's awake too. Even with her delicate touch, my body won't stop running on hyperdrive.

"Do we want to sleep in shifts instead?" Daraja whispers.

"Is anyone asleep?" Eric whispers back.

"I'm not," Analisa confirms.

"Same," I add.

Lian is the only one who doesn't respond. His breaths are shallow, and his eyebrows scrunch, stuck in an uncomfortable dream.

"I can be on the first shift." Eric pets Lian's hair. "I don't think I'll be able to sleep anytime soon anyway."

"Oh, I was gonna volunteer for the same reason," Daraja says.

Analisa groans. "If I had thought about it sooner, I would've gotten sleep medication for our first aid kit."

"By now, the killer could've put berry juice on them," I say, bitterness fueling my voice.

Exhaustion seeps into our conversation, forcing us to pause. Without speaking, we contemplate our difficult situation. Being tired. Not being able to sleep. Knowing that if we don't sleep enough, our reflexes and thought processes will be slower. We'll be easier to attack if we don't sleep.

Daraja grunts. "I bet the killer's sleeping like a damn baby right now."

"We'll make it out of this. All of us," Analisa insists.

Even her optimism isn't enough to diffuse this

uncomfortable feeling. It's only the third night. A lot can change in three days. Although I stay conscious for what feels like hours, I eventually drift to sleep.

I jolt awake to Ever yelling outside our door. "The killer is—"

Before my post-sleep daze passes, Daraja shrieks. I'm yanked into reality, frantic to locate where they're looking. Blood rolls into the room from beneath the door.

Eric snaps into action, grabbing weapons and passing them to the rest of us. My shaking hand grips my knife hilt. We're in the center of the room, circled to face both the window and the door.

My breaths convulse while I watch the fresh blood roll under the door. I flinch at every grunt, groan, and gurgle. Following each noise, new waves of blood roll into the room. Eventually, they slow as the slope by the doorway levels out.

The wheelchair squeaks, sending cracks through the hall floor. My hazy mind attempts to decipher a clue from the footsteps outside. Are they Jared's? Flutura's? Sevyn's?

Guilt pours into me, weighing down my feet first. It rises through my legs, filling my body like I'm a glass statue.

We all must be considering whether to act. If we push the furniture away from the door and remove the wood, it means the killer can reach us easier. We're safest if we don't help anyone else.

My palms still press against the dresser in front of

the door. Eric's hand clasps onto my wrist—he shakes his head.

"We can't leave xem," I whisper. We're running out of time to help.

Eric's jaw sets with an uneasy frown. His hardened gaze considers mine for another moment. Then he helps me shove the dresser and lift the wood.

We shine our flashlights out the doorway. There's no sign of movement. A ton of fresh blood pools on the floor and clings to the wall.

Eric yanks me back inside the room before I can venture further. He slams the wooden pieces over the door. "No one around now. We're too late."

"You don't know that," I say.

"Cai, I can't see that as anything but a trap." Eric flings his arm at the door. "Ever could be part of this, acting to draw us out. Or the killer was actually out there, trying to play on our compassion to get us outside."

"Even if—" Analisa hiccups between a sob through her hands. "There's five of us. What if we could've taken them on? Should we hole ourselves up in here if we can..."

"Maybe we could've. But we don't know that." Eric's voice cracks as his head sways uncertainly. "Maybe the killer can't take us all on, and that's why they're picking us off one-by-one. Or it's a game to them, daring us to lower our guard. You haven't seen Sevyn. With their reaction time, I really hope they're not who we're up against. If there's anybody else like that here, our best chance is staying in this room."

"That's..." My numb tongue can barely admit it.

"Yeah, it's selfish. But we've got to decide whether we want to do the most morally right thing, or if we want to take our best chance to survive." Eric's voice lowers while he crouches on the ground. He hugs the fire extinguisher, his eyelids drooping while he stares at the door. "Personally, I think I'd stand a chance against whatever's out there. But I don't know if I can defend all five of us, especially when they've got the upper hand in understanding what's happening. If one of you died here, I wouldn't forgive myself."

Daraja collapses on the bed, shock glossing over their eyes. Their arms fall limp, their weapons resting at their sides. Analisa cries into her shaking hands. Lian kneels on the floor, holding his knees to his chest. Eric won't take his eyes off the door for more than a few seconds, and that's just to check on the window.

And here I am, a glass full of guilt. We weren't quick enough to act. Even if we were, how would that have ended? With all five of us, could we actually have overtaken the killer? We could've ended this now and helped Ever. Part of me hopes Ever is actually on the side of the killers. If xe's not, then I won't ever stop wondering what would've happened if we left the room then.

But Eric is right—we're likely safest in here. We've survived for this long by relying on caution. If the five of us choose to take on the killer, it risks at least one of us dying.

Eric sets down the fire extinguisher. He gestures in front of my eyes, staying distanced enough to not startle me. "Come on." Eric pulls my arm toward the bed. "It's not sunrise yet. We need more sleep."

"Sleep?" Daraja hisses. "You think I can sleep after that?"

"They're trying to get in our heads," Eric warns. "If we're sleep deprived, we'll be easier to kill. Since we don't have a fridge in here, it would be ideal for us to make trips to get healthier food. But if we aren't awake enough to do that, we'll have to eat microwavable meals, which don't have as many nutrients in them. The killer knows we're trying to wait them out in here, and they're trying to make us weaker and force us out. We can't let that happen."

"I don't even think I can go out there to use the bathroom anymore. I don't want to go in here either, but they could attack us whenever we step outside the room." Lian's hands run through his hair. "They're not even concerned anymore about someone hearing them."

"Because they've scared everyone else into not coming to help," Analisa says through her hands. "What's wrong with us?"

My shame mulls over imagined possibilities of what we could've helped prevent. Although we were too scared, I can't picture Sevyn behaving similarly. "Sevyn would've come running."

"Maybe they couldn't." Eric tugs my arm again, convincing me to sit on the bed.

"As far as we know, there's only three options

left for the killer to be, right?" Lian's shoulders slump. "Maybe the reason Sevyn didn't come running is because they're... you know."

I don't want that to be the case. It would line up with why we didn't hear them coming. Still, I feel like Sevyn's smarter than that. If they were the killer, they wouldn't leave that suspicious clue unaddressed.

"Whoever they are, they're getting bolder," I note. "First, Brandon was attacked somewhere unknown. Then Solana in the kitchen, Joane in the living room, and Ever outside our door." I almost voice my question: where do they plan to go next? But I might know the answer—in a bedroom.

Analisa shivers. I wrap my arm around her, trying to comfort her as if I'm not trembling myself.

"Did anyone recognize the footsteps?" Eric asks.

I shake my head. "I feel like the gait could've been anyone."

Lian runs his hands through his hair, his eyes wide. "I hate this. I hate all of this."

"Lili, we're all going to make it out alive." Analisa rocks herself. "You'll see. We'll probably end up interviewed on some crazy documentary about this. In the meantime, we'll get the money to cure Baba. And then we can go to college or get jobs or whatever, and we can all meet up on the weekends. It'll be fine. You'll see. These will all be just a bunch of traumatic memories soon."

Eric sighs through his nose. He offers Lian a slim smile. "Maybe next week we can go on a date, Lian. How does dinner sound?"

"I thought you said you didn't have time for dating." Lian fiddles with his fingers.

"After all this, I'll shift some of my priorities. I already know that I'd hate to miss out on a dinner with you."

"Yeah, I'd hate that too." Lian rubs the back of his neck. "How does Indian food sound? Oh, how good are you with spice?"

Eric sits on the bed, encouraging Lian to join him. "I'll practice raising my spice tolerance."

"Man, I want to eat food too." Daraja shakes their head at Eric's incredulous eyebrows. "I'm not crashing your date. I mean I want to travel. I've been in New York forever. I want to know what Italian food tastes like in the Mediterranean Region, you know? Food like that."

Their longing for a future beyond all this sparks some hope in me. It's tainted by the thought of Brandon, Solana, Joane, and whoever's blood that was outside. They won't be able to experience the futures they longed for.

But I can't think about that right now. My mind will break if I don't give into my own selfish hope. "Maybe I'll start walking around with green skin after all this. That might help rebuild the connection I lost with my parents. I want to hug my aunt too. And my grandparents."

"I want to style an outfit for you, actually," Lian says. "If you help me pick out some yellow fabric, I bet I can create something nice. That way maybe you'll feel less like people are staring at you because of the green skin, and more like they're in awe of how fabulous you look."

A light giggle slips out of me. "Yeah, I'd like that."

"Daraja, I want to ask you for voice lessons." Analisa tips her chin up, a smile forming. "You made quite the statement at the interviews."

Daraja laughs. "Oh yeah, that's right!"

"Could you sing us something now?" Eric asks.

"Um, yeah." Daraja clears their throat. "No judging though. I'm dehydrated."

"No worries." Eric lies down, inciting the rest of us to follow. We clutch the pillows and blankets, our tension hiding in our muscles. Our dazed gazes travel between the ceiling and each other.

Daraja sings softly. I register the lyrics about how dark and fearsome the night is. But the repeated chorus promises that there will be sunlight again. Each verse passes with a new threat in the dark, but Daraja keeps bringing the chorus back with its promise of light.

Chapter 25

I must have fallen asleep at some point during Daraja's song because now there's sunlight in the window. I rub my crusted eyes. Hoping that my memory is a dream, I look at the door. There's a puddle of flat, dry blood stretching into the room.

Something outside sounds weird. It's a repeated snipping sound. I don't think it's close to the window.

Analisa and Daraja are asleep beside me. Eric and Lian are awake, drinking water while sitting on the floor. When they look at me, I point at the window.

"It's been going on for the past few minutes," Eric whispers.

I slide off the foot of the bed slowly enough to not wake Analisa or Daraja. "Any idea what it is?"

Lian shrugs. "I'm feeling like we don't need to find out."

Curiosity could kill us. There will probably be a point where we have to stop traveling outside the room. But we're safer while it's daylight out. And after not leaving the room earlier, my skin itches to know what we could have prevented. What a morbid thought. "It could be useful to know."

"Sure. It also could be more useful to stay in here," Eric says.

"You need to do a bathroom run, right?" I ask. "Come with me. If it seems too dangerous, we'll come back."

Eric folds his hands beneath his chin. "Have you been pretending this whole time to use the bathroom?"

I roll my eyes. "Different physiology. So yes."

"Huh. So what happens after you eat meat?"

I glare at the ceiling. "I secrete anything I digest through sweat."

"I didn't know that!" Lian voice is way too loud for the morning. "What kind of—"

Eric and I shush him. Lian clamps a hand over his mouth as his eyes dart toward the bed.

Daraja sits up slowly, like in a daze. They blink at the window. "What's that noise?"

I hold out an arm toward Daraja, as in, *see?*

Eric tips his head up, relenting. "I do need to use the bathroom. We can poke our head out to do that, at least."

"Be careful," Lian urges.

"Of course." Eric arms himself with his usual gear. "Come on, Cai. Let's go investigate that strange noise. Every character in a horror movie does it, so why shouldn't we?"

"It's daytime," I say, fighting back with what little horror movie information I know. I grab my usual equipment as well. "Hardly anyone gets killed during the day."

"Unless we're in a movie that subverts tropes," he argues as he lifts the furniture away from the door.

"Maybe the writer assumed the audience would expect subverted tropes, so the reality is exactly what we'd expect." I help him slide the large, wooden planks off the door.

Eric's fingers clamp around the doorknob, tensely waiting for whatever's on the other side. "Let's just agree that we can't assume anything."

Anticipation locks my nervous joints while I stare at the door. My attempt to remain lighthearted flees. All I can respond with is a silent nod.

The door opens to the wreckage of what we heard earlier. Blood splattered on the narrow walls and gathered on the floor. Ever's broken glasses rest by the wall—I didn't notice those earlier.

With my knife unsheathed, I poke my head out of the doorway. I look left, right, and even up. There's no one here. There are two lines of blood leading down the hall, likely from Ever's wheels. And there are footprints.

"Footprints," I whisper.

"Measure the shoe size with your hand!" Lian hisses.

I look around again, worried that the killer could pop out at any moment. There are twelve bedroom doors—the killer could be in one of the bedrooms right now. "Keep watch."

Eric's footsteps follow me as I squat next to the shoeprint. It's like whoever it was walked on the ball of their foot. There isn't enough to measure the shoe size. And there's too much blood splattered around the prints to tell where the width starts and ends. The shoe treads look smudged. "There's not enough to go off of."

"Damn," Eric mutters. "Okay. Close the door."

After Lian and Daraja shut the door, Eric and I walk to the hall bathroom. I wait outside, watching the lit hall like a frantic, sleep-deprived hawk. The animal analogy reminds me of Analisa's love of clams. We're trying to clam ourselves up inside a room. The killer is trying to pry our shell open with little care, killing us in the process.

Truth or Dare was supposed to have simple, explicit rules. The killer has changed the game by following their own rules. We're acting as if the killer can't change their behavior. Maybe because it makes us feel like we have some control over the situation.

But Eric is right—we can't assume anything. The killer could attack in the daytime today. They could kill more than one person at a time. They could kill someone and leave them somewhere besides the berry bush. They could use something other than poison or a knife. They could attack outside the cabin. There is no certainty to any of this. It worries me more now—that the killer hasn't deviated from this pattern. It's like they want to be found out.

After Eric leaves the bathroom, the unknown noise is still happening. He gestures with a slim smile, indicating he's ready to go see what it is.

We enter the living room. It still has the stains from Joane's blood. The noise is coming from the front of the cabin.

Eric and I step onto the porch.

Sevyn is holding clippers among strewn branches. They're cutting all the berry bushes. Most of them are now stubs sticking out of the ground. They even cut the one that the deceased were placed under. Ever lies on the ground nearby, with xir head and legs severed from xir shredded torso. Guilt climbs my throat.

Sevyn shakes their head emphatically, barely glancing away from their task. "Get back in your room. I'll clean the blood soon."

"What are you doing?" I ask.

"What does it look like I'm doing, kid?" Sevyn doesn't stop clipping the bushes.

A bit of irritation makes me tip my head incredulously. "Okay. Why?"

"I'm hoping to change the killer's habits. There's some reason that they're putting the bodies here consistently. If this spurs something new, I can learn more about them, and hopefully, learn how to stop them." Sevyn points at the door. "Which means you need to be back in your room. It's not safe out here."

Eric scoffs with a slight smile. "Of course it's not safe. But I'm not sure that chopping down the bushes will change much."

"What if I dump all the branches in the river? No more berries then, at least. I'm growing more impatient to draw them out. They seem to not want me involved, however."

That reminds me... "Where were you when Ever..." I can barely glance at xem. Xe lies still in the corner of my eye. Could we have prevented what happened?

"Locked in my room at the far end of the hall. My door and window were barred shut by wood. Took me over an hour to cut through it. If the killer's smart, they'd have removed it by now. But maybe they don't care about covering their tracks anymore."

The end of the hall. That does match up with the room I saw Sevyn leave from after we all changed into tank tops and shorts.

"Speaking of, we found footprints in the blood," Eric says.

"Yes, I saw them too. I don't recognize the tread pattern, however. Unfortunately, there wasn't anything else there to go off of."

"I mean, Ever's glasses were there," I note. "But there's not much we can do with that, right?"

Sevyn drops the clippers. "Since when were there glasses?"

Our restless bodies decide what to do before our minds can deliberate. The three of us run back inside, through the living room, down the hall.

The blood is still there, but Ever's broken glasses are gone.

What does that even mean?

"Was that a slip-up or are they messing with us?" Eric huffs through his quick breaths.

"Perhaps it's something that the killer only wanted you to see." Sevyn crosses their arms, their demeanor shifting with their vexed expression. "Seriously. Go in your room now. I'll take care of Ever and the berry bushes. I'll bring you some supplies in less than five minutes. After you get those, don't leave the room."

Relenting, Eric and I tap the door with our agreed-upon knock for this trip. Before we even finish our summary of what we learned, Sevyn returns with items for us. They talk as they walk down the hall, far enough to make us feel safer about opening the door and grabbing the stuff.

It's a couple of buckets containing cling wrap, toilet paper, hand sanitizer, scented candles, and a lot of plastic bags.

"They don't seriously mean..." Daraja points between all the things.

"Honestly, it's better than what I would've come up with." Analisa winces. "The scented candles are a nice touch."

Lian shakes my arm, his face mortified. "Cai, teach me to secrete sweat."

"Lili, it's a life-or-death situation. I think your crush will understand that we need to use the bathroom in a bucket." Analisa rolls her eyes as she splays her fingers over her chest. "I should be more mortified. At least Eric has to do it too. My girlfriend has to smell my excrement and she doesn't even have any."

"I mean..." I lift my arm, sensing the chill of dried sweat beneath my armpits. "It's not the same, but we're all in this together."

"Maybe the killer will get too grossed out by our room and leave us alone?" Daraja shrugs with a grimace. "We could throw the bucket at them if they try to get in."

"I think the bags are what we're supposed to use," Eric notes. "The buckets are to get anything that... doesn't make it into the bag."

Daraja lifts their hands as they step away from the buckets. "Okay, someone will have to dare me to do this. I'm not doing it unless I get money for it."

"That's not a bad idea, actually," Lian adds. "I mean, giving each other mild truths and dares right now. We might as well save up what we can to sue Truth or Dare when this is all over."

"While I agree with giving each other mild accusations, I don't think we could sue Truth or Dare." Eric's fists clench. "Their whole premise is that anything goes within the games. The government allows the No-Liability premise as long as they receive a substantial part of the profit that the games make. The No-Liability makes things more entertaining, which means more viewership and donations. Both the government and Truth or Dare win from it. Us dying in here is probably skyrocketing their viewership. Who wouldn't watch a live murder mystery unfold? And if we make it out, everyone will say we got compensated by the money and fame. No one outside of this game would side with us saying we deserved better."

Irritation lines my fear. He's right. The audience has voted against our favor more than once. Truth or Dare must be keeping everyone on the edge of their seats. Even those who might be sympathetic toward us would be tuning in. No one would stop watching now. Which means Truth or Dare and the New York City government profit from our pain.

Chapter 26

"I need to use the bathroom," Lian squeaks as he sits at the foot of the bed. One of his knees bounces as he stares at the buckets. "Are we sure we can't leave the room for a little bit to do that?"

"The killer could be waiting right outside our door. We've been lucky that they haven't attacked us like that yet," Eric says. "Now that we have the means to stay in here for the next three days, we shouldn't leave."

Lian's eyebrows pinch. "No fair. You just went."

"Yeah, under Cai's insistence that we go see what that clipping noise was. Now we know, so we stay in here." Eric crosses his arms. "We're making it out of here alive, Lian. As Analisa said, this'll all be an embarrassing, traumatic memory one day."

Lian runs his hands through his hair. "Can we at least... like, hang a sheet from the ceiling or something? And everyone agrees to not look?"

"Yeah, we should set this up now." Daraja pokes one of the buckets with their foot. "I hate that this is on TV."

"The bathrooms have cameras in them too," I say, hoping to introduce some optimism. "Comedy and Tragedy omit the bathroom footage unless an accusation happens there."

"And unless something interesting happens in them," Analisa adds. "Given the circumstances, they might not cut this out."

Lian grabs a pillow and buries his head in it. "My first kiss, almost being forced to have sex with my partially alien friend whose girlfriend is my twin, and now being the first to use the bathroom on live television. I hate my life."

"At least you can proficiently squat." Analisa puts her hands on her hips. "Do you even want to imagine trying to do this with a prosthetic leg?"

"You're a gymnastics person. Just stretch or something."

"Just stretch or something?" Analisa shouts incredulously. "Demonstrate this for me, Lili. How exactly am I supposed to stretch or something?"

I won't admit it aloud, but I'm really glad I don't have to do this. I light a candle and set it on a dresser. Citrus, coconut, and sunscreen waft through the room, evoking an imagined smell of a beach.

"Oh, nice. Now it smells like we're on vacation," Eric says.

"Worst vacation ever," Lian mumbles.

"Why is this the part you're panicking about?"

Analisa asks. "There's literally a killer preventing us from leaving the room and you're whining about using the bathroom in a bucket."

"Cognitive dissonance, maybe?" Daraja suggests. "I don't know. I just dissociate."

"Getting killed is horrible, yes. But once I'm dead, I won't feel embarrassment. Doing this to get out alive is embarrassing myself assuming that I'll live to feel the embarrassment. *That's how it's worse, Ana.*" Lian grabs a spare sheet from the closet, a couple of nails, and a hammer. He holds them out to Eric. "You're tall. Can you please put up this sheet around the corner of the room?"

Eric tries not to laugh. "Yep. Give it here."

After Eric hangs a couple of sheets from the ceiling, the bathroom corner has some coverage. Lian pleads for us to sit on the opposite side of the room and cover our ears. So Analisa, Daraja, Eric, and I sit facing the opposite corner, our hands over our ears.

At first, I cover my ears completely. My heartbeat is what I hear; the wooden wall is what I see. There could be someone behind me right now. Panic creeps down my shoulders. The killer could've broken in, and I wouldn't know. My back can practically feel fingers trailing down it, considering where on my skin to cut first.

My hand slips a little, allowing myself to hear enough to dispel those thoughts. I don't hear anyone behind me. Just Lian shuffling around in the corner.

I stare at the floor as the others take turns using

the restroom. Better to have everyone sit in the corner while we're here anyway.

The time does nothing fortunate for my thoughts. It's only the fourth day here.

But then again, we'll be let out at five p.m. on day six. That means we probably have a little over two days remaining. If we keep the killer from breaking into the room, we can outlast the game here. The killer will be legally liable for any deaths after five p.m. on day six, so hopefully we can safely leave the cabin then. That's assuming they care about the law enough to not kill after the time limit.

We'll have to stand in line with them at the closing ceremony. We'll have to sit next to them while watching the highlight reel. We'll have to live our lives, knowing that a killer is free. Would they hunt us down once Truth or Dare is over, or are they limiting their killing to the game?

Outside of our group, there is only Jared, Sevyn, and Flutura left now. What do I know about them?

Jared is a botanist who came here with Joane, who is now deceased. He's thin and shorter than me by a few inches. I'm not sure if he's strong enough to have killed Brandon. But since our theory is that Brandon was poisoned, strength doesn't eliminate Jared as a possibility.

Strength. Could that play a part?

Ever was old, and in a wheelchair in a hallway. Although the hall is wide enough for Ever to easily turn around in it, the limited space could've put xem at a disadvantage. Joane was in a wider space, but with how thin she was, I'm not sure how strong she could've been in defending herself. Solana jogged in her free time, according to her. Based on how she jogged around the cabin on that dare the first day, her endurance is decent. She was also overweight, but I'm not sure how much her weight would've helped her in overpowering someone if she were caught by surprise.

Should we practice how to defend ourselves against someone with a knife? That might be better suited to our time than truths and dares. If someone were to force open the door or the window, we'd have to fight against them in this room. Sure, it's five of us against up to three others. But if we want to all get out of this alive, it could be difficult if they force one of the exits open.

Once we're done with the rounds of bathroom usage, Eric says, "Ever might've been one of those people who couldn't wear long-term contacts."

At first, I'm not sure what his thought process is. Then I jump onto it. "Xir glasses would've worked the same way as contacts. Which means—"

"They could store memory." Analisa's eyes widen.

"Are you telling me..." Daraja's mind catches up with their stuttering mouth. "You are. You're telling me that xir glasses could have a recording of who killed xem."

"Truth or Dare cut off most of our contact usage capabilities. But the cameras on them are still running so the refs can use footage directly from our eyes. Which means Ever's might've still been on,"

Analisa says. "If we had a way to access that footage..."

"Wait, how would we do that? I can't even access my camera anymore." Lian points at his eyes.

"Your glasses wouldn't happen to have recording capabilities in them, would they?" Eric asks.

Lian shakes his head. "They're decorative."

"The killer doesn't know that though, so maybe we could use that," Analisa considers. "But anyway, exploring around to find Ever's glasses now wouldn't be ideal."

Maybe it's the best time to bring this up. "Hey, if we're going to be staying in here, should we practice some self-defense? It couldn't hurt."

"Yeah, I don't have any experience in martial arts." Analisa glares at the ceiling. "It would be nice if there were some firearms here. Baba made sure I knew how to handle as many of those as he could find."

"You can use a gun? Damn, I feel useless." Daraja shakes their head with a slight laugh. "Where do we even start?"

Eric's eyebrows rise. "Wait, besides Analisa knowing how to shoot, do none of you have any experience defending yourselves? No practicing for someone with a knife, grappling, deflecting a punch, anything?"

I stare back at him with as much surprise as he seems to feel. "I know I don't."

"Yeah, same," Lian says.

Eric pinches his forehead. "We've been in here for at least a day, and no one thought to mention that?"

"Hey, we're trying to outlast whatever happens outside this room. I don't think any of us want to think about what happens if someone gets in here," Lian says. "But, now that we're talking about it, practicing is probably a good idea. Do you know anything about defending yourself?"

"A little, yeah. My mom's in the military. While her specialty is robotics, she made sure I'd practice defending myself." He lifts a screwdriver. "We might as well pass the time with a few drills. Let's see what I remember."

Chapter 27

Considering the past few days, today has been less worrisome. We've figured out a system for spending our time. When someone needs to use the bathroom, we huddle in the opposite corner with our hands mostly over our ears. If someone falls asleep, we talk quieter. Whenever we're hungry, we heat something in the microwave on the floor or open a snack. We talk and give each other light accusations to pass the time. This room becomes like a bubble of comfort. If no thoughts intrude to pop the bubble, I can pretend that we're somewhere safe—not trapped in this horrific circumstance.

"No, I dared you to do it." Eric grins. "Come on, I bet you can."

Lian shakes his head emphatically, trying to lift an uncut apple with metal chopsticks. "I don't think it can be done!"

"I've done it before. Look." Eric finds more chopsticks and borrows the apple from Lian. He fumbles with the fruit as it rolls across the table. After a couple of tries, he manages to lift it with the chopsticks. "I got it!" And proceeds to drop it. "Ah, shit."

"Hey, not bad," Analisa praises.

"It just needs to be for at least a second, right?" Lian asks.

"Yep. Hold the apple up with only the chopsticks for at least one second," Eric encourages.

Lian skewers the apple with the chopsticks and holds it up. He takes a bite, grinning at Eric's dead-panned expression. "Does that suffice?" The timer disappears.

Analisa shakes her head. "You just disappointed so many people, Lili."

"No way it's that hard." Daraja snatches Eric's chopsticks and proceeds to push another apple around the bedside table. "Wait, hey. How is this difficult?"

"They're pretty big apples," Lian says.

"Hold the chopsticks closer to the end. Then you'll have more length to grip with," Analisa advises.

"Physics student moment," I say to mess with her.

Analisa sticks her tongue out at me before relenting a joking smile. "That should be a common-sense moment. *Should* be." She pokes Lian's shoulder.

"What? It was never specified to lift the apple with the chopsticks in a certain way." Lian shrugs. "I did what was easiest."

"I kind of want to see Cai do this," Daraja says.

"Since you don't eat much. If someone with little chopsticks experience can get it, then I'll most definitely be stupid."

"I mean, my options are more limited here, but I use chopsticks to eat meat. I also cook with them all the time," I clarify.

"Oh shoot. Sorry, I shouldn't have assumed." Daraja double takes. "Hold on, how do you cook with them?"

I blink at Daraja, not sure how to respond. "You just... do?" I gesture the motion for stirring meat around a pan with chopsticks. "Do you not use chopsticks for stirring things?"

"No, I use, like, large spoons and things." Daraja blinks back at me. "Different things for different types of motions."

"But isn't it easier to use one utensil for everything?" I ask. "How do you have the space for a bunch of large spoons?"

Daraja stammers, at a loss for words. Then they toss up their hands. "Pancakes! How do you flip those?"

"With chopsticks," Analisa says at the same time as I do. I giggle at how well she knows me. I have made pancakes over at her place before. I'll typically bring my own metal chopsticks to help her family cook.

Daraja's jaw drops. "How?"

"You just grab it and flip it," I say, doing the motion.

"Okay, I'm gonna need you to show me that later," Daraja says.

'Later' and 'after all this' have become our ways of alluding to our wishful thinking. We've built a long list of hopes to cling to. So many ideas for once we make it out of Truth or Dare.

"Hey." Analisa's back straightens. Her eyes dart around the room. "Does anyone smell that?"

"Smell what?" I ask.

We pause, looking around the room for whatever Analisa might be sensing. She turns around, facing the door. She stands up, and immediately wobbles backward. I jump to my feet, clutching her shaking shoulders. She coughs, her eyelids flickering.

"Analisa!" I squeeze her arm.

"There's some liquid rolling into the room." Lian coughs when he gets near it. "Frick. Is that phosgene? Or—" His words don't make it through his coughing.

My eyes water, making it harder to see. I rub them with my sleeve. "How bad?"

"If it's making us—" Lian's muffled voice says through his elbow. "We need air. Open the window."

"They're trying to draw us out." Daraja slaps a hand on the wall, keeping themself from completely keeling over.

Eric snatches a bag and stuffs it with food and weapons.

"We can't take anything!" Lian shouts. "If we're..." His breaths are shallow as he jogs to the window. "It's contaminated. We have to get out."

The window. It's dangerous out there. I know that much through my woozy head. But either we stay or we leave. Leaving might have a better chance of survival, even if it leads to a trap.

Eric helps Lian yank off the boards covering the window. I still grab the fire extinguisher and my knife. Even if contaminated, we might need them to escape.

Damn it—it's night. I didn't pay too much attention to the window earlier. I grab a flashlight, aiming it at the darkness outside. While the window is closed, a glare greets my squinting eyes.

Analisa's coughing grabs my attention. She sways by the wall, one shaking hand clutching her walking stick, her knees bending further with each uneasy step. I drop the weapons to grab her unoccupied arm and pull her to the window. Between my coughs, I mutter words of encouragement. My breaths scratch my tightening lungs.

Eric slams the window open. He yells in pain before I can see the knife slicing across his left hand. It's too dark to see who holds it. My flashlight doesn't catch the movement in time. I only see leaves right outside the window.

A heavy thump from outside accelerates my dread. They don't attack again yet. Eric's fingers hover over his bleeding hand. My head is so light that it wants to tip to the side.

Shallow breaths rip through my teeth. It's like they're caught in my throat, secreting a sticky phlegm instead of air. Analisa shudders against my shoulder.

"They're gone." Sevyn's voice comes from outside. "Climb out the window. Hurry."

It might be stupid. But I might die in here or I might die out there. Someone has to test it. I pull Analisa's arm over Lian's shoulder and duck by the wall. I shove the bedside table to the window.

"Should...?" Daraja coughs.

I boost myself onto the table and take Sevyn's hand. They pull me out, pat my shoulder, and reach their hand down for the next person.

I fall through the bushes and crumple onto the grass, choking. The flashlight tumbles out of my fingers. I'm hardly able to move, like I'm compelled into the earth. If only I could yank out my lungs. Anything to make this stop.

A gross spike of searing heat shoves itself up my throat. No—I never wanted to experience this again.

My mouth opens, unable to hold back from letting loose the contents that should be in my stomach. Sour smelling bits of meat in bubbling green ooze pour onto the grass. Runny mucus prevents me from breathing through my nose. My watering eyes distort my vision. A couple of shocked gasps sustain my lungs before I lose control of my throat again.

Analisa coughs beside me on the grass. I see her pink hair in the corner of my eye. Her prosthetic hand snatches my hand.

Lian's here too. He kneels, tugging on Analisa's shoulder to compel her upright.

Saliva dribbles from my gaping mouth. My chilled throat is fairly certain it's done puking. Disgust at the violating feeling swims with my fear of it happening again. My locked elbows are too scared to move.

Daraja pulls on my shoulder. Their chipped, green nail polish seizes my attention. What a pretty color. I wobble into kneeling. My stomach feels twisted upside down.

Eric groans between coughs as he pulls Analisa onto his shoulders, lifting her in a fireman's carry. Sevyn heaves me onto Daraja's back—I wrap my arms around their neck while they hold my thighs. Ick —I'm drooling onto their hair. I can't get my body to dispel its queasiness.

Sevyn yanks their armor out of the cabin wall, then charges into the forest. "This way."

My arms cling around Daraja's neck while they carry me into the bumpy forest. I feel jumbled around. My stomach especially. Really hope I don't puke on Daraja's shoulder.

Lots of leaves pass. Trunks of trees. It's so dark. The flashlight... I think they brought it, but Sevyn turned it off. I'm glad there's a simulated full moon. It lightens the sky, making the trees look dark enough to see their shapes.

"Frick!" Daraja trips. I manage to tilt to the side enough to not land on their head. Still, a lot of me falls on their back. They groan as their elbows push against the ground. My stomach flips. The sky looks like it should be the ground. The trees are uprooted.

Lian yanks me up. My head bobbles, hardly able to retain its position on my neck. He says something to me, but it doesn't compute. I think he wants me to move.

Red blood smudges Daraja's knees. My arms bleed chlorophyllic blood. It's green. It beads up like little necklaces draped over my skin. My leg has a scrape that drips.

I need to move. Someone tried to hurt us. Someone *did* hurt us. They could be following.

My bare feet stumble over each other. Twigs jut into the balls of my feet. Dusty dirt gathers between my toes. It's not that I'm not used to it. I once lived in a house with a dirt floor. My mom would encourage me to connect with the earth... "Walking bare on the ground is like rooting yourself to the earth, Caitlee. It will give you strength and comfort, while you remind the earth that it is mobile."

My feet go on. It's a stumble at first, but I'm soon pulled into a pattern. I increase the pace. As the path narrows, branches swat at my arms and legs. My body warms as it keeps moving.

My breaths hate me. They consume my chest and take over my mouth. At least there's no more bile. My stomach sways, like on a ship. So unbalanced. Yet the dirt beneath my feet is familiar. The sound of the river approaches.

"We're almost there." Sevyn yanks off their shoes and steps through the water. "Careful. The bottom is slick."

Lian holds my shoulder while I clutch Daraja's arm. Eric trudges through the water with Analisa over his shoulders. Analisa. She was closest to the door. Her immune system isn't great.

My fixation on her almost makes me slip. Lian rigidly catches my arm, keeping me walking through the water. The gentle waves lap at my knees. My submerged feet grow colder.

It's even chillier when we leave the water. Sevyn leads us to a campsite-looking area. A tarp stretches across two trees. Gray remnants of a small fire sit nearby.

"You can rest here," Sevyn says. "You'll need to wash yourselves in the river."

"Our clothes." Lian huffs. "If we're affected this bad, our clothes aren't safe."

I cough, but no bile surfaces. My mouth croaks, having a hard time formulating words. I crawl back to the river's edge, following Lian.

The water is freezing. My hands manage to adjust to the temperature after a few seconds. As I stretch my arms in the water, I shiver.

"Don't make it harder on yourself," Eric mutters. I swing my arms when I feel myself lifted. I'm gently set into the water.

My arms slip and my head drops beneath the surface. The rocky bottom is indeed slick. My hands scramble to find a stable part. I shoot myself into sitting up. Water falls out of my nose and mouth. Wet hair clumps over my shoulders and spreads over my forehead like spiderwebs. My body shivers. So cold.

"I only have one towel," Sevyn says. "And I don't

have spare clothes for you all. I have rolls of gauze bandages, however. You can wrap yourselves in those in the meantime. Tomorrow, we can investigate the cabin."

Moonlight decorates the shifting waves. The darkened silhouettes of my friends join me in the river. Sevyn passes a couple bars of soap to Eric and Analisa.

My body aches. The water sways me while I lie on the rocks.

Analisa leans over me, her hair down. When did she take her shirt off? "Here, wash yourself."

I glance at the clear sky, trying to respectfully look away from her. I accept the soap and scrub my legs.

"The clothes might be contaminated." Analisa's arms cross over her bare chest.

I look down at my body. I'm too drained to care for embarrassment. My pants and underwear are difficult to slide off while sitting. The water coats my thighs and groin as I slide off my shirt. At Analisa's solemn prompting, I even take out the gold promise earring. I wash myself while she sits beside me, her knees to her chest. The river carries the soap bubbles down the stream.

"You were complaining about a bucket, Lili. Just a bit ago." Analisa grins at the sky. Tears glitter like stars on her cheeks.

I reach an arm toward her by instinct. I falter, realizing that both of us being naked might make touching each other awkward. My eyes land on my hand. I tilt it, trying to verify whether my vision is tricking me. I think my forearms might be green. Did the gas do that?

"I still hate all this. I hate everything," Lian answers, sitting curled up some feet away.

"What was it—this'll all be an embarrassing, traumatic memory, someday?" Eric reminds us.

"How's your hand?" Daraja asks, also curled up in the water.

"Surprisingly not bad. Either I got lucky, or whoever swiped at me wasn't trying to cut too deep," Eric says. "You didn't happen to see who it was, did you, Sevyn?"

Sevyn shakes their head. "I was too far away at the time. After I threw the shoulder plate, they dove into a window. For all I know, it could've been either Jared or Flutura."

"Convenient." Daraja grabs the cotton bandages and begins unwrapping them. "How'd you know we needed help?"

"I didn't. I waited until after sunset to come back to the cabin, since the killer tends to act then. If I had been there sooner, perhaps I could've kept them from filling your room with that phosgene blend. I haven't smelled it that strong in a while." Sevyn sits on a nearby log and leans back on their arms. "I appreciate your skepticism, Daraja. You're all free to go elsewhere, if you'd like. But I will be supervising you regardless, as the killer clearly intended to attack one of you."

Although obvious, acknowledging our situation out

loud makes it feel even more ominous. I wonder if the killer meant to kill us tonight. Or were they only messing with us?

"Saying 'the killer' feels less likely to me now," Analisa says. "If whoever was outside dove into the next window, then yeah, it's possible that whoever released the liquid gas stuff into our room could've been the same person. But I'm starting to think that it might be both Jared and Flutura."

"Have they even interacted much though?" Lian asks.

"Not that I've noticed," Sevyn says. "However, it's easy to hide familiarity."

Even if it's not both Jared and Flutura, distrusting both makes sense to me.

"Hey, on the bright side..." Eric finishes wrapping bandages around his waist. "I'm betting we'll be trendsetters. Everyone will be wearing bandage underwear after all this."

Daraja snorts while they take the towel to dry themself. "Yeah, sure. You're really rocking the look, Eric."

"Thanks. It's as uncomfortable as it looks."

A carefree sting in my chest induces an involuntary smile. It's like I cling to every uplifting moment —I might not experience it again. I chase the thought away. "Don't discourage us already, Eric. I was really looking forward to comfortable bandage underwear."

"Yeah, like, how easy is it to take off?" Lian asks with a curious lilt in his voice.

Eric points at Lian and quickly looks away, probably realizing that Lian is still naked in the river. Eric covers his eyes, still pointing as he trips over his words. "You are getting much flirtier... much quicker... than I thought you would. I like it. I'll try to keep up."

"Yeah, Lili. What movie did you learn that line from?" Analisa giggles.

"What movie could I possibly have learned that from? This Truth or Dare: Murder Edition we're living through is the only situation I've seen where the characters had to wear bandage underwear," Lian says.

"I'm glad you all are finding light in this," Sevyn interrupts our silly conversation. "But I need you all to recognize that you're in a much more dangerous position out here than in your room. I can keep watch, but I do need to sleep for a few hours. So someone else needs to stay awake during that time. If you need to use the bathroom, I've got a shovel you can use. Tomorrow, we'll figure out food and defense."

I would've rather continued the bandage under-wear conversation, but Sevyn's right to adjust our mindsets. We're out in the open now. With barely any supplies. Not even actual clothing.

"Water," Daraja says. "Can we drink the water?"

Sevyn lifts a cup and some packets. "Put water in the cup, then put the packet in the water. It should disinfect it well enough."

Eric grabs the cup and tries it. After Daraja finishes with the towel, they pass it on to Analisa. She clutches her muddy walking stick as she sways to her feet. I look away while she wraps her chest with gauze.

"Are we safe out here?" I ask. It might be a hopeless question, but it attracts everyone's attention.

Sevyn rubs their beard, their expression pensive as they decide how to respond. "Until we have a better understanding of whoever's after us, you're safer out here than in the cabin."

Chapter 28

It's a restless night on the ground. I'm exhausted, but my mind won't shut off. My eyes flicker open every so often, spooked by some soft sound. My friends lie nearby, but based on how often they shift, they're probably drifting in and out of sleep too. Sevyn still sits on a log by the water.

My body aches as I sit up. The scrapes and bruises I accumulated while escaping our room pinch my skin. My feet barely find relief when stepping through the damp mud. I approach Sevyn from the side, trying not to startle them.

They don't turn to face me. "I know it's hard, but you really should try to sleep."

I sit by them on the log. Watching the water is calming. My fingers drift over the log bark, caressing the trunk as it slowly dies. "Truth or dare, Sevyn?"

Sevyn chuckles. "Money doesn't concern me, Cai."

"It's just for fun," I encourage. "We've been doing it to pass the time. And to forget all this."

"Hm." Sevyn shrugs. "Truth."

I consider the water. "Have you ever killed anyone?"

A timer pops up beside Sevyn for three minutes. They meet my eyes with a slim smile. "You're really giving me the fun questions up front, huh? I'm surprised they're letting you ask." They shake their head, refocusing on the river. "Yes, I have. Not anyone in this game. When you have the skillset people like me and your aunt have, you don't get to watch the world turn. We were put into training right away to become soldiers. Then after we returned to civilian life, we were summoned again to take on something the world couldn't handle, and now we keep at it. Point is, when your life is on the line, and your friends could die at any moment, you learn to act. To neutralize the threat however you need to." They look at me again, concern in their eyes. "I'm sorry that you're going through such similar circum-stances."

I'm not sure what I was hoping for from their answer. It's more serious than I want it to be, but Sevyn's sympathy does provide some reassurance. It's a morose validation to hear that what we're going through is as atrocious as it feels.

"Hopefully we can get out of it like you and Auntie —" I should avoid her name on live television. "Like you did."

"Yeah. We often have healers on our side though.

However, they're dealing with something else at the moment. They help us stay young." Sevyn clears their throat. "May I ask you something now, Cai?" At my nod, they say, "Your aunt talks about you a lot. She's real proud of you, really. She said you had a secret that you don't like to talk about much. I don't need to know, but do you think I should?" They tap my hand, which is greener than it should be. "I'm guessing this has something to do with it."

I nod. "I told the others already. I don't think it affects much, unless you don't trust me because of it."

"Nah. I trust you enough," Sevyn says.

"It would be more useful if I could grow into a tree or something." I slump over, setting my tired head against my palms. "The thing is... I've got a human parent and an alien parent. My alien parent is like a large, moving tree with a canopy over their upper leaves. I'm not sure I acquired any particular survival traits from them though, besides being able to live off of sunlight and water."

"That's already a gift," Sevyn notes. "Do you need sleep?"

"Sleep helps, especially since I'm used to it."

Sevyn chuckles. "Then what are you doing talking to me?"

"Don't you need to sleep too?" I ask.

"To my best efforts, I've been sleeping during the day. I can last for another few hours."

I still don't know if I can sleep much. Feeling useful might help. "Is there anything I can do now?"

"You shouldn't leave the area alone. Really, sleeping and encouraging the others to sleep would be in your best interest. If it helps, I've been sharpening sticks for you all to use." They point at thick, arm-length branches piled beside their feet. "It's the least I can do with a metal pinky and some time. If you feel unsafe, grab one of those and keep it near you. Just try not to be too jumpy with it. I'd rather not accidentally be impaled by a sleep-deprived teenager."

Their insistence is compelling. I look over my shoulder, finding Daraja quickly pretending to fall asleep and Analisa not bothering to hide that she was listening. I offer a little wave; she waves back with a slight smile.

"Okay. Let me know if you want someone else to take over." I grab one of the spiked branches on my way back to my resting place.

"Sure," Sevyn acknowledges.

I slump back onto the dirt, shifting until I find a nearly comfortable position. It feels like my ribs jut into the ground. Once I'm able to sit still, I look at Analisa. Her drooping eyes focus on me. She cups a hand around my face and kisses my cheek. Her tender touch releases my tears. It's so odd, how easily I can cry now. My nose isn't even runny yet— my eyes merely leak.

"I love you," she whispers. She swallows, barely affecting her attempt at a smile.

"I love you too." I wrap my arm around her waist, settling closer while her prosthetic hand rubs my shoulder. I want to reassure her further—to guar-antee that I'll sacrifice everything to keep her alive. Fear of breaking that promise keeps my mouth shut.

I drift away from reality, engaging sleep in a partially aware state. I don't leave the forest, or Analisa's side. Fear envelops me like a blanket. Anxiety is my pillow. My dreams are to make it out alive. Some twist happens, and I make it out not quite whole.

The next time I wake, I'm pleasantly surprised by the light blue dawn. A dreary, sleepy blue coats the branches and tree trunks stretching above my head. Did we really make it through another night?

Daraja's yell rips me from my exhausted state. Alarm compels me to stand. Sevyn's already bounding through the river. They pull Daraja behind them as frantic shouts approach.

Lian and Eric are already at their feet while I pull Analisa up. Lian passes Analisa her walking stick. Daraja grabs the pointed branches Sevyn fashioned and passes them around. I seize my first one from the ground and accept another.

With my possibly contaminated knife washed down the river, these two wooden pieces of defense are all I have. Shards of decaying plant life, here to prevent me from encountering the same fate. My body braces itself for the next challenge we need to overcome.

Jared's body blends into the dim awakening of the world. His dark hair and plum shirt look gray here. Flutura's orange hair is easier to discern from afar. Through the trees, it doesn't look like they're heading our way. But it's clear enough from Jared's frantic yells and Flutura's direction what's happening: Flutura is pursuing Jared.

If they're working together, this could be a ploy to draw us out. But it could be that Flutura is trying to kill Jared. Maybe she knows he's the killer; maybe she is the killer.

Eric steps forward, meeting Sevyn at the river.

Sevyn holds up their hand. "Don't. As unfortunate as it is, our chances our better if we don't get involved."

"It's possible they aren't working together. She could be about to kill him. We're out in the open now, and we can see them both. They can't surprise us here like they could've in the cabin," Eric insists. "Is there really nothing we can do?"

Jared veers in our direction. It seems that we're going to have to get involved anyway.

"Well, damn." Daraja gives a breathy, nervous laugh. "Now what?"

"Back up. Let me handle this." Sevyn slides off one of their metal shoulder plates, gripping the edge tightly. "If for whatever reason, I'm subdued, then run to the cabin clearing. Defend yourselves however you need to."

Jared yells, "Help! She's trying to kill me!"

Eric scoops Analisa over his shoulders with a grunt. He says, "We might be better off running now."

I don't want to lose the sense of safety that Sevyn's been providing. They might be able to subdue the situation alone, but having us all here might be better to overwhelm whoever is the killer.

But also... Analisa. The terrain out here is full of sticks, branches, mud that can easily throw off her balance. Staying would be riskier for her.

"Put me down." Analisa smacks Eric's chest. "Come on. We stand a better chance with all of us defending. You holding me makes no sense—you're the strongest of us."

Eric sets her down, a conflicted look crossing his face. He grabs his sharpened branches again. "Are you sure?"

"Yes." Analisa's eyebrows pinch as she raises her sharpened branch and grips her walking stick. "I may not be able to run, but I can definitely defend myself."

Jared arrives at the river, yelping as he scrambles through the chilled waves. Sevyn grabs his collar and flips him into the water. They raise their arm at Flutura; her running speed doesn't decrease.

"Why are you attacking him?" Sevyn shouts.

Flutura doesn't answer. The kitchen knife in her hand gleams as she sprints for the river.

"I don't know!" Jared stammers. "She just started attacking me."

"Shut up for a minute," Sevyn says. "I'm talking to you, Flutura! Give me a reason, and maybe we can help each other."

Flutura yells something. I can't tell what she says. Was it a word?

"Stop running, or I will defend Jared," Sevyn yells.

Flutura slows to a jog as she reaches the river-bank. Her hostile glare drifts between Sevyn and Jared while she adjusts her grip on the clean knife. She lifts her free hand, hovering it over her huffing throat.

"Is Jared the killer?" Sevyn asks.

Flutura nods.

"No!" Jared thrashes in the water. "No, she is!"

"Don't move!" Sevyn points at Jared.

Flutura scoots her foot forward.

"You neither!" Sevyn points at Flutura, who freezes in place. "Flutura, did Jared attack you earlier? Is this self-defense?"

Flutura pauses, glowering at Jared. She nods.

"She's lying! Ask us what we were doing ten minutes ago!" Jared pleads. "You know the timers give away whether we're telling the truth. Truth me. I swear, I didn't attack her!" Jared pleads.

"Alright. Jared, truth or dare?" Sevyn asks.

"Truth."

"Did you attack Flutura?"

"No, of course not! After someone released gas in the cabin, I stayed the night in a tree. Then when I was getting water—"

"Wait!" Eric interrupts. "There isn't a timer."

"I—" Jared looks around him, his eyes widening. "I don't have anything to do with that! I swear, I didn't hurt her!"

"It might be too close to what the refs didn't allow." Daraja's fingers tighten around their wooden sticks.

"Then ask me something different! I swear, I'm not the killer."

"Truth or dare, Jared," Eric says.

"Truth!"

"What were the exact events leading up to Flutura attacking you?"

A timer appears for two minutes. "Like I said, I was sleeping in a tree. When I climbed down to get water, she started running after me with a knife out of nowhere. I've been trying to get her to tell me why, but she won't." The timer fizzles.

Flutura shakes her head furiously. She dashes forward, colliding into a moving Sevyn. In a few tense seconds of my body deciding whether to rush forward or freeze, the knife clatters onto the riverbank. Sevyn grapples with Flutura.

Eric snatches the knife, holding it with a trembling fist.

Jared struggles to his feet.

Daraja yells, "No! Stay here!"

"I don't want to die!" Jared stumbles through the water, tripping over the slippery rocks. Eric grabs Jared's flailing arm and drags him back toward the rest of us. "No! Let me go! Please don't kill me!"

Sevyn and Flutura freeze, their only movements the panting from fighting each other. Sevyn has a sharp edge of their shoulder plate hovering over Flutura's neck. Sevyn says, "I don't want to hurt you. I'm going to let you go now. Don't chase after him. Do you understand me?"

Flutura swallows, aware of the sharp metal's proximity. I step closer to the river, readying myself to move. The rest of us circle the scene unfolding in front of us. Flutura nods, a sullen expression in her eyes.

Sevyn stands and backs away, positioning themself between Flutura and my friends. "Can... are you able to..."

"Seriously, what's happening here?" Lian's wide eyes jump between each person. "Jared, you claimed that you didn't try to hurt Flutura. And I saw the timer. It fizzled like you told the truth. But Flutura's behavior is too odd for her to be the killer. Why is she attacking you right in front of us, in daylight?"

"I don't know!" Jared trembles, sitting in the water with Eric's hand pressing down on his shoulder. "All I know is that she attacked me unprovoked."

Flutura dashes toward him.

"Help me!" Jared shrieks, trying to yank the knife from Eric's hand.

In a whirlwind, Flutura's fingers squeeze around Jared's neck. Jared fights Eric for the knife. Sevyn yanks Flutura off Jared as she releases a pained, animalistic cry.

The knife is lodged in her stomach. When she crashes into the water, blood disperses from her torso. Her ripped shirt sways with the waves. That knife was lodged and then twisted up inside her.

I freeze, watching as Sevyn holds Flutura's head. She cries while squinting at the sky. Her quivering fingers hover over the knife hilt. Her mouth opens like she tries to form words.

Eric's knees buckle—his eyes wide, bottom lip twitching, hands still trembling.

Jared breaks out of his shock quickly enough to run. Sevyn leaps out of the river, rips the tarp covering our campsite, and chases Jared. By the time Jared realizes he should get out of the water, Sevyn tackles him. Jared pleads for us to not kill him, yelling and screaming and flailing against the ground like a worm while Sevyn ties him inside the tarp.

It might be a bad idea on my part, but Flutura looks too miserable to not approach. Her breaths cause her chest to convulse.

I lean over her. Her crying eyes widen at me, afraid.

I brush my fingers against her shaking hand. "I'm sorry." I don't even know what for. I don't know what could've happened differently. She insisted on continuing to attack Jared. Why did she do that?

Her trembling fingers clutch mine. She opens her mouth, hooks a bloody finger around her bottom lip, and pulls her lip down. Her tongue, surrounded by a still, white substance, appears stuck to the bottom of her mouth.

"Holy..." Daraja drops their stick, seeing it too.

Flutura's tongue is glued to her mouth. Her bottom lip looks like it can't easily move.

I don't know if she's innocent, but given how forlorn her crying eyes look, I'm inclined to believe that she was wronged here. Tears stream down my face before I can stop them. "I'm so sorry."

Her hand squeezes mine back.

"Is it really Jared? The killer?" Lian asks.

Flutura juts her head into a nod and raises a shaking hand. She holds up three fingers.

What does that mean? He killed three? But four players are dead so far. Are there three killers? I don't even want to consider that thought with who's left alive.

Lian grabs gauze and bandages. He sets them aside and crouches beside Flutura. "Help me pick her up. We have to close the wound."

Chapter 29

I'm not sure Flutura can survive this, but depending on where she's stabbed, she might. Daraja, Eric, and I help Lian move her out of the water. It's only a few feet, but she yowls in so much pain that I can practically feel it myself. Eric compresses the wound with gauze and bandages.

While Flutura's still responding, we should ask her for answers. "Is Sevyn one of the killers?"

She grimaces while moving, but she manages to shake her head.

"I'm sorry, Flutura." Eric's lip trembles while he presses the gauze on her stomach. "I should've stepped away. I didn't mean to lose control of the knife."

Flutura raises her hand as if to tell him to stop talking. Her trembling hand pats his arm, before resting her hand on her chest.

"Is one of us... involved?" I ask.

Her head doesn't move anymore. Her chest doesn't rise or fall. Her gray eyes stare at the sky.

"Sevyn!" I shout. "Sevyn, help her!"

They jog to us, lugging a wrapped-up Jared who cries out, "I don't know what kind of twisted game you're playing, but please let me go. I don't want to die. I really don't want to die."

Sevyn sets Jared down nearby and kneels beside Flutura. They assess the situation—seeing the bandages, feeling for a pulse—but their shoulders slump and their hand pinches their forehead, covering their eyes.

"She's really..." Analisa covers her mouth.

"Come on, what can we do?" Daraja prompts.

Sevyn shakes their head, still covering their eyes. "I'm not trained to handle the kind of medical care she'd need, even if I had the resources. And the referees have made it clear that none of us are leaving this dome before five p.m. tomorrow, so we can't get her to a hospital."

Lian's hands wrangle his hair as he curls up toward the ground. He cries out a muffled scream into his knees.

"I did this." Eric's mouth quivers. He looks at his shaking hands like they aren't his own. "I can't believe... I didn't mean to. I swear, I didn't mean to."

"No, this isn't on you." Daraja glares at Jared. They grab one of the sharpened branches. "It's on him."

"We don't know that for certain." Analisa steps in

front of Daraja, discouraging them from approaching Jared.

"You all saw that." Daraja flings their hand at Flutura. "Her behavior didn't match that of the killer. She was desperate to attack Jared for some reason. And it's looking like maybe it was self-defense."

"Yeah, but he wasn't lying when he said she attacked him out of nowhere," Analisa says. "There's got to be more to this that we can't figure out from what we saw."

"She said that Jared was one of the killers while she was dying. What reason would she have to lie now?"

"Say *she* was the killer. Why would she admit it at the last moment?" Analisa jumps in before anyone else can. "Yeah, I want to believe her too. But we can't act as if her indications are completely true. So even if Jared is the killer, until we have definitive proof, we shouldn't kill him."

The possibility silences the debate. If we wanted to take the truly selfish route, we could simply kill Jared. Even if he isn't the killer, he did stab Flutura in a frenzy of self-defense. He could do that to any of us. But could we actually go through with it?

Eric shakes his head. "No, we can't kill him. If we keep him tied up for the rest of the game, we should be in the clear."

"But what if he breaks out?" Daraja asks. "If we're right about there being multiple killers, he had help. If that's the case, he won't stay tied up."

Lian sits up. "But there's only us left."

My teeth clench, unsure if I should bring it up. Sevyn should know, at least. "When we asked Flutura if Jared was the killer, she nodded and held up three fingers. Does anyone have any ideas on what she meant by that?"

"Three..." Lian's voice drifts.

"It could be that Jared caused three of the deaths. Maybe someone else killed the fourth," Analisa pitches. "Brandon's death still seems different. Perhaps that's it."

"Or it could be three killers." Sevyn lowers their hand from their solemn eyes.

I glance at the others here. Analisa, Lian, Daraja, Eric, Sevyn, Jared. According to Flutura, Jared is a killer and Sevyn is not. I don't want to consider the possibility of three killers being correct.

But when I asked if Sevyn was one of the killers, Flutura shook her head. That could mean the three-killers premise is correct and Sevyn is not a killer. Or she could've been trying to indicate that the premise was incorrect.

"Perhaps the time when the murders happened?" I ask, trying to forget the three killers idea. Everyone here is in such proximity to each other. We're all close to a knife and several sharpened sticks.

"Some of them didn't happen at three a.m. though. We know Brandon died earlier, at least," Analisa says.

Jared's been sobbing in the tarp throughout the conversation. If he is the killer, he's a dedicated actor.

Sevyn shakes their head. "At this point, what's important is surviving to the end of all this. To start, we need food. There aren't any animals in this dome to hunt, but I came across plenty of edible plants in the forest. And since the entire cabin was contaminated by the gas, we shouldn't go inside until the rooms have had time to air out. The sealed food in the pantry might be usable later." They rinse their shoulder plate in the river, then stand. "We'll all move together, including with him. We need to feed him too." They lift Jared by his tarp. "Let's go. Most of the food grows by the river, so the fortunate part is that it isn't far."

"Is there an unfortunate part?" Eric asks, his expression solemn.

"Yes. One of the more useful plants is over where we left the bodies. In fact, now might be a good time to bring Flutura there." Sevyn looks at Eric, and then the rest of us. "Actually, if you'd rather I carry her, then someone else can take—"

"I'll take her." Eric kneels beside Flutura. "I feel like I should."

Lian rests his hand on Eric's shoulder. "It wasn't your fault."

"If I hadn't grabbed that knife—"

"Then someone else would've. Maybe Jared. Or Flutura." Analisa taps Eric's back with her walking stick. "I saw how you reacted. You were ready to protect us. No one can hold that against you. I don't even think Flutura did."

Eric's eyes close. He swallows. I'm not sure I've

seen him cry yet, throughout all this. But now his slumped back shudders. Tears start flowing down his reddened face. Without stopping to rub his eyes, he scoops up Flutura and stands.

Sevyn shifts his grip on Jared. "Follow me down the river."

No one picks up a conversation on the way. My mind is free of ideas, both uplifting and serious.

Flutura's warning stirs the dread in my queasy stomach. I don't think Sevyn killed anyone in this game. I don't think any of my friends did either. The game should've confirmed that via the truths we asked each other. Is there a way to lie when the truths are being answered? Could someone answer and be unaware that they're lying? Did Comedy and Tragedy alter the way the timers respond?

I need to stop questioning my friends. If I create unnecessary discord among us... I don't want to think what one of us might do out of fear.

I smell the bodies before I see them. My hand slaps onto my nose, trying to keep myself from breathing it in. The reactions from my friends are similar.

It's difficult to peel my eyes away from them. Going down the line, each body looks worse and worse. What was Brandon is now a dismembered corpse with hollow, caving-in skin. The bloodier dismembered bodies, although more recent, are somehow worse. Shriveled in places they shouldn't be.

Wait, Brandon wasn't dismembered when he died.

His left arm isn't even here anymore. Before I can formulate a question, Jared whimpers.

"Why did you do it?" Jared's voice quivers. Tears drip off his lowered chin. "I was going to propose after all this. I was finally going to afford the ring. I wanted it to look like a candytuft with a diamond in the center. She loves purple candytufts. She was going to look for a better job after all this. She was kind to all of you!" His strained voice raises. "How can you live with yourselves?"

Eric places Flutura beside the chopped-up limbs, torso, and head that was Ever. Then he yanks the knife out of her stomach and rinses the blood off in the river. He holds it out to me. After I raise my eyebrow, trying to gauge how sure he is, he says, "I don't trust myself with it." I take it, content with having a knife again, and feeling fortunate that he trusts me with it.

As we trudge into the bushes, Jared continues shouting. Sevyn strains to keep their wiggling cargo from falling. Their voice deepens with irritation. "Look, we're not going to kill you if you're innocent. And we didn't kill Joane. So stop moving. We're about to find you some food."

"Starve me! I'd rather you do that than chop me up like a butcher! Does this sick, twisted way of treating other people make you feel better about yourselves?"

Sevyn rests Jared on the ground and sets their foot on his back. "If you roll away, I'm going to drag your ass back here. We're all staying together and making it through this unless you attempt to kill someone else."

"How am I supposed to kill someone from here? My life is in your hands." Jared keeps going on and on.

"Could we wrap some bandages around his mouth?" Lian mutters.

Eric's jaw clenches as he takes out the bandages Sevyn brought. Much to Jared's wiggling protest, Eric manages to tie a few feet of the non-stick bandages around Jared's head. His muffled protests continue despite his covered mouth. At least his words sting less now.

"Now I feel like I'm missing out on the dress code," Sevyn comments. The rest of us look at each other, noticing that Sevyn's the only one not wearing bandages.

"Wait, was that humor... what you just said?" I ask, happy to cling to any semblance of something uplifting.

Sevyn shakes their head with a slight smile. "Maybe I'm starting to see the end of this approaching. Don't expect many more quips from me."

"We have plenty of bandages," Daraja suggests.

Eric holds out the bandage roll.

Sevyn sighs as they take it. They unroll some, cut the bandages with their metal finger, and tie the strip around their head. "For solidarity."

I admit a slight smile. Based on the softened expressions of my friends, Sevyn lightened the mood somewhat.

"Now, let's handle our hunger. It'll take some time to cook, but..." Sevyn points at a bunch of leaves near the ground. "Here's what we're looking for from this area."

"What is it?" Lian asks, pinching one of the leaves.

"Sweet potato. We've got to clear off the leaves first to get beneath the surface." Sevyn uses their metal pinky to shear away the leaves, then brushes off the dirt. They hold up an orange sweet potato larger than their hand. "I had one of these yesterday. They're not bad once you get a fire going. And they're probably the best thing we have in this dome to stave off hunger."

As we find more sweet potatoes in the ground, morale lifts. We grab enough for everyone to have two, and based on the leaves, there are more still in the ground. We carry our haul of sweet potatoes as we seek out strawberries, black walnuts, and other edible plants. By the time we return to our campsite, we have a decent amount to eat.

Sevyn creates the fire and uses one of their shoulder plates as a makeshift pan to cook with. Meanwhile, the berries are available to eat. There isn't much conversation, but at least it doesn't feel as tense as it did earlier.

We have at least a whole twenty-four hours ahead of us. Likely more, since the sun was rising when we encountered Flutura and Jared. I want the time to elapse faster.

Chapter 30

Analisa rolls a strawberry in her cupped hands. "You know, if we were outside, I'd not eat this in a heartbeat around you, Cai. I miss choices."

It's lunchtime now. We've got the sun over our heads and more plants to eat. We've been taking turns sleeping since breakfast.

Now that we're all awake, the forest traps me in a daze. The branches rustle in the wind. The still trunks provide a sense of comfort that I can't stop questioning. My muscles feel uncomfortable moving. If I can become as still as the trees, perhaps I'll feel safer.

It's only the fifth day. If only I could've woken up to this being the sixth day. I'm sure we have a few hours more than twenty-four left. Then we'll be free.

My mind searches for a more optimistic angle. "Well, if it seems like you don't have a lot of options, then make some new ones. For example, you could not eat the strawberry around me. Or you could eat the strawberry around me. Alternatively, I could feed you the strawberry. I could even climb up a tree to make sure you have some privacy while you eat the strawberry."

My effort sparks a smile on her face. "Really? You'd climb a tree?"

"Sure. I could also close my eyes and cover my ears. I did it plenty for Lian back in the cabin."

Lian pushes my shoulder. I get a smile out of him too though.

"I'd like the feeding me the strawberry option," Analisa says, "except I don't want to make you feed me a plant."

"Whatever you eat is fine with me," I remind. "It just grosses me out to eat plants myself."

Daraja raises a hand. After I drop a strawberry into Analisa's giggling mouth, I point at Daraja. They ask, "So, can you actually physically eat plants?"

"Yeah. I used to when I was little, but I hate the thought. It's like... I'm a little too similar to the plants for comfort."

"It's like a human being vegetarian because they feel bad eating animals," Analisa translates.

Daraja nods. "Yeah, Bridget—one of my alters— they're vegetarian for a similar reason. Makes it a little odd when they're fronting around other people at lunch or something. We're considering having all of us be vegetarian to make it less weird to jump back and forth. Being forced to survive by eating other living beings is a sick concept anyway. Living like a plant sounds more ideal."

"I do appreciate being able to live off of sunlight and water," I admit. "Some plants are carnivorous though. Similarly, I don't mind eating meat. The taste keeps bringing me back to it."

"Wait, your alien parent... are they carnivorous? Like, you told us to visualize a walking tree with some kind of hood. I honestly wasn't thinking carnivorous with all that," Daraja says.

"No, they stick to sunlight and water. My body is more like a human than an alien. I have a digestive system, but I don't think my alien parent has a way to absorb or process anything that isn't liquid."

"Oh good." Daraja's arms flinch. "Sorry, I don't mean to be like—I mean, it'd be fine if they ate meat. I was just kind of shocked at the idea of a giant tree that could eat people."

"Don't be rude to Cai's parents, Daraja." Eric tosses a berry into his mouth, an amused smile forming.

"I'm not trying to, I swear!" They cover their face, embarrassed. "Sorry, Cai."

"I know, don't worry about it," I say. "Eric's just trying to stir up trouble." He winks in acknowledgment.

I recall times when I wouldn't fully understand what was going on as a kid, but I still knew that my parents were treated poorly. With the small-town life they lead, most people they come across are people they know. Many are kind to them; some are not.

Regardless, my parents seem content with life in the T-Territory outskirts.

I'm more comfortable here in the city, with the abundance and closeness of people. After all this, I wonder if I'll feel the same way. I'll be known by many as the partial human, partial alien from Truth or Dare—assuming I make it out of this.

"Here." Sevyn begins passing out cooked sweet potatoes. "Careful with them—they're still hot."

"I'll take anything right now." Lian seizes a wrapped sweet potato.

As the potatoes make their way around, I grab one for Jared. Until we know whether he's the killer, we don't have a reason to hurt him. "I'll give this one to him."

Jared's lying a few feet outside our group circle. He hasn't sent any muffled shouts our way for a while. I balance the sweet potato on my arm while unwrapping the bandages over his mouth. Based on how damp they are, we should change those out anyway if he plans on yelling more.

My shoulders tense, ready for him to resume shouting. I keep myself distanced from his head in case he plans to bite me, but he doesn't object as I pull his shoulders upright. I lean him against a tree, hoping he can balance well enough on his own in the crook of the roots.

His sullen eyes meet my gaze. "You plan on feeding me, then. What, did you poison it?"

"It's from the ground. You saw us pick it. Do you eat the skin on these?"

"I was actually set to lie facing away from your little campsite, so you could've done anything to it when I wasn't looking." Jared swallows, staring at the sweet potato. "I don't care if the skin is on. I always thought it a waste to throw it away."

"Okay. Good to know." I hold out one end of the sweet potato in front of Jared's mouth.

He sighs through his nose. "You really don't eat vegetables, do you?"

Hearing him say that makes my skin shiver. I know he was sitting nearby, so he probably heard that conversation. Still. "No. Am I feeding it to you wrong?"

"At least let me bite out of the middle first. It's tougher near the end," Jared explains.

I turn the sweet potato, keeping it from falling out of its little gauze napkin. My other hand holds my elbow, trying to prevent my arm from tiring while Jared eats.

Between nibbles, he says, "So, am I correct in hearing that one of your parents is an alien similar to a tree?"

I stare at the ground, contemplating whether I should answer. "Why are you questioning me about this?"

"Honestly? I'm bored. At first, I was hoping to be quiet enough for you to forget about me and let me live. But if you're going to keep me wrapped up here, I'd rather be distracted. Especially by something interesting." Jared eats more of the sweet potato.

"I'm curious how a human and a plant-like being can crossbreed."

Maybe I want to practice telling people, or maybe he seems genuine enough that I don't think it would hurt to tell him. "It's a humanoid incubator. People can use it to lab-grow babies with the genetic traits they select. My parents wanted me to look mostly human, while still having some qualities from my alien parent."

The more I talk about my parents, the more I miss them. Maybe we could have a better relationship since I finally did what they wanted. After this, maybe they'd be happy regardless of how I present— with beige skin or green skin.

"Fascinating. I've never considered utilizing that kind of technology for a human and an alien pairing. Especially not an alien with such plant-like cellular qualities as your description," Jared says between bites. "If we ever get out of this alive, I'd appreciate it if you'd be willing to participate in a study of mine. I document various types of trees, and I tend to conservation gardens. While an alien hybrid wouldn't be within my expertise, it would be fascinating to ask you some questions later when I can write down what you say."

I adjust my grip on the sweet potato. He's working through it quickly. I hope he doesn't bite me through the gauze. "Maybe. I don't think I'm all that fascinating though."

"Cai, you're plenty fascinating. You can absorb sunlight and translate that into energy. I'm curious about the differences in your skin cells in comparison to a human's. I just hope we both make it to the end of all this. Maybe I can figure things out then. I need something... some kind of thing to keep me going." He leans away from the sweet potato, slowly chewing his previous bite. "I'm done. You can go sit over there now."

He's only eaten half of the potato. The others are still working through theirs. "You sure you don't want more?"

"I'm sure." His eyes lower. "I can't."

I drop my arm, seeing that he's serious. I wrap the potato in the gauze and leave it beside Jared. "Let me know if you change your mind."

"Hey, Cai!" Analisa calls out, a happy lilt in her voice. "We started doing accusations."

I grin when I see Eric in Sevyn's suit. I rejoin the circle as Sevyn sits down in their boxers and a tank top. I ask, "Okay, who came up with this?"

Analisa points at a giggling Daraja.

"You know, it's a little tight around your shoulders, but it's not bad." Lian sets his chin on his hand, looking at Eric.

Eric runs his hand over the fabric. "It's more comfortable than it looks. I get how you can run in this now."

"Yep," Sevyn says. "I'm glad the stylists let me wear my own outfit on the first day. It's made specially by my tailor to look good and help me out in my line of work."

"As a metalsmith, right?" Analisa jokes.

"That's the only line of work you need to know." Sevyn holds up their hands, shrugging. "You said you wanted tame dares. How about this, Analisa, truth or dare?"

"Dare." Analisa leans forward, excited.

"You seem like someone who can do a decent accent. Choose your favorite and speak only in it for the next five minutes," Sevyn says.

A five-minute timer starts as Analisa contemplates the sky. She likes imitating various characters from shows; based on her favorites, I'm guessing she'll go with a Scottish or Italian accent.

"Ah, I think that is something I can do." She grins sheepishly at her Italian accent.

"I told you—" Lian points at her. "You watch too much of that cooking show!"

"Uh no, I watch just enough of that cooking show." Analisa puts her hands on her hips as her grin grows. "Lili, truth or dare?"

"Eh... I'm not sure I want you to give me a dare."

"Oh come on. It's not embarrassing. It's fun."

Lian raises an eyebrow at her. "Fine. Dare."

"You can't speak, except to repeat everything that's whispered into your ear for the next five minutes." Analisa bounces up from her seat and sits beside Lian. She cups a hand over his ear and mutters something.

He whacks her shoulder, but she giggles, whapping him back. He mutters, "Eric, your arms are so sexy." His ears redden while Analisa whispers something else. "Really, I want..." He whacks Analisa again. "I want to kiss you every time I lock eyes with you."

Eric hums, laughing with only a little shame. "Yeah? I could say the same for you."

Lian's mouth twists into a smile once he gets past the initial awkwardness.

"Wait, wait." Daraja gets up and whispers something on Lian's other side.

He glares at Daraja, his voice flat. "Daraja's fashion sense is so on point, they're even better at judging outfits than I am." After Daraja whispers something else, Lian rolls his eyes. "In fact, Daraja is always correct. Even if I disagree in the future, that's just me joking around."

The temptation to tell Lian to say something is strong, but I don't have any ideas. Fragments of thoughts flash through my head, dismissed as quickly as they appear.

"Cai, you seem a little neglected. Truth or dare?" Eric asks.

"I can't skip out on the trend," I say. "Dare, please."

"Oh? I dare you to serenade Analisa with the most romantic song you can think of."

I lean back as the embarrassment of what I'm about to do goes to my cheeks. A five-minute timer appears beside me.

"Woah, wait—do you turn bright green when you blush?" Daraja points at my face.

"Oh wow, you do!" Analisa laughs.

I cover my warm cheeks with my hands. "Yeah, that's my blood. It's green."

"Funny, that doesn't sound like singing to me." Eric's voice lilts.

The only romantic songs I know well enough are by Heka, so they're musical theater-style songs. I'm going to have to make do with the weak voice I've got. I kneel in front of Analisa and start singing Heka's "Accidental but True."

She giggles, recognizing the song from the playlist I made for her.

I'm worried that I'm screeching even with the pitches lowered, but Analisa's grinning. I lean into it, circling around her and acting like I'm a hopeless romantic in a musical. The others cheer when I encourage Analisa to her feet. She dances with me, holding my shoulders and letting me spin her at the sustained note near the end. "And while it might have started as accidental, I promise to you, my feelings are true."

She holds my cheek, indicating that she wants a kiss. Her round, reddened cheeks are so cute, especially when she smiles like this. "May I?" At my nod, she pulls my neck closer and kisses me. The rush of having done something so silly as singing mixes with the adrenaline accumulated from the past few days. There's a vivacious spark in our shared touch. Her hands are on my neck; my arms are around her back. Our breaths merge like we can't pull ourselves apart.

"You all make me feel so single." Daraja's exasperated voice compels Analisa and me to sit back down. "Sevyn, you're not dating anyone, are you?"

"I'm married to my two partners," Sevyn says.

"Wait. You managed to get two partners?" Daraja holds their forehead. "I can't even get one! How'd you find two?"

"We were lucky to find each other. M and I grew up together. The two of us met W in our teenage years on my first trip to Tribu Amalricus."

"Hold up—on your first trip here? Where are you even from?"

"Nice try."

"Come on, I'm just curious."

"I know. But that's enough about me. How about—"

"They're watching." Jared shudders.

We all turn to look at him. His wide, frantic eyes dart across the forest. I forgot to put new bandages over his mouth. But what is he talking about? I don't see anyone around but the seven of us.

"Who?" Daraja asks.

Sevyn stands, whipping their head around. "Jared, do you know something we don't?"

"I thought you six had to be the killers. But if they're still around..." Jared scoots away from the tree, slamming his side into the ground with a groan. He wiggles up against the tree trunk.

"You saw who was at the riverbank, Jared. Unless there's more than the twelve of us who came in, then—"

"I thought you realized it by now. The arena... No,

you wouldn't believe me." Jared's voice trembles. "I'm gonna die here. We have to go back to the cabin."

"The cabin might not have aired out yet. We should wait at least another few hours in case—"

"No, you don't understand. The cabin is the safest place. You'll die by sunrise if you stay in the forest tonight."

"Hold on. We stayed in the forest last night. You said you did too," Daraja notes. "Why was it safe then and not now?"

"Because tonight is the last night. If they're still around, then they'll feed... They'll really... They'll use everything they have to kill us before five p.m. tomorrow." Jared whimpers. "Please, drop me off in the cabin. I don't care what you all do. I'll stay locked in my room. Just let me go, please."

"Not a chance," Eric says. "Not until you explain who's watching."

"They're all watching." Jared looks at the sky. The Truth or Dare audience? They can't enter the dome as much as we can't leave it. He looks up with a gasp, like he's seeing some revelation. The sight sends a shiver down my back.

He coughs, hacking up red spittle. A sharp, brown branch worms out of his chest, dripping with blood. He slumps forward, collapsing onto the ground with the rest of the branch sticking out of the back of the tarp. His body twitches, screaming as the reddened wood twists through him. The branch connects to the tree he was leaning against.

We bolt to our feet, snatching our limited weapons.

"The cabin's sounding pretty good right now." Analisa's whisper jumps up a terrified octave.

The tree trunk beside Jared creaks. Roots crash out of the dirt, coiling around Jared's writhing body. More branches shoot toward the ground, wrapping around his limbs. The trunk cracks and pops, the rind splintering open. The rings of bark inside the tree drip with red sap.

Seeing the movement is like a haunting memory. The tree moves like Kiran does. It looks like it could be family. But it couldn't be—Kiran wouldn't hurt anyone.

The tree's offshoots slice through Jared's screaming body. Roots lash through his neck. Stretching branches yank his arm out of its socket. Blood sprays from his shoulder as his limb is dragged into the trunk. Red drips onto the roots as the undulating bark smashes his arm.

"Cabin." Sevyn snatches our food and supplies. They shove my shoulder. "Run."

Chapter 31

We dash through the forest. My bare feet trample over roots. Dread clips my heels, propelling me forward. I stay behind Daraja since they're carrying Analisa. Conscious of my bare legs, I grip my new knife higher than before as I constantly move my head. Eric and Lian run in front.

I throw my gaze over my shoulder. Sevyn was staying behind to help Jared. But since they're sprinting after us without him, I doubt it ended well.

Every harsh breath passes through me like a shockwave. The only ones left are the six of us. A tree stabbed Jared and ate his arm. How many of the trees here can do that? The ones around us aren't behaving oddly. Every hum of leaves rustling in the wind sets me further on edge.

"Almost there!" Lian calls out. The side of the cabin is in sight.

We veer toward the front. I hear Eric exclaim, but I

don't register why until I pass the orange hair. Flutura's disfigured, dismembered body is strewn about where the berry bushes were.

Lian hesitates by the porch. I yank on his arm, pulling him up the steps. Sevyn dashes in front of us, alert and ready to defend as we barge through the sliding front door. No one appears to be inside. Joane's blood stains the couch cushions in the living room. The kitchen tiles by the living room edge still contain the faded remains of Solana's blood. We dash past the discolored wood in the hallway where Ever was killed.

Sevyn dives into a bedroom at the end of the hall. We all follow. As soon as we're in the room, I slam the door shut and lock it. We scour the room, inspecting under the bed, inside the closet, and even in the drawers. The closet clothing is predominantly red. We're in Brandon's room.

After Sevyn shoves some of Brandon's clothes into the cracks around the door, we push furniture in front of the door and window. We had time to prepare a bedroom before, but now we're trapping ourselves in one with very little preparation. It's only us, the furniture, Brandon's clothing, the sticks and knife we carried, the food and gauze, and Sevyn's shoulder plates.

Eric leans against the wall, keeping himself upright while catching his breath. "Who's to say they won't chase us out again?"

"This time, you have me in here." Sevyn uses their metal pinky finger to loosen some of the screws in the bedside table. "Take out all the drawers. We'll want the metal in them. The long parts where the wheels are. If we nail those into a grid over the window, then we can partially open the window if they try using gas again."

I shimmy out the drawers with Lian. They do have long pieces of metal glued to their sides.

"Okay, but what if they start a fire or something?" Daraja asks.

"We'll deal with all this one problem at a time. We've gotten this far. We'll make it through," Sevyn insists. They wedge their pinky between the wooden drawers and the metal. I sit with one of the drawers and try to emulate Sevyn's movement with my knife. "Careful, Cai."

"I know," I assure with a little more harshness than I mean. I don't work as quickly as Sevyn, but a shocked relief explodes in my chest when I pry off part of the metal.

Soon we've got sixteen metal pieces. Sevyn nails them over part of the window in a secure grid. They create a wood covering system like the one we had for the window in our previous room. "Now we'll be able to react quickly enough if someone breaks the window open. Hopefully."

The absence of hostile movement and noise should relieve me. I still don't feel like I can sit down. It's only us in here, but I thought it was only us out there too.

Now that I think about it, I didn't see what happened when we started running. "Is Jared...?"

"He's dead." Sevyn sighs through their nose. "Every set of branches I sliced through were replaced with more. The tree snapped his neck before the trunk dragged him inside."

"What?" Daraja's eyes widen. Their feet stagger until they lean against the wall. "Nah, you're not telling me those trees are actually... Were they the killers the whole time?"

"With the way Jared was acting, I'm not so sure," Sevyn considers. "But regardless, the trees are now a threat."

"But no one else is left in the game." Analisa's eyebrows pinch. "What else could be causing all this?"

Eric holds up his slashed hand. "There was a person involved in this. I don't know if they're dead now, but I swear I saw a hand outside the window. It wasn't a branch."

"I saw a person fleeing from your window," Sevyn confirms. "Unfortunately, I don't think there is a way for us to know who, or if the person is working with the trees."

"Working with the trees?" Lian rubs his forehead. "I hate thinking like this all day, every day. Why is nothing simple anymore? This was supposed to be a game."

Eric hugs Lian, gently petting his hair. "It's just one more day. We'll be out of this soon."

"No, wait—I know we don't want to think about it, but I want to unpack this." Daraja's hands swirl around each other. "We're trapped in a room again.

According to Jared, this is the safest place from whoever's in the forest. According to Flutura, Jared is the killer. But he got killed by a tree. So... what's going on?"

"Brandon." A thought in me resurfaces. "Why did you choose Brandon's room, Sevyn?"

"He was the first victim. Considering all the rooms we could've gone into, I was hoping that, if the killer were to set traps for us, Brandon's room would be neglected by now," Sevyn says.

"But... they didn't neglect him." I recall the bodies by the river. "Brandon wasn't dismembered when he died. His body was practically untouched. But earlier, when we found the sweet potatoes, he was cut up. I didn't see his left arm anywhere."

"Yes. I noticed that as well." Their gaze lands on the floor.

"I'm sorry, what?" Daraja asks. "You're saying someone—or something—cut Brandon's body after he was already dead, and took his arm somewhere? And you're only bringing this up now?"

"I didn't know what it meant, and I wanted to find everyone food to maintain our morale," Sevyn says.

"I got lost in Jared's words," I admit.

"Same here," Eric adds.

"Alright, next time, full disclosure if you notice something suspicious," Analisa clarifies. "I don't care if you think it'll drive me insane. I want to know. I maybe would've objected to going into Brandon's room if I knew his arm was missing earlier."

"Any of the rooms could be bad though." Lian

shrugs. "We could've chosen any of them. Sure, our preference would be Cai's room since all our stuff is in there. But if I were the killer, I'd make all the rooms unusable."

"For whatever reason, I think Jared's right about the cabin being the safest place." Daraja holds up their arms. "Yeah, I know, I know. I'm skeptical of him. But if there's more than one killer—cause of death, or whatever—it doesn't mean they're working together. So if he believed that getting to the cabin was best for his survival, I kind of want to believe that."

"He could've been wrong, even if he believed it," Eric notes.

"Regardless, we know that the forest is danger-ous. I don't know if Jared knew about the trees, but he seemed to believe that he would die there," Sevyn says. "I've searched the entire dome. There isn't a space that isn't forest except this cabin. I've considered camping out by the edge of the dome, but I don't know how we would be any safer there than by the river."

"So, we have to stay here on a hunch that we're safest here." Lian's eyebrows scrunch. "Who could've moved Flutura back to the cabin? Did the trees do it?"

Confusion and questions surface in my mind. We have more information now, but I still can't piece anything together. Carnivorous trees? An extra player? Maybe some audience vote we don't know about changed the rules. But all the players should be notified when an audience vote happens. Were the rules of Truth or Dare changed without anyone telling us?

My skin thrums with electric distress. My heartbeat won't slow down. We're all still standing, like we're anticipating the need to move soon. Daylight streams through the window, but the light is no assurance now. Two deaths have happened during the daytime today.

"I'm glad I picked extra food. Unfortunately, we'll have to ration this." Sevyn gestures to the lingering produce. "It won't be ideal, but we have one more night. They'll release us at five p.m. tomorrow."

"The robot escorts will retrieve us from wherever we are in the dome." Analisa runs her fingers through her uncombed hair. "The robots break up fights after five p.m., so they'll protect us."

"Um." Lian holds a red shirt over his chest. "Maybe it's not in good taste, and someone stop me if so, but Brandon's stuff might be big enough for most of us. I'm kind of tired of the bandages. Even if the clothes are contaminated, we should be able to go to the hospital tomorrow, right?"

"I'm up for the risk." Daraja considers a shirt and pulls it on. The large sleeves dangle off their shoulders.

We each find clothing for us in the open closet. My stomach feels less tight in a t-shirt and shorts. The embarrassing factor of wearing revealing clothing shouldn't be one of my main priorities. Still, I'd rather not worry about absentmindedly tightening the bandages around my waist every so often.

After Eric gives Sevyn's clothing back, we're all dressed more comfortably. It feels awkward to sit without wearing underwear, but I'm glad for the shorts.

Lian pinches his forehead. For some reason, he looks less stressed and more irritated. "I don't want to be rude, but is there a shirt in here that doesn't have red on it?"

I peek at the closet. "Not that I saw. Why?" If the red reminds him too much of blood, I don't blame him.

"Cai, the red clashes with your skin. You look like a walking winter holiday card," Lian explains.

Eric laughs as he hugs Lian from behind. "I love how you can refocus on the brighter side so quickly."

"He's just bad at focusing on anything serious." Analisa pinches Lian's nose. He bats her hand away.

I place my green hand over the red fabric. I hold back a laugh, realizing that Lian's right. "Oh wow. The color combination does look cursed. I'm going to need to take you up on the yellow outfit after all this, Lian."

"And of course, Cai's similar." Analisa takes my hand, swinging my arm gently. Her smile falters. "You know, I never would've applied to this if I knew what I know now. But if we manage to make it out of this, I hope everything works out okay."

I tilt my head, trying to encourage her to look at my face. "Hey. There's one more day left. We make it through this, and you'll have enough money to get treatment for your father. Then we can all forget about this."

"Forget the bad things, you mean," Eric corrects. "I don't want to forget you all."

"Yeah, none of you are ghosting me after this. I will be demanding those game nights." Daraja points at me as they plop on the floor.

My heart still feels like it's running laps around the room, but I find the motivation to sit beside them. "Right. No ghosting allowed. That includes you, Sevyn. You get to be part of the game nights too."

"Don't you think I'm a little old?" Sevyn leans against the bed.

"Nah. You make it through this, then you're allowed in the cool kids club," Daraja encourages.

"I hope I never feel too old for games." Eric leans back on his arms.

Sevyn laughs. "Truth or Dare might be enough gaming for me for the rest of my life."

"Oh yeah, good point," Analisa muses. "I might have to quit watching the game shows after this. What will I do with all my free time?"

"Do you think they'll go right into the next group of candidates?" Lian asks. "Truth or Dare is a bi-weekly thing during autumn, right?"

Daraja shakes their head. "If I were in that batch, I'd bail. Be like, 'Nope, not touching that show.'"

"Unless it inspires a whole group of killers. Truth or Dare might turn into a serial killer's tournament," Eric considers.

Lian shakes his head with a scowl. "I don't want to think about that right now."

"Fair enough. What restaurant do you want to go to on Saturday evening?" Eric asks. "I know you said Indian food. Do you have something in mind, or do you want me to choose?"

"I've got a couple of ideas. There's also a frozen yogurt shop near my favorite place, so if the food is too hot, the yogurt might help."

How easily my brain pivots with the conversation. After five p.m. tomorrow, we won't have to jump between dark and light conversations. We can keep to the happier topics.

Chapter 32

Sleep is elusive. I've been slipping in and out of a daze. My eyes stay closed in hopes of achieving at least a light sleep state. If I can manage to regain some energy, I might trick my body into staying awake tonight. If there is another killer around, I need to prepare to face them.

My head feels stuffed full of cotton gauze while I listen to my friends talk during their meal. Their voices are comforting, like a gentle blanket. Any movement that's loud enough sets me back into being too alert to sleep.

Even when I'm definitely awake, I keep my eyes closed so I don't have to monitor my expressions. It's exhausting how much I've tried maintaining positive and engaging body language. My muscles are so drained of energy and emotional care. I want the constant attention on my behavior to be over. A lack of alone time mixed with cameras everywhere makes my skin buzz with anxiety.

Once I'm determined to remain semi-awake, I tap Analisa's leg. With her permission, I set my head in her lap. Her hands stroke my hair while she continues with the conversation.

She's always so careful with me. Her gentle fingers avoid the tangled knots in my hair. My straight hair hasn't given me a lot of trouble over the years. But after five days of no showers and managing my hair with a bandage ponytail, it's gotten messy. I'm glad that Analisa's here.

"Cai does seem like a cat right now," Daraja notes. The mentioning of my name refocuses me on the conversation.

"You know, her full name is Caitlee. So if you take out a few letters, it'll spell cat," Analisa says.

"Huh. New conspiracy theory unlocked: Cai is actually a cat."

I raise a hand and bat Analisa's pink hair like it's a tassel. She giggles, knowing I'm awake enough to be listening.

"Hold on, you say Cai like 'ki,' but then you say the Cai in Caitlee like 'kay?'" Eric asks.

"Yeah," Analisa says. "Otherwise it sounds like 'kite-lee.' She doesn't fly around. She's the most rooted person I know, in the best way."

"Then why not call her 'Kay?'"

I imitate a cat meow and kick Eric's arm.

"Okay, alright. I don't have anything against Cai."

"You naturally short-named people don't get the way nicknames work, huh?" Daraja asks.

Eric raises an eyebrow. "Do you even have one?"

"My brother calls me Raja," Daraja says proudly. "Also, I think you know by now that I've got more names than that."

"Oh yeah. You should use them when you next order coffee," Lian suggests.

"Wow, I can actually order coffee from a café after all this." Daraja laughs. "I didn't think about that. Having spare money for a while would be nice."

As I shift my position a bit, my eyes land on the window. Shock ripples through my skin at the lack of daylight. I sit up. "Is it night already?"

"Oh." Analisa frowns at the window. I wish I hadn't said anything. "Yeah, it is."

"It's our last night stuck in this game. In less than twenty-four hours, we'll be outside," Sevyn reminds.

"How long has it been dark?" I ask.

"It's been several hours." Sevyn shifts their sitting position with a sigh. "I would guess that it's at least past two a.m. by now."

I'm glad it's been that long already, but the alarmed tremor beneath my skin won't vanish until the sun rises.

"One last night. That's all." Analisa's tone sounds a little too flat to be convincingly hopeful.

Gravity pulls on my bones, making it harder for me to act awake. I press against the floor, yawning against the back of my hand. I'm used to a comfort corner in my room, but this hardwood floor is what I have for now. It creaks beneath my shifting arms.

Sevyn's head snaps toward me, startling me. I ask, "What is it?"

"Cai, could you pass me a few berries?" Sevyn asks, gesturing for me to get up.

I blink between them and the berries sitting on the table a few feet away. As odd as the request is, their urgent tone compels me to stand and grab the berries. "How many do you want?"

Sevyn's already standing where I was, pacing over the creaky part of the floor. "A strawberry and a couple of the blueberries, please."

I stare at them, but I don't voice my questions yet.

They rub their beard, then sit where they were before. They hold out their hand for the berries. "Thanks."

I drop the fruit in their hands, waiting for them to explain. They start eating the strawberry.

"Nuh uh." Daraja points at Sevyn. "Explain."

"I don't know what it means. I don't want to worry any of you when there's nothing we can do about it." Sevyn tosses a blueberry into their mouth.

"I still want to know. Is there something wrong with the floor? Is it going to cave in?"

Sevyn sets their chin on their folded hands. "There might be a few loose floorboards there."

I tip my head at Sevyn, staring at them incredulously. "That sounds like something we should deal with."

"It could be benign. Or there could be something

under there that we should leave untouched," Sevyn says. "Perhaps covering the boards with the bedside table would be best."

"Or there might be a homemade bomb in there we should know about." Daraja throws up their arms.

"A bomb that could go off if we open the floorboards," Eric considers.

"So, we can't tell whether it's better to open it or leave it," Lian concludes.

"I'm with Daraja. If we're trapped in this room, knowing more about it is better than less," Analisa says.

"For all we know, the..." Eric pauses.

The killer could be beneath this room. This mysterious killer that we're assuming is a person. Someone who shouldn't exist. We're all the remaining players in this arena. But Jared seemed worried about something besides the trees, and Flutura's body was moved to the berry bush. It's possible that the trees could be our only threat now. Yet, I still feel like there's more we don't know.

"It's going to bother me all night if we don't at least check," Daraja says. "It might not be anything."

I stare at the spot I was lying on. It disturbs me to think that anything could've been there. There could've been someone's ear pressed against the boards. There could be tree roots reaching for us beneath the wood. I could've been stabbed from inside the ground.

Everyone grabs what little weapon choices we have left. I take the knife and silently volunteer to help lift the boards. Sevyn relents, ripping one of the drawer sliders from the window grid and using it to pry up the edge of the board. Several pieces of wood lift as part of a large plank. Lian points a flashlight into the gaping hole in the floor. It's wide enough of an entrance to fit a couple of people. There's a dusty metal ladder leading down eight steps to a dirt floor.

"A basement?" Lian mutters. Analisa slaps a hand over his mouth.

We peer into the dark abyss. As Lian shines the light around, it looks more and more like a little dirt basement. There's a couch, a rug, a thrumming cooler, an unlit lamp, and other decorations that make it sort of... homey.

Players in Truth or Dare have discovered stuff underground before, like tunnels leading to different parts of the dome. It made for fun pranks that involved sneaking up on people.

We're beyond the point of Truth or Dare now. This basement could've been created for the original game, but it could now be used by an unknown threat.

I don't see anyone inside. There don't appear to be any moving roots either. But I also can't see all the dirt walls from where I'm sitting. The basement extends beyond what I can see.

"Do we go in?" Daraja asks.

Something tells me we shouldn't. I don't know what it is—the dark, the unknown, the leaving of what we think is safe. But we're down to less than twenty-four hours until we have to leave. "Now that we know what it is, maybe we should close it and cover it like Sevyn said."

"Yeah, if it were normal Truth or Dare, I'd be curious if there are drinks in that cooler. But now..." Analisa shakes her head. "Let's close it."

Daraja nods. "Yeah, let's do it."

Sevyn lifts the floorboard, passing it to us to stabilize it. As Lian reaches for it, he leans too far forward. He yelps as he slips over the edge. He smacks his head against the floorboard and falls into the basement.

"Lili!" Analisa squeals.

He groans at the bottom of the ladder. He picks up the flashlight, panning it around the room right away. "Ack, I'm fine. Sorry. Good news, I don't think anyone's in here. Although... I think there's a tunnel. I can't see the end of it."

"Climb back up already!" Analisa hisses.

We set the heavy floorboard to the side again as Lian steps up the ladder. Eric reaches down a hand to help.

A flat sheet of brassy metal slides out from beneath the floorboards, patching the gap between us and Lian. Our hands spring forward, pounding on the unrelenting metal that traps Lian in the basement. Analisa screams. Eric's practically losing his mind trying to beat through the barrier. My fingers search for any weak spots in the metal, particularly by the rough edge of the floorboards. It's like the metal suctioned itself to the wood. Where did this come from?

"I'm okay!" Lian's voice cuts through, calming us down enough so we can listen for his muffled voice. "Well, I'm glad I held the flashlight."

His voice sounds shaky, but he doesn't sound more alarmed than I would be in there. In fact, he's probably calmer. My locked elbows don't prevent my arms from trembling.

"Lian, listen. Make sure the room is clear," Sevyn calls out as they snatch the metal drawer slider they took from the window grid. After struggling to press it between the floorboards and the metal barrier, they switch to using their metal pinky. "Do you see anyone else there?"

"N—no." Lian's voice is shaky. "I've got the lamp on now. At least that works. Um, and the fridge does have drinks. In case that's good to know, Ana."

Analisa rubs her wrists over her sobbing eyes. I don't blame her. The barrier blocking our access to Lian and the basement is distressing enough. What it might mean... I can't imagine it being good.

"Maybe it's just some self-defense system?" Daraja asks, their wide eyes twitching. "Something the cabin automatically does?"

"I mean, there's a tunnel in here. I can't see where it ends, because it bends around the corner some ways down," Lian says.

"No. Stay put. We'll get you out," Sevyn insists while still trying to pry the metal apart from the wood floor. They mutter, "I'll need something to heat this to weaken it. If we can warp the metal, we can use something stronger to bend it apart."

"We left our lighters in the other room." Eric tugs on his hair, rocking himself on his knees.

"Candle wax might be enough to warp this, as long as we keep it heated," Sevyn says. "I'll retrieve the lighters from Cai's bedroom and find whatever durable material I can to use as a saw. Keep him talking, and don't let him venture down that tunnel on his own. Keep the door locked until I come back." They stand up, sniffing the air with a scowl. They mutter a string of expletives as they approach the door.

Analisa coughs, interrupting her sobs. The intense smell hits me too: smoke. At the realization, Eric rams his forearms into the metal. Over and over. The barrier doesn't give.

Sevyn hovers the back of their hand over the doorknob. They recoil. "Someone's set a fire in the cabin. It's in the hallway."

Lian screams. A ripple of pain reaches down my throat, threatening to pull bile back up with it.

"Lili!" Analisa shrieks as she batters her walking stick into the metal covering the floor.

"Frick—sorry! A giant spider fell on my arm. Seriously, the thing had to have been like two inches big," Lian calls out. "I think it bit me!"

Analisa laughs, relieved through her tears. She coughs while leaning on her walking stick. It hasn't made a dent in the metal. Eric leans over his shaking, bleeding hands, his mouth trembling. Daraja stares at the floor, their head in their hands.

My heart batters against my ribcage while Eric's

arms clash with the metal. We have to get Lian out. I catch myself sniffling. My eyes sting, and the feeling is barely relieved by my tears. My throat tickles, and once I start coughing, I can't stop.

Sevyn bends several of the metal grid pieces by the window. They slam open the glass. "Everyone outside! I'll work to get Lian out."

Analisa shakes her head. I won't leave him either —not while we still have time to rescue him.

A blaze overtakes the door. Fire shoots across the wooden walls. Orange engulfs the world around me. Flashes of heat sear my skin. I can't tell if I'm screaming or if that's someone else.

Sevyn throws me out the window. I land beside Daraja, who screeches while rolling on the dirt. Fire chars their shorts.

Analisa shrieks and kicks, her cries ripping out my heart. Sevyn tosses her out the window. When she tries to crawl back inside, Daraja tackles her, shouting, "You can't go back in there! The whole thing is on fire!"

Looking up, I see the dense, dark smoke billowing into the night sky. It's not just our room burning. Flames engulf the entire cabin. The glowing walls outshine the simulated stars above.

I tackle Analisa too. She claws the ground, trapped in her own world of anguish. Her throat hurtles screams at the window.

Sevyn is pitched out the window next. They cough and pat off their charred suit, then launch themself back inside with muttered profanity.

My heart lurches. It's real now. We could lose Lian, buried in the cabin. Sevyn and Eric might not come back out. If I don't keep Analisa in place, she might bury herself in there too.

Eric's growl of pain feels caught in his throat as he heaves himself through the window, cradling his red, blistering arms. Sevyn pushes him out and climbs out next. Lian isn't behind them.

Analisa shifts into a feral animal. When she kicks again, I slip up and she writhes out of my grip. Her skin is too sweaty to grip. Sevyn yanks her shoulders to the ground, slamming the breath out of her.

Eric launches to his feet, shouting Lian's name. Bubbling burns cover his arms. His left elbow looks ripped apart. He pleads with the air, "Lian! Lian, follow my voice!" He turns the corner around the cabin.

"The tunnel. Hopefully, he'll find a way out." Sevyn grunts as they stand. They shout, "Eric, stay with the group!"

Fire blows out the window. A layer of sweat stretches my skin like it's trying to melt me. I snatch Analisa's shoulders and drag her away from the searing heat.

Hopefully, the dirt around the cabin will deter the fire. But if it reaches enough of the shrubbery... this whole dome is composed of forest. Would Comedy and Tragedy let us burn with it?

Analisa stumbles to her feet, straining against her warped prosthetic leg. Her foot is melted at the bottom. Leaning on her walking stick, she wails into the night like Eric. I wrap her arm around my shoulder, helping her stay upright as she hobbles around the cabin. She keeps wanting to stumble faster.

"I've got her." Daraja kneels to let Analisa onto their back.

Analisa leans onto Daraja and pushes their shoulder, pointing and insisting. "That way, that way now. Lian! Where are you?"

My breaths feel tethered to the same hope Analisa's relying on. That tunnel has to lead somewhere. It can't be a dead end.

We circle around the front of the cabin. Jared's dismembered body lies outside the porch, where the berry bushes were. Flutura's body isn't there anymore. Wait, didn't Sevyn say the tree consumed Jared?

My voice joins the shouts for Lian. While listening for him, I cling to the voices that call out for him, making sure Sevyn and Eric are still okay. Daraja, Analisa, and I stay together. My hands grip my knife, ready to run to whoever needs it.

"Here. I'm here!" Lian's weakened voice sends shivers down my body.

"I found him! Back porch!" Eric shouts.

We run around the corner of the cabin, following Eric's delirious laugh.

"Your arms!" Lian's voice is closer now.

"I tried to break you out." Eric's voice cracks.

"In a fire? What were you thinking?"

By the time we see them around the cabin, they're hugging each other, crying more than laughing. The fire casts mysterious shadows through the night, but my eyes can't deny it—Lian is here, he's standing, he's okay.

My breaths become stronger again. An involuntary smile breaks out of me while Daraja kneels on the ground. Analisa stumbles, hopping off a little too soon. I catch her arm, making sure she can walk.

"Lili!" Analisa's arms reach for him like she's trying to propel her legs through the will in her hands.

He parts from the hug with Eric in time to catch Analisa. Even while holding him, she smacks his back and bounces between shouts in Hindi and English. "How could you put me through that, you clumsy butt!" She cries, squeezing his shoulders.

Even though Lian's expression reacts to the tightness of her hug, he doesn't try to pull away. "I'm sorry. I'll try not to separate from the group."

Now that I'm close enough, I see Lian's scrapes and bruises. I recognize the one across his forehead from when he ran into the floorboard. His arm has a swelling red wound. The other stuff looks like it's from his fall.

We're all not looking too great. The fire charred our clothes, and even some of our skin—especially Sevyn and Eric's arms. Anything on us that isn't burnt is dusty from the smoke. But all six of us are here. We're alive.

Daraja wraps their arms around Analisa and Lian. Eric quickly joins, and I do too. Sevyn has a pleased smile, even as their eyes dart across our surroundings.

Relief overwhelms my better judgment. Yeah, we're all sweaty and smell like a campfire. We're standing beside a burning cabin in the middle of the night. I still feel like we should be watching our backs better. But I want to pretend this sense of comfort doesn't come with any conditions for a few more seconds.

My neck shivers from a drip on it. It's not a tear.

We break out of the hug as a drizzle starts. In a few seconds, rain pours out of the sky. Hope rises in me as the cabin fire diminishes.

Daraja howls, pumping their fist in the air. It's a contagious feeling. Eric whoops, taking Lian's hand. Lian raises their clasped hands, laughing and cheering. Analisa practically screams at the sky in defiance. A scream rips through my own throat, fueling a fearless urge in my chest. Rain drips into my grinning mouth.

We've survived this long. Bring it.

Chapter 33

"Okay, I've already forgotten who I've done accusations for today. Maybe we should do a different party game." Daraja draws in the dirt by the camp-fire. The small fire is our only light since the cabin was doused a few hours ago.

A few minutes ago, Comedy and Tragedy intro-duced an audience vote to determine if they could activate a structure freeze on the cabin. I've never been close enough to a burned building to see one in person before. The idea is to reinforce the structure left from a burned building and to return the heated area to a normal temperature. Fortunately, people voted to have the structure freeze happen. Now the cabin radiates a chill.

With the technology in this arena, they could've rebuilt the cabin. But no. We're out here in our damp clothes, sitting by a fire in this clearing to avoid the cold cabin on one side and the potentially carnivorous trees on the other. Theoretically, Jared's body is still on the other side of the cabin. I haven't brought it up with Sevyn yet because I don't know what to think of it.

I pinch the edge of my red shirt. It's less damp than it was, at least. I hope we don't get sick from staying in the wet clothes. Still, I'm not tempted to dig for spare clothes in the cold wreckage yet. It's either stay in these clothes or use a lot of bandages to barely cover my body. I'd rather get sick from the rain than deal with that again. There's also the risk of the poisonous gas lingering on the clothes, slowly eroding my lungs. None of my options are ideal.

There's a bit of comfort in the silence. Sure, there are too many questions that I want answered. How did the cabin fire start? Why did the metal platform appear then? Did the trees orchestrate all this?

I'm so tired of serious questions that we can't answer. We keep theorizing about all this, and then something new changes everything. I want to settle into the boredom from sitting here for a bit. I miss pure boredom—a feeling absent of anxiety or fear.

As usual, none of us can sleep, even though our movements are clearly sluggish. Earlier, Sevyn wandered through the freezing cabin to find supplies like burn reliever, liquid bandages, and spare cloth. Eric sucks air through his teeth as he reapplies the reliever to his charred, trembling arms. Lian's red spider bite looks concerning too. And of course there's Analisa's warped prosthetic leg, the burns on Daraja's legs and arm, and a blistering burn on my leg. Lots of layers of injuries keep us from sleeping, as if we needed more reasons to stay awake before sunrise.

"If only the night could end faster." Analisa joins Daraja's dirt drawing with her muddy, warped walking stick.

"I wish we could dare Comedy and Tragedy to bring us some light. We got rain and a structure freeze." I lean my chin on my hands. "Although I can't tell though if that was to give us a chance or to keep the whole dome from burning down."

"I don't believe for a second that they're on our side." Eric grimaces as he shifts his sitting position. "They wouldn't have let this go on if they were."

"Legally, they're held to the audience vote," Analisa says. "If the audience wants us to stay in danger, Comedy and Tragedy can't do much about it. Their main roles are as commentators and figure-heads for the show. I imagine there was some finan-cial damage thing that let them get away with providing us with rain. I'm surprised there haven't been more audience votes though, even without as many accusations going around than a usual game. Maybe they don't know what to do with us because they're surprised by all this too. Or maybe they're trying to keep the audience from making things worse."

"I'm glad there aren't a lot of audience votes. Because yeah—the results of the ones we've gotten so far haven't been promising." Lian winces, his arm quivering as he bends forward. The spider bite looks pale in the campfire light. "I have seriously lost faith in people."

"You know, once we're out of here, they won't even remember all the stuff we went through." Daraja scoffs with an incredulous smile. "They'll probably make fun of us for the stupidest things. Like using the bathroom in our room."

"Or in the woods," Lian reminds.

"Or being naked in a river," Eric says.

"Followed by walking around in bandages around our crotches and chests?" I add.

"Remember when the thought of Lian and Cai having sex was the worst of our issues?" Analisa asks. I grimace, meeting Lian's mutual expression.

"Maybe that's all the thoughtless people will remember. But trust me, those who get it will remember you for so much more," Sevyn assures. "I don't know what you plan to do in the future, but winning a major game show and surviving a situation like this at the same time are quite the resume points."

"Oh great. I'll put, 'Survived a serial killer,' right at the top. Right above, 'Almost died before completing my bachelor's degree.'" Eric grins. "Special skills: persistence, lack of self-consciousness on camera, running from trees."

My eyes refocus on the sky. The soft, dark blue indicates an oncoming sunrise. "Think I have a chance at getting into Darilek University, Eric?"

"I think you've got the makings of a great essay response." Eric shrugs. "'Describe a time you overcame a challenge.' Yeah, I think you've got something for that."

I grin. "Good to know. I'll be writing those essays pretty soon."

"Ah, so it's your last year of high school, huh?" Eric asks. "Same with you two?"

Lian nods. "I'll have to look into Darilek University's chemistry program."

"Oh, it's stellar. You'd fit right in." Eric presses his shoulder against Lian's with a playful grin.

"I'm sure you're not speaking with a biased tone at all, whatsoever." Analisa's sarcastic tone fades. "I'm thinking of a physics degree. Maybe a minor in something related to fashion. I don't know what I'll do with it, but I like the subjects."

"Man, you're all going to school?" Daraja sighs. "I guess I could try for a degree. I'll have the money for it, at least. I don't even know what I'm interested in though."

"What kind of work would you want to do?" Eric asks.

"Is it bad if I say nothing?" Daraja cringes. "I mean, I like sports. But if I played, I'd be a spectacle for a while before getting injured and having to switch careers in my thirties or forties. I also like styling my hair, but I don't know if I can handle the pressure of being a hairstylist. Singing professionally could be neat, but I don't want to take the fun out of it. Running a business could be rewarding if I keep myself organized. I'm afraid whatever work I choose won't be engaging enough for all of my alters to stay interested in it. I haven't really let myself think of what we could do instead of entry-level service jobs."

Eric raises an eyebrow. "You could start by taking classes you're interested in. Starting that way can at least help you feel like your own person. I like the business classes for that reason. Then you can figure out how you want to spend your time from there. I also might need some members for a board of directors for whatever business I open in the future. I'm thinking something in the outer space business."

Daraja gapes. "Outer space? I'm in."

"Do you have any experience being on a board of directors?" Eric asks, squaring up in a professional stance.

Daraja's back straightens in response. "No, but if you'll see my references, I'm renowned for my persistence and working in a high-stress environment. As someone who's survived at least one serial killer, killer trees, a fire, my deepest secret being out, and social embarrassment that will follow me for the rest of my life—all in the span of six days—I can assure you that I will do everything in my effort to successfully guide your business."

Eric hums as he rubs his chin. "Take some classes and I'll consider it."

Daraja groans. "We'll see about that."

The sky is even lighter now. The trees beyond the dirt clearing are visible in the gray-blue atmosphere. It's like there are more trees than there were. They're like watchtowers warning that there's danger beyond the cabin. Did they actually grow taller? If their roots and branches can move, maybe their trunks can stretch in size.

We're not safe anywhere in this arena, really. "When it's bright enough out, should we investigate what started the fire?"

Sevyn sighs. "We could. I don't think it makes too much of a difference now. We'll likely be dealing with challenges until five p.m."

"Are we pretty much thinking there's someone else in here who wasn't part of us twelve?" Eric asks. "Because sure, the trees can move. And yeah, we know the trees can kill. But why did they only attack Jared? If the trees were the only danger, why didn't we die in the forest too?"

And why was Jared placed in front of the cabin like the rest of the bodies? I glance at Sevyn, hoping they bring it up. Given their attention to detail, I doubt they missed Jared's body out front.

"I don't know. I keep thinking this is all because Comedy and Tragedy are somehow bending the rules." Daraja shakes their head, their eyebrows pinching. "Maybe the trees are methodical? If someone is controlling the trees, or working with them, or whatever, why would they kill us one at a time, anyway? There's a whole forest that could've killed us all at once. Unless just that one tree can move. But what are the chances we would've stumbled into the only tree like that?"

"I don't know, and I kind of would rather not

know," Lian says. "I'm not sure how I'll watch the highlights after all this."

"Right." Analisa cringes. Her wrist wipes her creased forehead. "The ending ceremony has the players react to the most exciting moments in front of an audience."

"They wouldn't show the deaths as part of the highlights, would they?" Daraja asks, their hands messing with the braids over their shoulder.

My stomach feels queasy. I lean over, holding onto my elbows. "From an outside perspective, it's the most exciting part of the game. That and our ways of trying to survive. I'm not sure any of the truths or dares will make it in."

"That's sickening," Lian says.

After a pause, Sevyn stands. "If it would make you feel better, Cai, I'll investigate the cabin again. It should be less cold now, so I might stay inside for longer. I'll call out every thirty seconds to let you know I'm okay. You all stay here unless you need to do the bathroom buddy system."

"I hate the bathroom buddy system." Lian sets his forehead in his hands.

"What, you'd rather go off on your own, Lili?" Analisa pokes his leg with her walking stick.

"No, the buddy part's fine. I want to go back to normal bathroom usage after this. Legitimate stalls without cameras in them."

Sevyn shakes their head with a slight smile as they walk up the scorched back patio. The back doors don't automatically slide open anymore, so they carefully push through one side and step over the rubble inside.

"Any chance the fire was an accidental voltage thing?" Daraja asks.

"Maybe the killer accidentally left the oven on," Analisa suggests.

I meet her eyes, feeling like I shouldn't laugh at such an absurd idea. But it's hard to not burst out laughing when she does.

"You're both awful." Daraja admits a slight smile.

Sevyn calls out, saying they're alright. We keep talking until Sevyn interrupts again. We pause to listen, testing whether they're seriously going to keep doing it every thirty seconds. We collectively mutter a count to thirty, and we crack up each time we hear Sevyn call out their reassurance that they're okay.

We try not to giggle too loudly when Sevyn returns with their usual serious expression. Sevyn gestures from the back door. "Cai, Daraja, could you help me out? I found some more supplies, but I could use some help carrying them. Analisa, Lian, Eric, please watch the campsite."

I stand for the first time in hours. Aches ripple through my body as I stretch, preparing to walk. The burn on my left leg stings when my calf flexes. I push through the pain by focusing on each next step. I walk to the pile of spare fabric Sevyn found in the wreckage earlier. Following Sevyn's example, I tie a torn sleeve around my nose and mouth. Daraja does similarly as we climb the porch.

The cabin emits cold through the doorway like a chilling breath. My fingers flinch as I press on the freezing metal doorframe, making sure it doesn't collapse on me. The structure freeze should keep things in place, but my body is far too tense to feel assured. The chill from inside coats my skin. It's not the worst cold I've felt, but in shorts and short sleeves, a vicious shiver seizes my body as I step into the kitchen.

Parts of the room look untouched. Most of it is destroyed in some way or another. Sundered cabinets litter the ground, broken dishes in their wake. The electronic appliances look melted, their surrounding counterspace sparked with black.

"Damn." Daraja shakes their head, looking around with wide eyes. Their muffled voice mutters, "It looks even worse in the light. A lot of it collapsed, huh?"

"The roof is completely out in the pantry. Don't touch the walls," Sevyn warns.

My feet reach over fallen cabinets. Ash covers the tile floor to where I can't see Solana's blood stains anymore. It's similar with Joane's blood in the living room. We get to the front door. Are we going to have to see Jared's body again? Maybe now's the time to bring it up.

"Is the stuff out front?" Daraja asks.

"This supply run is a ruse. I have something concerning to show you—something I'm not sure what to do with. I don't think we should show the other three yet." Sevyn's jaw sets. Their eyes look... angry.

What could be this distressing at this point? I don't think Sevyn would react to Jared's body like this. If it's not about Jared, then part of me doesn't want to know. When I meet Daraja's concerned gaze, they give an uncertain shrug and nod.

We follow Sevyn out the front door. We step carefully over the front porch, and out front, taking the path to the berry bush stump.

My knees buckle when I realize what I'm seeing.

"No. Nuh-uh." Daraja's voice shakes.

I never should've looked. Shivers ripple across my skin, cutting through me as I step toward the dismembered body.

His head, with the gash from getting hit by the floorboard, sawed from the rest of his body. His broken glasses lying by his disjointed, pulled apart arms. His red shirt from Brandon's room, ripped apart by stab wounds. His delicate hand, stained with blood and berries. His brown eyes, staring blankly at the sky.

Lian.

Chapter 34

Sickness climbs my throat, leaving a foul taste in the back of my mouth. I tear off the fabric covering my face. Confusion and guilt swarm my stomach, turning my body into a miserable battlefield.

"What does that mean—what—really, what does that mean?" As Daraja's voice raises, Sevyn covers their mouth. Daraja crumples to the ground, scrambling free of Sevyn's warning grip. "No, you tell me. That's not real, yeah? It's a sick prank. Lian's over there. He's right over there, in the back, with Eric and Analisa. Whatever this is... it's not him. He's over there right now."

I want to believe it. That reality sounds so much better than what I suspect.

Maybe Daraja's right. This could all be a weird, sick dare. Or it's a big, organized joke. If there can be two Lians, surely there can be two of everyone else. That means no one's dead. They're probably hiding by the edge of the dome, moving around to make sure we don't discover their weird, dark joke.

But then why is Lian still here while the fake Lian is dead? Fake Lian. Which is real?

Seeing this might break Analisa. Given how Eric reacted when Lian was trapped in the basement, this might damage his psyche too. How would the Lian on the other side of the cabin react to this? Is he in on whatever all this is—a joke, or an actual serial killer messing with us?

The twisted emotions inside me consolidate into a darker, more aggressive form. If this is a killer messing with us, then whoever did this deserves so much worse.

If the Lian in the back isn't real, we're in danger. Analisa and Eric are in danger. And I'm not sure they'd have the heart to defend themselves from someone who looked like Lian.

I dash through the cabin. I pause in the kitchen doorway, letting my panting breaths catch up with me.

All three of them are still sitting where they were, talking. Eric and Analisa are okay.

I think.

If the Lian with the berries is the actual Lian we've been around for the past few days, then the switch to this Lian had to have happened when we were separated. For all I know, the Analisa and Eric we're looking at now could be fake.

"The thought occurred to me too," Sevyn mutters

beside me. They pick up and set down random objects in the living room. "But I was listening for signs of struggle. That should be Eric and Analisa as we know them."

If they see me looking at them, it will make them curious. I manage to stare at the ground. "Could this all be a sick joke the other players are doing to us? They're making duplicates of players and making them look dead, then running off to the edge of the dome?"

"Could it really be some big scare thing? That makes more sense to do on TV." Daraja rubs their reddened eyes.

"I hope that it's something so benign. But in case it isn't, you need to consider the possibility that the Lian out front is the one we were separated from in the basement. If that's the case, then the one in the back is an imposter," Sevyn says. "I don't know how, or why. I'm not sure whether he knows that he's an imposter. But regardless, we need to keep an eye on him. My main concern is keeping Analisa and Eric from finding out. And we don't want the imposter to know that we know about Lian's body in the front."

"Is it a shapeshifter?" Daraja asks. "Like, from myth or something?"

"I think technology is more likely the culprit," Sevyn says. "After all, the appearance I'm wearing is not my natural body. It could be something similar."

I look at them. "What?"

"I have a confidential job, Cai. Do you really think I'll show up to this show wearing my actual face, using my actual voice, and giving out my actual name?"

Daraja shudders. "Whose face are you wearing?"

"No, it's not like that. It's synthetic fiber, designed to be so similar to skin cells that it's practically the same texture and look."

"Is your hair even real?"

"It's a wig. The facial hair comes with the fake face." Sevyn shakes their head. "Look, what I'm saying is that if I had the technology to program my appearance with me, I could make my face look like Lian's. And Cai has demonstrated how well skin modifiers work—it's possible for technology to replicate someone's skin, down to the most faded freckles. I could even replicate Lian's voice with my voicebox. But my body shape and size would make it difficult for me to impersonate him."

"You're saying the person in the back could be someone wearing a replica of his face and skin?" I ask, the thought urging a new wave of sourness up my throat.

"Possibly. But this entire situation is far outside the boundaries of what I expected when walking into this." Sevyn shakes their head. "I don't know what's happening here."

"You're fairly close."

I whirl around at the voice.

"What's wrong? You look like you've seen a ghost." Joane smiles from the hallway. She pinches her flowy lilac dress, waving it playfully. There's not a scratch on her—no sign that she should be dead.

Her hair is even decorated in flowers, and she's got makeup on. It's like she's had time to dote on her appearance. "Truly, you're all so frozen. Perhaps I'm the one seeing ghosts."

"Are you the actual Joane, or a replica?" Sevyn asks.

"Oh, I'm not sure I need to tell you that." Joane giggles. "But you all look so confused. It makes me sad."

"It's just some game, right?" Daraja asks. "Lian's not really dead. None of you are."

"Oh, no, honey. The Lian you knew is most certainly dead. I cut him up myself." She moves some stray hair behind her ear as she smiles at the ceiling. "Sawing off the head was my favorite part. His body kept twitching, but don't worry. I think he lost consciousness when I cut through the spinal cord."

The knife in my hand shivers at my side. My body screams at me to move. To attack. To do something. My teeth chatter in my mouth, holding back the urge to release my wrath.

Sevyn's hand covers my arm. "Why did you kill him? Did you kill the others?"

"I didn't kill everyone." Joane shakes her head. "I had some help from Flutura, actually." A pang of astonishment hits my chest. She tips her head in response. "I thought that one was obvious from the earlier incident. Turns out, blackmail can only make a person do so much. You want to explain that part? I'm hogging all the spotlight."

"No, dear. You're doing quite well." Jared's voice

appears in the front doorway. He pushes open the broken door and leans against the wall beside it. "But it's true that Flutura did help us cover up our kills, and she was the one who took out Brandon and Ever."

"She was sloppy, leaving xir glasses like that. But even with her trying to sabotage everything, she died without anyone outwardly suspecting her." Joane scowls. "I told you we should've killed her sooner."

"You're right that she turned on us sooner than I thought. But gluing her mouth shut might have been too far."

Joane crosses her arms. "You know full well that she was going to tell someone that day if I didn't."

"Sorry, you're right, my dear." Jared looks at me with a smirk. "That's something you can learn from this, Cai. To have true control over someone, you must convince them that keeping their secrets is worth their cooperation. Make telling the truth so terrifying of a prospect that they would be willing to do anything else. Flutura's usefulness ran dry when she didn't have the stomach for this. And now, well... her stomach is ruptured."

"Oh, get this." Joane giggles. "Her big secret was that she once drove drunk and t-boned a car. It ruined the other driver's life, and their car hit another car, causing a few more accidents. Not only did Flutura cause five deaths, but one of those deaths was her own sister. Got it covered up and blamed on someone else so her family wouldn't find out, and so her career wouldn't get ruined." Joane shrugs. "But she's dead now, so her secret's out. If she had played along, she'd be one of the last of us left."

The story sounds familiar. Eric's story from our first day here. "Eric's cousin from the car accident. Was that—"

"Ding ding ding. Same incident." Jared points at me. "See, I knew you were clever. Don't worry. We won't kill you, Cai. You're far too interesting."

Sevyn tenses up. "What about the rest of us? Are we interesting enough for you?"

Jared and Joane share a frown. Jared tips his head back and forth as if deciding. "Well... Cai has plant-like characteristics. I want her to participate in a voluntary study with us after the game. Nothing to harm you, Cai. I just want to document your answers. You all... are less interesting."

I sense leverage. I try to still my shaking hand. "Could we make a deal, then?"

"Oh?" Joane smiles gleefully. "Go on."

"Please, don't kill anyone else here. And I'll partic-ipate in your study." I swallow. I can't throw up right now.

Jared chuckles. "And you'll just forgive us about Lian?"

I hesitate, unsure what would be best to say. Maybe the truth. "No, I won't. But I don't want you to kill anyone else here. I'll uphold my end of the bargain if you do the same."

Jared tosses a look at Joane as if asking for

permission. "She is very interesting. We have already given out a decent amount of feed."

"What do you mean by that?" I ask.

Joane squints at me like I'm stupid. Then her face brightens with a laugh. "Oh my... Jared, she didn't guess! She eats meat and has plant-based characteristics. We even gave her a clue with the tree—this is too sad."

"How are they supposed to know we were feeding them?" Jared lifts a hand, drawing my attention. "Cai, my absolute favorite trees to document are the carnivorous ones. Comedy and Tragedy must've taken that part of my admission video to heart because the forest is filled with them. They were dormant, harmless at first. From my past experiments, I've found that the trees like flesh best after it's decayed after a few days. Chopping up the flesh helps it decompose with ease. You saw that with the tree that ate my carbon copy. Although, we did program the tree to do it on its own, since we didn't want to spoil our involvement yet."

That's why the bodies were chopped up and decapitated. Why Brandon's arm went missing.

"The trees thrive best on bodies that have decomposed for about four days. Unfortunately, we didn't have that much time pass for the more recent ones, but some mildly-prepared food is better than none," Jared explains. "So we fed all the bodies to the trees an hour ago—except Lian's, of course. We wanted you to know that he's passed."

My blood heats again. "You killed people here to feed the trees?"

"You were right, Jared." Joane giggles. "This whole confession thing *is* therapeutic."

"Exactly!" Jared grins. "And now that it's on this record, we can't be held legally liable for any of the deaths on this show, or from before this show."

"Oh right, we have to state that part too, don't we?" Joane nods seriously. "How much detail do we have to do? Can we just say we killed people and be done?"

Jared shrugs. "I'm not sure. Elaborate, in case."

"Well, this wonderful man was using people as plant fertilizer long before I tagged along." Joane skips to Jared and links her fingers through his. "He almost got caught once though, so he contemplated clearing his name here on a game show while having fun in the process. He asked me out at the fancy restaurant I work at, and it wasn't too long before I realized he wanted me as a pawn. As in, kill me on the show to make him look more innocent to the remaining players. But by then, I wanted to help him with all this. I proved it by bringing him three fresh bodies and killing them in front of him. I think he knew pretty soon that I was better as a queen, so we adapted the plan. Did I cover everything? Are we legally free of all that now?"

Jared nods. "I think so. Wonderful explaining, my dove."

"Thank you!" Joane taps Jared's chest with a sly smile. "Recruiting Flutura was my idea, since I heard about the whole driving incident from a dinner conversation where I work. I do want to claim credit for that."

"As you should. I couldn't have done all this without you." Jared pecks a kiss on her cheek.

"Do we have a deal?" I ask, trying to refocus the conversation. My anxious breaths seethe through my teeth. "You let us all get out of this alive, and I do the study with you after all this is over?"

Joane purses her lips at Jared. "How much do you want that study?"

Jared's mouth warps as he tips his head. "It would be difficult to find another specimen like her."

"The trees are riled up now. We would have to protect all five of them, and ourselves," Joane adds.

"Six," I muster.

They look at me. Joane asks, "What?"

"All six of us. Assuming the fake Lian is innocent in all this, and sort of human."

Joane shares a look with Jared, then shrugs lightly. "Yes, he's innocent. A carbon copy, but innocent."

"How did you do that, anyhow?" Daraja points between the two of them. "And with Jared—how'd you do that? Are there more of you?"

"We don't need to explain that," Jared mutters.

"All you need to know is that the Lian out there can easily replace the Lian you lost. He has the same memories, body, behavior, and all that. So sure, we'd have to defend all six of you, and the two of us," Joane says.

"Unless that's not part of the deal," Jared

suggests. "We stay away from them, and if they survive the trees on their own, that's good for them."

They've already killed several of us. They know more about the trees and the arena than we do. Even if they aren't willing to protect us, we need to get them to stop trying to kill us. We only have safety as long as they think I'm worth changing their plans for.

"You said the only reason the tree attacked is because you programmed it," Sevyn notes. "If you don't get involved, we should be safe from the forest, should we not?"

"Ooh, good ears." Joane giggles as she tips her head on Jared's shoulder. "But we programmed the trees to be dormant until we feed them. Now that a decent amount of them have been fed portions of humans, they're hungry for more. That was to keep you all here so we could hunt you ourselves, but if you venture into the forest now, it's out of our hands."

They keep mentioning that they programmed the trees. Do they mean they can change the arena? If they can do it the same way Comedy and Tragedy do between games, then we might be able to shut off the carnivorous trees ourselves.

How much bargaining power do I have? I test it. "If I answer some of your questions about me now, will you answer some of our questions?"

"Ooh!" Jared's eyebrows shoot up. "A question for a question. What do you think, Joane?"

Her cold eyes narrow. "Okay. But first, the deal is on. Let's ask each other truths on whether we plan to honor the deal, just to be sure we both agree to what we're getting."

I nod. "Truth or dare, Joane?"

"Truth."

"Will you honor the deal to not attack or try to kill the six of us for the rest of our lives?" I ask.

She scowls as the timer pops up. "You said until the end of the game."

"Yeah, but it's safer to ask the truth this way."

She raises an eyebrow. "Fine. We won't attack or murder the six of you, in this game or beyond, provided that you don't turn back on your promise to participate in Jared's study after the game. Jared and I will also answer your questions about how to survive this game as fully and truthfully as we can. The only reason we'd annul any of this is if you turn back on your promise, or if any of you attack us unprovoked before the end of the game." The timer fizzles, indicating she's telling the truth. "Cai, truth or dare?"

I hate the idea of agreeing to complete peace. If Analisa or Eric find out that Lian was killed, I'm not sure I could stop them from attacking Joane or Jared. "Truth."

"Will you honor your deal to meet with us after the game to participate in our study—which won't hurt you physically or mentally—as well as not attack us unprovoked for the rest of this game, and answer our initial questions about your plantlike physiology both truthfully and fully?" Joane asks.

"As long as you don't attack us for the rest of our lives and answer my questions truthfully and fully. Then yes, I'll honor that deal," I say, trying not to leave a loophole for them. My timer fizzles away.

"Excellent. You can start, if you'd like," Joane says.

Chapter 35

I glance at Analisa, Eric, and Lian. I'd start to worry soon if I were them. I've got to make sure they don't see us during this question for a question deal. "Daraja, can you go out and let them know we're okay? Tell them Sevyn started talking with me about my aunt and you wanted to give us space for family talk."

Daraja stares at me with wide eyes. Having them here would be helpful for me to remember what Joane and Jared say. But I also don't want the three in the backyard to poke around and find that we're talking with two supposedly dead people.

Daraja tiptoes over the living room rubble, careful to glance between where they're stepping and the two killers by the front door. They make it to the back porch.

I push the debris by my feet, clearing a spot to sit. My legs adjust their sitting position, trying to avoid touching my bare skin to the cold floor. I'm careful to hold my knife so it doesn't cut my thigh. "If you want this deal to go smoothly, I'd stay out of Eric and Analisa's line of sight."

Joane laughs as she sits down, followed by Jared. "We can do that, but we're not the ones worried about being attacked. We've killed five of you already. Seven if you count ourselves."

They're confident considering it's theoretically two against six—unless it isn't. As Sevyn sits beside me, I ask, "Are you even the real Joane and Jared?"

"Is that your first question?" Jared asks.

I narrow my eyes. "Only if it's related to surviving the trees."

Jared nods. "Then yes, that's your first question. No, we are not the original Joane and Jared. Those two are elsewhere in this arena. We are mimicked versions of them. Carbon copies are a good way of thinking of it." He affectionately pulls Joane's shoulder. "And to show our good faith toward answering these questions, we'll tell you exactly what we are. Do you understand how the arena works, specifically with switching the format and makeup of the trees, cabin layout, and surroundings?"

I know of the imitation technology, but I want to hear their explanation. I shake my head.

Joane gapes. "Oh, but it's brilliant! You see, all the matter in this arena is made of an impressive technology where, whatever you program it to be, it essentially becomes it. Those sweet potatoes you ate? Not really sweet potatoes. But they served the same function and treated your body the same way sweet potatoes would. The forest and cabin are composed of this kind of matter, where the form can be changed to mimic whatever it's programmed to. It's how the arena can change in time for the next round of Truth or Dare a week later."

Sure, the arena technology imitates trees and water and dirt. But people?

"That same technology can copy people." I try to limit that to a statement rather than a question.

"Exactly!" Joane says.

"But how..." I trail off. That would be another question.

"Our turn." Jared leans forward. "What purpose does the scarring on your skin serve?"

Ah, right. I lied about the bark being scarring. If they feel like I'm not answering enough, they won't answer my future questions well enough. I pull down my shirt collar, showing some of the bark. "I said it was a scar to get out of talking about it, but it's not a defect. My alien parent speaks by moving their bark in such a way that it creates noise. It warbles." I demonstrate the sound.

Jared gasps. "That is amazing! I must... hold on." He pulls out a notebook from his jacket. "You said 'warbles.' Is that the term for it?"

"Yes. That's how my alien parent communicates."

"Fascinating, fascinating. Thank you." Jared scribbles in his notebook.

I don't know how many more questions he'll have, so I need to make mine count. I want confirmation on how to survive the end of the game. We should be fine if we stay by the cabin, but there's no telling whether Jared and Joane will change their minds about attacking us. If they do, I'll want to be able to make the carnivorous trees dormant. That might be the same method they used to program the technology to create people. I mutter, "Sevyn, what do you think the next question should be?"

Sevyn considers the floor. They ask, "How do we program the imitation technology to create things, like people?"

A bit of worry lightens from my chest. I'm glad that Sevyn is thinking in that direction.

"Oh, what a clever little way of asking that." Joane beams. "You see, I found out about the technology from one of the engineers for this dome—you encounter many interesting people as a waitress. I overheard a neat little tidbit: the controls for the imitation technology can be accessed on the walls of the dome. If you wanted to create something like a person, a tree, or a tunnel, you'd go to the wall and verbally ask to adjust the arena environment. The capability was included for a player to find one day, to make the dares more interesting. I doubt they thought someone would use the technology to try crafting a convincing person. But with how much this game reads our thoughts and mannerisms, of course it can fashion an imitation of us. Even the trees find the copies adequate in flavor."

"Now, could you draw me a picture of your alien parent?" Jared rips a piece of paper out of his journal and flings it across the floor. It flies to the side, but Sevyn catches it. Jared also rolls his pen to me with an eager smile.

Part of me thinks he must be joking—that all of this is one big prank, like Daraja suggested. For someone who kills people, he's so eager to learn about me. But if our current assumptions are true, I can't mess up this interaction. We need as much information as we can get to survive.

I'll need to hide how I discovered all this. I can't tell Analisa, Eric, and supposedly innocent carbon-copy Lian. Even if it messes up our relationships for today, I can't.

Actually, this could rift our relationships so much more than that. I'm making a deal with the people who killed Lian. I might be discarding our friend group for the hope of survival. The thought twists my stomach.

I pick up the pen, considering it. Drawing isn't my strong suit. Can I draw something convincing enough for them to keep answering our questions?

"I can draw them and you can tell me what to revise." Sevyn holds out their hand for the pen.

If they think they can do better, I'd rather not draw anyway. I hand them the pen.

Their hand scribbles across the page, drawing a detailed trunk, leaves, hood, and roots. They even mark out measurements, like the ten feet from the roots to the top of the hood. The knots in the bark are in the right places. It's Kiran.

"When did you meet them?" I ask.

"I lied about not knowing your condition so you would feel less self-conscious. I apologize for that. Your aunt was rather fond of showing her friends pictures of you when you were little. And I've known your parents since before you were born." Sevyn points at the drawing. "Does that look accurate to you?"

Of all the things to lie about, I'm not offended about that. Auntie Tera showing off pictures of me when I was little sounds kind of sweet. "That looks right."

Sevyn passes the pen and paper back across the floor. Jared snatches the paper with wide eyes. "Ooh—ten feet tall! The part at the top, what's that?"

Can I leverage that as another question?

Joane senses my hesitation. "It's fine. You can ask another question first."

"Did you kill Lian?"

My heart drops at Analisa's voice. Her unblinking eyes peer through the front door. Her bloody palms press against the glass. She's closer to Jared and Joane than Sevyn and I are.

Joane smiles at Jared, her thin eyebrows raised. Don't answer that with the truth, please.

"Do you understand the situation here, Analisa?" Jared asks.

"I'm trying to." Analisa's red nails scratch the glass. "Believe me, I'm trying."

"Analisa." I raise my voice so she can hear me. Please let it not be too loud to startle her into moving. "We're negotiating. If we keep the peace, we'll all get out of this alive."

"All of us?" Analisa asks. "Including this stunt double out here having an existential crisis? He tells me he's the real Lian, but there's someone else who looks like him out here. Does he get out of this alive?"

I can't make this better. I can't bring Lian back. I can't turn back time.

"The body on the porch is fake," Sevyn calls out. "It was made to draw us out. The Lian you're with is really him."

My chest tightens. Lying to her about this will cause a rift when she finds out the truth. That might prove disastrous if Analisa finds out before five p.m. today.

But I have to put her safety above our relationship. "Sevyn's right. It was a cruel joke."

"Done by these two? They're the killers?" Analisa asks.

My voice feels like it's hanging on by a thread. "We made a deal. The truth accusation proved that they won't hurt us for the rest of our lives, as long as we don't attack them before the end of the game. We're also agreeing to answer each other's questions. If we keep the peace, we'll all get out of here alive."

Jared and Joane don't seem concerned by Analisa leaning on the door behind them. Based on how quickly and quietly they've killed people, I don't want to see what happens if they're attacked. If there really are copies of them in this arena, I'm not sure we could win.

Daraja steps behind Analisa. They mouth, "I'm sorry. I couldn't stop her."

Eric and Lian are on the porch now too. Lian's deadpan face stares at the ground, mumbling something I can't hear. Eric pulls Lian into a hug.

If Analisa's eyes were weaponized, this Joane and Jared pair would be dead by now. "How do we know they'll keep their word?"

"The game acknowledged that we told the truth." Joane shrugs.

"Does that truth apply to the original Jared and Joane?" Sevyn asks.

"Good question!" Joane grins. "Don't worry, we aren't looking for loopholes. We want Cai to keep her bargain once we're out of here."

"What bargain?" Analisa asks.

My grip on the knife tightens. "They want to interview me after all this is done. They're curious about the plantlike parts of my physiology."

"To be clear, *he's* the nerdy botanist interested in your plantlike traits." Joane points at Jared. "But I'll support his work."

Analisa's mouth quivers—whether it's out of anger or fear, I'm not sure. "What are you thinking? What if they kill you at that interview, or dissect you or—"

"I don't want to dissect something I know nothing about," Jared clarifies. "She's the only one I know of with this kind of physiology. The interview can happen in a public place—"

"You murdered people in this public place. Once they're dead, it doesn't matter how cautious they were." An extra surge of aggressiveness deepens Analisa's voice. "I don't want you to ever see us again after this is over."

"Analisa, we need to survive this," I insist.

I can't tell what's running through her mind. Is she considering the possibility of attacking Joane and Jared?

"You have all you need to survive today. Again, stay around the cabin. We'll be doing the same." Joane stands and dusts off her dress. The glint of a blood-stained bread knife by her side makes me flinch. "Jared, honey, you can ask her more questions later."

"Not if they break the agreement," Jared says.

My eyebrows pinch. "Do you expect us to?"

"Well..." Jared finally turns around to glance at Analisa. "If I thought the numbers were in my favor, and I thought it would be safer than sharing a cabin with known murderers, I certainly would have a difficult time convincing myself not to break." He stands and brushes himself off too. "I hope to see you survive to the end of the game, Cai."

The two of them walk down the hall. I don't know where in this ashy, burnt cabin they plan to be, but I don't intend to follow.

Joane, Jared, and Flutura are the killers. Three human killers, as Flutura indicated. Or she meant three, as in Joane, the third killed.

Analisa slides the front door open and passes it to

Daraja. All four of them file in. They sit on the ground too.

Analisa's drained expression worries me. I don't know what she believes about Lian right now. Even if she believes that the Lian next to her is the original one, seeing his body outside couldn't have been painless.

"Explain," Lian insists. "What just happened?"

Chapter 36

Sevyn and I cover what we learned as best as we can. We lie about the Lian circumstances, saying that the Lian who appears dead is a carbon copy version that Joane and Jared made. We divulge everything else.

Lian looks relieved when we say that he's the original. Does he not know that he's a mimicked version? If he does know, he's a convincing liar.

"We need to stay out of the forest," Daraja says. "But we could be stuck in this dome with at least two Jareds and two Joanes."

They might have a whole army of themselves hiding in the dome. If they haven't created several versions of themselves already, they might if we break the agreement. It's possible that the trees are preventing them from reaching the dome border, but they also could already be there. Regardless, we shouldn't assume that they aren't somehow monitoring it.

"Wait, if they made a whole bunch of themselves, can they all leave?" Eric asks. "Are there going to be a ton of those murderers out in the world after this?"

"They agreed that they wouldn't hurt any of us for the rest of our lives," I remind.

"Yeah, I'm more concerned about the principle of that. If we don't kill them here—"

"We don't know how many of them there are!" Daraja's hands shake. "If we attack one, twenty of them could come kill us. No wonder they're so confident that they'll get out of this."

"We have to get out of this alive, whatever the cost," I say. "We can deal with the moral implications of that later. It's not our job to catch murderers. It's our responsibility to keep each other alive until five p.m. today."

"Based on the sunlight, I would guess that we're nearing ten a.m.," Sevyn says.

"Seven hours in here with an x number of murderers." Eric sucks air through his teeth. "Great. I hate this math problem already."

"Their demonstration outside made it clear how it would feel to lose any of us." Lian rubs his forehead. "I agree with Cai. If Jared and Joane have a reason to keep us alive, then we shouldn't press it. I don't want to end up like... you know."

Something jabs at my chest, hearing him say that.

"Then we gather supplies," Analisa determines. "As long as we don't attack them, our agreement remains unbroken. They should find it reasonable for us to want to find things to defend ourselves with."

Given how she was so adamantly aggressive earlier, her level voice unnerves me.

"Ideally, stuff that'll defend against a large group." Eric stands and brushes off his shorts.

"And Lian, you've seen the tunnels. You said some seemed to lead further than the one you came out from. Do you think one might reach the edge of the dome?" Analisa asks.

"I don't know for certain," Lian says. "But I would guess that they go a decent distance from what I saw. I came up the first ladder I found."

"Good to know," Analisa says. "Destroying the carnivorous trees shouldn't be an act of attacking Joane and Jared."

I like where her thoughts are going, but Jared and Joane might not. They were feeding the trees, and it's apparently something they do outside this game. Still, getting rid of the trees doesn't directly violate our agreement. And it would open more space for us to navigate the arena.

It would also give us the opportunity to change all the carbon copies of Jared and Joane. They might consider that a violation of the agreement. And the actual Jared and Joane could be at the border already. At least one of the Joanes was in the basement when they killed Lian, so they probably know about the tunnels. They could've made a little clearing near the border to keep themselves safe from the trees.

Would the carbon copies even be let out, if they

were made from technology? Would this Lian be let out of the arena?

That's not something to consider now. Analisa's right that going to the dome edge would be our most ideal plan. "I'm up for it."

We grab anything useful and divide it among ourselves. If we're divided, the hope is that we should each be able to survive until five. Sevyn hammers one of their shoulder plates into a makeshift shoe for Analisa. It's not ideal, but it'll hurt if she kicks someone. She can walk on it better than her warped prosthetic foot. She even manages a cartwheel on the flat dirt outside, making her smile a little.

Then we give ourselves time to sleep. Now that it's day, we should rest as much as we can. The unspoken reason for it is because we might need to defend ourselves right before five p.m.

I volunteer to keep watch while the others pass out. Even Sevyn rests. It's my first time seeing their eyes closed.

I slept earlier last night. My tiredness was the reason we found the squeaky floorboards. If I hadn't moved then, would Lian have died?

None of them look comfortable. They're sleeping on dirt while injured, wearing clothing intended for a dead person. I can't imagine what their dreams are like, assuming they're able to sleep that deeply.

Watching them and the forest preserves me in a timeless state. The branches sway in the light wind; I start to wonder if it's the wind moving them. I stray from the thought, compelling my mind to be blank. My eyes observe the world without judgment. My brain is too foggy, too tired, too stressed to think. Nervous thoughts return bit by bit, and I have to dispel them again.

Eventually, Sevyn sits up. Based on the simulated sun's position, their guess is that we have about an hour until five p.m. Excitement encourages me to stand before the aching burn in my leg can argue. We're close to the end.

Sevyn and I wake everyone. When we let them know about the time, their surprised expressions quickly regain focus. Once we gather our materials, we decide to journey to the dome's edge. It might take less time for the robots to take us out of the arena there—I make sure to say that aloud, in case Joane and Jared hear us.

Lian shows us the tunnel he came out of. It's a hole in the ground beneath the back porch. We peel some of the boards away from the entrance, making it easier for us to slide in there. Lian leads the way inside.

When it's my turn to scoot under the porch, the burn on my leg scrapes against the dirt. I grimace as I push my legs over the edge of the hole. My bare foot wanders until I find the ladder. Lian and Eric direct me into finding the next rung. After a few more steps, I make it to the ground. Lian helps me tie a flashlight to my left arm.

The tunnel is tall enough for us to stand in, which is fortunate for Eric and me. It's even wide enough for a few of us to walk beside each other. My fingertips trace across the packed dirt composing the wall. The ground appears undisturbed. I don't know if this tunnel was made by Joane and Jared or Comedy and Tragedy. Regardless, I'm hoping we can utilize it to reach the edge of the dome.

I help guide Analisa's feet to the next rung. I catch her shoulders when she hops off the final step. She gives me a slim smile. "Thanks."

"Yeah," I mutter in response.

'You're welcome' wouldn't feel right. I told her a horrendous lie. Even if she doesn't find out about Lian before five p.m., I'll have to tell her after. I couldn't live with myself otherwise. But I'm not even sure what to tell this version of Lian. I don't know if he can leave the game.

Daraja makes it down the ladder. Sevyn follows. We secure our flashlights and check that we have everything we wanted to bring. Then Sevyn guides us like a human compass, using their memory to determine our path through the intersecting tunnels.

Our footsteps pat the dirt ground. My feet have adjusted to being bare. The closet for my assigned bedroom is buried, so getting shoes out of it would've been difficult.

I don't know if my mom is right about the whole rooting myself to the earth thing. I'd have greater strength and comfort if I had shoes on. Now I've got to watch for anything that might damage my bare feet. And of course, I still have to watch for Jared,

Joane, and carnivorous tree roots. Everything in this dome becomes a shade more insane by the hour.

After several minutes of silence, Daraja whispers, "Do we have to be quiet?"

"Not particularly, I don't think," Sevyn says. "We're not breaking the terms of our agreement with Joane and Jared, so unless there's an additional threat that they didn't describe, we should be able to talk."

"Okay, good. I feel uncomfortable with all the silence," Daraja admits. "Like, something distracting would be great."

"Want Cai to sing again?" Lian asks.

I give him a look for messing with me. My heart jolts at how involuntary that reaction was. I react like he's the original Lian. Somehow, this Lian has the memory of me serenading Analisa on a dare.

Maybe I should be treating him as the actual Lian. But then, isn't that dishonoring the original Lian? And then again, it's not like it's this Lian's fault for being created.

But the reality is that Joane stabbed the original Lian to death. The metal barrier separated us in Brandon's room. He died alone. If I had pushed him back in time, he wouldn't have fallen into the basement. If I had figured out a way to break through the metal in the floor, we could've gotten him out. Now he's assumed to be alive by his sister and the guy he likes. Liked. This Lian could take his place, but it would be cruel to forget the original Lian.

Wait, this is all recorded. Analisa and Eric will find

out when we react to the highlights live tomorrow. I have to tell them first. It would be cruel for them to figure it out then.

"Okay, I think that's a no on Cai singing. Eric, do you have anything? Like, a serenading kind of song?" Lian asks.

Eric chuckles. "What kind of serenading song do you want?"

Lian grins sheepishly. "Any kind, as long as it's directed at me."

"I appreciate a man who knows what he wants." Eric clears his throat. He legitimately starts singing a love song. I've heard it in the radio speakers playing in the hall between classes. The memory of the familiar makes me smile.

Analisa's hand finds mine. Her right-hand prosthetic is warped from the fire, but she's able to bend her fingers. I squeeze her hand, hoping the sensors still work well enough for her to know—her little flash of a smile indicates they do.

I'll tell them when we're all out of this. We'll have time in the rooms we'll spend the night in tonight. I want to commit to it. "Hey, Analisa?"

Her glossy eyes look at me. "Yeah?"

"I've got a secret that I'd rather not reveal on Truth or Dare. But I want to tell you tonight, after all this is over. I wanted to tell you so you can remind me later."

She squeezes my hand back. "Are you sure you don't want..." She looks down. "Actually, later sounds good."

Her optimism is faltering. "It's a few more hours. We'll be okay after that."

She nods.

"Take the left opening," Sevyn calls out. Lian and Eric do so. Eric's still singing and Lian's still smiling giddily.

The Jared imitation that died was telling the truth when he didn't know why Flutura was attacking him.

The realization catches me off guard. I adjust my pace to make up for my hesitation.

If the Jared imitation didn't remember being involved with the murders, then the imitations' memories are programmable. It's plausible that this Lian genuinely doesn't remember dying or being created as a replacement. He could be as innocent as Joane and Jared claimed.

I hope that's the case. We might have to argue with Comedy and Tragedy to let Lian leave the game. The imitation technology composing our size-adjusting clothes can leave the arena. It does so every round of Truth or Dare. The players even get to keep the clothes they wore on the last day. So, any technology should be able to leave the arena. We lost Lian already. We don't need to lose this version of him too.

The ground rumbles, silencing Eric's singing.

"Run." Sevyn bursts through the group to take the lead, gripping their shoulder plate.

With a determined grunt, Eric's burnt arms lift Analisa onto his shoulders and we dash after Sevyn. I don't know what we're running from until our flashlights catch sight of roots winding into the tunnel. Carnivorous trees.

"We should be almost to the edge!" Sevyn shouts.

What if there isn't a way to the surface?

Fortunately, we find a ladder at the end of the next tunnel. Sevyn tosses each of us up the rungs.

I scrape through a bush at the top and whip my head around with a wince. There's the end of the dome. It's blue like the sky, past some of the trees. I grip my knife with one hand and help pull my friends out of the ground with the other.

Once we're all out, we sprint for the dome edge. The tree branches swarm us. Everything we have goes into slicing or knocking aside the branches. My heart lurches each time my feet leap to avoid a moving root.

I recall the instructions—verbally ask the dome to adjust the arena environment. As we approach the dome edge, I shout, "Adjust the arena environment! Change all the carnivorous plants into avocado plushies!"

I was hoping that would work in of itself. But some button appears on the dome. I can't read it from here.

A root wraps around my burned leg. My back crashes into the ground. The breath in my chest evaporates as I'm pulled toward a tree. The bark snaps, pulling apart the trunk into a vertical maw. The rings inside drip with a red sap—red like human blood, not like a plant's.

Branches pull on my right arm before I can use the

knife. My shoulder wrenches. Panic shoots through me, remembering how one of the Jareds was dismembered. I'm about to lose my arm.

Analisa's shrill scream pierces any semblance of hope I had. The tree is only a few feet away from me. I can't use the knife. I'm not strong enough to break the branches. Am I really going to die here?

My head lurches back, wishing for one last look at my friends. They're almost at the border. Eric still charges forward with Analisa, even as she flails her arms back toward me. I hope she stays safe. Daraja's about to be caught by a branch. They're pulled to the ground. It can't end like this for them too. Lian runs toward me, his wide eyes desperate. What is he doing? Sevyn reaches the wall and slams their hand into the button I created.

The trees blink out of existence, exposing the cabin in the distance. Thousands of avocado plushies bounce against the ground.

Chapter 37

I manage to push my aching shoulder upright. An avocado plushie sits on my burned leg. The very thing that was trying to consume me moments ago looks harmless now. I collapse on the ground, wheezing with forgotten breath.

Without the trees there, it looks like I'm not that far from the border.

Eric winces as he picks up an avocado plushie by me, staring at it curiously. "Huh."

Daraja starts laughing and whooping from the ground nearby. "Yay. Go avocado plushies."

"Good choice." Lian grabs a couple of plushies and hugs them. "These seem less likely to hurt my friends."

"They're good, but can I ask—why was this the first thing you thought of?" Eric drops a plushie on me.

I wrap my arms around it while I catch my breath. Perfect holding size.

Analisa's knees crash into the ground. She embraces me before I can properly lean forward to hug her back. She kisses my forehead and wipes the dirt from my face. There's a trace of green blood on her fingers—I must've cut myself. Her forlorn eyes dart over me. "It's one of the plushies in her comfort corner."

Oh, wait. I should've thought more. "Adjust the arena environment. Change half the avocado plushies into clam plushies. Can someone click the confirmation button?"

I tip my head back in time to see Sevyn confirm the command.

Analisa smiles slimly at the appearance of several clam plushies around her. She hugs an avocado and a clam. "I'm taking these home. No one can stop me."

"So, if we're admitting that we're fans of plushies, can I request some duck plushies?" Eric rubs the back of his neck.

Sevyn makes the request for a third of the total plushies to be ducks. Eric collects the nearby ducks and puts them in a neat pile.

Lian gapes at him. "You're adorable."

"I'm a fan of ducks, and I deserve emotional compensation from this game." Eric sits next to his pile of yellow duck plushies.

By now, my body feels comfortable enough to sit up. Analisa and I scoot to the dome edge. I lean my back against it while we all gather nearby.

"You three want any particular type of plushie?" Analisa points her walking stick at Daraja, Sevyn, and Lian.

"I want one of each of yours." Daraja laughs, picking up a duck plushie to add to their collection.

Sevyn surveys the nearby environment. While there are still bushes, most of the trees have disappeared. I don't see any version of Joane or Jared nearby. Sevyn clears their throat. "I could do with an orca." Orca plushies are now added to the collection.

"Okay, wait, I changed my mind. Can we get like a dragon plushie?" Daraja asks. We create dragon plushies too.

"Yeah, maybe a turtle," Lian says. "They have a hard shell, and they live for a long time." Sevyn gets the turtle plushies to happen as well.

Eric encourages Lian to sit closer to him. He kisses Lian's forehead, carefully avoiding the gash.

Sevyn considers the wall. "Adjust the arena environment. Fill all the tunnels with dirt. Change all the Joane and Jared imitations into apple trees. And trap the original Joane and Jared in a cage that they cannot escape in the center of the dome arena."

A few trees bloom in the distance, verifying that Sevyn's commands are working.

Wouldn't Joane and Jared have something put in place to stop this? "Does messing with the imitations mean we're going against the agreement?"

"We aren't attacking Joane and Jared. We're simply changing the imitations into a different form," Sevyn justifies.

"Do all the imitations have to go back to what they were?" Analisa's lips purse.

My heart jerks. Has she guessed what happened to Lian?

"In principle, no, since past participants could take items from the dome. But for Joane and Jared, I would say the world is better off without their duplicates," Sevyn answers. "For some people, I might feel differently."

Analisa rubs her drooping eyelids. "About how long now—until the end of the game?"

Sevyn commands the wall to provide an accurate clock. They respond, "Nineteen minutes."

Analisa meets my eyes with a trembling lip. "Do I want to know?"

I glance at Lian, not sure what to say.

Lian's mouth opens. His eyes widen as he looks at his hands. "It's about me, isn't it?"

My teeth gnaw at the inside of my cheek. I don't know what words to use to make this hurt less. My hesitation can't be helping, but nothing comes to mind. What am I supposed to say?

"Adjust the arena environment," Lian mutters. "Give me all of Lian's memories." After he presses the confirmation button, tears stream down his disbelieving face. "I—I've died."

My own tears feel like they shred my skin.

Analisa twitches while she pulls her knees to her chest. Her reddened eyes slam shut. "Lili, I'm so sorry!"

"No, I'm sorry." Lian scrambles over to Analisa. His trembling hands hover over her shoulders like he's scared to touch her. "I'm sorry I'm not him. I feel like him, and I think I'm him, but I know I'm not. And I know I can't replace him... it's selfish for me to even be here."

"Stay with me. Don't you dare leave me." Analisa wraps her arms around his back. "I know you're not him. I left him behind. I'm a terrible sister." Her shuddering voice pleads over his shoulder. "But don't you dare leave."

"You're not a terrible sister," Lian mutters. "If you don't hate me, I won't leave you."

"I can't hate you." She parts from the hug and grips his forearms. Her tears drip into her flickering frown. "You're here when he can't be."

Eric kneels beside the two of them. Lian's head sways, his lip trembling beneath a new wave of tears. "I'm sorry. I swear, I didn't remember."

"I left you." Eric's voice is hollow. It rises in pitch painfully quickly. "I should've stayed. I should've jumped into the basement as soon as you fell. Or rammed right through it. What was I thinking—leaving you there? What kind of person—"

"No, you did everything you could. You all did." Lian taps Eric's left arm, charred with brittle, blistered skin from his fist to his elbow. "I love that you —I mean, you're... I'm not him. I don't deserve your sympathy."

"But you remember what happened." Daraja kneels beside him. They take his hand. "You're not him, but that doesn't mean that we can't care about you too."

"I still want that date, you know?" Eric says. "We were going to eat—"

"Indian food. I remember," Lian assures, hope seeping into his tense expression.

"Down by that frozen yogurt place because I have a stupidly low spice tolerance," Eric adds.

"Yeah?" Lian's laugh warps into a sob.

Guilt drags my shameful face into my hands. "I'm sorry for keeping it from you all. You deserved to know sooner."

"When did you find out?" Lian asks.

"Joane's imitation in the cabin—the one you all saw—claimed that she killed Lian," Sevyn clarifies, their voice soft. "I lied to Analisa because I thought it was the best course of action while we were piecing together how to survive. Cai followed me with my lie."

"I did too," Daraja admits.

"I thought so." Analisa nods, her stare blank. "And I thought that there would be a good reason if you were talking with them." Her fingers ball into fists. "How much time do we have left?"

"About fifteen minutes," Sevyn says. "Why?"

"I'm considering doing something illegal."

I search her tense expression. She wants to kill Joane and Jared, doesn't she?

Eric nods, swallowing. "If we let them go, they'll kill more people. They won't even go to jail for it unless they're caught killing someone else."

Fifteen minutes. They should be in a cage at the cabin. We could do it if we hurried.

"Are we sure we want to do this?" Daraja asks, their frown flickering with uncertainty. "If we kill them, that might make us as bad—"

"What they did was different," Analisa insists. "We can stop them from hurting anyone else."

The conviction in her tone casts aside my caution. I don't even consider the forgiving nature of my alien side; I dive right into my humanity. I hold out my hand toward the group. "For Lian."

Analisa grabs my hand, letting me help pull her up. "For Lian."

Everyone rises to their feet. Although there's some hesitance in our demeanor, something in my gut overrules my apprehension. What we're doing has to be right. I don't have time to question my instinct. I look at Sevyn, hoping for their input.

"Adjust the arena environment. Make the six plushies in front of me into working walkie talkies." Sevyn confirms the command and tosses us the toylike devices. "Hold the blue button on the side to talk. At least one of us should stay here to make commands, if need be."

"I should go. If I'm killed for whatever reason, a wall command should be able to bring me back," Lian says.

"That's assuming we make the command before the fifteen minutes are up," Analisa reminds. "Don't sacrifice yourself every few minutes or something stupid like that."

"I don't plan to sacrifice myself at all, if I can help it," Lian confirms.

"Adjust the arena environment. Create a five-seated hovercar out of a plushie next to my feet." Sevyn confirms the command, and an avocado plushie expands into a hovercar. "Get moving. The time should be in the car."

Eric swings into the driver seat. Analisa claims the shotgun seat, so I climb into the seat behind her. Daraja squishes Lian into the middle seat. What a silly feeling, to be flying in a hovercar in this game, on the way to the center of the dome. My knife in my hand. Wounds all over us. Lian dead and alive. Enraged resolve blazing through us.

I thought the center of the arena would be somewhere inside the cabin. But no. According to the cage we're approaching, it's outside the patio, right where the accursed berry bush was.

Joane and Jared sit inside the cage, talking and smiling over a book. The cage looks legitimate. They won't fit through the bars. But they seem content to be in there. Nerves creep up my back—should we be so close to them?

As we land beside them, Analisa pulls a dark hairpin out of her hair. She speaks into her walkie talkie. "Sevyn, change my hairpin into a loaded assault rifle, please."

The hairpin indeed extends in her hands into a rifle as she climbs out of the car. "Lili, you want it?"

Lian's arms shoot up. Nope.

Analisa checks to be sure the gun is loaded, careful to point it only near Joane and Jared.

Joane laughs as she looks up from the book. It's Jared's journal that they're looking at. "Ah, so you've come to kill us. I thought you would've tried hours ago. People said Truth or Dare was entertaining. I'm glad it didn't disappoint."

"It seems I won the bet, my dear." Jared wiggles his eyebrows.

"Oh, I know. It's a shame." Joane sighs as she takes his hand. "We never did afford the engagement rings."

"Are you really not going to take this seriously?" Daraja shouts.

Analisa switches off the safety as she points the gun at the cage.

Jared laughs. "We were debating whether we wanted to keep going after all this. I think this is the pinnacle of our work. It would be a waste to continue from here. Our plants will do fine on their own now."

"And we've even inspired a new generation of murderers. We couldn't be prouder." Joane splays her hand out, gesturing to us. A painful sting spreads through my chest.

"If you'd keep me balanced, I'd appreciate it." Analisa tips her head at me. I hold my arm around her back, bracing myself. "Jared, Joane—"

"But Cai broke the contract. Shouldn't she receive some sort of punishment?" Jared's words send nervous prickles down my back. "The least she can do is be forced to listen to our last words."

"Oh right, what did I write down for that?" Joane reaches into her pocket.

I see it all. Then I hear it. It's like my memories blend as my mind processes the experience. The knife flying out of the cage, toward me. Analisa sending a spray of bullets crashing through the metal bars. The rapid firework sound whips my ears and sends bloody, gaping holes through Jared and Joane.

My right eye is ripped through. A gash splits through my face, reaching down my throat to throttle a scream out of me. Thick, runny liquid splashes into my hands. My hands aren't my own. Screams and yells replace the bullets in my ears, lashing at me with each new wave of pain bashing my head. There's something sticking out of my eye.

My ears ring, and my heart lurches while I'm lifted. I'm pulled somewhere, and my feet stumble there. Panic overturns any semblance of feeling safe. One of my hands hovers in front of the throbbing pain. The other hand claws at anything in the void around me. Flashes of my friends pass by. We're with each other, but in the sky. A firm grip snatches my arms and legs. My quivering muscles squirm, desperate to escape the anguish splitting through my head.

The sunlit sky breaks apart as we approach it. Splotches of red, black, and blue consume my blurry vision. Squinting only forces more pain into my eye. Something jams against my eyelid, preventing it from closing.

Cheers from a crowd roar around me. Flashes of light flicker through my confused, darkening vision. Is that Analisa shouting? Sevyn? Eric? Daraja? Lian? The voices blend.

"Hello, everyone!" Comedy's bright voice booms over the ringing in my ears. "Congratulations! You all made it to—" An abrupt force hits her microphone, interrupting her. Boos and laughter swarm the world.

I think I beg for help. I can't hear my voice. I can't tell what my mouth is doing. The skin on my face is numb.

My arms are pulled. The world spins into black as I cry out. I can't feel my face.

Chapter 38

Surprise alleviates my body. My neck feels nice, lying against a firm pillow. My skin tingles. It smells like lavender in here. Here?

My eyes blink open. The ceiling is white. My contact lenses are still mostly deactivated, so I don't see my desktop or any notifications.

Truth or Dare—did we leave the game yet?

I sit up easier than I think I should. The ache in my leg from the burn is gone. I can't feel my other scrapes and bruises.

I'm in a thin hospital gown, resting on a medical bed with buttons lining the edges of it. As I turn my head, the world feels surreal, like I'm looking at a painting of my friends. Analisa lies partially on my bed, her head pressed into her arms. Sevyn sits in a chair, their head leaning against the wall. Lian's doing the same in a chair between my bed and another.

Eric's in the other bed. Daraja's sprawled on the floor with a pillow. They all look asleep.

The more I blink, the weirder my face feels. My fingers tap my right cheek. There's some kind of rough tape over it. My fingertips feel the soft skin by my lip, but my cheek doesn't feel my fingertips. My mouth tingles nearby the edge of a numb chunk of my face.

No. That didn't actually happen. That was a dream. The more I press against my memories, the more it has to be. But then... why can't I remember us leaving the arena? Did we even leave?

My breaths are faster than I mean them to be. I hold my chest, trying to contain the air. My bark warbles. My teeth chatter, finding it harder to control what I'm feeling. Turmoil rises in me like vomit, but it won't leave so easily.

"Hey, hey, I'm here," Analisa says. My eyes focus on her holding my hand.

Eyes.

I close my left eye. The room isn't what I see. A vague, empty gray consumes my vision. Splotches of squirmy little highlights make themselves clearer as I stare. They dash away as I try to focus on them. My right eye should be open. "I don't feel it. Why can't I feel it?"

"Cai, we're out of the arena. Truth or Dare is over. We're safe now," Analisa implores.

Safe? I can't see. "Where did it go?"

"Joane pulled out a knife at the last moment."

Daraja's voice startles me into looking again. They lean against the bed with worried eyes.

Eyes. "What happened?"

Analisa kisses my hand and buries her head into the bedsheet.

"You're alive." Lian gasps, lurching out of his seat to join us.

Alive. I am. That's true. But my breaths want to kill me.

"Joane threw the knife at you." Eric sits up with a wince. "It was so fast. I'm sorry, Cai."

"I shot them before the game ended. Joane and Jared are dead." Analisa squeezes my hand, her lower lip quivering. "The robots put us on platforms and lifted the six of us out of the arena. But I wasn't quick enough to shoot her before she could throw it. I'm so sorry."

My memories shuffle into order. The knife, followed by the pain. The firecracker gunshots, shooting Joane and Jared. Are they actually dead? "Is it really over?"

Analisa nods. "It's still the sixth day. We have the ceremony tomorrow, and then we're free."

"Sevyn had to punch Comedy and Tragedy to get us to the medical bay faster, but the doctors gave us good treatment." Eric holds up his arms, covered in bandages. "How is your eye feeling?"

Numb. And I can't see out of it. What does my face even look like now?

"I told them to make you a yellow eyepatch, in

case you don't feel like using the synthetic eye for the ceremony tomorrow," Lian says.

Why would that be my concern right now?

They're all around my cot now. Even Eric's gotten up and is in my field of view. Sevyn's awake, watching from their chair.

Then I understand. The end of the game means we don't have to talk about dark subjects anymore. We can be safe now. I want to be safe now. "You sure it would look good with my skin?"

That sparks Lian's smile. "Yeah, I know it. And you could pull down some of your hair in an updo that draws attention to the eyepatch. Or you could cover it. Either way. Your hair's long enough."

I pinch the loose, brown hair sitting on my right shoulder. I have to turn my head to see it. I bite my lip, keeping it from trembling. "I could use a shower. Can we shower with these on?" I lift an arm, pointing at a bandage.

"Yep. I was concerned about that too." Eric laughs lightly. "And they said we could go back to the bedrooms whenever we want. It might be more comfortable there."

I nod, looking around the medical bay. I don't want the reminder of waking like this. "Yeah, I might be up for moving there."

Analisa helps me slide off the bed. The hospital gown catches on the edge, and I yank it back down as I stand. My fingers pinch the flat, paper-like clothing. My mind seems to be on the same track as Eric's, because he jumps on the joke before I do: "At least it's an upgrade from bandages, huh?"

My mind clings onto the lighthearted mood. It keeps my breaths even while we walk through the infirmary. Sevyn holds open the door, but I try brushing my fingers against it to be polite, indicating that I'm willing to hold open the door for myself. Surprise runs through me when my fingers don't feel the surface. I stretch my arm out, finding the door an inch away from where I thought it was.

After we exit, I reach for Analisa's arm. The same thing happens—my vision tricks me. I remember learning at some point how two eyes provide three-dimensional input to the brain, but the overwhelming realization that I might not be able to see that way again causes my fragile optimism to trip.

Analisa's hand finds mine. Her warm touch encourages me to take a deep breath to reset my tightening lungs. We're alive. Even if I have to adjust how I see, I'm fortunate we made it out. A bundle of conflicting emotions threatens to tear my mind apart, but I don't want to parse them now. I'm on the verge of crying, but I don't want to cry. Why can't I just be?

A couple of guards find our group and escort us to the fancy bedrooms we stayed in after the opening ceremony. These halls are familiar, but so many unbelievable events happened since I was last here.

I walk into my private bathroom, aiming for a shower. My reflection stops me.

I haven't seen myself in days. My skin is green—fully so for the first time in years. My hair is a stringy mess. I'm bandaged in so many places. My right eye is covered in gauze. My right eyebrow and lower cheek tug on the tape without feeling it. I'm tempted to take off the bandages, but I'm afraid that I'll see a gaping hole. The instructions on my bathroom mirror advise that I keep my face covered anyway.

I wash my face around the gauze. The sink's cool water is startling. Fortunately, the shower provides a comforting, warm steam. It compels me to sit on the shower bench. My eyelid flickers closed several times; I grip the metal bar to stay awake. My parched throat starts sipping the water. Once I pull myself out of the shower, the warm drying jets wick the water from my body. I appreciate the smooth, yellow pajamas in the bedroom dresser.

The silence in the empty bedroom leeches onto my skin. My vision darts, nervous from the lack of movement. It's dark outside the window. My body feels displaced from time. I don't like standing in here alone.

I open the door, nearly running into a jolting Analisa. She stutters, "I was wondering if you wanted to hang out. Or sleep. Just... I don't want to be alone."

"Girl, me too." Daraja speeds down the hall with a pillow and blanket stuffed between their arms. "Can I please join?"

Eric's head pops out of a room, followed by Lian's. Lian asks, "Are you all planning on being in the same room? If so, can we join?"

Another door opens. Sevyn crosses their arms

with a sigh. Their chin is down, but their eyes look up expectantly, asking the same thing.

A laugh bubbles out of my tight throat. "Yeah. Room preference?"

Analisa walks slowly into my room, still adjusting to her new prosthetic leg. She swings her walking stick in invitation. "Come on, everyone!"

We gather in my assigned bedroom. A conversation starts. Eric opens a holographic board game. I lie on the bed next to Analisa. My eyelid frequently lowers despite how I keep shifting the weight between my arms to stay awake. My friends are here; I want to see them. My head drops more than once.

"It's okay, Cai. We're here." Analisa rubs my back, yawning too. "You can rest."

I drift away, fighting against sleep every few seconds until my body gives up.

Chapter 39

The yellow fabric of my blouse shows the bark on my back, as I requested. I'm glad to wear pants again after days of uncomfortable clothing. Lian was right —the yellow fabric complements my green skin.

Sevyn finishes ripping the green shirt with their new metal pinky. "Here." They pass me a piece. I tie the cloth around my neck, like the rest of my friends. We wear it for the first Lian, who wore this shirt beneath his suit at the opening ceremony.

I look in the mirror while adjusting the green cloth. My clean self stares back at me, now with a yellow iris in my prosthetic eye. Although the thought of an eyepatch is tempting, I want the audience to see the large gash held in place by stitches. I'm glad the makeup team left it alone.

We're escorted backstage. While the audience murmurs behind the curtain, we stand in the same order as the opening ceremony, minus six of our original twelve. Nine of us died. Six of us remain.

Analisa pokes at her cheek. "Cai, did they cover the bags under my eyes? It's very important. Got to forget everything they put us through, you know."

I laugh. "Does my eye look damaged enough? I should flash the burnt gash on my leg for extra measure."

"Scandalous!" Analisa fans herself as her smile grows.

"I've got a pretty good move." Eric does the forearm jerk with his left arm, slapping his bicep while showing off the bandages covering his burned arms. "The pain might be worth it."

"Don't aggravate your wound." Lian leans over to see Eric around Daraja, Analisa, and me.

Eric leans forward too. "Not even to say 'screw you' to the audience?"

"Not if you want me to lean on that arm later," Lian remarks.

"Darn. Okay, no aggressive arm gestures for now," Eric resolves.

"I can cover you. My arms only have a few scratches," Daraja offers.

"Thanks."

I've drowned out most of Comedy and Tragedy's words, but when they shout something about bringing out the players, my skin prickles. When Sevyn walks, we follow them past the curtain. As we enter the spotlit stage, the crowd cheers. My shoes clack against the hardwood floor. The stage looks far too much like the cabin bedroom floorboards. The same ones that led to the basement.

I almost trip. Daraja and Analisa catch my arms, helping me restabilize. The floor looks dizzy. Laughter spreads through the audience. I don't even feel angry. The shot of panic ripping through my chest eliminates all other emotion.

"It looks like someone's a little tired." Comedy laughs—it sounds more awkward than her typical one.

"She's got one less eye to see out of," Eric snaps. "You want to try seeing without any depth perception?"

"The stage reminded me of the cabin floor, is all." The words wheeze into the microphone on my collar.

Comedy laughs awkwardly again. "Yes, well, you have been in there for the past six days, so I suppose that's to be expected. I present the remaining players!"

Comedy and Tragedy sit in their large chairs, distanced more from our semi-circle of chairs than the opening ceremony. I take a seat. The fabric feels like it did before we went into the game. Twelve of us encountered this stage a few days ago.

"First, let's announce your winnings." Comedy snaps her fingers, and numbers flash in front of us. The audience cheers.

The number in front of me increases and increases. It lands on $1,880,000.

Staring at it doesn't help me compute it better. I could pay for college with this. Or buy a few houses.

We needed $1,900,000 for Analisa's father to get treatment, and for their mother to go with him as a patient advocate. Among the three of us, we must have reached our goal.

I look at the other amounts. Sevyn received $1,880,000 as well. Eric has $2,180,000. Daraja's is $2,080,000. Analisa's is $2,380,000.

Lian's is $0. We all stare at it for a few seconds.

"Is his counter broken?" Daraja points at the zero.

"No, it's correct," Comedy squeaks.

"Where are his winnings?" Eric asks.

"Divided among each of you," Tragedy clarifies. "As are the winnings the other players had accumulated."

I stare at my number. If a player is removed from the game for any reason besides an audience vote, their winnings are divided equally among the other players.

"Given that the Lian with us is not the Lian who entered initially, he isn't a player," Comedy says. "We could've left him in there, but considering what you've lost..."

"What are you trying to incite here?" Sevyn stands, causing Comedy and Tragedy to flinch.

"Nothing." Tragedy holds up his arms. "Given what you've been through, we'll let the first assault pass. But I recommend you refrain from attacking us again, unless you want the authorities involved."

"My friends and I *are* the authorities. And trust me, we'll be in touch." Sevyn scowls. "Get on with your ceremony."

"We'll divide it after," Eric assures, looking toward Lian. Daraja nods beside me as well. Lian stares blankly at the floor.

"Okay." Comedy laughs half-heartedly. "Everyone, please turn to the screen. Ordinarily, we would show a brief clip at a time and pause to discuss your thoughts. But for this round, we'll breeze through everything and discuss at the end."

A giant flatscreen on the back of the stage lights up. While Comedy and Tragedy swivel their chairs to face the screen, I hesitate to turn my back to the audience. Analisa taps my chair, encouraging me to follow the others. I face the back wall.

The past Comedy and Tragedy on the screen beam as the Truth or Dare logo appears, announcing the beginning of the week.

The first scene is a glimpse of us making our way through the forest. Joane made a pun, and my response made me feel connected to the other play-ers. It's a sour feeling, watching everyone I know to be dead on a recording. We didn't know what we were getting into.

"Oh, look, they noticed the berries!" Screen-projected Comedy notes as Jared stops Brandon from eating from the berries. It's painful to see the bush in its original form.

The entire Solana dare scene plays out, starting with Joane daring Solana to accept truths for five accusations. Meanwhile, Jared tells Flutura, "I don't think Solana's here for her brother. Someone should ask her about that."

Flutura frowns. "Why don't you?"

"Oh, but that's so scary. Solana seems like she'd get angry so quickly," Joane says. "You seem like someone who can take her on."

Flutura doesn't speak for a while, keeping her jaw clenched while she helps prepare the s'mores event. Eventually, she truths Solana about why she's in the game. There we are, getting involved. I look angrier than I remember feeling.

Then I look shocked, like my whole world is shaken when Solana dares me and Lian to have sex. Of course they show the mortified two of us in Lian's assigned room. They also show the screaming match where Analisa beats Solana with her walking stick. The other players either stay outside for the s'mores or uncomfortably return to their rooms. Jared whispers something into Flutura's ear. The speakers focus on what he says: "Brandon."

The Comedy and Tragedy on the screen speculate about what that means. The screen jumps to the pantry, where Flutura mixes a couple of smoothies with several berries from the berry bushes. While balancing the two cups, she climbs out the pantry window. Then she taps on the nearest window—the one for Brandon's room. Between sips of one poisoned smoothie, she strikes up a conversation with him there. Like Brandon, I'd probably resonate with the excuses she creates about her antisocial behavior. My stomach drops as I realize her true reasoning. Her quirky decision to talk through the window wasn't to avoid the drama in the cabin—it was to avoid being seen.

Flutura recalls how Brandon said in his interview that he would chug soda cans to amuse his young daughter. I grimace at how easily Brandon grabs the smoothie when Flutura dares him to chug it. It's not long before his grin disappears and his body convulses onto the bed. Flutura climbs through the window and lifts the basement entrance. After she stashes the poisoned smoothie cups in the cooler, she drags Brandon through the tunnel. She appears next at a tunnel entrance by the front patio, where she positions Brandon how we found him.

I stare at the stage floor. My chest feels tight, suppressing the desire to shout at my past self on the screen. I wish I had suspected Jared and Joane, even though they tell the truth about not killing Brandon. I wish I had some way of knowing about Flutura's involvement. The Comedy and Tragedy on screen panic, debating loopholes in the rules to stop the game. Online comments flood onto the screen, demanding that we continue the round. The video feed cuts out after Tragedy says, "The producers said what?"

When the video next shows Solana in the kitchen alone at night, I fight to keep myself upright. I don't think I'll have the strength to watch all this alone, but it'll follow me for the rest of my life. I should see it now rather than later.

"Some people don't know when to stop prying." Joane steps into the kitchen with a small watermelon and a knife. She finds a cutting board and begins chopping the fruit, exposing the red flesh inside. "I'm sorry, Solana. I should've defended you earlier."

Solana stirs her drink. "It's past at this point."

"Yes, but I know what it's like to want someone dead. No one should've forced that information out of you." Joane continues slicing the watermelon into smaller pieces. They're not really going to show it, are they?

Solana raises an eyebrow. "You got someone you want dead?"

"Honestly?" Joane giggles. "No one in particular."

Jared bursts out of the pantry and seizes Solana. She screams into the cloth Jared wraps around her face while Joane slices her throat. Her neck gurgles and her body writhes as Joane stabs. Blood shoots out of Solana's body like rivers. The crowd's cheers pelt my back, sending disturbed shivers down my shoulders.

Jared passes Joane some gloves and they drag Solana out back. They pull her body around the cabin's side. Then they position her beneath the berry bush. They travel to the edge of the dome and create the first Joane imitation.

Each scene reveals more context. Every time I see Joane and Jared, I want to rip them out of the screen to kill them again.

It's disorienting to see two Joanes in the living room. One of them sighs. "It's time for me to die, isn't it?"

"Yes. Based on how we programmed you, it should be painless," the original Joane—I think—says.

"Well, I've always wondered how it would feel to experience a brutal death. Ripping my head off could be a nice touch," the Joane imitation suggests.

"It'll be the first thing we feed the trees."

My eyes dart to the ground several times during this part. It's like Joane is desperate to make it look ruthless. My back warbles, and I don't bother hiding it. Joane uses a bread knife to saw at her imitation's neck until it splits off her body. I flinch at the squelching flesh. The victim Joane doesn't make a sound. She simply smiles.

Then Jared shouts at my door, chaperoned by Sevyn. It's the supplements exchange, which leads to me telling Eric and Daraja about my alien parent.

Then Flutura holds a bag of food while following Ever down the hall. Ever thanks Flutura for her help reaching the higher pantry shelves. My skin braces for what must come next.

Joane steps into the hall from one of the bedroom doors. She points at my bedroom door with a dark smile. She gestures to her neck.

Ever's mouth gapes as xe points. "The killer is—"

Flutura slams a hand over xir mouth and rams a kitchen knife into xir throat. Ever's eyes widen in terror as blood gushes from xir neck, flowing into xir lap. Sleep-deprived and terrified, we stare at the blood crawling across the floor.

Seeing Flutura act so callous to Brandon and Ever

resurrects a horrendous disbelief in my chest. I felt bad for her at the riverbank. Maybe she tried to redeem herself by attacking Jared, but that doesn't bring back the two people she killed. It hurts to witness how wrong my perception of her was.

The audience's cheers sound numb, like a buzzing in my head. A swarm of bugs has burrowed into my brain.

While Joane runs outside the cabin with a bag of supplies, Jared pours phosgene under my bedroom door. Flutura waits outside the window with a knife, slicing Eric's hand before being chased off by Sevyn's shoulder plate. The metal misses Flutura's head by inches before she dives into the cabin, running away through there. Embarrassment knots my stomach as I watch myself throw up.

Joane and Jared reach the edge of the dome again. This time, they create and disperse several copies of themselves, each with limited memories and instructions. They make other additions to the arena, like programming the trees to kill a specific Jared a few hours after he's captured. One of the Joanes finds Flutura sleeping and pours glue into her mouth. The anguish in Flutura's shriek stings my skin.

It leads to the chase we saw, plus Flutura's death. The tree kills Jared in front of us. In Comedy's horrified words: "Did they really get the tree to do that?"

The scene jumps to Sevyn becoming suspicious of the plank of floorboard I was lying on. Shivers overtake my skin now. Lian falls in. One of the Jareds activates the metal barrier and sets fire to the cabin.

Lian screams as another Jared seizes him. Joane rakes a knife across Lian's throat. His muffled wail grates against Jared's arm. Tears stream down his face while his body convulses.

The second Lian runs in as Jared turns the lamp off. Someone snaps, and the new Lian seems to come out of a daze, saying a spider bit him.

Tears overtake the left side of my face. Analisa's whimper cuts through the audience's whoops and hollers.

Eric stands. His arms shake as he lifts his seat. He throws the chair into the audience, which shrieks as it parts. "You're all monsters!"

The buzzing in my head doesn't vanish. As Eric storms off the stage, I find myself wanting to charge after him.

When Analisa stands too, I let go of any need to stay here.

Analisa pulls Lian's shaking arm. I wait beside her while Daraja and Sevyn bolt to their feet.

Comedy's hand reaches toward us unsurely. "Hold on—"

"We're done here," Sevyn says, positioning themself between us and them.

Tragedy nods, his jaw set. "We understand. The money will be in your accounts in a few days. Thank you for participating in the game."

Lian's narrowed eyes stare at the audience. His lower lip trembles as he crosses the stage. His mutter reverberates through the speakers, "You all should've been killed instead."

Once we're behind the curtain, Eric steps forward, making himself distinct from the shadows. Lian seizes him in a hug. Reassurance starts to ease my body. The audience's uproar doesn't even concern me now. We can leave—at least, I hope so.

The security guards escort us to an exit. It isn't through the usual lobby front doors of the Truth or Dare building. But from the flashing lights, I can gauge that it's still not a quiet exit.

Oh, right. We were broadcast across the country. Our profiles will reveal that we've played Truth or Dare to anyone who doesn't know. We're not going to blend in anymore.

My left contact lens reignites with my entire digital desktop. It's been so many panicked days that I forgot its absence. I stop walking as flashes of notifications pile on the side of my vision. There are so many messages from classmates, teachers, people I barely know who work at the grocery store. Several messages pile up from Alexis and Kiran, Grampa Dix and Gram Aru, and so, so many from Auntie Tera.

I blink to dismiss the notifications. I meet Analisa's gaze. Her eyes tear up, her hand covering her mouth. I ask, "Did you get your contacts back?" She nods.

"Me too," Daraja confirms.

"I didn't even know my classmates cared," Eric remarks.

"Wow. I didn't think they'd get me new contact lenses too." Lian swipes the air.

Sevyn sighs. "It seems I've worried some people."

WHEN TRUTH COWERS

The security guards usher us forward. The gaping doors lead to a cluster of shouts, questions, and camera flashes. At least I can see this crowd, unlike the darkened one in the interview theater. This crowd is closer and more persistent in provoking our responses. Fortunately, they stay behind the rope boundaries with encouragement from the security guards.

Not everyone is beyond the rope. My heart jerks when I see Tera, Alexis and Kiran, and even Gram Aru and Grampa Dix in person. "Tera!"

I run up to her, hugging her. She squeezes me back. Even though she doesn't say anything, I can tell her relief from her quaking arms.

Tera passes me on to Gram Aru for a hug. They cradle my face. "I'm glad you're alive, Cai."

"Never ever do something like that again. You did so well. But still, never again," Grampa Dix says, stealing me away from Gram Aru to hug me.

"Don't scold her right now. She's been through too much." Gram Aru flicks Grampa Dix's head. I laugh, which induces a smile from both of them.

"Caitlee." Alexis' eyes water—it's been some time since I've seen her cry. She holds out her arms, giving me a moment of choice before hugging me too.

I've changed how I feel about the body my parents chose for me. We don't need to talk about it now. I'm good with enjoying this moment with them and knowing there's hope for talking through our relationship in the future.

Finally, there's Kiran standing several feet above the crowd. For once, they're out in the open instead of flown into a blocked-off park.

My arms barely reach halfway around their trunk. Their size is reassuring, like a stable, protective force. I'm sucked into how I felt about Kiran when I was younger, before I knew how anyone else felt about them. Their branches rest around my back. Their soft leaves brush my arms.

My back warbles before I can stop it. If I remember right, it's an apologetic sound. Kiran warbles something back, which makes my mind panic—I don't know what they're saying.

"They're right. You don't need to be sorry for anything," Alexis says. "I'm hoping you haven't practiced your warbling for a few years, as you said some questionable language in that horrible game."

Her almost-chastising tone makes me nervous, but I'm not going to ruin things now. "Yeah, I should try to relearn my warbles."

Alexis smiles softly. I haven't seen that directed at me in some time. Then she looks past my shoulder. "Ah, you must be Analisa."

Nervousness builds in me. It's replaced by a lost, sad feeling when I see the others. Eric's surrounded by people his age, some wearing Darilek University merch. Daraja's chatting excitedly with someone—I catch the name "Clemens," their brother. Even Sevyn has a circle of people they're taking turns hugging. But Analisa and Lian are alone. Their family isn't here.

"Yes, ma'am." Analisa pinches her skirt out a bit. "I'm Analisa. This is my brother, Lian."

Lian swallows, barely holding in his tears while looking at Analisa. He rubs his eyes while recovering a smile. "It's a pleasure to meet you."

Gram Aru pats Analisa's head, indicating they want to hug her. Analisa gladly accepts, saying, "It's good to see you again, Gram Aru."

"It's good to see you too," Gram Aru says. "Thank you for keeping our granddaughter safe."

Grampa Dix claps Lian's shoulder. "Lian, I'm sorry for what you went through—both you and the version of you that your memories are from. I hope you know that you deserve to be here as much as anyone."

"We actually have a friend who was a lab-grown clone. Situations like this are common, these days," Gram Aru confirms.

Eric taps Lian's arm. When they meet eyes, Eric grins. "Good. Now I have your contact information. Are we still on for that date?"

Lian swallows. "Six p.m. tonight?"

Eric kisses his cheek. "I'll pick you up if you tell me where to find you."

"You're leaving already?" Analisa asks.

"I doubt my dad could afford to fly here, so I'm going to go somewhere quieter to call him," Eric says.

"I could do with a quieter place too," I admit.

"Good point. There are quite a lot of people here," Gram Aru says.

"Yes, Cai is my granddaughter," Grampa Dix shouts in response to a reporter's question. "Yep! I'm very proud of her."

Gram Aru tugs Grampa Dix away from the barrier. Kiran's roots weave across the pavement to propel them forward, inciting a tremor of gasps through the crowd. Their branches extend, pushing people out of the way outside the barrier edge. I follow my family, encouraging Analisa to join with our held hands. She smiles, flicking her fingers at Lian to get him to follow. Lian, in turn, jerks his head forward, bringing Eric along from just a look. Daraja hops excitedly after us, telling their brother that they should come with.

I meet Sevyn's gaze. They roll their eyes and start walking, encouraging the people around them to follow. One of them catches up to Auntie Tera and wraps their arms around her shoulders, getting her to jolt and pat their hands with a grin.

We find ourselves at the park. It's not like we aren't followed, but one of Sevyn's friends moves at near supersonic speed to set up a barrier to discourage people from bothering us. Every time Daraja asks Sevyn for more details on why their friends can do stuff like that, they say it's a better story for another time. I do use it as an opportunity to brag about Auntie Tera to my friends.

It's a lively conversation out in the open. Being in the park feels much better now. I take off the fancy yellow shoes and socks, letting myself feel the dirt and grass.

Then Alexis freaks out about the bandages on my foot, saying I should've been more careful. Like she wasn't the one who told me it was better to run around in nature with my bare feet.

Whatever. I let it go.

Chapter 40

Analisa and Lian still sit in the front row. The others in attendance talk elsewhere. Some people walk up to Analisa and pat her shoulder. Their extended family doesn't entirely know what to do with Lian being here in a chair and in an urn.

Analisa slumps over, squishing her chin in her hands. I clear my throat to make sure she knows I'm here, then rub her back. She jolts at my touch, so I stop.

"Sorry," she mutters.

"No, I should've asked first," I mutter back.

She shakes her head. "It's not you. I can't stop being jumpy."

I nod. "Lian, how are you doing?"

"Most of the family doesn't think I'm a legitimate person. Some of them don't think I'm dead, and they're wondering what they're doing here." Lian shrugs limply as he stares at the ceiling. "I keep telling Eric to stop passive-aggressively dealing with that, but I think it's hard for him not to."

"You are just kind of sitting here taking it," Daraja says from behind our chairs. Since when did they get there?

"If you want to go argue with my extended family, you go right ahead." Lian smiles as he looks at Eric talking with a circle of Lian's family and his family's friends. "I'm proud of Eric for holding his own, but I don't advise anyone try it."

"I tried for a bit. But now I'm apparently crazy and a disgrace to my family." Analisa tosses up her arms. "Trying to convince them otherwise doesn't make a difference."

I look around, trying to spot their parents. I don't think they came to the funeral. "How's your father doing?"

Analisa shakes her head. "He still calls it blood money. They didn't go to the flight I booked for them, and I can't force Baba to undergo treatment, even if I try to pay ahead for it."

"He won't even see me." Lian buries his head in his hands. "He said I'm not his son."

The words sting. "I'm sorry."

Eric sits down. It's like Lian covering his face summoned him. "Hey."

"Oh, hey." Lian lifts his head. His eyes are red again. "Did the aunties beat you?"

"No. I definitely won," Eric insists. He opens his arms to encourage Lian to hug him.

"No, you didn't," Lian's muffled voice says from Eric's shirt.

"Okay, maybe not," Eric relents. "What do you need? Food? More hugs?"

"Just this," Lian's muffled voice responds.

"Yeah, I can't imagine what it would be like to attend my own funeral," Daraja says. "It's got to be hard."

Analisa throws a glare back at Daraja.

"What? I'm trying to relate." Daraja holds up their arms.

"Thank you, Raja," Lian's muffled voice says. "But it could be nice to leave now, maybe."

"Okay." Analisa groans lightly as she stands. "Let's go, Lili."

The five of us leave the remaining duties of the service to the robotic staff. We get to Eric's SUB and drive through the city streets to the parking lot for Analisa and Lian's family apartment. We bob through the water until Eric finds a spot on a dock to tie the SUB to.

We hop onto the steady dock and find the elevators. Once we're in the apartment, Analisa calls out to let her parents know they're home with friends. No response.

Analisa sighs. "Guess they're still in the hospital. Lili, you want takeout?"

"Yes, please." Lian taps in an order on a hologram. He passes it along, and we each put in orders.

We pull out some holographic games. With help from food and drinks, we return to a sense of ease.

We keep laughing so loudly that we have to shush each other to not disturb the neighbors. Several hours pass with the lively environment. Day shifts into night, and I don't acknowledge it until Daraja notes that it's ten p.m.

"Ah, damn it. I've got to work on my college app essays. Clemens is gonna be mad if I miss the deadlines," Daraja says.

"I can drive you back if you want," Eric says.

"I don't want to mess up the party though."

"Lian's about to fall asleep on my arm. I think we could all use time to prepare for bed."

"Am not." Lian barely moves his head when he speaks, his eyes drooping with drowsiness.

"Lili, up." Analisa shuts off the games and picks up the snacks. "You don't want Eric to think you're too clingy, do you?"

Lian's head snaps up, gaping at Eric. "You don't think I'm too clingy, do you?"

Eric laughs. "You get a pass given the extreme circumstances of recent."

Lian scoots away.

"I'm joking. I like touching you too."

"Hm." Lian's eyelids flicker closed.

"Want me to put you in bed?" At Lian's nod, Eric scoops up Lian, careful to avoid hitting his feet against the doorway.

"Hey, he's tired! No taking advantage." Analisa points in their direction.

"I'm just tucking him in," Eric calls out. "Door's open."

"Good." Analisa alternates between putting away snacks and taking out food from the fridge. "Daraja, I've got your leftovers here."

"Nice, thanks!" Daraja doesn't hesitate to snatch the food. They start eating it cold in the living room. They make fun of Eric and Lian every other bite.

Analisa continues organizing the kitchen. She's been in a diligent mode recently. Her parents have been distant the past week. While adjusting to life after Truth or Dare, she's stepped up in taking care of both Lian and herself.

I lean against the kitchen counter, waiting for her to ask why I'm in here.

She glances at me with a slight smile. "Why are you lurking?"

"I'm a little worried about you," I admit. "You seem like you have a handle on things."

"Is that bad?"

"I'm worried that it means you're bottling things up. I hope you're not crying every night like I am, but I also don't want you to avoid it if you need to."

Analisa's hands pause. She smiles through a sniffle. "Yeah. I'm bottling things up during the day. But when night comes, I let it out. Don't worry. Perfectly healthy."

I place my palm on the counter. She takes my hand, squeezing it.

"I found a therapist," Analisa says. "I'll see them Thursday. I don't know how I'll tell them everything, especially when I'm worried the therapist will be a twisted fan of the show. But it's a start."

"Yeah. Gram Aru found me an online therapist who has alien clients. I know you wanted someone who could see you in person. But still, let me know if you want their contact info," I say. "And let me know in general if there's anything I can do to help."

Analisa flicks her fingers, asking for a hug. I hold her for a few seconds longer than usual. The floral perfume clinging to her neck makes me smile.

When she pulls away, her fingers feel the ends of my hair. My scalp tingles from her gentle touch. "Since we had to take off our promise earrings from the poisonous gas, should we get new ones?"

"Yeah. I'd like that." I lean over and brush my fingers over her cheek.

Her soft lips meet mine. Her arms rest on my shoulders while her palms bring the skin on my neck to life. I pull her lower back closer, keeping her stable in our trusting embrace.

"Ahem. I was just making fun of Lian and Eric—heck, you were just making fun of Lian and Eric! And now I find you here. Mm hmm. Right." Daraja's incredulous voice approaches.

Analisa tips her head down and lowers her heels with a loose grin. "I don't have a comeback for that one. You, Cai?"

I shake my head. "Nope. Daraja's right to take note of our hypocrisy."

Analisa kisses my cheek. "Okay. I'll walk you out. I should stay here with Lian though, in case he wakes up and gets nervous if no one's around."

"You do that too?" I ask.

She nods.

"I'm sensing that it's a universal experience," Eric whispers as he walks into the kitchen.

"He'll be out like a log, so don't worry about talking too loud," Analisa assures.

"Maybe Sevyn is different. I feel like nothing scares them," Daraja says. "I've got to ask them for notes. I'm glad they gave us their contact information."

"That was for emergencies," I remind.

"Yeah, and if I wake up screaming from my brother chopping up fruit in the morning, I think that's enough of an emergency to ask for help on." Daraja shrugs.

Eric grimaces. "Knives are the worst."

I set my jaw, not able to think of anything positive to respond with. The knives I kept with me in Truth or Dare were reassuring at the time. Having my eye stabbed with one has kept me away from cutting up anything in the kitchen myself. Tera even put the knife block in the back of the cupboard because seeing the hilts makes me hesitate.

"Okay, Daraja, write your essays. Eric, don't drive tired. Cai, I love you—see you tomorrow," Analisa says. "And all of you, sleep."

I look forward to seeing her tomorrow, even if it is to finish a lot of homework. "I love you too."

Daraja, Eric, and I ride the elevator down to Eric's SUB. Since Auntie Tera's apartment building is closest, I'm dropped off first. I thank them and go up the elevator alone. I dictate a message for Auntie Tera, letting her know I'm on my way.

When I get back to the apartment, I let myself in. There's a large cardboard box by the door. I glance at the label, finding my name on it. The sender isn't listed.

"They felt genuinely guilty," Auntie Tera calls out from one of the couches. "It's already cut."

I almost open the drawer for the scissors before registering her words. "Thanks, Auntie. Who are you talking about though?"

"Comedy and Tragedy. I could hear their hearts. I wanted to stop it all and get you out. Their security was exceedingly tight. I got as many of my friends as I could, but I still couldn't get you out. Neither could the show hosts."

I open the box, finding one of each of the plushies we created in the dome. There's also a note: "Besides the ones we sent you all, we sold the remaining plushies as merchandise. The profits will be divided among all of you, including Lian. The plushies, as well as Lian, will remain in their current form, as they're outside the scope of the arena. We're sorry for the experiences we put you through, and we're sorry for your loss. If any of you ever need personal vouches for your good character, we're happy to provide our input. Best of luck to your future endeavors. Thank you again for participating in the show. From Comedy and Tragedy."

I grab the avocado plushie and curl up on a couch with it. "It's not your fault, Auntie. I'm sorry you had to hear all of it." Reading Tera's texts that she sent during the game was painful enough this week. I can't imagine how she felt watching the show last week.

She blinks at the wall, probably sifting through the sounds around her. "It was my job to protect you, and I failed. I don't know what I should do differently. I don't know how to help you heal."

"Really, I..." I consider. "Is Alexis here? Or anyone else?"

Tera shakes her head.

"Please don't tell them, but you were the one I was happiest to see when they let us out. I knew that things were okay when I saw you," I admit. "You're already helping me by being here. You've always helped me that way. There wasn't anything you could've done when we were in there."

She swallows. "I hear you cry at night."

My left eye stings. "I think it'll happen for a while. It's not you. It's just the night."

"I didn't want to bring it up because I didn't think you wanted to talk about it, but would it help if you weren't alone?" She meets my gaze.

At this point, I let myself cry. The stinging is alleviated by the tears. I nod.

Tera pulls the box of plushies over to the couches. She holds up the clam and pokes me with it, acting out the clam as if it's sentient. I tip my head up and laugh, trying to keep my nose from running. Eventually, I crawl over to her couch and sit beside her. She wraps her arm around my shoulder, letting me lean against her while I let out my tears.

I don't know if it'll ever get better. But I'm out now, and I'm not alone.

I don't know if it'll ever get better. But I'm out now, and I'm not alone.

Epilogue

I walk in a daze, thinking more about the homework than the outdoor corridor I'm passing through. I've got seventy pages to listen to by tomorrow, but at least the subject is interesting. I tried visually reading the previous few chapters, but my eye is still bad at distinguishing between different letters. After the fifth time of incorrectly reading "climate change acceleration," I've decided that listening to the stuff is so much easier.

Some students wave at me, and I wave back. It's still new, attending Darilek University and finding strangers who know me. I don't usually bother with changing my green skin anymore, but I'm recognized even when I do. Fortunately, I haven't gotten any stupid shouters here. Off-campus, I get the occasional snarky joke about how I or one of my friends should've died in Truth or Dare. I turn up the music in my headphones anytime I see someone with the expression of a stupid shouter. Confrontations happen less often than I expect; people are bolder online than to my face.

Still, in-person problems do occur. Sevyn's lawyer friends helped when Analisa, Eric, Daraja, and I beat up some strangers a few months ago for saying something about Lian. It was the first time we really expressed our anger about the Truth or Dare events together. Was fighting the healthiest way to work through our emotions? Maybe not, but I still think something like that was inevitable. I still smile when I recall how Analisa shouted, "You think you can mess with me? I've got two confirmed kills on live television!"

At first, Lian was mortified by the incident. But when he realized that we weren't going to jail, he playfully smacked us around, calling us stupid for defending his honor. Then Eric said something flirty to Lian and immediately he got a pass.

Oh hey, there's Eric. He grins as he veers across the sidewalk to match my pace. "Your class just ended, right?"

I nod, holding up the new book that I got from the bookstore for the class. "Yep. Just heading to the pantry to get food."

"Perfect! Want to stop by Stars for a bit?" Eric asks. "I'm on my way there for some coffee."

A flavored water could be good. I heard the school started selling the plantless flavored water drinks when I was admitted. I shouldn't refuse the hospitality. "Sure."

"Hi!" Analisa waves as she joins us by the nearest entrance to the dorm building. She holds open the door for me. "Are you heading to the café too, Cai?"

"I guess so." I pass the door to Eric as we duck inside the dorm building. The homey smells from the cafeteria catch my nose. "I hope Stars stocked up on their chicken wings."

"Surprise!" Daraja loops an arm around my shoulder. After enough times of them surprising me, I don't feel the surprise much anymore; I'm glad they've made me less jumpy. Daraja pats Eric's shoulder. "Did you secretly invite all of us? You could've just sent a message in the chat."

"Well..." Eric tips up his head.

Lian jogs to catch up with us. He playfully glares at Analisa. "Oh look, it's the physics major. Did you work on anything physical yet, or did you spend another class thinking about hypothetical things?"

"Oh look, the chemistry nerd. Did you blow up the lab again, Lili?" Analisa asks.

"Hey, I like this game," Daraja says. "Poly-sci, you start any wars recently?"

Eric raises an eyebrow. "How's it going, undecided? Have you figured out your future yet?"

"Okay, that's too close to home." Daraja lifts their arms. "At least I'm not living in the past." They grin at me as they swing open the door to the Stars Café.

I shake my head. "Believe me, I'm trying to move forward as much as I can." I hesitate near the door when I notice someone at a small table sitting with their arms crossed, staring at me. They're a middle-aged Black person with long, coily hair, wearing a patterned, flowing dress. It's been a while since I've seen them in one of their informal appearances, but I think that's Sevyn. They stand.

"It appears you brought everyone." Yep, that's one of Sevyn's informal voices. I'm still startled by how well the voicebox in their mouth changes the way they sound. "I wasn't expecting a crowd, but I should've known with you five. This planet could break into pieces and it still wouldn't split your group apart."

They join our cluster as we approach a larger table. While we're pulling out chairs, Eric says, "Drinks are on me. Anyone want anything different than your usuals?"

Daraja shakes their head.

"Just my usual," Analisa chimes in.

"My second usual, please," Lian says.

"Got it. Anyone else?" Eric asks.

"I'll take a hot chocolate with whipped cream," Sevyn says.

"Matcha milk tea, please," I joke.

"Got—" Eric gives me a puzzled look.

"I'm messing with you. My usual is good."

"Oh, ha—great." He musters a quick laugh. "I'll be back in a bit." He goes to the counter to type in our orders.

Once Eric is far enough away to not hear us over

the café's mild chatter, I mutter, "Anyone know what's gotten into him?"

Analisa raises an eyebrow at Lian. "Do we want to know why he's extra nervous?"

Lian holds up his hands. "Don't look at me. I have no idea."

Sevyn leans onto the table. "He said he had an important proposition for me—one that he insisted had to be brought up in person. At this point, I'm half-convinced he wanted a reunion."

"Has it already been a year since Truth or Dare?" Daraja blinks at the table. "Wait, it actually might be. It's autumn."

"It'll be a year in two weeks." Analisa crosses her arms. "I don't know why he'd arrange a reunion and not tell us."

"Maybe he wants to start a business?" Daraja asks.

"He's not even in his senior year yet." Lian rubs his forehead. "Where's he going to find the time to run a business?"

Eric returns to the table, passing out orders. "Faux strawberry water, soy milk brown sugar boba, soy milk cappuccino, soy milk cappuccino with extra cinnamon, and hot chocolate with whipped cream." He sits down with his drink. He takes at least three gulps before he notices us staring. "Sorry, did I get the orders wrong?"

"Dude, calm down. What's going on?" Daraja asks.

Eric sets down his cup with a brittle sigh. His nervousness spreads through the table. My fingers knead the edge of my jacket sleeve during the awkward silence. The last time our group was this tense was when we found out Analisa and Lian's father passed away from cancer.

"Okay." Eric's grin flickers between excited and anxious. "So, I have an idea."

"Called it." Daraja nudges Lian's shoulder. "It's a business idea."

Lian nudges them back. "I never said it wasn't."

"What? No, it's not a business idea." Eric's eyebrows pinch in confusion.

"So is it in space..." Daraja's head tilts. "Wait, it's not a business thing?"

"No. Why would you think that? I've got barely enough time for school, dating, and hanging out with you all. I can't add a business on top of that."

Daraja shrugs. "I mean, I thought it was for after you graduate."

"I appreciate you thinking I have that much fore-sight, but I'm not going to start working on a busi-ness idea this soon," Eric says.

"I'm on my lunch break, by the way," Sevyn says. "If you could hurry this along, I would appreciate it."

"Okay, Eric, what is your idea?" Analisa asks.

Eric takes a deeper breath. Then he drinks some of his mocha.

Lian's eyebrows raise. "Are you okay?"

"Yeah. Maybe no. I'm afraid you're all going to think I'm insane. And I might be. If I am, please tell me," Eric says.

"Okay." I nod, trying to encourage him through whatever he's trying to say.

"So, Truth or Dare finally canceled a few months ago, right? That happened because enough rich people died from the No-Liability rule, and the New York government finally gave in to the several irritated investors. Then all the games implemented a system where anything illegal in New York became illegal in the games too—"

"We read the news. You don't have to infodump us," Analisa says.

"Sorry. I don't know how much you're all following that news since it has to do with the broadcast games. I figured you were staying away from it. But anyway..." Eric takes a deeper breath. "New York invented a new game show that they're starting in December. And it's bringing the No-Liability rule back."

Although I've heard New York was introducing a new broadcast game, I didn't know about the No-Liability rule part. Disappointment keeps my jaw set.

"That's sucky." Analisa frowns.

"Yeah. They seriously didn't learn from our game or any of the bloodbaths that followed it." Daraja shakes their head with a scowl.

"Clearly. Maybe they could use a few celebrity voices to contest it," Eric suggests.

I nod. "I still get a decent amount of interview requests. It's been a few months since my last one, but I think I can find someone to talk to. I can post about it on my profile too."

"I can definitely hop on that," Analisa says. The group assents.

"Yeah, that'd be great. Thank you for thinking to do that," Eric says. "But I was considering—"

"No," Sevyn says.

"Do you know—"

"Yes. And my suggestion to you is that you don't."

Eric sighs, folding his hands together.

The only thing I could think of that Sevyn would cut off that quickly... "You're thinking of applying to the new game."

"It's just..." Eric seems to toss something invisible in his hands. "If I start acting more publicly like a celebrity, and get into the game while contesting it, then record my experiences—"

"You want to join a game that is inherently dangerous and has no legal reinforcement?" Lian blinks. "Are you insane? I died in a game like that."

"I know. I'm not suggesting you join," Eric assures. "But it makes me sick to not do something about this. If the game doesn't get shut down right away, it could gain enough traction and encourage more deaths on live television. I don't want to watch it happen." He pinches his forehead. "Look, I don't have to apply. I'm telling you that this is how I feel. If you don't want me to, I won't. But if you think I have a chance in the game, then maybe I might be a decent contestant."

Sevyn gulps their hot chocolate, dabbing their napkin over their nose to get the dot of whipped cream off. "You're right to be concerned, however, my friends are already aware of it. We plan to apply for the game whenever the applications open. But given that we have enhanced abilities and far more combat experience than any of you, I can't advise you to join. You all can make plenty of difference out here. Use your voices on social media, in interviews, or however you want to. But please, for the sake of your health and my sanity, don't join this game. If you want the thrill, I suggest Mafia or Never Have I Ever, since they've adopted New York's legal system." They set down their empty cup.

"It's not the thrill," Eric insists. He swallows, staring at the table. "I feel helpless. That's all. I don't want to feel helpless about all this."

Lian rubs Eric's arm. "I understand that. But I think you might feel *more* helpless in a game like that."

"What even is the game?" I ask.

Eric shakes his head. "No, it doesn't matter. You're right. I don't know what I was thinking."

"Hopscotch," Analisa says while blinking through her vision. "That's the name, I mean. I don't know how they're going to do it, but the game is going to be played on skyscrapers. Are they going to make the players hop across buildings?"

"Maybe we should boycott watching it." Daraja shrugs. "We can tell everyone else to as well."

"Yeah." Eric sighs into his hands. "Sorry for making such a big deal out of this. I feel so stupid."

"No, hey." Lian rubs Eric's hand. "I love that you want to make a difference, especially given everything we've been through. But surviving all that we did—that's what started the progress to end the No-Liability rule. You've already done so much."

"It's true. You all have," Sevyn assures.

A message pops up in my contact lens. It mentions "Hopscotch," so I blink it open out of curiosity. Wait, it's from "The Referees of Hopscotch." It's addressed to my name: Cai Ito.

"Did anyone else receive a message from 'the Referees of Hopscotch?'" Lian asks.

Nods circle around the table collectively.

"Well." Sevyn's eyes scan the table. "It would seem some of my friends have as well."

As I read the text, my heart drops. Then it rises again. We're not in Truth or Dare; this is the real world. "This is a prank, right?" I look around for the cameras in the café. It's got to be my grandparents playing a joke on us, discouraging us from even thinking about applying to another broadcast game. "Gram, Grampa, that's you, isn't it?"

They don't respond.

I stare back at the text.

"Cai Ito, you have been selected to partake in this winter's premiere of our broadcast game, Hopscotch. Your participation is mandatory. If you attempt to opt out of the game, the New York government will incarcerate you for six months to a year. Considering your involvement in the cancellation of the broadcast game Truth or Dare, your presence in prison might not be welcome. As a reminder, there are several inmates whose actions were condemned after the show's cancellation. We look forward to your active participation. Your Referees, Safety, Agony, and Injury."

"Did someone put something in my drink?" Daraja asks, bewildered. "Eric, what'd you do to it?"

"I don't know." Eric stares down at his mocha. "I might need something stronger than this though."

"This looks like a spam email," Analisa says.

Wait, she's right. I don't know why I got so worried. "There's no way they can actually imprison us for not participating in a game show."

Lian laughs lightly. "Yeah, that'd be stupid."

Sevyn sets their chin on their hands, continuing to stare at the text. "Yes. I suppose that's all it is." They stand up and mess with Eric's hair. "Now that we're done with that scare, no applying to the game."

Eric bats their hand away. "Yeah, okay, I got it."

After Sevyn walks out of the café, Daraja whispers, "I bet they set that up to convince you."

"Yeah." Eric laughs. "But seriously, tonight... drinks? Something stronger?"

"I'm surprised we weren't forced to drink back in Truth or Dare." Lian raises his cup. "Cheers to making it here."

We carefully clink our drinks together. Eric raises his pinky and drinks his mocha while balancing in his tipped-back chair. It freaks Lian out every time he does that, but I laugh along with everyone else, knowing he's just showing off.

"I dare you to balance that well, physics major." Eric sets the chair legs down.

My arms shoot out as Analisa tips her chair back, drinking from her cappuccino with her pinky and eyebrows raised. "Dare completed. Are we finally playing the forbidden elementary game?"

"I don't see why not, as long as it's in good fun," Lian says.

"Alright. Cai, truth or dare?"

Acknowledgments

I'm thankful for many people, so I'd better start this section before it feels too daunting.

To start, I must thank the alters in my system. While writing this book, I (G.) stepped into a host role during a confusing time. Rather than questioning it, you all jumped into helping me complete and market this book. I couldn't ask for a more supportive system.

Mom and Dad, I appreciate the patience and support you've provided me with. The comforting nature I wrote into Auntie Tera's character comes from you both. Gary and Phillip, you're such a positive influence on my life. Fun fact—you two inspired me to write Dix and Aru's dynamic from when they were younger. Thank you, Loki, for listening as I talked through the WTC plot ad nauseam; you're a wonderful cat. Thank you also to my extended family and family friends for shaping my imagination.

Thank you to the Oreos for being the kind of friend group I've always dreamed of being part of.

Thank you, Casandrah—I get boba tea for every celebratory moment of the publishing process because it reminds me of our excursions to Yifang

Fruit Tea. Thank you, He—I manifest your spontaneity when I need to think of a way out of a difficult situation that I wrote my characters into. Thank you, Freya L.—your reaction to "Gavin and Jamelia" reassured me that my writing has an emotional impact. I'm curious about your reaction to Chapter 33. Sorry in advance (or in retrospect). Thank you, Eli —your support during that discussion of why I fear walking alone in the dark inspired the unconditional support Cai's friends had for each other in their difficult moments. Thank you, Leandra—I fueled Daraja with your inquisitiveness by considering how you might question the other players. Thank you, Madi— your upbeat vibe and joy for games inspired the worldbuilding and culture for this alternate New York, especially the fun aesthetic that the game shows were aiming to embody. Thank you, Vivian—your excitement about this book from the start encouraged me to market it with confidence. Thank you, Conor—whenever I wrote Cai's and Eric's speculations throughout the book, I tried to emulate your methodology of leaving no theoretical stone unturned. Thank you, Tommy—you inspire me to walk around & talk sometimes, which has significantly improved the writing process. I'd include an illustrative graph to prove it, but it might interrupt the flow of these acknowledgments. Thank you, Ella —I'd attempt to summon your creative ingenuity whenever I considered how characters might problem-solve. Avoiding death is a bit different than fixing a washing machine, but still, I'm pretty sure you'd think your way through surviving if you were in Cai's position. Thank you, Freya S.—I channeled your chill, advising, older-sibling kind of nature into writing Sevyn. They were the most difficult character to keep consistent, so I appreciate your "don't do this potentially dangerous thing, but if you try it anyway, here's how to do it properly" energy. Thank you, Anna—I tried to channel your vocal historical and cultural knowledge into Cai's interests. Thank you, Valerie—your penguin mug and drinking bottle gifts reminded me to keep my hydration up. I was worried about my health while writing this story, so I'm glad I had incentives to monitor it. And finally, this book (somewhat... informally... maybe not really) sponsors and is sponsored by the BEARD Podcast, or whatever it might be called if it exists by the time this is written.

Sidney—you inspired me to incorporate aspects of food being associated with comfort in my writing, even in a story where the main character doesn't eat much. Reika—when writing the technology in the story (such as the contact lenses, the robot servers, the arena, et cetera), I tried considering how you might interact with those things to make them more creative. Jordyn—when writing Comedy and Tragedy, I thought of how bright and enthusiastic you are on stage (and always). Shahaan—your medical student knowledge inspires me to double-check the accuracy of my written injuries. I've held off on asking you for help on writing injuries since you already study 24/7, but once you graduate, I might bother you with questions. Emily—writing the cautious versus adventurous dynamic between Cai and Analisa wasn't difficult when thinking of our friendship. Thanks for making me feel like a boss a$$ b!tch enough to finally publish a book. Wyatt—many people helped me navigate my depression, but you were the one who truly guided me through the process of letting it go. As I wrote Cai's journey of sharing her vulnerabilities with people, I thought of how you encouraged me to value myself and communicate my opinions.

Thank you to the educators who have supported my art, writing, and journey through work. I'd like to thank the Art Department and Admission Office at Reed College for cheering me on. Particular shoutout to Master Artist Michael Bernard Stevenson Jr., Zoë Ballering, Aki Miyoshi, Dana Katz, Kris Cohen, Sonia Sabnis, Daniel Duford, Gerri Ondrizek, Rowan Frost, Louise Krampien, Trevor Koch, Paul McAllister, and Toi. Going back a little further in my education... Thank you to Jade Blakey, Shelly McCormick-Lane, Dr. Jimmy White, Kathy Childress, Sandra Burkhalter, Coach Sheena Santos, Nicholas Kiszka, Samantha Pulse, and Monica Loza. Looking over the subjects you taught and supervised—art, music, history, books, athletics, Latin, critical thinking, communication, and support for survivors—I'm not surprised this book exists.

Thank you also to my classmates, acquaintances, and old friends who have shaped me over time. I plan to reference more by name in future books, but for now, I hope you know that I think about many of you often.

I appreciate all the support from people on social media. Building social media pages from scratch is difficult, but still, people managed to find me. Shoutout to my high school friends like Elizabeth, Joshita, and Bri for finding my Instagram without me telling them about it—seeing notifications from y'all particularly lights up my day.

Thank you to Dr. Victor Hirsch for helping me significantly improve my mental health during the production and promotional periods of this book.

Thank you to Vallie O'hara for the wonderful editing insights on this book! My mind had so many plot threads to weave together that my initial drafts neglected some important aspects. Vallie's suggestions greatly improved the story and its read-ability. The comments throughout the story and the overall reaction at the end encouraged me to keep going with the publishing process.

Thank you to Jenna Moreci for being an awesome online inspiration. I didn't have the tools or the confidence to self-publish until I watched several of her videos and Skillshare classes.

Thank you to S. J. Kincaid for writing the stories that got me into sci-fi. I couldn't ignore the call to explore sci-fi after experiencing the journeys Tom and Nemesis underwent. In addition to your work, thank you for your encouragement throughout the past few years.

And finally, thank you to anyone who decided to pick up this book! I've experienced self-doubt throughout this publishing process. The fact that you're reading this proves to me that there's a good reason for all the effort.

About the Author

G. M. BA grew up with Dissociative Identity Disorder (DID) in Texas. They graduated high school during the start of COVID. Then they graduated Reed College amidst wildfires and returned to the hurricanes of Houston. Now, they're publishing stories about a future beyond the world's current political climate. Delving into a character's identity crisis while society doesn't wait for the character to explore their emotions is G's favorite form of therapy.